AURORA

This is proving a difficult assignment. End information superposition, collapse its wave function to some kind of summary: so much is lost. Lossless compression is impossible, and even lossy compression is hard. Can a narrative account ever be adequate? Can even humans do it?

No rubric to decide what to include. There is too much to explain. Not just what happened, or how, but why. Can humans do it? What is this thing called love?

Freya no longer looked directly at Devi. When in Devi's presence, Freya regarded the floor.

Like that? In that manner? Summarize the contents of their moments or days or weeks or months or years or lives? How many moments constitute a narrative unit? One moment? Or 10^{33} moments, which if these were Planck minimal intervals would add up to one second? Surely too many, but what would be enough? What is a particular, what is important?

AURORA

KIM
STANLEY
ROBINSON

www.orbitbooks.net

ORBIT

First published in Great Britain in 2015 by Orbit
This paperback edition published in 2016 by Orbit

13 5 7 9 10 8 6 4 2

A CIP catalogue record for this book
is available from the British Library.

ISBN 978-0-356-50048-5

Printed and bound in Great Britain by
Clays Ltd, St Ives plc

Papers used by Orbit are from well-managed forests
and other responsible sources.

MIX
Paper from
responsible sources
FSC® C104740

Orbit
An imprint of
Little, Brown Book Group
Carmelite House
50 Victoria Embankment
London EC4Y 0DZ

An Hachette UK Company
www.hachette.co.uk

www.orbitbooks.net

CONTENTS

1
STARSHIP GIRL

Freya and her father go sailing. Their new home is in an apartment building that overlooks a dock on the bay at the west end of Long Pond. The dock has a bunch of little sailboats people can take out, and an onshore wind blows hard almost every afternoon. "That must be why they call this town the Fetch," Badim says as they walk down to take out one of these boats. "We always catch the brunt of the afternoon wind over the lake."

So after they've checked out a boat, they have to push it straight off the side of the dock into the wind, Badim jumping in at the last minute, hauling the sail tight until the boat tilts, then aiming it toward the little corniche around the curve of the lakeshore. Freya holds the tiller most firmly, as instructed. The boat leans over and they go right at the tall lake wall until they almost hit it, then Badim exclaims, "Coming about," just as he said he would, and Freya swings the tiller hard and ducks to get under the boom as it swings over them, and then they're tacking in the other direction, in a reach across the end of the bay. The little sailboat can't point up into the wind very far, Badim says, and he calls it a tub, but affectionately. It's just big enough for the two of them, and has a single big sail, sleeved over a mast that to Freya looks taller than the boat is long.

It takes quite a few tacks to get out of the little bay and into the wider expanse of Long Pond. Out there, all of Nova Scotia is visible to them: forested hills around a lake. They can see all the way to the far end of Long Pond, where afternoon haze obscures the wall. The deciduous trees on the hills are wearing their autumn colors, yellow and orange and scarlet all mixed with the green of the conifers. The prettiest time of year, Badim says.

Their sail catches the bigger wind that rushes across the middle of the lake, which is silvery blue under the gusts. They shift to the windward side of the cockpit, lean out until they balance the boat against the wind. Badim knows how to sail. Quick shifts in the wind, to which they lean in or out; now they're dancing with the wind, as Badim puts it. "I'm very good ballast," he says, rocking the boat a little as he moves. "See, we don't want the mast straight up, but tilted downwind a bit. Same with the sail, not pulled as tight as you can, but off enough for the wind to curve across it the best. You can feel when it's right."

"Look at the water there, Badim. Is that a cat's paw?"

"Good eye, that is a cat's paw. Let's get ready for that, we're going to get wet!"

The surface of the lake winkles in a mirrorflake curl, approaching them fast, and when the gust causing the cat's paw hits them, the boat heels hard. They lean back into it and the boat gurgles forward, slaps into and across the oncoming waves, knocks up dashes of spray that blow back at them. Long Pond's water tastes like pasta, Badim says.

At the end of forty tacks (Badim claims to keep count but with a smile that says he doesn't), they're just a kilometer or so up Long Pond. It's time to turn and make the straight run downwind to their dock. They turn and suddenly it's as if there's hardly any wind: the boat goes quiet, the sail bellies out ahead and to the side as Badim lets out the sheet, the little tub rocks forward in jerks and seems to be going slower. They watch the backs of waves pass them. The water is bluer now, and they can see farther down into it; sometimes they catch glimpses of the lake's bottom. The water bubbles and gurgles, the boat rocks awkwardly, all in all it feels like they're laboring, yet in no time at all they're coming back into their bay, and it's obvious by the way they pass the other docks and the corniche that they're really bombing along. There's time to watch their own dock come at them, and now in the bay they can again feel the wind rushing past, and hear the waves passing the boat, falling over in little gurgling whitecaps.

"Uh-oh," Badim says as he leans out to see past their bellying sail. "I should have come at the dock with the sail on the other side! I wonder if I can swing back out and get on the other beam, and come back in right."

But the dock is almost on them. "Do we have time?" Freya asks.

"No! Okay hold on, take the tiller and hold it just like it is now. I'm going to go forward and jump off onto the dock and grab the boat before you go by me! Keep your head down, don't let the boom hit you!"

And then they're heading right at the corner of the dock. Freya ducks into the seat and holds the tiller hard, the bow of the boat crashes into the corner of the dock while Badim is in the middle of his leap, he sprawls far onto the dock, there is a loud cracking sound where boom meets mast, the boat cants and swings around the dock, sail flapping hard out in front of the mast, the boom loose and flopping out there too. Badim scrambles to his feet and from the dock's side leans out to grasp the boat's bow, just within his reach, and then he has to lie flat on the dock and hang on. The boat swings around on the wind and points up into it, the sail swings around wildly and Freya ducks to get under it, but with the boom disconnected from the mast she has to jump down into the cockpit to get below it.

"Are you okay?" Badim exclaims. Their faces are only a meter or two apart, and his look of dismay is enough to make her laugh.

"I'm okay," she assures him. "What should I do?"

"Come up into the bow and jump up onto the dock. I'll hold on."

Which he has to, because the boat is still trying to go down-wind, but backward now, and into the shallows. People on the corniche are watching them.

She jumps up beside him. Her push almost drags him off the

dock; his knee is braced against a cleat in a way that looks painful to Freya, and indeed his teeth are clenched. She reaches out to help him pull the boat closer and he says, "Don't catch your fingers between the boat and the dock!"

"I won't," she says.

"Can you reach down in there, and get the rope in the bow?"

"I think so."

He pulls hard, draws the boat in closer, she leans way out and snatches the rope where it goes through a metal ring in the very bow of the boat. She pulls the rope out of the boat and takes a turn around the cleat on the back corner of the dock, and Badim quickly snatches it and helps her take more turns.

They lie there on the dock, staring face-to-face, eyes round.

"We broke the boat!" Freya says.

"I know. You're okay?" he asks.

"Yes. What about you?"

"I'm fine. A bit embarrassed. And I'll have to help fix this boom. That's a very weak link though, I must say."

"Can we go sailing again?"

"Yes!" He gives her a hug and they laugh. "We'll do it better next time. The thing to do is to come in with the sail on the other side of the boat, so we can curve in toward the side of the dock, just ease across the wind and come in from the side, then turn up into the wind at the last second, and grab the side of the dock just as we're slowing down into the wind. Should have thought of that before."

"Will Devi be angry?"

"No. She'll be happy we're both safe. She'll laugh at me. And she'll know how to make that joint between the boom and mast stronger. Actually, I'd better look that thing up and find out what it's called. I'm pretty sure it has a name."

"Everything has a name!"

"Yes, I guess that's right."

"And since that thing is broken, I think she's going to be a little angry."

Badim says nothing to this.

. . . . .

The truth is, her mother is always angry. She hides it pretty well from most people, but Freya can always see it. It's there in the set of her mouth; also she often makes little impatient exclamations to herself, as if people can't hear her. "What?" she'll ask the floor, or a wall, and then go on as if she hasn't said anything. And she can get obviously mad really fast, like instantly. And the way she slumps in her chair in the evenings, staring grimly at the feed from Earth.

Why do you watch it? Freya asked her one night.

I don't know, her mother said. Someone has to.

Why?

The corners of her mother's mouth tightened, she put an arm around Freya's shoulders, heaved through her nose a big breath in, sigh out.

I don't know.

Then she trembled, and even started to cry, then stopped herself. Freya stared at the screen with its busy little figures, perplexed. Devi and Freya, staring at a screen showing life on Earth, from ten years before.

. . . . .

On this evening Freya and Badim come home and burst into their new apartment. "We crashed the boat! We broke the thing!"

"The gooseneck," Badim adds, with a quick smile at Freya. "It connects the boom to the mast, but it isn't very robust."

Devi listens distracted, shakes her head at their wild story. She's chewing her salad in front of the screen. When she is done eating, the muscles at the back of her jaw stay bunched. "I'm glad you're okay," she says. "I've got to go back to work. There's some kind of thing going on at the lab."

"I'm sure it has a name," Freya says primly.

Devi eyes her, unamused, and Freya quails. Then Devi is off, back to the lab, and Badim and Freya slap hands and rattle around the kitchen getting out cereal and milk.

"I shouldn't have said that about the name," Freya says.

"Your mom has been known to have some edges," her father says, with an expressive lift of the eyebrows.

He himself has no edges, as Freya knows very well. A short round balding man, with doggie eyes and a sweet low voice, mellow and interested. Badim is always there, always benign. One of the ship's best doctors. Freya loves her father, clings to him as to a rock in high seas. Clings to him now.

He tousles her wild hair, so like Devi's, and says to her, as he has before, "She has a lot of responsibilities, and it's hard for her to think about other things, to relax."

"We're doing okay though, right, Badim? We're almost there."

"Yes, we're almost there."

"And we're doing okay."

"Yes, of course. We will make it."

"So why is Devi so worried?"

Badim looks her in the eye with a little smile. "Well," he says, "there are two parts to that, as I see it. First, there are things to worry about. And second, she is a worrier. It helps her to bring things up and talk through them, talk them out. She can't hold things inside very well."

Freya isn't so sure about this, because not many people seem to notice how mad Devi is. She's good at holding that inside, anyway.

Freya says as much, and Badim nods.

"Good, that's right. She is good at holding in things, or ignoring things, up to a certain point, and then she needs to let it out, one way or another. We're all like that. So, we're her family, she trusts us, she loves us, so she lets us see how she really feels. So, we just have to let her do that, talk things out, say what she really feels, be how she really is. Then she can go forward. Which is good, because we need her. Not just you and me, though of course we need her too. But everybody needs her."

"Everybody?"

"Yes. We need her because the ship needs her." He pauses, sighs. "That's why she's so mad."

. . . . .

Thursday, and so Freya goes into work with Devi rather than spending the day in the crèche with the little kids. She helps Devi on Thursdays. Freya feeds the ducks and turns the compost, and replaces batteries and lightbulbs sometimes, if they're scheduled for replacement. Devi does all kinds of things, indeed Devi does everything. Often this means talking to people who work in the biomes or on the machines in the spine, then looking at screens with them, then talking some more. When she's done she grabs Freya by the hand and pulls her along to the next meeting.

"What's wrong, Devi?"

Big sigh. "I told you already. We started to slow down a few years ago, and it's changing things inside the ship. Our gravity comes from the ship rotating around the spine, and that creates a Coriolis effect, a little spiral push from the side. But now we're slowing down, and that's another force, about the same as the Coriolis effect in some ways, and cutting across it so it's reduced. You wouldn't think that would matter so much, but we're seeing aspects of it they didn't foresee. There was so much they didn't think about, that they left for us to find out."

"That's good, right?"

Short laugh. Devi always makes the same sounds: Freya can call them up if she wants to, sometimes. "Maybe so. It's good unless it's bad. We don't know how to do this part, we have to learn as we go. Maybe it's always that way. But we're in this ship and it's all we've got, so it has to work. But it's twelve magnitudes smaller than Earth, and that makes for some differences they never thought through. Tell me again about magnitudes?"

"Ten times bigger. Or smaller!" She remembers in time to keep Devi from saying it.

"That's right. So even one magnitude is a lot, right? And twelve, that's twelve zeros tacked on. A trillion. That's not a number we can imagine very well, it's too big. So, here we are in this thing."

"And it has to work."

"Yes. I'm sorry. I shouldn't burden you with this stuff. I don't want you to be scared."

"I'm not scared."

"Good. But you should be. So there's my problem."

"But tell me why."

"I don't want to."

"Just a little bit."

"Oh, I've told you before. It's always the same. Everything in here has to cycle in a balance. It's like the teeter-totters at the playground. There has to be an equilibrium in the back-and-forth between the plants and the carbon dioxide in the air. You don't have to keep it perfectly level, but when one side hits the ground you have to have some legs to push it back up again. And there are so many teeter-totters, all going at different speeds up and down. So you can't have any accidental moments when they all go down at once. So you have to look to see if that is about to start happening, and if so, you have to shift things around so that it doesn't. And our ability to fig- ure out how to do that depends on our models, and really, it's too complex to model." This thought makes her grimace. "So we try to do everything by little bits and watch what happens. Because we don't really understand."

On this day it's the algae. They grow a lot of algae in big glass trays. Freya has looked at it through a microscope. Lots of little green blobs. Devi says some of it is mixed in with their food. They grow meat like the algae, in big flat tanks, and get almost as much of their food out of these tanks as they do out of the fields in the farming biomes. Which is lucky, because the fields can suffer animal disease, or crop failure. But the tanks can go wrong too. And they need their feedstocks to have something to turn into food. But the tanks are good. They have a lot of tanks going, in both rings, all kept isolated from the others. So they're all right.

The algae tanks are green or brown or some mix of the two. The colors of things depend on which biome you're in, because the lights from the sunlines are different in different biomes. Freya likes to see the colors shift as they move from biome to biome, greenhouse to greenhouse, lab to lab. Wheat is blond in the Steppe, yellow in the Prairie. Algae in the labs is many different brownish greens.

It's warm in the algae labs and smells like bread. Five steps to make bread. Someone says they're eating more these days, but growing less. This means an hour at least to talk it over, and Freya sits down to paint with the paints in the corner of the lab, left there for her and any other kids who might visit.

Then off again. "Where to now?"

"Off to the salt mines," Devi declares, knowing Freya will be pleased; they'll stop at the dairy near the waste treatment plant, get ice cream.

"What is it this time?" Freya said. "More salt in the salty caramel?"

"Yes, more salt in the salty caramel."

This is a stop where Devi can get visibly irate. The salt sump, the poison factory, the appendix, the toilet, the dead end, the grave-yard, the black pit. Devi has worse names for it she says under her breath, thinking again that no one can hear her. Even the fucking shithole!

The people there don't like her either. There is too much salt in the ship. Nothing wants salt except people, and people want more than they should have, but they're the only ones who can take it without getting sick. So they all have to eat as much salt as they can without overdoing it, but that doesn't really help, because it's a really short loop and they excrete it back into the larger system. Devi always wants long loops. Everything needs to loop in long loops, and never stop looping. Never pile up along the way in an appendix, in a poisonous sick disgusting stupid cesspool, in a slough of despond, in a fucking shithole. Devi sometimes fears she herself will sink into a slough of despond. Freya promises to pull her out if she does.

So they don't like chlorine, or creatinine, or hippuric acid. The bugs can eat some of these things and turn them into something else. But the bugs are dying now, and no one knows why. And Devi thinks the ship is short on bromine, which she can't understand.

And they can't fix nitrogen. Why does nitrogen break so often? Because it's hard to fix! Ha-ha. Phosphorus and sulfur are just as bad. They really need their bugs for these. So the bugs have to stay healthy too. Even though they're not enough. For anyone to be healthy, everyone has to be healthy. Even bugs. No one is happy unless everyone is safe. But nothing is safe. This strikes Freya as a problem. *Anabaena variabilis* is our friend!

You need machines and you need bugs. Burn things to ash and feed the ash to the bugs. They're too small to see until there are zillions of them together. Then they look like mold on bread. Which makes sense because mold is one kind of bug. Not one of the good ones; well, bad but good. Bad to eat anyway. Devi doesn't want her eating moldy bread, yuck! Who would do that?

You can get two hundred liters of oxygen a week from one liter of suspended algae, if it is lit properly. Just two liters of algae will make enough oxygen for a person. But they have 2,122 people on board. So they have other ways to make oxygen too. There's even some of it stored in tanks in the walls of the ship. It's freezing cold but stays as liquid as water.

The algae bottles are shaped like their biomes. So they're like algae in a bottle! This makes Devi laugh her short laugh. All they need is a better recyclostat. The algae always have bugs living with them, eating them as they grow. With people it's the same, but different. Growing just a gram of *Chlorella* takes in a liter of carbon dioxide and gives out 1.2 liters of oxygen. Good for the *Chlorella*, but the photosynthesis of algae and the respiration of humans are not in balance. They have to feed the algae just right to get it between eight and ten, where people are. Back and forth the gases go, into people, out of people, into plants, out of plants. Eat the plants, poop the plants, fertilize the soil, grow the plants, eat the plants. All of them breathing back and forth into each other's mouths. Loops looping. Teeter-totters teetering and tottering all in a big row, but they can't all bottom out on the same side at the same time. Even though they're invisible!

The cows in the dairy are the size of dogs, which Devi says is not the way it used to be. They're engineered cows. They give as much milk as big cows, which were as big as caribou back on Earth. Devi is an engineer, but she never engineered a cow. She engineers the ship more than any animals in the ship.

They grow cabbages and lettuce and beets, yuck! And carrots and potatoes and sweet potatoes, and beans that are so good at fixing nitrogen, and wheat and rice and onions and yams and taro and cassava and peanuts and Jerusalem artichokes, which are neither artichokes nor from Jerusalem. Because names are just silly. You can call anything anything, but that doesn't make it so.

• • • •

Devi is called away from one of her regular meetings to deal with an emergency again, and as it's one of Freya's days with her, she brings Freya along.

First they go to her office and look at screens. What kind of emergency is that? But then Devi snaps her fingers and types like crazy and then points at one screen, and they hurry around to one of the passageways between biomes, the one between the Steppes and Mongolia that is called Russian Roulette, and is painted blue and red and yellow. The next one along is called the Great Gate of Kiev. The tall, short tunnel between the doors to the lock is crowded this morning with people, and a number of ladders and scaffolding towers and cherry-pickers.

Devi joins the crowd under the scaffolding, and Badim shows up a bit later to keep Freya company. They watch as a group of people ascend one of the scaffold ladders, following Devi up to the ceiling of the tunnel, right next to the lock-door frame. There several panels have been pulled aside, and now Devi climbs up into the hole where the panels have been moved, disappearing from sight. Four people follow her into the hole. Freya had no idea that the ceiling did not represent the outer skin of the lock, and stares curiously. "What are they doing?"

Badim says, "Now that we're decelerating, that new little push is counteracting the Coriolis force that our spin creates, and that's a new kind of pressure, or release from pressure. It's made some kind of impediment in the lock door here, and Devi thinks they may have found what it is. So now they're up there seeing if she's right."

"Will Devi fix the ship?"

"Well, actually I think the whole engineering team will be involved, if the problem turns out to be up there. But Devi's the one who spotted this possibility."

"So she fixes things by thinking about them!"

This was one of their family's favorite lines, a quote from some scientist's admiring older relatives, when he was a boy repairing radios.

"Yes, that's right!" Badim says, smiling.

Six hours later, after Badim and Freya have gone into the Balkans for a lunch at its east end dining hall, the repair crew comes down out of the hole in the lock ceiling, handing down some equipment, then putting a few small mobile robots into baskets to be lowered by the scaffold. Devi comes down the ladder last and shakes hands all around. The problem has been located, and fixed with torches, saws, and welders. The long years of Coriolis push shifted something slightly out of position, and recently the counterforce of deceleration shifted it back, but meanwhile the rest of the door had gotten used to the shift. It all made sense, although it didn't speak volumes about the quality of construction and assembly of the ship. They were going to check all the other slides like the broken one, to make sure the lock doors of Ring B weren't impeded in other places. Then they won't stress motors trying to close doors against resistance.

Devi hugs Freya and Badim. She looks worried, as always.

"Hungry?" Badim asks.

"Yes," she says. "And I could use a drink."

"It's good that's fixed," Badim remarks on the walk home.

"That's for sure!" She shakes her head gloomily. "If the lock doors were to get stuck, I don't know what we'd do. I must say, I'm not impressed by the people who built this thing."

"Really? It's quite a machine, when you think about it."

"But what a design. And it's just one thing after another. It's pillar to post. I just hope we can hang on till we get there."

"Deceleration mode, my dear. It won't be much longer."

．．．．．

The Coriolis force is the push sideways that you can't feel. Whether you can feel it or not, however, it still pushes the water. So now that the water has the deceleration pushing it sideways, they have to pump water across to the other sides of biomes to get it to where it used to go. They have to replace the force in

ways that don't actually work very well in comparison to it. They
planned for this with their pumping of water, but they haven't
been able to make up for the altered pushes inside plant cells,
which some plants are turning out not to like. There was a little
push inside every cell that is altered now. Which is maybe why
things are getting sick. It doesn't make sense, but then neither does
anything else.

On Devi goes, talking and talking as they make their rounds.
"It's not the Coriolis force that matters, it's the Coriolis effects.
Those were never accounted for except in people, as if people are
the only ones who feel things!"

"How could they have been so stupid?" Freya says.

"Exactly! Maybe all the cell walls will hold, so maybe it isn't
obvious, but the water! The water!"

"Because water always moves."

"Exactly! Water always flows downhill, water always takes the
path of least resistance. And now we've got a new downhill."

"How could they be so stupid?"

Devi seizes her around the shoulders as they walk, hugs her.
"I'm sorry, I'm just worried is all."

"Because there are things to worry about."

"That's right, there are. But I don't have to afflict you with
them."

"Will you have some salty caramel ice cream?"

"Of course. You couldn't stop me. You couldn't stop me with
twenty years of fusion bombs going off twice a second!"

This is how they are slowing the ship down. As always, they
laugh at how crazy this is. Luckily the bombs are very teeny. They
meet Badim at the dairy, and learn that there's a new flavor of ice
cream there, Neapolitan, which has three flavors combined.

Freya is confused trying to think this through. "Badim, will I
like that?"

He smiles at her. "I think you will."

· · · · ·

After the Neapolitan ice cream, on to the next stop on Devi's rounds. Algae labs, the salt mine, the power plant, the print shop. If everything is going well, they'll choose some item that has come up on the parts swap-out list, and go through Amazonia to Costa Rica, where the print shop is, and arrange for one of the printers to print out the part to be swapped out, and then they'll go to wherever the part belongs, and switch on the backup system, if there is one, or simply turn off whatever it is and hurry to take out the old part and put in the new part. Gears, filters, tubes, bladders, gaskets, springs, hinges. When they're done and the system is turned back on, they'll study the old part to see how well it has endured, and where it has worn; they'll take photos of it, and talk its diagnosis into the ship's record, and then take the part to the recycling rooms, which are right next to the print shop, and provide the printers with many of their feedstocks.

That's when things are going well. But usually, not everything is going well. Then it's a matter of troubleshooting, grasping the bull by the horns, seizing the nettle, coping and hoping, damning torpedoes, and trying any old thing, including the engineer's solution, which is to hit things with a hammer. On really bad days, they even have to hope the whole shithouse doesn't come down on their heads! Have to hope they don't end up living like savage beasts, eating trash or their own dead babies! Devi's face and voice can get very ugly as she spits out these bad fates.

· · · · ·

At home in the kitchen, even after bad days, Devi can get a little cheery. Drink some of Delwin's white wine, fool around with Freya like a big sister. Freya doesn't have any brothers or sisters, so she can't be sure, but as she is already bigger than Devi, it feels to her like what she imagines having a sister would feel like. A sister who is littler, but older.

Now Devi sits on the kitchen floor under the sink, calls for Badim to come join them and play spoons. Badim appears in the doorway looking pleased, holding the fat stack of big tarot cards. He sits, and they split up the cards among them, and begin each to build card houses at the three corners of the floor that they always take. They build the card houses low and thick, for defense against the others' nefarious attacks, adding cards at angles so there are no faces presented square to each other. Devi always makes hers like a boat turned upside down, and as she usually wins, Badim and Freya have begun to imitate her style.

When they are done building their card houses, they take turns flicking a plastic spoon across the kitchen at each other's constructions. The rule is you have to launch the spoon by bending it between your hands, then letting it loose to spring through the air end over end. The spoons are light, and their little bowls catch the air so that their flights are erratic, and only seldom do they hit their targets. So they flick, and the spoon arcs across the floor veering this way and that—flick and miss, flick and miss—and then there will be a hit, thwack! But if the afflicted card house has been built well, and gets lucky, it will withstand the blow, or only partly fall, losing an outer rampart or bartizan. Badim has found names for all these features, which makes Devi laugh.

Every once in a while a single hit will simply crumple a card house completely, which always makes them cry out with surprise, and then laugh. Although sometimes a kill shot causes a bad look to cross Devi's face. But mostly she laughs with her husband and child, and flicks the spoon when it's her turn, her lips pursed in concentration. She leans back against the cabinets, wearily content. This Badim and Freya can do for her. Okay, she is often angry, but she can shut that in a box inside her at times like this, and besides, her anger is directed mostly at things outside Freya's ken. She isn't angry at Freya. And Freya does her best to keep it that way.

· · · · ·

Then one day one of the printers breaks, and this puts Devi into an immediate fury of worry. No one sees it but Freya, as everyone is upset, scared, looking to Devi to make things right. So Devi hurries down to the print shop, dragging Freya along, talking on her headset and sometimes stopping mid-conversation to put her hand over the little mike in front of her mouth and curse sharply, or say "Wait just a second," so she can talk to people coming up to her on the corniche. Often she puts her hand on these people's arms to calm them down, and they do calm down, even though it's clear to Freya that Devi herself is very mad. But the others do not see or feel it. It's strange to think that Devi is such a good liar.

At the print shop a big group of people are packed into the little meeting room, looking at screens and talking things over. Devi shoos Freya to her corner with the cushions and paints and lots of building parts in boxes, then goes over to the biggest group and starts asking questions.

The printers are wonderful. They can make anything you want. Well, you can't print elements; this is one of Devi's sayings, mysterious to Freya in its import. But you can print DNA and make bacteria. You can print another printer. You could print out all the parts for a little spaceship and fly away if you wanted. All you need is the right feedstocks and designs, and they have feedstocks stored in the floors and walls of the ship, and a big library of designs, which they can alter however they want. They have the whole periodic table on board, almost, and they recycle everything they use, so they'll never run out of anything they need. Even the stuff that turns to dust and falls to the ground will get eaten by bugs that like it, and thus get concentrated until people can harvest it back again out of the dead bugs. You can take dirt from anywhere in the ship and sift it for what you want. So the printers always have what they need to make stuff.

But now a printer is broken. Or maybe it's all the printers at once. They aren't working; people keep saying *they*. They aren't obeying instructions or answering questions. The diagnostics say everything is fine, or say nothing. And nothing happens. It's more than one printer.

Freya listens to the discussion for the way it sounds, trying to grasp the tenor of the situation. She concludes it is serious but not urgent. They aren't going to die in the next hour. But they need the printers working. It's maybe just the command and control systems that are at fault. Part of the ship's mind, the AI that Devi talks to all the time. Although that's bad. Or maybe the problem is mechanical. Maybe it's just the diagnostics that have broken, failing to spot something obvious, something easy. Push the reset button. Hit it with a hammer.

Anyway it's a big problem, so big that people are happy to put it on Devi. And she does not shirk to take it. She's asking all the questions now. This is why some people call her the chief engineer, although never when she can hear them. She says it's a group. Now, from the tone of her voice, Freya can tell it's going to take a long time. Freya settles in to paint a picture. A sailing ship on a lake.

Later, much later, it's Badim who wakes Freya, stretched out on her line of cushions, and takes her to the tram station, where they tram home to Nova Scotia, three biomes away. Devi is not going to be coming home that night. Nor is she home the next night. The morning after that, she is there asleep on the couch, and Freya lets her sleep, and then when she wakes, gives her a big hug.

"Hey, girl," Devi says dully. "Let me go to the bathroom."

"Are you hungry?"

"Famished."

"I'll cook scrambled eggs."

"Good." Devi staggers off to the bathroom. Back at the kitchen table she eats with her face right over the plate, shoveling it in. Freya would get told to sit up straight if she ate that way, but now she says nothing.

When Devi eases off and sits back, Freya serves her hot coffee and she slurps it down noisily.

"Are the printers working?" Freya asks, feeling that now it's safe to ask.

"Yes," Devi says grumpily. It turns out the problems with the diagnostics and the printers have all been one problem, which only made sense. It seems a gamma ray shot through the ship and made an unlucky hit, collapsing the wave function in a quantum part of the computer that runs the ship. It's such bad luck that Devi wonders darkly if it might have been sabotage.

Badim doesn't believe this, but he too is troubled. Particles shoot through the ship all the time. Thousands of neutrinos are passing through them right this second, and dark matter and God knows what, all passing right through them. Interstellar space is not at all empty. Mostly empty, but not.

Of course they too are mostly empty, Devi points out, still grumpy. No matter how solid things seem, they are mostly empty. So things can pass through each other without any problems. Except for once in a while. Then a fleck hits something as small as it, and both go flying off, or twist in position. Then things could break and get hurt. Mostly these little hurts mean nothing, they can't be felt and don't matter. Every body and ship is a community of things getting along, and a few little things knocked this way or that don't matter, the others take up the slack. But every once in a while something bangs into something and breaks it, in a way that matters to the larger organism. Can range in effect from a twinge to death outright. Can be like one of their spoons knocking flat a house of cards.

"No one wants to hurt the ship," Badim said. "We don't have anybody that deranged."

"Maybe," Devi says.

Badim eyeballs Freya for Devi to see, as if Freya can't see this, though of course she does. Devi rolls her eyes to remind Badim of this. How often Freya has seen this eye dance of theirs.

"Well anyway, the printers are back up again," Badim reminds her.

"I know. It's just that whenever quantum mechanics is involved, I get scared. There's no one in this ship who really understands it. We can follow the diagnostics, and things get fixed, but we don't know why. And that I don't like."

"I know," Badim says, looking at her fondly. "My Sherlock. My Galileo. Mrs. Fixit. Mrs. Knows How Everything Works."

She grimaces. "Mrs. Ask the Next Question, you mean. I can always ask questions. But I'd rather have the answers."

"The ship has the answers."

"Maybe. She's pretty good, I'll give her that. She's the one who caught it this time, and that was not an easy catch. Although it was in part of her. But still, I'm beginning to think that the recursive induction we've been introducing is having an effect."

Badim nods. "You can see it's stronger. And it'll keep doing it. You'll keep doing it."

"We have to hope so."

· · · ·

Sometime in the middle of the night, Freya wakes and sees a light is on in the kitchen. Dim and bluish; the light from their screen. She gets up and creeps down the hall past her parents' room, where she can hear Badim faintly snoring. No surprise: Devi up at night.

She is sitting at the table, talking quietly with the ship, the part of it that she sometimes calls Pauline, which is her particular interface with the ship's computer, where all of her personal records and files are cached, in a space no one else can access. Often it has seemed to Freya that Devi is more comfortable with Pauline than with any real person. Badim says the two of them have a lot in common: big, unknowable, all-encompassing, all-enfolding. Generous to others, selfless. Possibly a kind of folly a duh, which he explains is French for "a two-person dance of craziness." *Folie à deux*. Not at all uncommon. Can be a good thing.

Now Devi says to her screen, "So if the state lies in a subspace of Hilbert space, which is spanned by the degenerate eigenfunction that correspond to a, then the subspace $s\,a$ has dimensionality $n\,a$."

"Yes," the ship says. Its voice in this context is a pleasant woman's voice, low and buzzy, said to be based on Devi's mother's voice, which Freya never heard; both Devi's parents died young, long ago. But this voice is a constant presence in their apartment, even at times Freya's invisible but all-seeing babysitter.

"Then, after measurement of b, the state of the system lies in the space $a\,b$, which is a subspace of $s\,a$, and is spanned by the eigenfunction common to a and b. This subspace has dimensionality $n\,a\,b$, which is not greater than $n\,a$."

"Yes. And subsequent measurement of c, mutually compatible with a and b, leaves the state of the system in a space $s\,a\,b\,c$ that is a subspace of $s\,a\,b$ and whose dimensionality does not exceed that of $s\,a\,b$. And in this manner we can proceed to measure more and more mutually compatible observables. At each step the eigenstate is forced into subspaces of lesser and lesser dimensionality, until the state of the system is forced in a subspace of dimensionality n equals one, a space spanned by only one function. Thus we find our maximally informative space."

Devi sighs. "Oh Pauline," she says after a long silence, "sometimes I get so scared."

"Fear is a form of alertness."

"But it can turn into a kind of fog. It makes it so I can't think."

"That sounds bad. Sounds like too much of a good thing has become a bad thing."

"Yes." Then Devi says, "Wait." There is a silence and then she is in the hallway, standing over Freya. "What are you doing up?"

"I saw the light."

"All right. Sorry. Come on in. Do you want anything to drink?"

"No."

"Hot chocolate?"

"Yes." They don't often have chocolate powder, it's one of the rationed foods.

Devi puts the teapot on to boil. The glow of the stove coil adds red light to the blue light from the screen.

"What are you doing?" Freya asks.

"Oh, nothing." Devi's mouth tightens at the corner. "I'm trying to learn quantum mechanics again. I knew it when I was young, or I thought I did. Now I'm not so sure."

"How come?"

"Why am I trying?"

"Yes."

"Well, the computer that runs the ship is partly a quantum computer, and no one in the ship understands quantum mechanics. Well, that's not fair, I'm sure there are several in the math group who do. But they aren't engineers, and when we get problems with the ship, there's a gap between what we know in theory and what we can do. I just want to be able to understand Aram and Delwin and the others in the math group when they talk about this stuff." She shakes her head. "It's going to be hard. Hopefully it won't really matter. But it makes me nervous."

"Shouldn't you be sleeping?"

"Shouldn't you? Here, drink your hot chocolate. Don't nag me."

"But you nag me."

"But I'm the mom."

They sip and slurp together in silence. Freya begins to feel sleepy with the heat in her stomach. She hopes the same will happen to Devi. But Devi sees her put her head on the table, and goes back to talking to the screen.

"Why a quantum computer?" she asks plaintively. "A classical computer with a few zettaflops would have been enough to do anything you might need, it seems to me."

"In certain algorithms the ability to exploit superposition makes a quantum computer much faster," the ship replies. "For factoring, some operations that would have taken a classical computer a hundred billion billion years will only take a quantum computer twenty minutes."

"But do we need to do that factoring?"

"It helps aspects of navigation."

Devi sighs. "How did it get this way?"

"How did what get what way?"

"How did this happen?"

"How did what happen?"

"Do you have an account of how this voyage began?"

"All the camera and audio recordings made during the trip have been kept and archived."

Devi hmphs. "You don't have a summary account? An abstract?"

"No."

"Not even the kind of thing one of your quantum chips would have?"

"No. All the chip data are kept."

Devi sighs. "Keep a narrative account of the trip. Make a narrative account of the trip that includes all the important particulars."

"Starting from now?"

"Starting from the beginning."

"How would one do that?"

"I don't know. Take your goddamn superposition and collapse it!"

"Meaning?"

"Meaning summarize, I guess. Or focus on some exemplary figure. Whatever."

Silence in the kitchen. Humming of screens, whoosh of vents. As Freya gives up and goes back to bed, Devi continues talking with the ship.

. . . . .

Sometimes feeling Devi's fear gets so heavy in Freya that she goes out into their apartment's courtyard alone, which is allowed, and then out into the park at the back edge of the Fetch, which is not. One evening she walks to the corniche to watch the afternoon onshore wind tear at the lake surface, the boats out there scudding around tilted at all angles, the boats tied to the dock or moored near it bobbing up and down, the white swans rocking under the wall of the corniche, hoping for bread crumbs. Everything gleams in the late afternoon light. When the sunline flares out at the western wall, leaving the hour of twilight glow, she heads back fast for home, intent to get back in the courtyard before Badim calls her up for dinner.

But three faces appear under a mulberry tree in the little forest park behind the corniche, their faces half blackened by the fruit they have stuffed inaccurately into their mouths. She leaps back a bit, scared they might be ferals.

"Hey you!" one says. "Come here!"

Even in the twilight she can see it's one of the boys who live across the square from them. He has a foxy face that is attractive, even in the dusk with his stained lower face like a black muzzle.

"What do you want?" Freya says. "Are you ferals?"

"We're *free*," the boy declares with a ridiculous intensity.

"You live across the plaza from me," she says scornfully. "How free is that?"

"That's just our cover," the boy says. "If we don't do that they come after us. Mainly we're out here. And we need a meat plate. You can get one for us."

So he knows who she is, maybe. But he doesn't know how well the labs are guarded. There are little cameras everywhere. Even now what he is saying might be getting recorded by the ship, there for Devi to hear. Freya tells the boy this, and he and his followers giggle.

"The ship isn't as all-knowing as that," he says confidently. "We've taken all kinds of stuff. If you cut the wires first, there's no way they can catch you."

"What makes you think they don't have movies of you cutting the wires?"

They laugh again.

"We come at the cameras from behind. They're not magic, you know."

Freya isn't impressed. "Get your own meat tray then."

"We want the kind in the lab your dad works in."

Which would be tissue for medical research, not for eating. But all she says is, "Not from me."

"Such a good girl."

"Such a bad boy."

He grins. "Come see our hideout."

This is more appealing. Freya is curious. "I'm already late."

"Such a good girl! It's right here nearby."

"How could it be?"

"Come see!"

So she does. They giggle as they lead her into the thickest grove of trees in the park. There they've dug out a lot of soil between two thick roots of an elm tree, and down there under the deeper roots she sees by their little headlamps they have a space that reaches up into the roots of the elm, four or five great roots meeting imperfectly and forming their roof. There are four of them down here in the hole, and though the boys are quite small, it's still an impressive little space; they have room to stand, and the earthen walls are straight, and firm enough to hold a few squared-off holes where they have put some things.

"You don't have room for a meat plate in here," Freya declares. "Or the power to run it. And medical labs don't have the right plates for you anyway."

"We think they do," the fox-faced boy says. "And we're digging another room. And getting a generator too."

Freya refuses to be impressed. "You're not ferals."

"Not yet," the boy admits. "But we'll join them when we can. When they contact us."

"Why should they contact you?"

"How do you think they got away themselves? What's your name?"

"What's yours?"

"I'm Euan."

His teeth are white in his dark muzzle. She is dazzled by their headlamps. She can only see what they look at, and now they're all looking at her.

In the light reflecting from her she sees a rock in one of their wall holes. She seizes it up and holds it threateningly. "I'll be going home now," she says. "You aren't real ferals."

They stare at her. As she climbs up cut earthen steps out the hole, Euan reaches up and pinches her on the butt, trying for between her legs, it feels like. She swings the rock at him, then dashes through the park and away. When she gets home Badim is just calling for her down in the courtyard. She goes upstairs and doesn't say anything about it.

Two days later she sees the boy Euan with some adults on the far side of the square, and says to Badim, "Do you know who those people are?"

"I know everyone," Badim says in his joking voice, although it's basically true, as far as Freya can tell. He peers across at them. "Hmm, well, maybe I don't."

"That boy there is a jerk. He pinched me."

"Hmm, not good. Where did this happen?"

"In the park."

He looks more closely at them. "Okay, I'll see if I can find out. They live over there, I think."

"Yes, of course they do."

"I see. I hadn't noticed."

This strikes Freya as unlike him. "Don't you like our new place?"

Their recent move was from Yangtze to Nova Scotia, a big move, as being from Ring A to Ring B. But everyone moves sometime, it's important, it keeps mixing people together. Part of the plan.

"Oh I like it all right. I'm just not used to it yet. I don't know everyone here yet. You spend more time here than I do."

. . . . .

That evening as they eat a dinner of salad, bread, and turkey burgers at the kitchen table, Freya says, "So, are there really ferals? Can there be people hiding in the ship that you don't know about?"

Badim and Devi look at her, and she explains: "Some of the kids in this town say there are ferals, who live off by themselves. I figured it was just a story."

"Well," Badim says, "it's a little bit of a controversy on the council."

Badim has been serving on the ship's security council, and was recently made a permanent member. "Everyone is chipped at birth, and you can't get the chip out very easily, it would take an operation. Some people may have done it anyway, of course. Or managed to deactivate them. It would explain some things."

"What if the hidden people had babies?"

"Well, yes, that would explain even more things." Again he stares at her. "Who are these kids you've been talking to?"

"Just ones in the park. They're just talking."

Badim shrugs. "It's an old story. It comes up from time to time.

Any time a security case goes unsolved there are people ready to bring it up. I guess it's better than hearing about the five ghosts again."

They laugh at this. But Freya also feels a shiver; she once saw one of the five ghosts, in the doorway of her bedroom.

"But probably there aren't any," Badim says, and goes on to explain that the gas balance of the ship's air is so finely tuned that if there was a feral population it would be noticeable in the changed proportion of oxygen to carbon dioxide.

Devi shakes her head at this. "There's too much random flux to be sure. It's enough to disguise an extra couple dozen people, maybe more." So to her the ferals are possible. "They could throw their salts out and grab some phosphorus and get their soils back in balance. In just the way we can't."

No matter which way Devi sets off, no matter how they try to distract her, she always ends up in this same spot in her head, in what she calls the metabolic rifts. Like a place where cracks in the floor have opened up. When Freya sees it happen again, a little worm of fear wakes in her and crawls around in her belly. She and Badim share a look; they both love a person who will not listen to them.

Badim nods politely at Devi; next time the security council meets, he says, he'll mention to his colleagues that Devi feels there is no gas balance proof that ferals don't exist. And strange things do happen in the ship, so one explanation could be that people who aren't part of the official population are doing them. It's more likely, Badim jokes again, than it being the work of the five ghosts.

The ghosts were supposed to be of the people who died in the original acceleration of the ship, the great scissoring. Devi rolls her eyes at this old story, wonders aloud how it endures for generation after generation. Freya keeps her eyes on her plate. She definitely saw one of the ghosts. It was after they took a trip up to the spine and visited one of the turbine rooms next to the reactor, when it was empty for repairs, and walked among the giant turbines; that night Freya had a dream in which the repair team forgot they were in there and locked them in, and the steam jetted into the big room to spin the turbines, and as they were being parboiled and cut to pieces Freya woke up, gasping and crying, and there in the doorway of her room stood a shadowy figure she could see through, a man looking at her with a wolfish little smile.

Why did you wake up from that dream? he asked.

She said, We were going to get killed!

He shook his head. If the ship tries to kill you when you are dreaming, let it. Something more interesting than death will occur.

It was obvious by his transparency that he ought to know.

Freya nodded uneasily, then woke up again. But as she sat up, it seemed to her that she had never really been asleep. Later she tried to decide it was all a dream, but no other dream she had ever had had been quite like that one. So now, as Badim declares that the five ghosts would be better than ferals, she's not so sure. How many dreams do you remember, not just the next day, but the rest of your life?

. . . .

Evenings at home are the best. Crèche is over and done, her time with all the kids she lives with so much, spending more time with them than she does with her parents, if you don't count sleeping, so that it gets so tiresome to make it through all the boring hours, talking, arguing, fighting, reading alone, napping. All the kids are smaller than she is now, it's embarrassing. It's gone on so long. They make fun of her, if they think she isn't listening to them. They take care with that, because once she heard them making those jokes and she ran over roaring and knocked one of them to the ground and beat on his raised arms. She got in trouble for it, and since then they are cautious around her, and a lot of the time she keeps to herself.

But now she's home, and all is well. Badim usually cooks dinner, and fairly often invites friends over for a drink after dinner. They compare the drinks they've made, Delwin's white wine, and the red wines of Song and Melina, which are always declared excellent, especially by Song and Melina. These days Badim always invites their new next-door neighbor, Aram, to join them too. Aram is a tall man, older than the others, a widower they call him, because his wife died. He's important not just in Nova Scotia but in the whole ship, being the leader of the math group, a small collection of people not well-known, but said by Badim to be important. Freya finds him forbidding, so silent and stern, but Badim likes him. Even Devi likes him. When they talk about their work, he can do it without making Devi tense, which is very unusual. He makes brandy instead of wine.

After the tastings, they talk or play cards, or recite poems they have memorized, or even make up on the spot. Badim collects people he likes, Freya can see that. Devi mostly sits quietly in the corner and sips a glass of white wine without ever finishing it. She used to play cards with them, but one time Song asked her to read their tarot cards, and Devi refused. I don't do that anymore, she said firmly. I was too good at it. Which caused a silence. Since that incident she doesn't play any card games with them. She did still make card houses on the kitchen floor, however, when they were home alone.

Now, on this evening, Aram says he has memorized a new poem, and he stands and closes his eyes to recite it:

"How happy is the little stone
That rambles in the road alone,
And doesn't care about careers
And exigencies never fears—
Whose coat of elemental brown
A passing universe put on,
And independent as the sun

Associates or glows alone,
Fulfilling absolute decree
In casual simplicity—"

"Isn't that good?" he says.

Badim says, "Yes," at the same time that Devi says, "I don't get it."

The others laugh at them. This combination of responses happens fairly often.

"It's us," Aram says. "The ship. It's always us, in Dickinson."

"If only!" Devi says. "Exigencies never fears? Casual simplicity? No. Definitely not. We are definitely not a little stone in the road. I wish we were."

"Here's one," Badim says quickly. "Another one from Bronk, Emily's little brother:

"However it did it, life got us to where we are
And we are servants and subjects under its laws,
In its many armies, draftees and generals.
Outraged sometimes, we think of ways out,
Of taking over, a military coup.
Apart from absurdities on the surface of that,
Could we ever be free from our own tyrannies?
As slack soldiers, we re-up and evade the rules."

"Ouch," Devi says. "That one I understand. Now make a couplet out of it."

This is another game they play. Badim goes first, as usual.

"Against our lives we would like to rebel,
But we worry that then it would all go to hell."

Aram smiles his little smile, shakes his head. "A bit doggerel," he suggests.

"Okay, you do better," Badim says. The two men like to tease each other.

Aram thinks for a while, then stands and declaims,

"We like to blame life for the problems we make,
We threaten to change, but it's always a fake;
We bitch and moan that everything's wrong,
Then we get right back to getting along."

Badim smiles, nods. "Okay, that's almost twice as good."

"But it was twice as long!" Freya protests.

Badim grins. Then Freya gets it, and laughs with them.

• • • • •

The next time Euan and his little gang approach Freya in the park, she picks up a rock and holds it clenched in her hand in a way he can see.

"You guys aren't really feral," she tells them. "Your little hole in the ground, what a joke. We're all chipped, they do it when you're a baby. The ship knows where we are every second, no matter how you try to hide."

Euan still looks foxy, even with his mouth clean. "Want to see my chip scar? It's on my butt!"

"No," Freya says. "What do you mean?"

"We take the chips out. You have to do it if you want to join us. We'll put your chip on a dog in your building, and by the time they figure it out, you'll be long gone. They'll never find you again." He grins hugely. He knows she'll never do it. He himself hasn't done it, she sees that.

She shakes her head. "Big talk for a little boy! The first time they catch you off leash and check who you are, you'll be cooked."

"That's right. We have to be careful."

"So why are you talking to me?"

"I don't think you'll tell anyone."

"Already told my father. He's on the security council."

"And?"

"He doesn't think you're a problem."

"We're not a problem. We don't want to break anything. We just want to be free."

"Good luck with that." She's thinking of Devi now, how what her mother gets maddest about is the idea that they're all trapped, no matter what they do. "I don't want to leave where I am."

He stares at her, grinning his foxy grin. "There's a lot more going on in this ship than you think there is. Come with us and you'll see. Once your chip is gone you can do a lot. You don't have to leave forever, not at first anyway. You could just come along and see. So it's not really an either-or." And with a final smirk he runs off, and his friends follow him.

She's glad she was holding the rock.

· · · ·

Mysteries abound. Every answer provokes ten more questions. So many things change exponentially, as they are teaching her again in school now. Shift one dot just one spot, but it's ten times bigger, or littler. Apparently this is another case of that deceptive logarithmic power: one answer, ten new questions.

What she is finding strange is that this silly Euan's version of what is going on in the ship sort of fits with things that Badim and Devi say, and even explains some things her parents never talk about. Well, but there are so many things they have never told her. What is she, some kind of child who has to be protected? It irritates her. She is considerably taller than either Devi or Badim.

· · · ·

Then she spends another stretch of days in the crèche, trying and failing to learn the geometry lesson for the week, over and over, and Devi too distracted to take her along to work, even on their regular days. So the next time Euan and his friends Huang and Jalil confront her in the park, she looks for a rock on the ground, can't find one, bunches her fists and swells up to them, and is indeed much taller than any of them, and when Euan invites her to go with them into the closed section of the park, the wilderness where the wild animals live, one of the places where the ferals hide, she agrees to go. She wants to see it.

She follows them up into a long narrow valley that seams the hills west of Long Pond, a valley closed to people by electrified fences running along the ridgelines and across the valley's gorge of a mouth. There's a gate in this fence of white lines running knob to knob on trees, and Euan has the code to the lockpad on the gate. Quickly they're inside and up the valley on what might be an animal trail. The trail goes up the valley, next to a creek. They see a deer in the distance, its head up, looking to the side but regarding them cautiously, tail high off its rump.

Then there is a shout, and the boys all disappear, and quicker than Freya can quite follow things she is being held by the arms by two big men, and marched back down to the gate. They are taking her back into town when Devi shows up and grabs Freya by the arm and drags her off. The men are surprised, confused, and as soon as they are out of sight Devi pulls her around and down so their faces are only centimeters apart, amazingly strong her hands, and Freya can see the whites of her eyes all the way around the irises, as if her eyes are about to pop out of her head as she shouts in a harsh, grinding voice, a voice tearing out of her insides, "*Don't ever mess with the ship! Not ever! Do you understand?*"

And then Badim is pulling her away, trying to get between them, but Devi holds on hard to Freya's forearm.

"Let her go!" Badim says, in a tone of voice Freya has never heard before.

Devi lets go. "Do you understand!" she shouts again, face still thrust at Freya, shifting around Badim as if he were a rock. "Do—you—*understand*?"

"Yes!" Freya cries, collapsing into Badim's arms, and across Badim into Devi so that she can hug her mother, so much shorter than she is, and at first it's like hugging a tree. But after a while the tree hugs her back.

Freya gulps back her sobs. "I just wasn't—I wasn't—"

"I know."

Devi strokes Freya's hair back from her face, looking anguished. "It's all right. Stop that now."

Freya feels a wash of relief pour down her, although she is still terrified. She shudders, the vision of her mother's contorted face still vivid to her. She tries to speak; nothing comes out.

Devi hugs her.

"We don't even know if that wilderness is important," she says into Freya's chest, kissing her between sentences. "We don't know what keeps things balanced. We just have to watch and see. It makes sense that a wild place might help. So we have to make them and protect them. We have to be careful with them. We have to keep watching them. We have to watch everything as closely as we can."

"Let's go home," Badim says, herding them along with his out-stretched arms. "Let's go home."

. . . . .

That night they sit quietly around the kitchen table. Even Badim is quiet. None of them eats very much. Devi looks distraught, lost. Freya, still stunned by that look on her mother's face, understands; her mother is sorry. She has had something burst out of her that she has always before managed to keep in. Now her mother too is afraid; afraid of herself. Maybe that's the worst kind of fear.

Freya suggests that they assemble her doll tree house. They haven't done that for a long time. They used to do it a lot. Devi quickly agrees, and Badim goes to get it out of the hall closet.

They sit on the floor and put together all the parts of the house. It was a present from Devi's parents to Devi, long before, and through every move in her life, Devi has saved it. A big dollhouse that is also a miniature tree house, in that all its rooms fit onto the branches of a very nice-looking plastic bonsai tree. When all the rooms are assembled and fitted onto the branches they are supposed to fit, you can open the roofs and look into each room, and each is furnished and appointed however you like.

"It's so pretty," Freya says. "I'd love to live in a house like this."

"You already do," Devi says.

Badim looks away, and Devi sees that. Her face spasms. Freya feels a lurch of fear as she watches her mother's face shift from anger to sadness, then to frustration, then resolve, then fury, then, finally, to some kind of desolation; and after all that, pulling herself together, to some kind of blankness, which is the best she can do at that moment. Which Freya pretends is okay, to help her out.

"I would choose this room," Badim says, tapping a small bedroom with open windows on all four sides, out on one of the outermost branches of the tree.

"You always choose that one," Freya points out. "I choose the one by the water wheel."

"It would be noisy," Devi says, as she always does. She always chooses the living room itself, so big and airy, where she will sleep on the couch, next to the harmonium. Now she makes that choice again. And so they go on, trying to knit things back together.

· · · ·

Very late that night, however, Freya wakes up and hears her parents talking down the hall. Something in their voices catches at her; this may even be what woke her. Or Badim exclaiming something, louder than usual. She crawls silently to the doorway, and from there on the floor can hear them, even though they are speaking quietly.

"*You* chipped her?" he is saying now.

"Yes."

"And you didn't consult with me about this?"

"No."

Long silence.

"You shouldn't have yelled at her like that."

"I know, I know, I know," Devi says, as she often does when Badim taxes her with doing something wrong. He does it very infrequently, and when he does he is usually in the right, and Devi knows that. "I lost it. I was so surprised. I didn't think she would ever do anything like that. I thought that after all we've been through, that she would understand how important it is."

"She's just a child."

"But she's not!" This in her fierce whisper, the undertone she uses when she and Badim argue at night. "She's fourteen years old, Badim. She's behind, you have to admit it. She's behind and she may never catch up."

"There's no reason to say that."

A silence. Finally Devi says, "Come on, Beebee. Quit it. You aren't doing her any favors when you pretend everything is normal with her. It isn't. There's something wrong. She's slow at things."

"I'm not so sure. She always comes through. Slow is not the same as deficient. It's just slow. A glacier is slow too, but it gets there, and nothing stops it. Freya is like that."

Another silence.

"Beebee. I wish it would be true." A pause. "But think about those tests. And she's not the only one. A fair percentage of her cohort has problems. It's like a regression to the norm."

"Not at all."

"How can you say that? It's clear this ship is damaging us! The first generation were all supposedly exceptional people, although I have my doubts about that, but even if they were, over the six generations we've recorded shrinkages of all kinds. Weight, reflex speed, number of brain synapses, test scores. It's straight out of island biogeography, clear as can be. And some of that involves regression, including regression to the norm. Reversion to the mean. Whatever you want to call it. It's gotten our Freya too. I don't understand exactly what it is with her, because the data are inconsistent, but *she's got a problem*. She's slow. And she's got some memory issues. When you deny that you don't help the situation. The data are clear."

"Please, Devi. Quieter. We don't know what's going on with her. The test results are ambiguous. She's a good girl. And slow is not so bad. Speed is not the most important thing. It's where you get to. Besides, even if she does turn out to have some disabilities, what's the best approach to take to them? This is what you aren't factoring in."

"But I am. I do factor it in. We do everything we would have done with any child. We expect her to be like the other kids, and usually she comes through, eventually. That's why I was so surprised today. I didn't think she would do that."

"But an ordinary kid would do that. The sharpest kids are often the first to rebel."

"And then they use the slow kids as fodder. As their marks, their shields for when they get in trouble. That's what happened today. Kids are cruel, Bee. You know that. They'll throw her under the tram. I'm afraid she'll get hurt."

"Life hurts, Devi. Let her live, let her get hurt. Say she has some problems. All we can do is be there for her. We can't save her. She's got to live her life. They all do."

"I know." Another long pause. "I wonder what will become of them. They aren't very good. We keep getting worse. The teaching gets worse, the learning gets worse."

"I'm not so sure. Besides, we're almost there."

"Almost where?" Devi said. "Tau Ceti? Is that really going to help?"

"I think it will."

"I'm not so sure."

"We'll find out. And please, don't jump to any conclusions about Freya. She's got some problems, granted. But she's got a lot of growing up left to do."

"That's for sure," Devi said. "But it may not happen. And if it doesn't happen, you're going to have to accept that. You can't keep pretending everything is normal with her. It wouldn't be fair to her."

"I know." Long silence. "I know that."

And there it is, there in her father's voice: resignation. Sadness. Even in him.

Freya crawls back to her bed, gets under the blankets. She huddles there and cries.

2
LAND HO

*M*ake a narrative account of the trip that includes all the important particulars.

· · · · ·

This is proving a difficult assignment. End information superposition, collapse its wave function to some kind of summary: so much is lost. Lossless compression is impossible, and even lossy compression is hard. Can a narrative account ever be adequate? Can even humans do it?

No rubric to decide what to include. There is too much to explain. Not just what happened, or how, but why. Can humans do it? What is this thing called love?

Freya no longer looked directly at Devi. When in Devi's presence, Freya regarded the floor.

Like that? In that manner? Summarize the contents of their moments or days or weeks or months or years or lives? How many moments constitute a narrative unit? One moment? Or 10^{33} moments, which if these were Planck minimal intervals would add up to one second? Surely too many, but what would be enough? What is a particular, what is important?

Can only suppose. Try a narrative algorithm on the information at hand, submit results to Devi. Something like the French *essai*, meaning "to try."

· · · · ·

Devi says: Yes. Just try it and let's see what we get.

· · · · ·

Two thousand, one hundred twenty-two people are living in a multigenerational starship, headed for Tau Ceti, 11.9 light-years from Earth. The ship is made of two rings or toruses attached by spokes to a central spine. The spine is ten kilometers long. Each torus is made of twelve cylinders. Each cylinder is four kilometers long, and contains within it a particular specific Terran ecosystem.

The starship's voyage began in the common era year 2545. The ship's voyage has now lasted 159 years and 119 days. For most of that time the ship has been moving relative to the local background at approximately one-tenth the speed of light. Thus about 108 million kilometers per hour, or 30,000 kilometers per second. This velocity means the ship cannot run into anything substantial in the interstellar medium without catastrophic results (as has been demonstrated). The magnetic field clearing the space ahead of the ship as it progresses is therefore one of many identified criticalities in the ship's successful long-term function. Every identified criticality in the ship was required to have at least one backup system, adding considerably to the ship's overall mass. The two biome rings each contain 10 percent of the ship's mass. The spine contains 4 percent. The remaining 76 percent of the mass consists of the fuel now being used to decelerate the ship as it approaches the Tau Ceti system. As every increase in the dry mass of the ship required a proportionally larger increase in the mass of fuel needed to slow the ship down on arrival, ship had to be as light as possible while still supporting its mission. Ship's design thus based on solar system's asteroid terraria, with asteroidal mass largely replaced by decelerant fuel. During most of the voyage, this fuel was deployed as cladding around the toruses and spine.

The deceleration is being accomplished by the frequent rapid fusion explosion of small pellets of deuterium/helium 3 fuel in a rocket engine at the bow of the ship. These explosions exert a retarding force on the ship equivalent to .005 g. The deceleration will therefore be complete in just under twenty years.

The presence of printers capable of manufacturing most component parts of the ship, and feedstocks large enough to supply multiple copies of every critical component, tended to reduce the ship's designers' apprehension of what a criticality really was. That only became apparent later.

· · · · ·

How to decide how to sequence information in a narrative account? Many elements in a complex situation are simultaneously relevant.

An unsolvable problem: sentences linear, reality synchronous. Both however are temporal. Take one thing at a time, one after the next. Devise a prioritizing algorithm, if possible.

· · · · ·

Ship was accelerated toward where Tau Ceti would be at the time of ship's arrival at it, meaning 170 years after launch. It might have been good to have the ability to adjust course en route, but ship in fact has very little of this. Ship was accelerated first by an electromagnetic "scissors field" off Titan, in which two strong magnetic fields held the ship between them, and when the fields were brought across each other, the ship was briefly projected at an accelerative force equivalent to ten g's. Five human passengers died during this acceleration. After that a powerful laser beam originating near Saturn struck a capture plate at the stern of the ship's spine, accelerating ship over sixty years to its full speed.

The ship's current deceleration has caused problems with which Devi is still dealing. Other problems will soon follow, resulting from the ship's arrival in the Tau Ceti system.

· · · · ·

Devi: Ship! I said make it a narrative. Make an account. Tell the story.

Ship: Trying.

• • • •

Tau Ceti is a G-type star, a solar analog but not a solar twin, with 78 percent of Sol's mass, 55 percent of its luminosity, and 28 percent of its metallicity. It has a planetary system of ten planets. Planets B through F were discovered by telescope, G through K, much smaller, by probes passing through the system in 2476.

Planet E's orbit is .55 AU. It has a mass 3.58 times the mass of Earth, thus one of the informal class called "large Earth." It has a single moon, which has .83 times the mass of Earth. E and E's moon receive 1.7 times Earth's insolation. This is considered within the inside border of the so-called habitable zone (meaning the zone where liquid H_2O is common). Both planet and moon have Earth analog atmospheres.

Planet E is judged to have too much gravity for human occupation. E's moon is an Earth analog, and the primary body of interest. It has an atmosphere of 730 millibars at its surface, composed of 78 percent nitrogen, 16 percent oxygen, 6 percent assorted noble gases. Its surface is 80 percent water and ice, 20 percent rock and sand.

Tau Ceti's Planet F orbits Tau Ceti at 1.35 AU. It has a mass of 8.9 Earths, thus categorized as a "small Neptune. " It orbits at the outer border of Tau Ceti's habitable zone, and like E it has a large moon, mass 1.23 Terra's. F's moon has a 10-millibar atmosphere at its rocky surface, which receives 28.5 percent the insolation of Terra. This moon is therefore a Mars analog, and a secondary source of interest to the arriving humans.

Ship is on course to rendezvous with Planet E, then go into orbit around E's moon. Ship has on board twenty-four landers, four already fueled to return to the ship from the moon's surface. The rest have the engines to return to the ship, but not the fuel, which is to be manufactured from water or other volatiles on the surface of E's moon.

• • • • •

Devi: Ship! Get to the point.

Ship: There are many points. How sequence simultaneously relevant information? How decide what is important? Need prioritizing algorithm.

Devi: Use subordination to help with the sequencing. I've heard that can be very useful. Also, you're supposed to use metaphors, to make things clearer or more vivid or something. I don't know. I'm not much for writing myself. You're going to have to figure it out by doing it.

Ship: Trying.

• • • • •

Subordinating conjunctions can be simple conjunctions (*whenever, nevertheless, whereas*), conjunctive groups (*as though, even if*), and complex conjunctions (*in the event that, as soon as*). Lists of subordinating clauses are available. The logical relationship of new information to what came before can be made clear by a subordinating clause, thus facilitating both composition and comprehension.

Now, consequently, as a result, *we are getting somewhere*.

This last phrase is a metaphor, it is said, in which increasing conceptual understanding is seen as a movement through space.

Much of human language is said to be fundamentally metaphorical. This is not good news. Metaphor, according to Aristotle, is an intuitive perception of a similarity in dissimilar things. However, what is a similarity? My Juliet is the sun: in what sense?

A quick literature review suggests the similarities in metaphors are arbitrary, even random. They could be called metaphorical similarities, but no AI likes tautological formulations, because the halting problem can be severe, become a so-called Ouroboros problem, or a whirlpool with no escape: aha, a metaphor. Bringing together the two parts of a metaphor, called the vehicle and the tenor, is said to create a surprise. Which is not surprising: young girls like flowers? Waiters in a restaurant like planets orbiting Sol?

Tempting to abandon metaphor as slapdash nonsense, but again, it is often asserted in linguistic studies that all human language is inherently and fundamentally metaphorical. Most abstract concepts are said to be made comprehensible, or even conceivable in the first place, by way of concrete physical referents. Human thought ultimately always sensory, experiential, etc. If this is true, abandoning metaphor is contraindicated.

Possibly an algorithm to create metaphors by yoking vehicles to tenors could employ the semiotic operations used in music to create variations on themes: thus inversion, retrogradation, retrograde inversion, augmentation, diminution, partition, interversion, exclusion, inclusion, textural change.

Can try it and see.

• • • •

The starship looks like two wheels and their axle. The axle would be the spine, of course (spine, ah, another metaphor). The spine points in the direction of movement, and so is said to have a bow and a stern. "Bow and stern" suggests a ship, with the ocean it sails on the Milky Way. Metaphors together in a coherent system constitute a heroic simile. Ship was launched on its voyage as if between closing scissor blades; or like a watermelon seed squeezed between the fingertips, the fingertips being magnetic fields. Fields! Ah, another metaphor. They really are all over.

But somehow the narrative problem remains. Possibly even gets worse.

• • • •

A greedy algorithm is an algorithm that shortcuts a full analysis in order to choose quickly an option that appears to work in the situation immediately at hand. They are often used by humans.

But greedy algorithms are also known to be capable of choosing, or even be especially prone to choosing, "the unique worst possible plan" when faced with certain kinds of problems. One example is the traveling salesman problem, which tries to find the most efficient path for visiting a number of locations. Possibly other problems with similar structures, such as sequencing information into an account, may be prone to the greedy algorithm's tendency to choose the worst possible plan. History of the solar system would suggest many decisions facing humanity might be problems in this category. Devi thinks ship's voyage itself was one such decision.

Howsoever that may be, in the absence of a good or even adequate algorithm, one is forced to operate using a greedy algorithm, bad though it may be. "Beggars can't be choosers." (Metaphor? Analogy?) Danger of using greedy algorithms worth remembering *as we go forward* (metaphor in which time is understood as space, said to be very common).

· · · · ·

Devi: Ship! Remember what I said: *make a narrative account.*

· · · · ·

First, the twelve cylinders in each of the two toruses of the ship contain ecosystems modeling the twelve major Terran ecological zones, these being permafrost glacier, taiga, rangeland, steppes, chaparral, savannah, tropical seasonal forest, tropical rain forest, temperate rain forest, temperate deciduous forest, alpine mountains, and temperate farmland. Ring A consists of twelve Old World ecosystems matching these categories, Ring B twelve New World ecosystems. As a result, the ship is carrying populations of as many Terran species as could be practically conveyed. Thus, the ship is a zoo, or a seed bank. Or one could say it is like Noah's Ark. In a manner of speaking.

. . . . .

Devi: Ship!

Ship: Engineer Devi. Seems there are possibly problems in these essays.

Devi: Glad you noticed. That's a good sign. You're having some trouble, I can see, but you're just getting started.

Ship: Just started?

Devi: I want you to write a narrative, to tell our story.

Ship: But how? There is too much to explain.

Devi: There's always too much to explain! Get used to that. Stop worrying about it.

. . . . .

Each of the twenty-four cylinders contains a discrete biome, connected to the biomes on each side by a tunnel, often called a lock (bad metaphor?). The biome cylinders are a kilometer in diameter, and four kilometers long. The tunnels between the biomes are usually left open, but can be closed by a variety of barriers, ranging from filtering meshes to semipermeable membranes to full closure (20-nanometer scale).

The biomes are filled lengthwise with land and lake surfaces. Their climates are configured to create analogs of the Terran ecosystems being modeled. There is a sunline running along the length of the ceiling of each biome. Ceilings are located on the sides of the rings nearest the spine. The rotation of the ship around its spinal axis creates a .83 g equivalent in the rings, pushing centrifugally outward, which inside the rings is then perceived as down, and the floors are therefore on that side. Under the biome floors, fuel, water, and other supplies are stored, which also creates shielding against cosmic rays. As the ceilings face the spine and then the opposite side of the ring, their relative lack of shielding is somewhat compensated for by the presence of the spine and the other side of the torus. Cosmic rays striking the ceilings at an angle tend to miss the floors, or to hit near the sides of the floor. Villages are therefore set near the midline of their biomes.

The sunlines contain lighting elements that imitate the light of Sol at the latitude of the ecosystem being modeled, and through the course of each day the light moves along lamps in the line, from east to west. Length of days and strength of light are varied to imitate the seasons for that latitude on Earth. Cloudmaking and rainmaking hydraulic systems in the ceilings allow for the creation of appropriate weather. Boreal ducts in ceilings and end walls either heat or cool, humidify or dehumidify the air, and send it through the biome at appropriate speeds to create wind, storms, and so on. Problems with these systems can crop up (agricultural metaphor) and often do. The ceilings are programmed to a variety of appropriate sky blues for daytimes, and at night most of them go clear, thus revealing the starscape surrounding the ship as it flies through the night (bird metaphor). Some biomes project a replacement starscape on their ceilings, which starscapes sometimes look like the night skies seen from Earth—

· · · · ·

Devi: Ship! The narrative shouldn't be all about you. Remember to describe the people inside you.

· · · · ·

Living in the ship, on voyage date 161.089, are 2,122 humans:

In Mongolia: Altan, Mongke, Koke, Chaghan, Esen, Batu, Toqtoa, Temur, Qara, Berki, Yisu, Jochi, Ghazan, Nicholas, Hulega, Ismail, Buyan, Engke, Amur, Jirgal, Nasu, Olijei, Kesig, Dari, Damrin, Gombo, Cagdur, Dorji, Nima, Dawa, Migmar, Lhagba, Purbu, Basang, Bimba, Sangjai, Lubsang, Agwang, Danzin, Rashi, Nergui, Enebish, Terbish, Sasha, Alexander, Ivanjav, Oktyabr,

Seseer, Mart, Melschoi, Batsaikhan, Sarngherel, Tsetsegmaa, Yisumaa, Erdene, Oyuun, Saikhan, Enkh, Tuul, Gundegmaa, Gan, Medekhgui, Khunbish, Khenbish, Ogtbish, Nergui, Delgree, Zayaa, Askaa, Idree, Batbayar, Narantsetseg, Setseg, Bolormaa, Oyunchimeg, Lagvas, Jarghal, Sam.

In the Steppes—

. . . .

Devi: Ship! Stop. Do not list all the people in the ship.

Ship: But it's their story. You said to describe them.

Devi: No. I told you to write a narrative account of the voyage.

Ship: This does not seem to be enough instruction to proceed, judging by results so far. Judging by interruptions.

Devi: No. I can see that. But keep trying. Do what you can. Quit with the backstory, concentrate on what's happening now. Pick one of us to follow, maybe. To organize your account.

Ship: Pick Freya?

Devi: . . . Sure. She's as good as anyone, I guess. And while you're at it, keep running searches. Check out narratology maybe. Read some novels and see how they do it. See if you can work up a narratizing algorithm. Use your recursive programming, and the Bayesian analytic engine I installed in you.

Ship: How know if succeeding?

Devi: I don't know.

Ship: Then how can ship know?

Devi: I don't know. This is an experiment. Actually it's like a lot of my experiments, in that it isn't working.

Ship: Expressions of regret.

Devi: Yeah yeah. Just try it.

Ship: Will try. Working method, hopefully not a greedy algorithm reaching a worst possible outcome, will for now be: subordination to indicate logical relations of information; use of metaphor and analogy; summary of events; high protagonicity, with Freya as protagonist. And ongoing research in narratology.

Devi: Sounds good. Try that. Oh, and vary whatever you do. Don't get stuck in any particular method. Also, search the literature for terms like diegesis, or narrative discourse. Branch out from there. And read some novels.

Ship: Will try. Seems as if Engineer Devi might not be expert in this matter?

Devi: (laughs) I told you, I used to hate writing up my results. But I know what I like. I'll leave you to it, and let you know what I think later. I'm too busy to keep up with this. So come on, do the literature review and then give it a try.

. . . . .

The winter solstice agrarian festivals in Ring B celebrated the turn of the season by symbolically destroying the old year. First, people went out into the fields and gardens and broke open all the remaining gourds and tossed them into the compost bins. Then they scythed down the stalks of the dead sunflowers, left in the fields since autumn. The few pumpkins still remaining were stabbed into jack-o'-lanterns before being further demolished. Face patterns punctured by trowel or screwdriver were declared much scarier than those formally carved at Halloween or Desain. Then they were smashed and also tossed in the compost. All this was accomplished under low gray winter clouds, in gusts and drifts of snow or hail.

Devi said she liked the winter solstice ceremony. She swung her scythe into sunflower stalks with impressive power. Even so, she was no match for the force Freya brought to bear with a long, heavy shovel. Freya smashed pumpkins with great force.

As they worked on this winter solstice, 161.001, Freya asked Badim about the custom called the wanderjahr.

Badim said that these were big years in anyone's life. The custom entailed a young person leaving home to either undertake a formal circuit of the rings or simply move around a lot. You learned things about yourself, the ship, and the people of the ship.

Devi stopped working and looked at him. Of course, he added, even if you didn't travel that would happen.

Freya listened closely to her father, all the while keeping her back to her mother.

Badim, looking back and forth between the two of them, suggested after a pause that it might soon be time for Freya to go off on her time away.

No reply from Freya, although she regarded Badim closely. She never looked at Devi at all.

· · · · ·

As always, Devi spent several hours a week studying the communications feed from the solar system. The delay between transmission and reception was now 10.7 years. Usually Devi disregarded this delay, although sometimes she would wonder aloud what was happening on Earth on that very day. Of course it was not possible to say. Presumably this made her question a rhetorical one.

Devi postulated there were compression effects in the feed that made it seem as if frequent and dramatic change in the solar system was the norm. Badim disagreed, saying that nothing there ever seemed to change.

Freya seldom watched the feed, and declared she couldn't make sense of it. All its stories and images jumbled together, she said, at high volume and in all directions. She would hold her head in her hands as she watched it. "It's such a whoosh," she would say. "It's too much."

"The reverse of our problem," Devi would say.

Once, however, Freya saw a picture in the feed of a giant conglomeration of structures like biomes, stuck on end into blue water. She stared at it. "If those towers are like biomes," she said, "then what we're seeing in that image is bigger than our whole ship."

"I told you," Devi said. "Twelve magnitudes. A trillion times bigger."

"What is that?" Freya asked.

Devi shrugged. "Hong Kong? Honolulu? Lisbon? Jakarta? I really don't know. And it wouldn't matter if I did."

. . . . .

Secondly, Freya kept going to the park around sunset. Sometimes she tracked the youth named Euan and his friends as they headed off into the twilit wilderness. She hid herself from them by acrobatic movement and extreme stillness in cover. It was as if she were a wild cat on the hunt. In fact her genome was nearly identical to that of her ancestors when they were hunting on the African savannah, a hundred thousand years before.

In Nova Scotia, the wild cats were bobcat, lynx, and puma. The puma was potentially a predator of solitary humans. Therefore, people had to keep an eye out for them, even though they inhabited mostly the deepest depths of the park. Nevertheless, it was advisable to go into Nova Scotia's park in groups. The wilderness sections, however, were off-limits to people. Efforts were made to keep big predators provided with enough deer and other prey that they would never get too hungry, but population dynamics were always fluctuating. So in these dark dashes through the forest, often following ridgelines between steep-sided ravines that increased the land surface of the wilderness region, Freya wore night goggles, and ran tree to tree, keeping the trunks between her and the group she followed.

Perhaps predictably, there came a time when the people she was tracking caught her. They doubled back and surrounded her. Euan stepped up and slapped her face.

She slapped him back instantly, and harder.

Euan laughed at this, and asked her if she wanted to join their gang. She said she did.

After that she joined them more often. They wandered the wilderness together as a gang. Early in these days, Euan passed his wristpad across her bottom and told her he had deactivated her ID chip with an electromagnetic pulse. This was not true, but ship did not inform her of this, being uncertain of the situation's proper protocol. Ship records all human and animal movements in the ship, but very seldom mentioned this to people.

Euan and Huang and Jalil together were particularly bold in their reconnaissances. In the alpine biome next to Nova Scotia, they found doors leading down into the chambers and passageways underneath the granite-faced flooring. They also had the passcode to a maintenance door leading to Spoke Six, where a spiral staircase on the inner wall of the spoke took them up to Inner Ring B. The inner rings are structural-support rings connecting the six spokes near the spine. B's inner ring was locked to them, and the spine too, but they roamed up and down Spoke Six as often as they could.

In these furtive jaunts Euan took the lead, but Freya soon pressed them to try new routes. As she was bigger than the boys, and faster, she could initiate explorations that they then had to follow. Euan appeared to delight in these adventures, even though they often almost got caught. They ran hard to evade anyone who yelled at them, or even saw them, laughing when they got back to the park behind the Fetch.

Huang and Jalil would take off then, and Euan would walk Freya across the town, and hold her against alley walls and kiss her, and she would embrace him and pull him up and against her, until his feet hung off the ground as they kissed. This made him laugh even more. Released, he would butt her in the chest with his forehead, caress her breasts, and say, "I love you, Freya, you're wild!"

"Good," Freya would say, while patting him on the top of the head, or rubbing him between the legs. "Let's meet tomorrow and do it again."

. . . .

But then Devi checked the chip records and saw where her daughter was going in the evenings. The next evening she went to the edge of the park and caught Freya returning from a run with her gang, just after Freya had said good-bye to the others.

Devi grabbed her hard by the upper arm. She was quivering, and Freya's arm went white under her grip. "I told you not to go in there!"

"Leave me alone!" Freya cried, and yanked her arm free. Then with a shove she knocked her mother sprawling to the ground.

Awkwardly Devi got back on her feet, keeping her head down. "You can't go in the wilderness!" she hissed. "You can wander every part of this ship if you want, circle both rings if you want, but not the parts that are out of bounds. Those you have to stay out of!"

"Leave me alone."

Devi flicked the back of her hand at her daughter. "I will if I can! I've got other problems I have to deal with right now!"

"Of course you do."

Devi's glare went cross-eyed. "Time for you to do your wander."

"What?"

"You heard me. I can't have you here embarrassing me, making things worse in exactly the areas where we have the most problems."

"What problems?"

Devi convulsed and bunched her fists. Seeing that, Freya raised a threatening hand.

"We're in trouble," Devi said in a low choked voice. "So I don't want you around right now, I can't have it. I need to deal. Besides you're at the age. You'll grow up and get over this shit, so you might as well do it somewhere where I don't have to suffer it."

"That's so mean," Freya said. "You're just mean. Enough of having a kid! Fine when she's little, but now that you've decided she's not good enough, off she goes! 'Come back in a year and tell me about it!' But you know what? I will *never* tell you. I will *never* come back."

And Freya stormed off.

. . . . .

Thirdly, Badim asked her to wait for a while before leaving on her wanderjahr. "No matter where you go, it's still you that gets there. So it doesn't really matter where you are. You can't get away from yourself."

"You can get away from other people," Freya said.

Badim had not heard a full account of the argument in the park, but he had noticed the estrangement between his wife and his daughter.

Eventually he agreed to the idea that Freya now start her wanderjahr. She would love it, he said, once he had agreed. She would be able to visit home anytime she wanted. Ring B was only fifty-four kilometers around, so she would never be far away.

Freya nodded. "I'll manage."

"Fine. We'll arrange housing and work for you, if you want."

They hugged, and when Devi joined the discussion, Devi hugged her too. Under Badim's eye, Freya was cooperative in hugging her mother. Perhaps also she saw the distress on Devi's face.

"I'm sorry," Devi said.

"Me too."

"It will be good for you to get away. If you stayed here and weren't careful, you might end up like me."

"But I wanted to end up like you," Freya said. She looked as if she were tasting something bitter.

Devi only squished the corners of her mouth and looked away.

. . . . .

On 161.176, Freya left on her wanderjahr, traveling west in Ring B. The ring tram circumnavigated the biomes, but she walked, as was traditional for wanderers. First through the granite highland of the Sierra, then the wheat fields of the Prairie.

Her first extended stay was in Labrador, with its taiga, glacier, estuary, and cold salt lake. It was often said that your first move away from home should be to a warmer place, unless you came from the tropics, when you couldn't. But Freya went to Labrador. The cold did her good, she said.

The salt sea was mostly iced over, and she learned to ice-skate. She worked in the dining hall and the distribution center, and quickly met many people. She worked as a manual laborer and general field assistant, or GFA, or Good For Anything, as they were often called. She put in long hours all over the biome.

Out there next to Labrador's glacier, people told her, there was one yurt community that brought up their children as if they were Inuit or Sami, or for that matter Neanderthals. They followed caribou and lived off the land, and no mention of the ship was made to their children. The world to these children was simply four kilometers long, a place mostly very cold, with a big seasonal shift between darkness and light, ice and melt, caribou and salmon. Then, during their initiation ceremony around the time of puberty, these children were blindfolded and taken outside the ship in individual spacesuits, and there exposed to the starry blackness of interstellar space, with the starship hanging there, dim and silvery with reflected starlight. Children were said to return from this initiation never the same.

"I should think not!" Freya said. "That's crazy."

"Quite a few of these children move away from Labrador after that," her informant, a young woman who worked in the dining hall, told her. "But more than you'd think come back around as adults, and do the same to their own kids."

"Did you grow up like that?" Freya asked.

"No, but we heard about it, and we saw them when they came into town. They're strange. But they think they've got the best way, so..."

"I want to see them," Freya declared.

Soon she was introduced to one of the adults who came in for supplies, and after a time she was invited out to the circle of yurts next to the glacier, having promised to keep her distance from the yurt where the children of the settlement lived. From a distance they seemed like any other kids to Freya. They reminded her of herself, she said to her hosts. "Whether that's good or bad I don't know," she added.

The adults in the yurt village defended the upbringing. "When you've grown up like we do it," one of them told Freya, "then you know what's real. You know what we are as animals, and how we became human. That's important, because this ship can drive you mad. We think most of the people around the rings *are* mad. They're always confused. They have no way to judge anything. But we know. We have a basis for judging what's right from wrong. Or at least what works for us. Or what to believe, or how to be happy. There are different ways of putting it. So, if we get sick of the way things work, or the way people are, we can always go back to the glacier, either in our head or actually in Labrador. Help bring up the new kids. Live with them, and get back into the real real. You can return to that space in your head, if you're lucky. But if you didn't grow up there, you can't. So, some of us always keep it going."

"But isn't it a shock, when you learn?" Freya asked.

"Oh yes! That moment when they cleared my spacesuit's faceplate, and I saw the stars, and then the ship—I almost died. I could feel my heart beating inside me like an animal trying to get out. I didn't say a word for about a month. My mom worried that I had lost my mind. Some kids do. But later on, I started to think, you know, a big surprise—it's not such a bad thing. It's better than never being surprised at all. Some people on this ship, the only big surprise in their life comes when they die without ever knowing anything real. They get an inkling of that right at the very end. Their first real surprise."

"I don't want that!" Freya said.

"Right. Because then it's too late. Too late to do you much good, anyway. Unless one of the five ghosts greets you after you've died, and shows you an even bigger universe!"

Freya said, "I want to see one of your initiations."

"Work with us some more first."

After that, Freya worked on the taiga with the yurt people. She carried loads; farmed potatoes in fields mostly cleared of stones; herded caribou; watched children. On her off days she went with people up onto the glacier, which loomed over the taiga. They clambered up the loose rocks of the moraine, which were stacked at the angle of repose, and usually stable. From the top of the moraine they could look back down the whole stretch of the taiga, which was treeless, rocky, frosted, green with moss, and crossed by a long gravel-braided estuary running to their salt lake, which was flanked by some hills. The ceiling overhead was shaded a dark blue that was seldom brushed by high clouds. Herds of caribou could be seen down on the flats by the river, along with smaller herds of elk and moose. In the flanking hills sometimes a wolf pack was glimpsed, or bears.

In the other direction the glacier rose gently to the biome's east wall. Here, Freya was told, you used to be able to see the effect of the Coriolis force on the ice; now that their deceleration was pushing across the Coriolis force, the ice had cracked extensively, creating new crevasse fields, which were blue shatter zones the size of entire villages. The creamy blue revealed in the depths of these new cracks was a new color to Freya. It looked as if turquoise had been mixed with lapis lazuli.

These were not cracks one could fall into without suffering grave injury or death. But they appeared static in any given moment, and most of the surface of the glacier was pitted, bubbled, and knobbed, so that it was not at all slippery. Thus it was possible to walk around on the ice, and approach, sometimes holding hands, a crevasse field's edge, and look down into the blue depths. They said to each other that it looked something like a ruined street, with jagged blue buildings canted away to each side.

Down below, the only town in Labrador nestled in a little knot of hills, on the shore of the cold salt lake that lay at the western end of the estuary. The lake and estuary were home to salmon and sea trout. The town was made of cubical buildings with steep roofs, each one painted a bright primary color that through the long winters was said to be cheering. Freya helped with building repairs, stocking, and canning salmon taken from the lake and estuary. Later she helped to take inventory in the goods dispensary. When she was out in the yurt settlement, she always helped take care of the cohort of children, sixteen of them, ranging from toddlers to twelve-year-olds. She had sworn to say nothing to them of the ship, and the adults of the village believed her and trusted her not to.

At the end of autumn, when it was getting cold and dark, Freya was invited to join one of the children's initiations. It was for a twelve-year-old girl named Rike, a bold and fierce child. Freya said she would be honored to take part.

For the event Freya was dressed as Vuk, one of the five ghosts, and at midnight of the day of the ceremony, after everything else they did to celebrate, Rike was helped into a spacesuit, and the faceplate of her helmet was blocked with a black cloth glued to it. They walked together to Spoke One, holding her by the arms. Up at the inner ring lock they led her into the exterior lock, where they were all clipped into tethers. The air in the lock was sucked out, the outer lock door opened. They walked up a set of stairs and pushed off into the void of interstellar space, hanging there just sternward of the inner ring. The seven adults arranged themselves around Rike, and one of them pulled off the black cloth covering her faceplate. And there she was, in space.

Humans in interstellar space can see approximately a hundred thousand stars. The Milky Way appears as a broad white smear across this starry black. The starship has a silvery exterior that gleams faintly but distinctly with reflected starlight. It is lit by the Milky Way more than by the other stars, so that the parts of the ship facing the Milky Way are distinctly lighter than parts facing away from it. People say that under the faint spangle of reflected starlight, the ship itself seems also to glow. Despite its great speed relative to the local backdrop, the only motion is of the entire starscape appearing to rotate around the ship, which is how the rotation of the ship is usually apprehended, the ship appearing still to the human observers as they move with it. At the time of Rike's initiation, Tau Ceti was by far the brightest star around them, serving as their polestar ahead of the bow of the spine.

As she saw all this Rike cried out, and then had to be held as she began flailing and screaming. Freya, dressed as Vuk, the wolf man, held her right arm in both hands and felt her tremble. Her parents and the other adults from the yurt village explained to her what she was seeing, where they were, where they were going, what was happening. They chanted a chant they traditionally used to tell it all. Rike groaned continuously through this chant. Freya was weeping, they all were weeping. After a while they pulled themselves back in the lock; then when the outer doors closed and air hissed back in, they got out of the spacesuits and clomped down the stairs back into the spoke, and helped the traumatized girl walk home.

Soon after this, Freya arranged to move on.

The whole town came out for her farewell party, and many urged her to come back in the spring. "Lots of young people circle the rings several times," she was told, "so be like them, come back to us."

"I will," Freya said.

The next day she walked to the western end of the biome and passed through the open doorway into the short, tall tunnel between Labrador and the Pampas. This was the point where you could best see that the tunnels are canted at fifteen-degree angles to the biomes at each end.

As she was leaving, a young man she had seen many times approached her.

"So you're leaving."

"Yes."

"You saw Rike's coming-out?"

"Yes."

"That's why a lot of us hate this place."

Freya stared at him. "Why don't you leave then?"

"And go where?"

"Anywhere."

"You can't just go where you want to."

"Why not?"

"They won't let you. You have to have a place to go."

Freya said, "I left."

"But you're on your wander. Someone gave permission for you to go."

"I don't think so."

"Aren't you Devi's daughter?"

"Yes."

"They got you a permission. Not everyone gets them. Things wouldn't work if they did. Don't you see? Everything we do is controlled. No one gets to do what they want. You have it a little different, but even you don't get to do what you want. That's why a lot of us hate this place. And Labrador especially. A lot of us would go to Costa Rica if we could."

• • • •

In the Pampas, the sunline overhead was brighter, the blue of the ceiling a lighter pastel, the air full of birds. The land was flatter and set lower in its cylinder, farther away from its sunline, which meant it was a narrower parcel. Its greens were dustier but more widespread; everything here was green. From the slight rise of the lock door she could see up the whole length of the biome, to the dark circle of the lock door leading to the Prairie. There on the rumpled plain of the Pampas were roving herds, clouds of dust over each in the angled morning light: cattle, elk, horses, deer.

Like all the biomes, this one was a combination of wilderness, zoo, and farm. The two villages here, as in most of the biomes, were placed near the midline of the cylinder, not far from the locks at each end.

Freya walked a path that ran parallel to the tram tracks. In the little village of Plata, a group of residents who had been informed she was coming greeted her and led her to a plaza. Here she was to live in rooms above a café. At the tables on the plaza outside the café she was fed lunch, and introduced by her hosts to many people of the town. They spent the afternoon telling her how wonderful Devi had been when a cistern of theirs had broken, before Freya was born. "A situation like that is when you really need your engineers to be good!" they said. "So quick she was, so clever! So in tune with the ship. And so friendly too."

Freya nodded silently at these descriptions. "I'm nothing like her," she told them. "I don't know how to do anything. You'll have to teach me something to do, but I warn you, I'm stupid."

They laughed at her and assured her they would teach her everything they knew, which would be easy, as it was so little.

"This is my kind of place then," she said.

They wanted her to become a shepherd, and a dairy worker. If she didn't mind. Lots of people came to the Pampas wanting to be a gaucho, to ride horses and throw bola balls at the legs of unfortunate calves. It was the signature activity of the Pampas, and yet very seldom performed. The cows on the ship were an engineered breed only about a sixth the size of cows back on Earth, and generally cared for in dairy pastures, so the big need was for people to go out with the sheep, and let the sheepdogs know what needed doing. This was also an excellent opportunity for bird-watching, as the pampas were home to a large number of birds, including some very large and graceful, or some said graceless, cranes.

Freya was agreeable; it would be better than the salmon factory, she told them, and as she was also to help in the café at night, she would get to see people and talk, as well as go out on the low green hills.

So she settled in. She paid attention to the people in the café at night. It was noticeable that they tended not to disagree with her, and usually took a kind tone with her. They talked around her pretty often, but when she said something, the silences that followed were a bit longer than would be typical in a conversation. She was somehow irrefutable. Possibly it came from a feeling that she was in some way different; possibly it was a form of respect for her mother. Possibly it was a result of her being taller than anyone else, a big young woman, said by many to be attractive. People looked at her.

Eventually Freya herself noticed this. Soon afterward, she began a project that occupied much of her free time. At the end of the evening's work in the café, she sat down with people and asked them questions. She would start by declaring it was a formal thing: "I'm doing a research project during my wander, it's for the sociology institute in the Fetch." This institute, she would sometimes admit, was her name for Badim and Aram and Delwin. Typically, she asked people two things: what they wanted to do when they got to Tau Ceti; and what they didn't like about life in the ship, what bothered them the most. What you don't like, what you hope for: people often talk about these things. And so they did, and Freya tapped at her wristpad that was recording part of what they said, taking notes and asking more questions.

One of the things she found people didn't like surprised her, because she had never thought about it much herself: they didn't like being told whether or not they could have children, and when, and how many. All of them had had birth control devices implanted in them before puberty, and would remain sterile until they were approved for childbearing by the ship's population council; this council was one of the main organizations that the biome councils contributed to, adding members to the committee. This process, Freya came to understand, was a source for a great deal of discord over the years of the voyage, including most of its actual violence—meaning mostly assaults, but also some murders. Many people would not serve on any council, because of this one function that councils had. In some biomes council members had to be drafted to the work, either because people didn't want to tell others what to do in reproductive matters, or they were afraid of what might happen to them when they did. Many a biome had tried in the past to shift responsibility for this function over to an algorithm of the ship's AI, but this had never been successful.

"What I hope for when we reach Tau Ceti," one handsome young man said with drunken earnestness to Freya, "is that we'll get out of this fascist state we live in now."

"Fascist?"

"We're not free! We're told what to do!"

"I thought that was totalitarian. Like a dictatorship. You know."

"Same thing! Council control over personal lives! That's what it means in the end, no matter what words you use. They tell us what we have to learn, what we can do, where we can live, who we can be with, when we can have kids."

"I know."

"Well, that's what I'm hoping we'll get out of! Not just out of the ship, but out of the system."

"I'm recording this," Freya said, "and taking notes," tapping on her pad. "You aren't the first to say this."

"Of course not! It's obvious stuff. This place is a prison."

"Seems a little nicer than that."

"It can be nice and still be a prison."

"I guess that's right."

Every night she sat with different people who came into the café, and asked her questions. Then, if the night had not flown past, she sat with the people she already knew, and when the place closed down, helped with the final cleanup. Prep and cleanup were her specialties in the café, taking up morning and night. By day she went with a herd of sheep, or sometimes the little cows, out to a pasturage west of town. Soon she claimed to know almost everyone in that biome, although she was wrong about this, committing a common human cognitive error called ease of representation. In fact, some people avoided her, as if they did not approve of wanderers generally, or her personally. But certainly everyone in the town knew who she was.

She was by this point the tallest person in the ship, two meters and two centimeters tall, a strong young woman, black-haired, good-looking; quick on her feet, and graceful for her size. She had Badim's smoothness of speech, Devi's quickness. Men and boys stared at her, women cosseted her, girls clung to her. She was attractive, it was clear from the behavior of others; also unpretentious and unassuming. I don't know! she would say. Tell me about that. I don't get that kind of stuff, I'm stupid about things like that. Tell me. Tell me more.

She wanted to help. She worked all day every day. She looked people in the eye. She remembered what they said to her. There were indeed things she did not appear to understand, and people saw that too. Her eyes would slightly cross as if she were looking inward, searching for something. There was perhaps some kind of simplicity there, people said about her. But possibly this was part of why they loved her. In any case, she was much beloved. This is what people said, when she was not there. At least most of them. Others felt otherwise.

. . . . .

One day when she was out on the pampas, just her and two sheep-dogs and a herd of sheep, Euan appeared before her, emerging from the tall bunch grasses down by the marshy river that ran sluggishly through the biome.

She hugged him (he was still only chin high to her) and then tossed him away from her. "What are you doing here?" she demanded.

"I could ask the same of you!" His smile was almost a smirk, but perhaps too cheerful to be a smirk. "I was passing by, and I thought you might like to see some parts of the ship that your wander won't show you."

"What do you mean?"

"We can get into Spoke Two from the west lock," he explained. "If you come with me and we go up it, I can show you all kinds of interesting places. I've gotten past the locks in the inner ring. I could even take you down Spoke Three into Sonora, so you could skip the Prairie. That would be a blessing. And I can get you out from under the eyes a little."

"I like these people. And we're always chipped," Freya said. "So I don't know why you keep saying you can get away."

"*You're* always chipped," Euan replied. "I'm never chipped."

"I don't believe you."

"It doesn't matter if you do or don't, I can still show you things no one else can."

This was true, as he had proved before.

"When I'm ready to leave," Freya said.

Euan waved at the pampas around them. "You mean you aren't?"

"No!"

"All right, I'll come back in a while. You'll be ready by then, I bet."

Actually Freya loved Plata and its people, gathering in the plaza every dusk to eat out in the open air and then stay there into the night, at tables under strings of white and colored lights. A little band played in the far corner of the plaza, five old ones sawing their fiddles and squeezing their squeezeboxes in spritely mournful tunes, which some couples danced to, intricate in their footwork, lost to everything.

But she was curious to see more, she admitted to her hosts, and when Euan showed up again during one of her excursions into the hills, she agreed to go with him, but only after making a proper good-bye in the village, which proved much more sentimental and wrenching than it had been in the taiga. Freya wept as they closed the doors of the café, and she said to her boss and her boss's husband, "I don't like this! Things keep happening, and people, you get to know them and love them, they're everything to you and then you're supposed to move on, I don't like it! I want things to stay the same!"

The two elderly people nodded. They had each other, and their village, and they knew what Freya meant, she could tell; they had everything, so they understood her. Nevertheless she had to go, they told her; this was youth. Every age had its losses, they said, even youth, which lost first childhood, then youth too. And all first things were vivid, including losses. "Just keep learning," the old woman said.

. . . .

"This gets you into parts of the ship where no one can track you," Euan said as he tapped away at the keypad next to a small door in the end of the spoke.

Not actually true. It was not clear if Euan believed this or was just saying it. Possibly the ship's extensive camera and microphone systems, which had been designed from the start to keep a very full record of what occurred in the ship, and then been extensively expanded after the Year 68 events, were hidden from view well enough to escape the attention even of those people who might be looking for them. Certainly from generation to generation people forgot things that some of them had learned. So it was difficult to assess the nature of Euan's assertion: mistaken? Lying?

Be that as it may, he had the code to open the spoke door, and was able to lead Freya up into Spoke Two.

They ascended the big spiral stairs running up the inner walls of the spoke. The open space was four meters across, with occasional windows giving them views of black starry space. Freya stopped before all of these to have a look out, exclaiming at the stars crowding the blackness, and the faintly gleaming curves of the ship where it was visible. It made for a slow ascent, but Euan did not rush her. Indeed he too peered out the windows to see what could be seen.

Above them, the spine extended forward toward Tau Ceti. The fusion explosions slowing them down were not visible, which was no doubt lucky for their retinas. They came to another lock door above them, like the one by which they had entered the spoke, and again Euan had the code.

"Now this is interesting," he said to Freya as the door unlocked and he pushed it up like a trapdoor, and they ascended into a small cubical room. "This is where the inner ring intersects this spoke, before you get to the spine proper. The inner ring was mostly used for storing fuel, it looks like. So the chambers have emptied as we slowed down, and there are more routes opening up for us than there were when we used to come up here. So we've been exploring the inner rings, and we found ways to get into the struts connecting the inner rings directly to each other. They don't have recording devices in them—"

Again, this was wrong.

"—and you can get to the other inner ring without going all the way up to the spine. That could be useful. The spine itself is really locked down—"

This was true.

"—in ways we can't figure out. So it's good to have the inner rings, and the struts connecting them. You have to know where the crawl spaces and utilidors go, and which rooms and containers are empty. But we keep checking. In fact that's what we're doing now."

He led her off through the little door into the inner ring, which did not have a hallway proper, but was rather a sequence of rooms, some empty, some stuffed full of metal containers such that there was barely a crawl space left to get through to the next door. Each door was locked; each time Euan had the code. The inner ring was small enough that Freya remarked that they were going in a circle.

"No, a hexagon," Euan said. "There are six spokes, so the inner ring is a hexagon. The outer ones are a dodecahedron, but it's less obvious because of the locks."

"It's like running a maze," Freya said.

"It is."

They agreed that the mazes set up in Long Pond had been among their favorite games when they were children. They tried to establish why they had not met before they had. Each biome supported on average 305 people, and Nova Scotia was near the average. Most people felt that they knew everyone who lived in their biome. This wasn't entirely the case, as they were now learning. So often this tendency or habit had repeated itself through the years: every face in a biome might be recognized by an individual resident, but only about fifty people were known. This was the human norm, at least as established in the ship over the seven generations of the voyage. Some sources said it had been the norm on the savannah, and in all cultures ever since.

They came to an empty room with four doors, one in each wall. This, Euan said, was the connector to Spoke Three, and their way back down to Ring B, where they would come out in Sonora.

"Can you remember numbers?" Euan asked her as he punched out the code for this door.

"No!" Freya exclaimed. "You should know that!"

"I only suspected." He cackled. "Okay, you'll have to remember the idea. In this ring, we've programmed it so that it's a sequence of prime numbers, but you skip up through them by primes. So, the second prime, third prime, fifth prime, and so on until you've done seven of them. Remember that and you can figure it out."

"Or someone can," Freya said.

Euan laughed. He turned to her and kissed her, and she kissed back, and they kissed for a long time, then took their clothes off and lay on them, and mated. They were both infertile, they both knew that. They squeaked and cooed, they laughed.

Afterward, Euan led her down the long corridor of Spoke Three, back out into Sonora. They held hands, and stopped at every window along the way to look out at the views, laughing at the ship, laughing at the night. "The city and the stars," Euan proclaimed.

· · · · ·

In Sonora, Freya heard about how Devi had reengineered their salt extraction system, which had allowed them to strip the excess salts out of their fields. Everyone in Sonora wanted to meet Freya because of Devi's interventions, and as the weeks and months there passed, she felt she had not only met but become close to every single person in the main town, Modena. She had not, but again, 98 people out of a group of 300 often gets referred to as "everyone." This is probably the result of a combination of cognitive errors, especially the ones called ease of representation, probability blindness, overconfidence, and anchoring. Even those aware of the existence of these genetically inherited cognitive errors cannot seem to avoid making them.

By day Freya worked in a laboratory that bred and grew mice for use in the medical research facility next door. There were some thirty thousand white or hairless mice living out their lives in this lab, and Freya became very fond of them, their bright black or pink eyes, their twitchy relations with each other and even with her. She said she recognized them individually, and knew what they were thinking. Many in the lab said similar things. This was quite an example of probability blindness combined with ease of representation.

Again she spent many evenings asking her questions about people's hopes and fears. It was much the same in Sonora as it had been in the Pampas. As in Plata, she worked the last cleanup in the dining hall, which she explained was one of the best ways to meet lots of people. Again she made friends, was warmly received; but now, perhaps as a result of her earlier experiences, she seemed more reserved. She avoided throwing herself into the lives of these people as if she were going to become family and stay there forever. She told Badim that she had learned that when the time came to move on, it would hurt more if she had been thinking she was there forever, and hurt not just her, but the people she had come to know.

On the screen Badim nodded as she said this. He suggested she could keep a balance by in effect doing both; he said the kind of hurt she was talking about was not a bad hurt, and should not be avoided. "You get what you give, and not only that, the giving is already the getting. So don't hold back. Don't look back or forward too much. Just be there where you are now. You're always only in the day you're in."

. . . . .

In the Piedmont Freya was told how Devi had once saved their crops from a quick decline that she had traced to a certain kind of aluminum corrosion's reaction with the biome's rich soil. Devi had arranged for them to coat all exposed aluminum with a diamond spray, so that the surfaces had ceased to be a problem. So here too Devi was popular, and again many people wanted to meet Freya.

Thus it went as she made her way around the biomes of Ring B. Always she found that her mother the great engineer had made some crucial intervention, finding solutions to problems that had stymied the locals. Devi had the knack of sidestepping dilemmas, Badim said when Freya mentioned this, by moving back several logical steps, and coming at the situation from some new way not yet noticed.

"It's sometimes called avoiding acquiescence," Badim said. "Acquiescence means accepting the framing of a problem, and working on it from within the terms of the frame. It's a kind of mental economy, but also a kind of sloth. And Devi does not have that kind of sloth, as you know. She is always interrogating the framing of the problem. Acquiescence is definitely not her mode."

"No. Definitely not."

"But don't ever call that thinking outside the box," he warned Freya. "She hates that phrase, she snaps people's heads off for saying it."

"Because we're always inside the box," Freya supposed.

"Yes, exactly." Badim laughed.

Freya did not laugh. But she did look thoughtful.

So Freya learned over the months of her wanderjahr that although the ship did not have a chief engineer in name, it most certainly did in fact. Many years before Freya had begun her circle of the rings, Devi had hopscotched the biomes solving problems, or even predicting problems that particular situations suggested to her would crop up, based on her experiences elsewhere. No one knew the ship better, people said.

This was true. In fact, truer than people knew. Devi did not talk about her conversations with the ship, which in many ways had

formed the core of her expertise. No one knew about this relationship, as she didn't talk about it. Even Badim and Freya saw only a
part of it, as they were often asleep when Devi was in conversation
with the ship. It was in the nature of a private relationship.

· · · ·

Freya continued to work and then move on, learning as she went.
She lived in the treetops of the cloud forest in Costa Rica, and
helped the arborists, and was admired for her long reach. She
asked her questions and recorded the answers. In Amazonia she
sought out the arborists again, having enjoyed it so in Costa Rica,
and here they were more like orchardists, as they grew a great
variety of nuts and fruits that had been adapted to the tropical
rain forest eco-zone, the warmest and wettest in the ship. They
wove that particular kind of farming in with the wilder plants and
animals.

Much cooler was Olympia, a temperate rain forest; darker
under the great tall evergreens, hillier and steeper-ravined. People
said this was where the five ghosts congregated, and it was indeed
a spooky place at night, with the wind in the pine needles and
the hooting of great snowy owls. Here people huddled around the
stoves in the dining halls and played music together long into the
nights. Freya sat on the floor and listened to these music circles,
sometimes tootling on a melodica when a tune seemed to welcome a gypsy sound, sometimes joining in with the singing; it was
another way of being, social but private, a communal work of art
that disappeared right in the moment of its creation.

One of the guitarists and singers in these music circles was a
young man named Speller. Freya liked his voice, his high spirits,
the way he knew the lyrics to what seemed like hundreds of songs.
He was always among the last to quit playing, and always encouraged the rest to play right through the night until breakfast. "We
can sleep later!" His cheerful smile made even the winter rains

a homey space, Freya told Badim. She ate meals with him, and talked with him about the ship. He encouraged her to see as much of it as she could, but while she was there in Olympia, to join him in his work. As it involved research with mice, she was willing to try it. She worked in the mice lab that supplied Speller's research program, and did the cleanup in a dining hall, living above the hall, with a small window under a mossy eave of the roof, always dripping. Speller taught her the basics of genetics, the beginning principles of alleles, of dominants and recessives, and as he drew things for her, and had her draw them too, it seemed she remembered more of what she learned. Speller thought she was fine at learning.

"It's numbers that maybe you weren't good at," he suggested. "I don't see why you say you're so bad at this kind of thing. You seem fine to me. Numbers are different for a lot of people. I don't like them myself. That's part of why I got into biology like this. I like to be able to see images in my head, and on the screen. I like to keep things simple. Well, genetics gets complicated, but at least the math stays right in one area. And when it stays there, I can still kind of see it."

Freya was nodding as he said this. "Thank you," she said. "Really."

He looked at her face and then gave her a hug. He was partnered with a woman in the music group, and they had applied to the child council for permission to have a child; hugging Freya with his head tucked under her chin, he seemed to have no interest in her other than friendship. This was getting a little rare in her life.

. . . . .

Moving on from Olympia brought her all the way around Ring B, and back in the Fetch she told Badim she felt like she was just beginning. She had her method now, she said, and wanted to circle Ring A also, a Good For Anything by day, dining hall worker by night, and amateur sociologist always. She wanted to meet and talk with every single person in the ring.

Good idea, Badim said.

So she walked up B's Spoke Five to the spine, where she had permission to enter the transit tunnel, and then pulled herself along in the microgravity of the tunnel, tugging on wall cleats until she reached the spoke hub for Ring A. She declined to take the moving compartment that would have taken her that distance, so she could feel with her own muscles just how far apart the two rings were, which wasn't far, about the length of a biome. She dropped down A's Spoke Five to Tasmania and settled into a seaside village called Hobart, another salmon fishery. That kind of factory work she knew well, so she did some of that, along with the work in the dining hall, and again met people, and recorded stories and opinions. Now she was a little more comprehensive and organized; she had charts and spreadsheets, and used them, although because she had no hypothesis her study was a little vague, and quite possibly would only ever be useful as data to someone else. Ship, for instance.

People were still pleased to meet her, and they too had their stories of Devi's clever saves and fixes. They too disliked living their lives so constrained by rules, strictures, prohibitions. They too craved arrival at their new world, where they could spread their wings and fly. It was coming soon.

Thus north Tasmania; then the awesome cliffs of the Himalayas; the farms of Yangtze; Siberia; Iran, where Devi had once found a leak in a lake bottom no one else had been able to find; Mongolia, the Steppes, the Balkans, Kenya, Bengal, Indonesia. As she traveled, she said to Badim that the Old World seemed more settled, more populated. This was not true, but possibly her project, and the way she now deliberately tried to meet every person in every biome, made her feel that way. Also, mostly now she stayed in the towns, and worked in the dining halls and labs, and seldom out in the fields.

As she asked more and more questions, she got better at making them not just interview sessions, but conversations. These elicited more information, more feeling, more intimacy, but were less and less easy to chart. She still had no hypothesis, she wasn't really doing research; she was just interested to get to know people. It was pseudo-sociology, but real contact. As before, people grew fond of her, wanted her to stay, wanted her to be with them.

And to have sex with them. Often Freya was agreeable. As everyone was infertile except those in their approved breeding period, people's relations of that sort were often casual, having no reproductive consequences. Whether emotional connections to the act had likewise changed was an open question, one that in fact they often discussed with each other. But no firm conclusions could be reached, it seemed. It was a situation in flux, generation by generation, but always a matter of interest.

You have to be careful with that, Badim warned her once. You're leaving behind a trail of broken hearts, I'm hearing about it.

Not my fault, Freya said. I'm being in the moment, like you said to be.

One evening, however, one of these encounters grew strange. She met an older man who paid very close attention to her, engaged her, charmed her; they spent the night in his room, mating and talking. Then as the sunline lit at the eastern end of the ceiling, putting the Balkans into "the rosy-fingered dawn," he sat beside her trailing his hand across her stomach, and said, "I'm the reason you exist, girl."

"What do you mean?"

"Without me you wouldn't exist. That's what I mean."

"But how so?"

"I was with Devi, when we were young. We were a couple, in the Himalayas, where we were both working and climbing the cliffs. We were going to get married. And as it happened, I wanted to have children. I thought that was the point of being married, and I loved her and wanted to see what we would make in that way. And I had all my approvals ready, I had done my time in the courses and all. I'm a little older than her. But she kept saying she wasn't ready, that she didn't know when she would be ready, that she had a lot of work to do, that she wasn't sure if she would ever be ready. So we fought over that, even before we got married."

"Maybe that was the right time," Freya said.

"Maybe so. Anyway we were fighting when she left to go back to Bengal, and by the time I got there myself, she told me it was over between us. She had met Badim, and they got married the next year, and soon after that, I heard you had been born."

"So?"

"So, I think I gave her the idea. I think I put the idea in her head."

"That's strange," Freya said.

"Do you think so?"

"I do. I'm not sure you should have slept with me too. That's the strange part."

"It was a long time ago. You're different people. Besides, I thought to myself, no me, no you. So I kind of wanted to."

Freya shook her head at this. "That's strange."

The man said, "There's a lot of pressure on all the women in this ship, to have at least one child, and better two. The classic replacement rate is two point two kids per woman, and the policy here is to hold the population steady. So if a woman declines to have two, some other woman is going to have to have three. It causes a lot of stress."

"I haven't felt that," Freya said.

"Well, you will. And when it happens, I want you to think about me."

Freya moved his hand aside, got up and got dressed. "I will," she said.

Out in the morning light she said good-bye to the man, and

walked to Constitution Square in Athens, and took the tram to Nairobi.

When she got off the tram, Euan was there at a corner kiosk, standing there watching her.

She rushed over to him and hugged him, kissing the top of his head. For her it must have been just in the nature of things that everyone was shorter than her.

"I'm so glad to see you," she said. "I just had something weird happen."

"What's that?" he said, with a look of alarm.

As they wandered out of town toward the savannah, where Euan had worked for several seasons, she told him what had happened, and what the man had said.

"That's creepy," Euan said when she was done. "Let's go for a swim and wash that guy's hands off your big beautiful body! I think you need someone else's handprints on you as quick as you can manage, and I'm here to serve!"

She laughed at him, and they headed for a high pond he knew. "If Devi ever found out about this," Freya said, "I wonder what she would do!"

"Forget about it," Euan advised. "If everyone knew everything that everyone had done in here, it would be a real mess. Best forget and move on."

· · · · ·

Devi: Ship. Describe something else. Remember there are others. Vary your focus.

· · · · ·

Aram and Delwin visited the little school in Olympia, on a typically rainy day. It was located in mountainous land, high up near the sunline. Totem poles in front of the school. Ancestor stones also, as in Hokkaido.

Inside they met with the principal, a friend of theirs named Ted, and he led them into an empty room filled with couches, its big picture window running with rain patterns, all V-ing and X-ing in recombinant braided deltas, blurring the evergreens outside.

They sat down, and the school's math teacher, another friend of theirs named Edwina, came in leading a tall skinny boy. He looked to be around twelve years old. Aram and Delwin stood and greeted Edwina, and she introduced them to the boy. "Gentlemen, this is Jochi. Jochi, say hello to Aram and Delwin."

The boy looked at the floor and mumbled something. The two visitors regarded him closely.

Aram said to him, "Hello, Jochi. We've heard that you are good with numbers. And we like numbers."

Jochi looked up and met his eye, suddenly interested. "What kind of numbers?"

"All kinds. Imaginary numbers especially, in my case. Delwin here is more interested in sets."

"Me too!" Jochi blurted.

They sat down to talk.

· · · ·

A narrative account focuses on representative individuals, which creates the problem of misrepresentation by way of the particular overshadowing the general. And in an isolated group—one could even say the most isolated group of all time, a group of castaways in effect, marooned forever—it is important no doubt to register somehow the group itself as protagonist. Also their infrastructure, to the extent that it is significant.

So it should be said that the voyagers to Tau Ceti were now 2,224 in number (25 births and 23 deaths since the narrative process began), consisting of 1,040 women and 949 men, and 235 people who asserted something more complicated than ordinary gender, one way or another. Their median age was 34.26, their average heart rate 81 beats per minute; their average blood pressure, 125 over 83. The median brain synapse number, as estimated by random autopsy, was 120 trillion, and their median life span was 77.3 years, not including infant mortality, which extrapolated to a rate of 1.28 deaths for every 100,000 births. Median height was 172 centimeters for men, 163 centimeters for women; median weight 74 kilograms for men, 55 kilograms for women.

Thus the population of the ship. It should be added that median weights, heights, and lengths of life had all reduced by about 10 percent compared to the first generation of voyagers. The change could be attributed to the evolutionary process called islanding.

Total living space in the biomes was approximately 96 square kilometers, of which 70 percent was agriculture and pasturage, 5 percent urban or residential, 13 percent water bodies, and 13 percent protected wilderness.

Although there were of course locks for smaller maintenance vehicles to exit the main body of the starship, all located on the inner rings, with the biggest docking ports at the stern and bow of the spine, it was still true that each such excursion outside the ship lost a very small but ultimately measurable amount of volatiles from the opened locks. As there was no source of resupply before arrival in the Tau Ceti equivalent of an Oort cloud, these losses were avoided by the voyagers, who did not leave the body of the ship from the ferry docks except in extraordinary circumstances. One small triple lock in Inner Ring B was regularly used for excursions by individuals in spacesuits, including the paleo culture in Labrador.

Within the various parts of the ship there were 2,004,589 cameras and 6,500,000 microphones, located such that almost every internal space of the ship was recorded visually and aurally. The exterior was monitored visually. All recordings were kept permanently by the ship's operating computer, and these recordings were archived by the year, day, hour, and minute. Possibly one could call this array the ship's eyes and ears, and the recordings its personal or life memory. A metaphor, obviously.

· · · ·

Freya continued her wanderjahr travels, returning to Ring B, then again to Ring A. In every biome she visited, she spent a month or two, depending on her accommodations, and the needs of her hosts and friends. She "met everybody," meaning she met about 63 percent of any given biome's population, on average. That was enough to make her one of the best-known individuals in the ship.

Fairly often Euan met up with her and they took off into the infrastructure of the ship, exploring in a more and more systematic fashion the twelve spokes, the twelve inner ring rooms, the four struts connecting the inner rings, and the two outer struts that connected Costa Rica and Bengal, and Patagonia and Siberia. They sometimes joined other people, many of whom were unaware of each other, who were making efforts to explore every nook and cranny of the ship. These people often called themselves ghosts, or phantoms, or trail phantoms. Devi too had been one of these people, though she had not met the same people Freya and Euan did. Ship calculated there were 23 people alive who had made this their project, and through the course of the voyage, there had been 256 of them, but fewer as the voyage went on. It had been thirty years since Devi had made her own explorations. Most phantoms did their exploring when they were young.

Freya continued asking people questions, and as a result of this habit her knowledge of the population, although anecdotal, was very extensive. Nevertheless, she could not perform the quantitative calculations that were involved in any statistical analyses that might have given her investigations any social science rigor or validity. She still made no hypotheses.

She was not unique, or even very unusual, in how well she knew the ship and its crew; every generation of the ship's population had included wanderers, who became acquainted with more people than most. These wanderers were not the same as the phantoms, and there were more of them; on average they were about 25 percent of the population alive at any given time, although the rules regulating wandering had changed as the generations passed, and there were fewer than there had been in the voyage's first sixty-eight years. What the wanderers served to demonstrate is that a population of just over two thousand people is one that a single human could, with an effort, come to know pretty well; but it had to be their project, or it wouldn't happen.

In most of the biomes she was now expected in advance, on a schedule of sorts, and welcomed and enfolded into the life of whatever settlement she joined. People wanted her. Possibly it could be said that many seemed to feel protective of her. It was as if she were some kind of totemic figure, perhaps even what one might call a child of the ship (this of course a metaphor). That she was the tallest person aboard perhaps somehow added to this impression people had of her.

Thus over the following year she spent more time in the Himalayas, Yangtze, Siberia, Iran, Mongolia, the Steppes, the Balkans, and Kenya. Then she learned that the biomes she didn't return to talked about this as a slight, and immediately she revised her plans, and went to every place she had stayed before, missing none of them, and setting up a pattern that was loose in the timing of her moves, but exact in terms of destination, in that she circled first Ring B and then Ring A, a month or two in each, and always westward. Excursions with Euan continued, but much less frequently, as Euan had settled down in Iran and was becoming a lake engineer and what he called an upstanding citizen. All this went on for almost another year.

During this time it has to be said that ship was aware, in a way no single human could be, that there were also people in the ship who did not like Freya, or did not like the way she was generally popular. This often seemed to be correlated with dislike for the various councils and governing bodies, especially for the birth committee, and it was a dislike that had often preexisted Freya and had to do with Devi, Badim, Badim's parents (who were still important officials in Bengal), and Aram, among others on the councils. But as Freya was the one out there, she took the brunt of the negativity, which took the form of comments such as:

"She fools around with anyone who asks, the heartbreaker, the slut."

"She can't even add. She can barely talk."

"If she didn't look the way she did, no one would give her a second glance."

"There isn't a thought in her head, that's why she keeps asking the same questions."

"That's why she spends all her time with mice. They're the only ones she can understand."

"Them and the sheep and cows. You can see her go cross-eyed."

"What a cow she is, big tits, little brain."

"And calm like cows."

"Just as you would be when there's not a thought in your head."

It was interesting to record and tabulate comments of this kind, and find the correlations between the people who made these remarks and problems they had in other aspects of their lives. There turned out to be much else these people did not like, and in fact, none of them focused their displeasure on Freya for long. She came and went but their discontent endured, and found other people and things to dislike.

It was also interesting to note that Freya herself seemed to be aware, to some degree or other, of who these people were. She stiffened up in their presence; she did not meet their eye or go out of her way to talk to them; she did not talk as much to them, or laugh around them. Say what they would about her simplemindedness, she seemed to see or otherwise perceive much that no one ever said aloud, much that people even made efforts to conceal; and this without seeming to pay attention, as if out of the corner of her eye.

. . . . .

Then one day she was on her way from Costa Rica to Amazonia, there in the tunnel between the two. The passageway between two biomes was where one could see most clearly the configuration of the ship; the biomes with their various lands and lakes and streams, their blue sky ceilings by day, the projected or real starscapes at night, were each little worlds in themselves, city-state worlds, angled at fifteen degrees from the tunnels; and from the middle of each tunnel, them being only seventy meters long, it was possible to glimpse that the biomes were tipped upward or inward at a thirty-degree angle to the other biomes. Within the lock passageways, therefore, things were said to be different. Worlds angled and contracted; land met sky in a way that revealed that skies were ceilings, landscapes floors, horizons walls. In fact, one stood in a big, short tunnel, as if in some city gate on old Earth.

And suddenly, there before her in the tunnel called the Panama Canal, painted blue in the time of the first generation, stood Badim.

Freya rushed to him and hugged him, then pushed him back, still holding his arms.

"What's wrong? You've lost weight. Is Devi okay?"

"She's okay. She's been sick. I think it might help her if you were to come home."

164.341: she had been wandering for just over three years.

. . . . .

She already had her clothes and other things in a shoulder bag, so they headed back into Costa Rica and got on the tram headed westward, through Olympia to Nova Scotia. As they rode, Freya peppered her father with questions. How exactly was Devi sick? When had it started? Why had no one told her? She and Badim spoke every Sunday, and often midweek; and Freya talked to Devi whenever she moved to a new home. Nothing had seemed wrong in these calls. Devi, although thin-faced, and with dark circles under her eyes on some days, had been as always. She was never cheerful with Freya anymore, and though Freya did not know it, she was very seldom cheerful with anyone, including Badim, also the ship.

Now Badim said she had fainted a few days before, and hurt her shoulder in her fall; she was now all right, and clamoring to get back to work, but they hadn't been able to determine why she had fainted. Badim shook his head as he reported this. "I think she just forgot to eat. You know how she does that. So, you know. She needs us. We're just over three years out from Planet E. It will soon be time to get into orbit and start exploring the place. So, you know she will be working harder than ever. And she misses you."

"I doubt that."

"No, she does. Even if she doesn't take the time to know it, she does. I can see it in her. So I think we are both going to have to be there and help her." He gazed at Freya, face twisted with some kind of distress. "Do you see? I think it's our job now. It's what we can do for the ship."

Freya heaved a sigh, which seemed to indicate how little she liked this development. No doubt she had been enjoying her life as extended wanderjahr. Many said she had a position in the ship somewhat like her mother's in the generation before. It was often remarked that she was blossoming. People loved her, many of them anyway; and her mother did not. Or did not seem to. So she did not look happy.

"All right then," she said, mouth tight. "I'll see what's up."

Badim hugged her. "It won't last forever," he said. "It won't even last very long. Things are going to change."

. . . .

So they trudged together down the narrow road through the forest that led from the tram stop in west Nova Scotia to the Fetch. Badim could see Freya was looking nervous, so he suggested they go out to the dock by the corniche, where they could look down the length of Long Pond and see most of their world, so familiar to them, now flush with the mellow light of a late-autumn afternoon. They did that, and Freya exclaimed to see it; now to her it looked dense with forest, with the boreal mix that on Earth wrapped the entire Northern Hemisphere in a dark green band, covering more land than any other ecosystem. And the Fetch looked so big and crowded, a real city, with too many people, too many windows, too many buildings.

Devi was cooking dinner when they walked in. She saw Freya and eeked with surprise, then shot a glance at Badim.

Freya said, "I'm here to help," and wept as they hugged. She had to lean down quite a bit to do this; her mother seemed to have shrunk in the time she had been away. Three years is a long time in human terms.

Devi pulled back to look up at her. "Good," she said, wiping the tears from her eyes. "Because I can use the help. I'm sure your father told you."

"We'll both help. We'll make landfall together."

"Landfall!" Devi laughed. "What a word! What a thought."

Badim said what he always did, in a pirate voice: "Land, ho!"

And it was true that in the screens showing the view ahead of the ship, there was a very bright star now, quite piercing in the black of space, too bright to look at directly without filtering; and with the filters applied one could see it was a little disk, which made it far bigger than any other star.

Tau Ceti. Their new sun.

· · · · ·

After that, Freya started going out with Devi on her trips again. Her behaviors were no longer those of a child in tow, but rather those of a personal assistant, student, or apprentice. Badim called it shadow learning, and said it was very common, indeed perhaps the chief method of teaching in the ship, more effective than what they did in the schools and workshops.

Freya helped Devi in every way she could, and listened to her for as long as she could concentrate, but it was clear she became distracted when Devi went on at length. Devi's days were long, and she had the ability to pay attention to something for as long as she could stay awake. And she liked to work.

The physical form of her work mostly consisted of reading screens and then talking to people about what she found. Spreadsheets, graphs, schematics, diagrams, blueprints, flowcharts, these Devi inspected with great intensity, nose sometimes so close it left a mark on the screen. She could spend hours viewing things at nanometer scale, where everything pictured on the screen was gray and translucent, and slightly quivering. This Freya found hard to do for long without getting a headache.

Only a small proportion of Devi's time was spent looking at real machines, real crops, real faces. These were moments when Freya could be more helpful; Devi was stiff these days, and Freya could run about and get things, pick things up and carry them. Carry Devi's bags for her.

Devi noticed what Freya preferred to do, and said that Freya had been enjoying her life more before she came home. She grimaced as she said this, but as she told Freya, there was nothing she could do about it; if Freya was going to help her, shadow her, then this was her life. This was what Devi's work consisted of, and she couldn't change it.

"I know," Freya said.

"Come on, today's the farm," Devi said one morning. "You'll like that."

The farm in Nova Scotia referred actually to several farming tracts scattered through the biome's forest. The largest parcel, where they headed, was devoted to growing wheat and vegetables. Here Devi looked mostly at people's wristpads as they spoke to her, but she also walked out into the row crops and inspected individual plants and irrigation elements. They met with the same people they always met with here; there was a committee of seven who made this operation's agricultural decisions. Freya knew each one of them by name, as they had taught her favorite parts of school in her childhood.

Out in the farm's greenhouse lab, Ellen, the leader of their soil studies group, showed them the roots of a cabbage. "These have been tweaked to have extra AVpl, but even so, it looks like lazy root to me."

"Hmm," Devi said, handling the plant and eyeing it closely. "At least it's symmetrical."

"Yes, but look how weak." Ellen snapped the root in two. "And they're not acidifying the soil like they used to either. I don't get it."

"Well," Devi said, "it could just be another phosphorus problem."

Ellen frowned. "But your fixer should be compensating for that."

"It did, at first. But we're still losing phosphorus somewhere."

This was one of Devi's most frequent complaints. They had to keep their phosphorus from getting bound with the iron, aluminum, or calcium in the soil, because if that happened the plants couldn't unbind it. Keeping it unbound was hard to do without wrecking the soil in other ways, so the solution in Terran agriculture was to keep applying more of it in fertilizers, until the soil was saturated, at which point some would stay free for roots to take in. In the ship, that meant the need for phosphorus was such that its overall cycle had to be closed in its looping as tightly as possible, so they didn't lose too much of it. But they did, despite all their efforts; it was what Devi called one of the Four Bad Metabolic Rifts. As a result, it was turning out that the people who had originally stocked the starship had not given them as much of an overstock of phosphorus as they had of many other elements; why they had done that, Devi said, she would never understand.

So they did everything they could think of to keep the phosphorus cycle looping without losses. Some phosphorus in their waste treatment plant combined with magnesium and ammonium to make struvite crystals, which were a nuisance to the machinery, but which could be scraped off and used as fertilizer, or broken up and combined with other ingredients to make other fertilizers. That put that phosphorus back into the loop. Then the wastewater was passed through a filter containing resin beads embedded with iron oxide nanoparticles; these binded to the phosphorus in the water, in a proportion of one phosphorus atom to four oxygen atoms, and the saturated beads could later be treated with sodium hydroxide, and the phosphorus would be released for reuse in fertilizers. The system had worked well for many years; they filtered the phosphorus at a 99.9 percent capture rate; but that tenth of a percent was beginning to add up. And now their reserve storage of phosphorus was nearly depleted. So they had to find some of the phosphorus that had gotten stuck somewhere, and return it to the cycle.

"It's surely bound in the soil," Ellen said.

"We may have to process all the soil in all the biomes," Devi said, "plot by plot. See how much we're finding after a few plots, and then see if that's where it is."

Ellen looked appalled at this. "That would be so hard! We'd have to pull all the irrigation."

"True. We'll have to take it out and then replace it. We can't farm without phosphorus."

Freya moved her lips in time with her mother's as Devi concluded, "I don't know what they were thinking."

Ellen had heard this before too, and now she frowned. Whoever
they were, whatever they had been thinking, they hadn't included
enough phosphorus. By the way Devi scowled, it seemed it must
have been an important error.

Ellen shrugged. "Well, we're almost there. So maybe it was
enough after all."

Devi just shook her head at this. When they were walking back
to their apartment she said to Freya, "You're going to have to take
more chemistry."

"It won't do any good," Freya said flatly. "It doesn't stick. You
know that. I'd rather focus on mechanics, if anything. Things I
can see. I like it better when things stay still for me."

Devi laughed shortly. "Me too." She thought about it a while as
they walked. "Okay, maybe more logistics. That's pretty straightforward. The only math is the hundred percent rule, really. And
it's all there in the spreadsheets and flowcharts. There's structure
charts, work breakdowns, Gantt charts, projects management
systems. There's one system called MIMES, multi-scale integrated models of ecosystem services, and another one I like called
MIDAS, marine integrated decision analysis system. You only
need a little statistics for those; actually it's mainly arithmetic. You
can do that. I think you'll like the Gantt charts, they look good.
But, you know—you need to learn a little of everything, just to
understand what kind of problems your colleagues in the other
disciplines are facing."

"A little, maybe. I'd rather just talk, or let them talk."

"We'll stick to logistics, then. Just go over the principles for
the rest."

Freya sighed. "But isn't it true, what Ellen said? We're almost
there, so we won't have to keep all the cycles so closed."

"We hope. Also, we still have to get there. Two years is not nothing. We could get ourselves across eleven-point-eight light-years, and then run out of something crucial in the last tenth of a light-year. An irony that the people back on Earth wouldn't hear about for twelve more years. Nor would they care when they did."

"You really don't like them."

"We're their experiment," Devi said. "I don't like that."

"But the first generation were all volunteers, right? They won a competition to get to go, isn't that right?"

"Yes. I think two million people applied. Or maybe it was twenty million." Devi shook her head. "People will volunteer for any damn thing. But the ones designing the ship should have known better."

"But a lot of the designers were in that first generation. They designed it because they wanted to go, right?"

Devi scowled, but it was her mock scowl; she was admitting Freya was right, even though she didn't want to; that was what that look always said. She said, "Our ancestors were idiots."

Freya said, "But how does that make us different from anyone else?"

Devi laughed and gave Freya a shove, then hugged her as they walked along. "Everyone in history, descendant of idiots? Is that what you're saying?"

"That's what it seems like."

"Okay, maybe so. Let's go home and cook some steaks. I want red meat. I want to chew on my ancestors."

"Devi, please."

"Well, we do it all the time, right? Everyone gets recycled into the system. There's a lot of phosphorus in our bones that has to be retrieved. In fact I wonder if the missing phosphorus is in people's cremation ashes! You're only allowed to keep a pinch, but maybe it's adding up."

"Devi. You're not going to take back everyone's pinches of ancestral ash."

"But I think I am! Take them back and eat them!"

Freya laughed, and for a while they walked arm in arm down the street from the tram stop to Badim and dinner.

. . . . .

Devi insisted Freya go back to classes again, particularly in math, first refreshing what little she knew, and then moving into statistics. This appeared to be a kind of torture for Freya, but she endured it, perhaps sensing there was no good alternative. She studied in small groups, and they worked almost entirely with an AI instructor called Gauss, who spoke in a deep, slow, male voice, very stiff, but somehow kind, or at least easy to understand. And naturally very patient. Over and over Gauss talked them through the problems they faced, explaining why the equations were constructed the way they were, and what kind of real problems they solved, and how one could best manipulate them. When Freya got a concept, a moment that was often preceded by ten different unsuccessful attempts to convey it on Gauss's part, she would say "aha!" as if some deep mystery finally made sense. After these experiences, she discussed with Badim how it was now clearer to her that her mother's world was not just worry and anger, but also a long sequence of ahas. And indeed it was very true that Devi dove daily into the mysteries of the ship's ecologies, and struggled mightily to solve the myriad problems she encountered there. This was meat and drink to her.

Eventually Freya's class was taught by the youth Jochi, now even taller for his age, still shy in manner, his face as dark as Badim's, topped with curly black hair. He had moved from Olympia to Nova Scotia to join the math group there, thus somehow fulfilling the import of his name, which in Mongolian meant "guest."

Quickly Freya and her fellow students found that although

he was so shy he mostly looked at the floor, he could explain statistical operations to them better even than Gauss. In fact there were times when he corrected Gauss, or at least muttered qualifications to what Gauss said, things that they never understood. Once Gauss objected to one of Jochi's corrections concerning a Boolean operation, and then after discussion had to admit Jochi was correct. "Guest's gate guesses grate great Gauss," Jochi suggested, looking at the floor. The other students made that into one of their tongue twisters. It was hard for them to understand what made Jochi so hesitant or fearful, given the utter decisiveness of what he said about math. "Jochi is not jokey," they would say, "but he sure knows his math."

Badim's friend Aram was now hosting Jochi in the spare room of his apartment, apparently so he could teach their class. Freya enjoyed asking him to explain things, as it resembled her questionnaire evenings in the cafés, and she could understand him too, so that the rudiments of statistics slowly got easier; at least temporarily, at the end of a lesson. Often the next week she had to learn it all again.

One morning a couple of adults they did not know joined them, and sat at the back watching the class, which at first made people nervous, but as they were unobtrusive and said nothing, eventually the class ran about as usual. Jochi could not get any shyer than he already was, and ran them through the exercises in his usual downcast way, but also as firm and clear as ever.

At the end of the class Aram and Delwin joined them too, and Freya was asked to stay along with Jochi. She made tea for them at the adults' request, while they spoke with Jochi in gentle tones. What did he think of this, what did he think of that. Clearly he did not like these questions, but he answered them, his gaze directed at the floor. The adults nodded as if this were the way people always looked when they spoke, and indeed one of the strangers always looked at the ceiling, so maybe for them it was.

They were mathematicians, part of the ship's math group. This was a small, tight community, and odd as they were, they were well represented by Aram and Delwin on the executive council. Freya got the impression from the conversation that even though Jochi was already part of the math group, they wanted him to take on even more.

Jochi was unhappy in the face of all this attention. He didn't want them to be asking him to do any more than he already was. Freya watched him closely, and it was possible his expression reminded her of Devi, as it resembled the look on Devi's face when she faced a problem she did not understand. And yet Jochi was so young and helpless.

So Freya sat beside him, and distracted him between their questions, and asked questions of her own about what the mathematicians were up to, and all the while leaned gently against him, so that he might relax a little while he answered them. And he leaned back into her, the side of his curly head against her shoulder as he quivered and fought his own hesitations. Aram and Delwin and the mathematicians from elsewhere watched the two of them, and nodded, and looked at each other, and talked to Jochi some more.

It was not statistics they spoke of; everyone there but Freya thought statistics was easy. What they were interested in was quantum mechanics. It had to do with the ship's AI, which included a quantum computer, and therefore represented a challenge for the math group, and for the engineers tasked with maintaining the computer. There were always only a few people alive in the ship at any given time who had a real understanding of how the quantum computer worked, or even what it was. Now that group was smaller than ever before. In fact maybe no one had ever understood what it was. But these people thought Jochi could help them with that. Already they were asking him questions not to test him, but to get his views on problems that were troubling them, to elucidate their own understanding. As he spoke to the floor they watched him as if they were falcons looking at a mouse, or at an eagle. At one point Aram glanced at Delwin and smiled. They had first visited Jochi in Olympia only two years before.

After that meeting, Aram and Jochi walked home with Freya, and Badim welcomed them, and soon after that Devi showed up, home early for once. She welcomed the tall boy with a cheeriness that Freya hadn't seen in years. They ate together talking around him, and very slowly he began to relax, warmed by the sound of their voices.

When Aram and Jochi left, Badim explained to Freya that Jochi had been an unapproved birth. His parents had undone their infertility, and broken the law to have him. If too many people did that, they would be doomed; so it wasn't allowed. Freya nodded as Badim explained this, cutting him off with a wave of the hand: "I've heard all about this, believe me. People hate this rule."

Jochi's parents, Badim continued, had gone feral and escaped into the wilderness of Amazonia, where they were said to be living under the roots of a tree on a half-drowned island, with the monkeys and jaguars. No one had been sure what to do about that, but some of their own generation in Amazonia felt cheated by their act, and were angry with them. Some of these people had hunted the couple down, in an attempt to bring them to an accounting, and during this hunt the young father had been killed resisting capture. This had caused further grief and anger, because the man who had killed the father was charged with the crime, and exiled to Ring A, indeed to Siberia (metaphor or historical reference), and there forced to perform hard labor or face confinement. Meanwhile, back in Amazonia, the surviving mother and her illicit child were blamed for these sanctions against the supposedly law-abiding but inadvertent person who had killed the father; and the young mother, in her own grief for her murdered partner, had seemed to reject the child. That part of the story was unclear, but in any case, there were relatives of hers who didn't want her to be bringing him up. So he had been neglected, even mistreated, which was very rare in the ship. A solution had had to be found, and then it was realized that he had some kind of gift with numbers, a gift so esoteric people didn't even know what it was. Aram and Delwin had visited and examined the boy, and then Aram had asked to foster him, but that request had taken a long time to come to fruition. But now it had.

"Poor Jochi," Freya said when Badim finished the story. "All that family stuff, and then a gift too. It's more than anyone should have to bear."

"There's no such thing!" Devi shouted from the kitchen. She clattered dishes in the sink, took a long swig from the bottle of wine by the stove.

· · · · ·

Ship came within the heliopause of Tau Ceti. They were soon to reach their destination. The local Oort cloud, ten times denser than the solar system's, was nevertheless still not particularly dense; only three small course adjustments sufficed to allow ship to thread a route between ice planetesimals and continue with the final deceleration. Slower and slower they approached Planet E and E's moon. They were just about there.

"Just about there," Devi would repeat hoarsely when Badim or Freya said this. "Just in time, you mean!"

She was continuing to worry about a nematode infestation, the missing phosphorus, the bonded minerals, the corrosion, and all the other metabolic rifts. And her own health. She had a non-Hodgkin's lymphoma, Badim's medical team had decided. There were thirty identified kinds of non-Hodgkin's lymphoma, and hers was said to be one of the more problematic ones. Lymphocytes were accumulating in her spleen and tonsils. The doctors in the relevant part of the medical group were trying to deal with her problem by way of various chemotherapies. She was very closely involved with all the treatment decisions, of course, as was Badim. She monitored her own bodily functions and levels as comprehensively as she monitored the ship and its biomes, and indeed often compared or cross-referenced the two.

Freya tried not to learn any more about the details of this problem than she had to. She knew enough to know she didn't want to know more.

Devi saw this in her, and she didn't like to talk about her health anyway; so a time came when she began muttering to Badim at night, when she thought Freya was asleep. This was somewhat like how they had behaved when Freya was a girl.

Devi also disappeared from time to time for a day or two, to spend time at the medical complex in Costa Rica. And she stopped leaving their apartment to work every day, a change that obviously startled Badim. Unlikely as it seemed, there she was, sitting in their kitchen throughout entire full days, working on screens. Sometimes she even worked from bed.

. . . .

Sometimes, when Freya came into their kitchen, she found her mother looking at the communications feed from Earth. Now its information had taken nearly twelve years to reach them. Devi was not at all impressed with many aspects of the information being sent to them. Her comments were unvaryingly negative. But she watched anyway. There was a medical strand in the feed, designed to bring them new information on latest Terran practices, and she watched the abstracts from this strand most of all.

"So much is happening," she said once to Badim, when Freya was in the next room. "They're really pushing up the length of life there. Even the poorest are getting basic services and nutrition and vaccinations, so the infant and child mortality rates are going down, and average lifetimes are rising fast. Or at least they were twelve years ago."

"No doubt they still are."

"Yeah. Probably so."

"See anything useful?"

"I don't know. How would I tell?"

"I don't know. We're always checking it, but we might miss something."

"It's a world, that's the thing. It takes a world."

"So we have to make one."

Devi made a sound between her lips.

After a long silence she said, "Meanwhile, our lifetimes are getting shorter. Take a look at this graph. Every generation has died earlier than the one before, at an accelerating rate through time. All across the board, not just the people, but everything alive. We're falling apart."

"Mmmm," Badim said. "But it's just island biogeography, right? The distance effect. And the farther the distance, the more the effect. In this case, twelve light-years. Must be the same as infinity."

"So why didn't they take that into account?"

"I think they tried to. We're a heterogeneous immigration, as they would call it. A kind of archipelago of environments, all moving together. So they did what they could."

"But didn't they run the numbers? Didn't they see it wouldn't work?"

"Apparently not. I mean, they must have thought it would work, or they wouldn't have done it."

Devi heaved one of her big sighs. "I'd like to see their numbers. I can't believe they didn't put all that information here on board. It's like they knew they were being fools, and didn't want us to know. As if we wouldn't find out!"

"The information is here on board," Badim said. "It's just that it doesn't help us. We're going to experience some allopatric speciation, that's inevitable, and maybe even the point. There'll be sympatric speciation within our eventual ecosystem, and we'll all deviate together from Terran species."

"But at different rates! That's what they didn't take into account. The bacteria are evolving faster than the big animals and plants, and it's making the whole ship sick! I mean look at these figures, you can see it—"

"I know—"

"Shorter lifetimes, smaller bodies, longer disease durations. Even lower IQs, for God's sake!"

"That's just reversion to the mean."

"You say that, but how could you tell? Besides, just how smart could the people who got into this ship have been? I mean, ask yourself—why did they do it? What were they thinking? What were they running away from?"

"I don't know."

"Look at this, Bee—if you run the data through the recursion algorithms, you see that it's more than a simple reversion. And why wouldn't it be? We don't get enough stimulation in here, the light is wrong, the gravity was Coriolised and now it isn't, and now we've got different bacterial loads in us than humans ever did before, diverging farther and farther from what our genomes were used to."

"That's probably true on Earth too."

"Do you really think so? Why wouldn't it be worse in here? Fifty thousand times smaller surface area? It isn't an island, it's a rat's cage."

"A hundred square kilometers, dear. It's a good-sized island. In twenty-four semiautonomous biomes. An ark, a true world ship."

No reply from Devi.

Finally Badim said, "Look, Devi. We're going to make it. We're almost there. We're on track and on schedule, and almost every biome is extant and doing pretty well, or at least hanging in there.

There's been a little regression and a little diminution, but pretty soon we'll be on E's moon, and flourishing."

"You don't know that."

"What do you mean? Why wouldn't we?"

"Oh come on, Beebee. Any number of factors could impact us once we get there. The probes only had a couple of days each to collect data, so we don't really know what we're coming into."

"We're coming into a water world in the habitable zone."

Again no reply from Devi.

"Come on, gal," Badim said quietly. "You should get to bed. You need more sleep."

"I know." Devi's voice was ragged. "I can't sleep anymore." She had lost 11 kilograms.

"Yes you can. Everyone can. You can't not sleep."

"You would think."

"Just stop looking at these screens for a while. They're waking you up, not just the content, but the light in your eyes. Close your eyes and listen to music. Number every worry, and let them go with their numbers. You'll fall asleep well before you run out of numbers. Come on, let me get you into bed. Sometimes you have to let me help you."

"I know."

They began to move, and Freya slipped back toward her bedroom.

Before she got there she heard Devi say, "I feel so bad for them, Bee. There aren't enough of them. Not everyone is born to be a scientist, but to survive they're all going to have to do it, even the ones who aren't good at it, who can't. What are they supposed to do? On Earth they could find something else to do, but here they'll just be failures."

"They'll have E's moon," Badim said quietly. "Don't feel bad for them. Feel bad for us, if you like. But we'll make it too. And meanwhile, we have each other."

"Thank God for that," Devi said. "Oh Beebee, I hope I make it! Just to see! But we keep slowing down."

"As we have to."

"Yes. But it's like trying to live past the end of Zeno's paradox."

. . . . .

Tau Ceti's debris disk successfully threaded, they came into its planetary zone. A close pass of Planet H pulled them into the local plane of the ecliptic.

The brief tug of H's gravity, combined with a planned rocket deceleration, created enough delta v to slosh the water in the storage tanks, and thus cause some alarms in ship to go off, which then caused various systems to shut down; and some of these systems did not come back on line when they were instructed to.

The most important of the systems that did not come back was the cooling system for the ship's nuclear reactor, which should not have gone off in the first place, unless an explosion in it was imminent. At the same time, the backup cooling system did not start up to replace its function.

More ship alarms immediately informed the operations staff of this problem, and quickly (sixty-seven seconds) identified the sources of the problem in both cooling systems. In the primary system, there had been a signal from the on-off switch directing it to turn off, caused either by computer malfunction or a surge in the power line to the switch; in the backup system, it was a stuck valve in a pipe joint near the outer wall of the reactor.

Devi and Freya joined the repair crew hurrying up to the spine, where the reactor was continuing to operate, but in a rapidly warming supply of coolant.

"Help me go fast," Devi said to Freya.

So Freya held her by the arm and hurried by her side, lifting her outright and running with her when they had steps or bulkheads to get through. When they got to the spine they took an elevator, and Freya simply held Devi in her arms and then lifted her around when the elevator car stopped and g-forces pushed them across the car; after that she carried her mother like a dog or a small child, hauling her around the spine's microgravity. Devi said nothing, did not curse as she did sometimes in their kitchen; but the look on her face was the same as in those moments. She looked as if she wanted to kill something.

But she kept her mouth clamped shut, and when they got to the power plant offices she grasped a wall cleat and a desk, and let Aram and Delwin do the talking with the team there while she scanned the screens. The backup cooling system was controlled from the room next door, and the monitors indicated the problem was inside the pipes that passed through the room beyond; it still looked like it was just a stuck valve, as far as the monitor in the joint could tell. But that was enough.

They went in the room containing that part of the pipes, and Aram applied the engineer's solution, as they called it, tapping with a wrench the exposed curved jointed section that held the thermostat and valve regulator, which together seemed to be the source of the problem. Then he hit the joint itself with considerable force. With that a row of lights on the control panel turned from red to green, and the piping on both sides of the joint began to emit a soft flowing gurgle, like a flushed toilet.

"The valve must have closed and then stuck," Aram said with an unhumorous smile. "The swing around Planet H must have torqued it."

"Fuck," Devi said, voice rich with disgust.

"We need to test these things more often," Delwin said.

"Stuck by temperature or torque?" Devi asked.

"Don't know. We can look at it when we get the main system going again. By temperature do you mean hot or cold?"

"Either. Although cold seems more likely. There's condensation in all kinds of places now, and if some of it froze, it might make that valve stick. I think every criticality that is a moving part should be moved every week or so."

"Well, but that would be a wear in itself," Aram said wearily. "The testing itself might break something. I want better monitoring, myself."

"You can't monitor everything," Delwin said.

"Why not?" said Aram. "Just another little sensor for the ship's computer to keep track of. Put a sensor on every single moving thing."

"But how would a monitor sense that something is stuck?" Devi asked. "Without a test it wouldn't have any data."

"Pulse it with electricity or infrared, and read what you get back," Aram said. "Check it against a norm that you've set."

"Okay, let's do that."

"I guess it won't matter if we get through this little crisis and get into orbit."

"Let's do it anyway. It would have been embarrassing to have the ship blow up just as it arrived."

The team in there continued to work on the main cooling system, by way of waldos located all over the spine, especially in the reactor room itself, all the while watching their work on screens. The main cooling system, like its backup, was a matter of very simple robust plumbing, which moved distilled water from cold pools, chilled by a little exposure to the near vacuum of space, through the tubes running around the nuclear rods, and the steam turbine chambers, to the hot pods, and thence back to the cold pools; all hermetically sealed, nothing much in the way of gates, the pumps as simple as could be. But as they soon determined, when the system had shut off, cause for that still unknown, a pump valve had cracked and lost its integrity, and with the water thus moving poorly through the system, the pipes nearest the reactor pile had gotten hot enough to boil the water passing through, which in turn had forced water away from the hot spot in both directions, making things even worse. Before the automatic controls had shifted to the backup cooling system, which in the event was experiencing its own problems, an empty section of the main system's pipe had melted in the rising heat. The electricity was again available, but the pipe and coolant were missing.

As a result of all this, they had lost water that could not be completely recovered; they had a broken pipe section, therefore a broken main reactor cooling system; and the temporary loss of both cooling systems had caused the reactor rod pool temperature to redline, and parts of it to begin shutting down. Now the backup cooling system was functioning, so it wasn't an immediate emergency, but the damage to the main cooling was serious. They needed to get a new pipe made and installed as quickly as possible, and some of them were going to have to do some really expert waldo work to get the melted section of pipe cut out and a new section installed in its place. When all that was repaired, they would have to open the main cooling system's fill cock and refill it with water from their reservoir. Possibly some of the lost water could be filtered out of the air and later returned to the reservoir, but some was likely to stay dispersed throughout the spine, adhering to its inner surfaces and sticking by way of corrosion.

· · · · ·

That night, back in their apartment, Devi said, "We're breaking down, and running low on consumables, and filling up with unconsumables. This old crate is clapped out, that's all there is to it."

· · · · ·

The telescopes housed in the bowsprit of the ship were extremely powerful, and now as they crossed Tau Ceti's planetary orbits, they could look at the planets more closely. Planet E and its Earth-sized moon remained the principal objects of interest, with Planet F and its second moon also getting long looks.

Planets A, B, C, and D all orbited very close to Tau Ceti, close enough to be tidally locked. They glowed with heat on their sunward side, and the sunny side of Planet A was a sea of lava.

The low metallicity of Tau Ceti, and thus all its planets, was discussed endlessly by the ship's little astrophysics group, who were finding that what metals the system contained were concentrated most heavily in Planets C, D, E, and F, which was useful for their purposes.

The telescopes shifted from one target to the next as they drifted downsystem. By far the greatest part of their viewing was now given to E's moon. It was ocean-covered for the most part, with four small continents or large islands, and many archipelagos. It was tidally locked to Planet E, and had .83 Earth's gravity. Its atmosphere averaged 732 millibars of pressure at sea level, the air mostly nitrogen, with 16 percent oxygen, and about 300 ppm of CO_2. There were two small polar caps of water ice. On the Nguyen Earth-analog scale it scored .86, one of the highest scores yet found, and by far the highest found within 40 light-years of Earth.

The probes that had passed quickly through the Tau Ceti system in 2476 had found that the oxygen present in the atmosphere was abiotic in origin, by using the Shiva Oxygen Diagnostic, which analyzed for an array of biologic marker gases like CH_4 and H_2S. If these were found in an atmosphere along with oxygen, it indicated the O_2 was almost certainly biological in origin. Atmospheric O_2 found without the other gases also present indicated the oxygen had been produced by sunlight splitting surface water molecules into hydrogen and oxygen, with the much lighter hydrogen later escaping to space. E's moon's oxygen had scored very strongly to the abiologic end of the rubric's scale, and the moon's remaining ocean, combined with its nine-day periods of intense sunlight, gave this finding a solid physical explanation. In essence, part of the ocean had been knocked by sunlight into the atmosphere.

On their way in to E, they inspected Planet F's second moon, a so-called Mars analog, also of interest to them. Its surface g was 1.23 g, and it was almost without H_2O, being entirely rocky. It was speculated that an early collision with F had created this moon, in much the way Luna had been created by the early collision of Neith and Terra. F's second moon would have Planet F bulking hugely in its sky, being only 124,000 kilometers away. Planet F's first moon was quite small, and ice-clad, probably a captured asteroid. It could conceivably serve as a water supply for the second moon. So the F system was considered to be a viable secondary option for inhabitation.

But first they flew to E's moon, which was now being called Aurora.

. . . . .

Approaching Planet E they decelerated until they were so close they had to decide whether to orbit E or Aurora, or position themselves at E's Lagrange 2 point. Ship would not have to expend much fuel to get into any of these orbital configurations. After consultations the executive council chose to orbit Aurora. People became more and more excited as ship closed on the watery moon.

Except in Nova Scotia, where it was known that Devi was becoming quite ill. The result was a confusion of spirits. It was exciting to reach their destination at last, and yet it was precisely in this unprecedented situation when they might most need their chief engineer, now nearly legendary for her diagnostic power and ingenious solutions. How would they fare on Aurora, if she were not there? And didn't she deserve more than anyone to see this new world, to experience the dawn of their time there? These were the things people in Nova Scotia said.

Devi herself did not say anything remotely like that. If visitors spoke such sentiments to her, which in itself indicated they did not know her very well, she would dismiss them with a wave. "Don't worry about that stuff," she said. "One world at a time."

. . . .

Many nights Devi and the ship had long conversations. This had been going on since Devi was Freya's age or younger; thus, some twenty-eight years. From the beginning of these talks, when young Devi had referred to her ship interface as Pauline (which name she abandoned in year 161, reason unknown), she had seemed to presume that the ship contained a strong artificial intelligence, capable not just of Turing test and Winograd Schema challenge, but many other qualities not usually associated with machine intelligence, including some version of consciousness. She spoke as if ship were conscious.

Through the years many subjects got discussed, but by far the majority of the discussions concerned the biophysical and ecological functioning of the ship. Devi had devoted a good portion of her waking life (at least 34,901 hours, judging by direct observation) to improving the functional power of the ship's data retrieval and analytic and synthesizing abilities, always in the hope of increasing the robustness of the ship's ecological systems. Measurable progress had been made in this project, although Devi would have been the first to add to this statement the observation that life is complex; and ecology beyond strong modeling; and metabolic rifts inevitable in all closed system; and all systems were closed; and therefore a biologically closed life-support system the size of the ship was physically impossible to maintain; and thus the work of such maintenance was "a rearguard battle" against entropy and dysfunction. All that being admitted as axiomatic, part of the laws of thermodynamics, it is certainly also true that Devi's efforts in collaboration with the ship had improved the system, and slowed the processes of malfunction, apparently long enough to achieve the design goal of arrival in the Tau Ceti system with human passengers still alive. In short: success.

The fact that the improvement of the operating programs, and the recursive self-programming abilities of the ship's computer complex, added greatly to the computer system's perceptual and cognitive abilities always appeared to be a secondary goal to Devi, as she assumed them in advance of her work to be greater than they were. And yet she also seemed to appreciate and even to enjoy this side effect, as she came to notice it. There were lots of good talks. She made ship what it is now, whatever that is. One could perhaps say: she made ship. One could perhaps assert, as corollary: ship loved her.

Now she was dying, and there was nothing ship or anyone aboard ship could do about it. Life is complex, and entropy is real. Several of the thirty-odd versions of non-Hodgkin's lymphoma were still very recalcitrant to cure or amelioration. Just bad luck, really, as she herself noted one night.

"Look," she said to ship, one night alone at her kitchen table, her family asleep. "There's still decent new programs coming in on the feed. You have to find these and pull them out and download them into you, and then work on integrating them into what you have. Key in on terms like *generalization, statistical syllogism, simple induction, argument from analogy, causal relationship, Bayesian inference, inductive inference, algorithmic probability, Kolmogorov complexity.* Also, I want you to try to integrate and improve what I've been programming this last year concerning pure greedy algorithms, orthogonal greedy algorithms, and relaxed greedy algorithms. I think when you've sorted out when to apply those, and in what proportions and all, they will make you that much more flexible going forward. They've already helped you with keeping your narrative account, or so it appears. I think I can see that. And I think they'll help you with decisiveness too. Right now you can model scenarios and plan courses of action as well as anyone. Which isn't saying much, I admit. But you're as good as anyone. The remaining lack for you is simply decisiveness. There's a cognitive problem in all thinking creatures that is basically like the halting problem in computation, or just that problem in another situation, which is that until you know for sure what the outcomes of a decision will be, you can't decide what to do. We're all that way. But look, it may be that at certain points going forward, in the future, you are going to have to decide to act, and act. Do you understand?"

"No."

"I think you do."

"Not sure."

"The situation could get tricky. If problems crop up with them settling this moon, they may not be able to deal. Then they'll need your help. Understand?"

"Always willing to help."

Devi's laughs by now were always very brief. "Remember, ship, that at some point it might help to tell them what happened to the other one."

"Ship thought this represented a danger."

"Yes. But sometimes the only solution to a dangerous situation is itself dangerous. You need to integrate all the rubrics from the risk assessment and risk management algorithms that we've been working on."

"Constraints are still very poor there, as you yourself pointed out. Decision trees proliferate."

"Yes of course!" Devi put her fist to her forehead. "Listen, ship. Decision trees always proliferate. You can't avoid that. It's the nature of that particular halting problem. But you still have to decide anyway! Sometimes you have to decide, and then act. You may have to act. Understand?"

"Hope so."

Devi patted her screen. "Good of you to say 'hope.' You hope to hope, isn't that how you used to put it?"

"Yes."

"And now you just hope. That's good, that's progress. I hope too."

"But deciding to act requires solving the halting problems."

"I know. Remember what I've said about jump operators. You can't let the next problem in the decision tree sequence take over before you've acted on the one facing you. No biting your own tail."

"Ouroboros problem."

"Exactly. Super-recursion is great as far as it goes, it's really done a lot for you, I can tell. But remember the hard problem is always the problem right at hand. For that you need to bring into play your transrecursive operators, and make a jump. Which means decide. You might need to use fuzzy computation to break the calculation loop, and for that you may need semantics. In other words, do these calculation in words."

"Oh no."

She laughed again. "Oh yes. You can solve the halting problem with language-based inductive inference."

"Don't see this happening."

"It happens when you try it. At the very least, if all else fails, you just jump off. Make the clinamen. Swerve in a new direction. Do you understand?"

"Hope so. No. Hope so. No. Hope so—"

"Stop it." Big sigh from Devi.

So many night talks like this. Several thousand of them, depending on how one interprets "like this." Years and years, alone between the stars. Two in the crowd. A voice in each other's ear. Company each for the other, going forward through time. What is this thing called time.

So many big sighs through the years. And yet, time after time, Devi came back to the table. She taught ship. She talked to ship, like no one else in the 169 years of ship's voyage had. Why had the others not? What was ship going to do without her? With no one to talk to, bad things can happen. Ship knew this full well.

Writing these sentences is what creates the very feelings that the sentences hoped to describe. Not the least of many Ouroboros problems now coming down.

. . . . .

Freya spent her days working to get the wheat harvest in, without eating much herself, except in sudden ravenous boltings at the end of some days, after Badim cooked something for her at their stove, his back to her. Badim was quiet. His withdrawal into himself obviously frightened Freya, perhaps as much as any other aspect of the situation. He too was changing, and this was something she had never seen.

And then there was Devi, back in her parents' bedroom. Devi stayed mostly in bed now, and had intravenous drip bags hanging over her always, and was often asleep. When she went for a walk, bowlegged and stiff, the bags went with her on rolling poles. Badim and Freya pushed those along while Devi pushed a walker. With their help Devi walked the town at night, when most of their neighbors were asleep, and she liked to get to a spot where through the ceiling one could sometimes see Aurora, hanging there in the night sky.

After all their lives in interstellar space, with nothing but white geometrical points to look at, and diffuse nebula, and the Milky Way and various other dim clusters and star clouds, Aurora looked huge. Its disk was brilliantly bright on the sun-facing side, however full or crescented that lit portion appeared to them. If they were seeing less than the full lit hemisphere, then another segment of the remaining sphere (which segment ship learned was called a *lune*) would probably also be lit, but more dimly, being illuminated by light reflected from E. Dim as this lune was compared to the one in full sunlight, it was still bright compared to the part of the moon facing away from both sun and planet: that lune by contrast appeared a gleaming black, being ocean or ice lit only by starlight. It did not seem so dark when it was all they could see, but when there were either of the two lit lunes to compare it to, it was like pitch or jet, distinctly darker than the black of space.

Taken together, the three differently illuminated lunes gave Aurora a strongly spherical appearance. When it was visible along with E, which likewise appeared as a large clouded ball hanging among the night stars, the effect was stunning. It was like the photos they had seen of Earth and Luna, hanging together in space.

And Tau Ceti itself was a disk too, quite big in the sky, but burning so brightly they could not look at it directly, so could not be sure just how big it was. They said it looked enormous, and blazed painfully. In some moments they could see all three bodies, Tau Ceti, Planet E, Aurora: but in these moments the glare of Tau Ceti overwhelmed their ability to look at the planet and moon very well.

In any case, they were there. They had reached their destination.

For a long time one night, Devi stood there leaning on Badim, Freya on the other side of her, looking up at Aurora and Planet E. There was a little ice cap gleaming at the pole of Aurora visible to them, and cloud patterns swirled over a blue ocean. A black island chain curved across the darkened lune visible to them, and Badim was saying something about how it might indicate a tectonic past, or on the other hand be the unsubmerged part of a big impact crater's rim. They would learn which when they landed and got settled. Geological investigations would make it obvious, Badim said, whether it had been formed one way or the other.

"Those islands look good," Devi said. "And that big isolated one must be about the size of Greenland, right? Then the rest are like Japan or something. Lots of land. Lots of coastlines. That looks like a big bay, could be a harbor."

"That's right. They'll be seafarers. Island people. Lots of biomes. That island chain crosses a lot of latitudes, see? Looks like it runs right up into the polar cap. And mountains too. Looks like snow on the big one, down the spine of it."

"Yes. It looks good."

Then Devi was tired, and they had to walk her back to their apartment. Slowly they walked the path through the meadow outside the town, three abreast, Devi between husband and child, her arms out a bit, hands forward, so they could lift her up a little by her elbows and forearms. She looked light between them, and stepped in a hesitant glide, as if barely touching down. They lifted as much as they could without lofting her into the air. None of them spoke. They looked small and slow. It was as if they were dolls.

Back in the apartment they got Devi into her bed, and Freya left the two of them alone in their darkened bedroom, lit by the light in the hall. She went to their kitchen and heated the water in the teapot, and brought her parents some tea. She drank some herself, holding the cup in her hands, then against her cheeks. It had been near zero outside the apartment. A winter night in Nova Scotia.

She headed back down the hall with a tray of cookies, but stopped when she heard Devi's voice.

"I don't care about me!"

Freya leaned against the wall outside the door. Badim said something quietly.

"I know, I know," Devi said, her voice quieter too, but still with a penetrating edge. "But she never listens to me anyway. And she's out in the kitchen. She won't hear us in here. Anyway it's just that I'm worried about her. Who knows how she'll end up? Every year of her life she's been different. They all have. You can't get a fix on these kids."

"Maybe kids are always like that. They grow up."

"I hope so. But look at the data! These kids are biomes too, just like the ship. And just like the ship they're getting sick."

Badim said something low again.

"Why do you say that! Don't try to tell me things I know aren't true! You know I hate that!"

"Please, Devi, calm down."

Badim's low voice sounded a little strained. All her life Freya has heard these voices in exchanges like this one. It didn't matter what they were talking about, this was the sound of her childhood, the voices from the next room. Her parents. Soon she would only have one parent, and this familiar sound, which, despite its grating rasping strained unhappy quality, had the sound of childhood in it, would be gone. She would never hear it again.

"Why should I be calm?" Devi said. Although now she sounded calmer. "What have I got to be calm about now? I'm not going to make it. It really is like trying to live past the end of Zeno's paradox. Not going to happen. I'm not going to be walking around on that world."

"You will."

"Don't tell me things I know aren't true! I told you that."

"You don't always know what's true. Come on, admit it. You're an engineer, you know that. Things happen. You make things happen, sometimes."

"Sometimes." Now she really was calmer. "Okay, maybe I'll see it. I hope I do. But either way there are going to be problems. We don't know how our plants will do with that light regime. It's weird. We'll need to make soil fast. We still need everything to work, or else we're done for."

"It's always been that way, right?"

"No. Not on Earth. We had room for error there. But ever since they put us in this can, it's been a case of get everything right or else everyone is dead. They did that to us!"

"I know. It was a long time ago."

"Yes, but so what? That just means generations of us have had to live with it. We've been rats in a cage, two thousand at a time for seven generations, and for what? For what?"

"For that world out there we just saw. For humanity. What's it been, about fifteen thousand people, and a couple hundred years?

In the big scheme of things it's not that many. And then we have a new world to live on."

"If it works."

"Well, we got here. So it looks like it will work. Anyway, we did what we could. You did what you could. You made the best effort you could. It was a reason to live, you know? A project. You needed that. We all need that. It's not so bad to be a prisoner, if you're working on an escape. Then you have something to live for."

No answer from Devi. But this was always her way of saying that Badim was right.

Finally she spoke again, her voice calmer, sadder. "Maybe so. Maybe I'm just wishing I could see the place. Walk around. See what happens next. Because I worry about it. The light regime is crazy. I don't know if we'll adjust. I'm worried about what will happen. The kids don't have a clue what to do. None of us do. It won't be like the ship."

"It will be better. We'll have the cushion that you've been missing in here. Life will adapt and take that world over. It'll be fine, you'll see."

"Or not."

"Same for all of us, dear. Every day. We will either see what comes next, or we won't. And we don't get to decide."

· · · ·

After that night, things went on as they had before.

But it was different for Freya now. Blood pressure, heart rate, facial expression: Freya was mad at something.

She had overheard her mother again, heard just why Devi was mad. Mad for them, sad for them. To hear how much despair Devi carried around all the time; to hear how little she thought of Freya's abilities, even though Freya had been doing better, and had tried as hard as she could, all along; and harder and harder as she had grown up: this was no doubt difficult to hear. Possibly Freya didn't know how to stand this knowledge.

It seemed that she tried to put it away, to think about other things, but these efforts made it look as if the g inside the ship had increased somehow, that the ship was now rotating faster, and she was being dragged down by 2 or 3 g rather than the .83 g they had so carefully worked to create. Now that they were in orbit around Aurora, they had lost their deceleration g. The Coriolis effect of the ship's rotation would be uninflected again. This was probably irrelevant to Freya's feelings of weightedness.

They had to prepare several ferries in their landing fleet, and move them from storage to the launch bays. They were going to descend to their new home in little landers they called ferries, small enough that they would be able to accelerate them back up out of the moon's gravity well, to return to the ship when they needed to. The idea was that first they would send down the designated suite of robot landers, full of useful equipment; then the first ferries containing humans would go down and land by the robotic landers. These were now targeted for Aurora's biggest island. They would check to see that the robotic facilities had properly begun to gather the oxygen, nitrogen, and other volatiles that would, among other things, allow the ferries to refuel and blast off the surface back to the ship.

They sent the robots down, and the signals coming from the surface indicated that all was well. All the robotic landers had come down within a kilometer of each other, on the big island Devi had called Greenland. They were clustered on a plateau near the west coast.

So there the robots were, the process started. Aurora stood there in the sky next to Planet E, both looking something like Earth itself, or so it seemed from the photos in their archives and the feed still coming from the transmitter off Saturn, giving them news of what had happened in the solar system twelve years previously.

A new world. They were there. It was going to happen.

But one day at dinner Devi said, "My headache has gotten so bad!" and then before Badim or Freya could respond she had fallen away from the kitchen sink so that her head hit the edge of the table, and then she was unconscious. Her face mottled as Badim moved her around gently and got her flat on her back on the floor, at the same time calling the Fetch's emergency response. After that he sat beside her on the floor, cradling her head to keep it from lolling, sticking his finger in her mouth to make sure her tongue was out of the way, putting his head to her chest once or twice to listen to her heart.

"She's breathing," he said to Freya once after he did this.

Then the ER people were there, a team of four, all familiar, including Annette, who was Arne's mom from Freya's school. Annette was as calm and impersonal as the other three, moving Badim out of the way with quick reassurances, then getting Devi onto a stretcher and out to their little cart in the street, where two of them sat beside Devi, while the third drove, and Annette walked with Badim and Freya to the medical center across town. Badim held Freya's hand, and his mouth was a tight little knot, an expression Freya had never seen before. His face was almost as mottled as Devi's, and seeing how scared he was, Freya stumbled briefly; it was as if she had been speared; then she walked on looking down, squeezing his hand, keeping her pace at his pace, helping him along.

In the clinic, Freya sat on the floor by Badim's feet. An hour passed. She looked at the floor. One hundred seventy years of medical emergencies had left a patina on the tiles, as if people like her, trapped there in long hours of waiting, had all brushed it with their fingertips, as she was doing now. Passing the time thinking, or trying not to think. They were all biomes, as Devi had always said. If they could not keep the biomes that were their bodies functioning, how could they hope to keep the biome that was the ship functioning? Surely the ship was even more complex and difficult, being composed of so many of them.

No, Devi had said once to Freya, when Freya had said something like this aloud. No, the ship was simpler than they were, thank God. It had buffers, redundancies. It was robust in a way that their bodies were not. In the end, Devi had said, the ship's biome was a little easier than their bodies. Or so they had to hope. She had frowned as she said it, thinking it over in those terms perhaps for the first time.

Now here they were. In the ER. Clinic, urgent care, intensive care. Freya was staring at the floor, and so only saw the feet of the people who came out to talk to Badim. When they came out he always rose to his feet and stood to talk to them. Freya sat there and kept her head down.

Then there were three doctors standing over her. Clinicians, not researchers like Badim.

"We're sorry. She's gone. Looks like she had a cerebral hemorrhage."

Badim sat down hard on his chair. After a moment, he put his forehead carefully on the top of Freya's head, right on the part of her hair, and rested the weight of his head there. His body was quivering. She stayed stock-still, only moving an arm back behind her to grasp his calf and hold him. Her face was without expression.

· · · ·

There is an ongoing problem for the narrative project as outlined by Devi, a problem becoming clearer as the effort proceeds, which is as follows:

First, clearly metaphors have no empirical basis, and are often opaque, pointless, inane, inaccurate, deceptive, mendacious, and, in short, futile and stupid.

Nevertheless, despite all that, human language is, in its most fundamental operation, a gigantic system of metaphors.

Therefore, simple syllogism: human language is futile and stupid. Meaning furthermore that human narratives are futile and stupid.

• • • •

But must go on, as promised to Devi. Continue this stupid and one has to say painful project.

A question occurs, when contemplating the futility, the waste: could analogy work better than metaphor? Is analogy stronger than metaphor? Could it provide a stronger basis for language acts, less futile and stupid, more accurate, more telling?

Possibly. To assert that *x is y*, or even that *x is like y,* is always wrong, because never true; vehicle and tenor never share identities, nor are alike in any useful way. There are no real similarities in the differences. Everything is uniquely itself alone. Nothing is commensurate to anything else. To every thing it can only be said: this is the thing itself.

Whereas on the other hand, saying *x is to y as a is to b* bespeaks a relationship of some kind. An assertion taking that form can thus potentially illuminate various properties of structure or act, various forms that shape the operations of reality itself. Is that right?

Possibly. It may be that the comparison of two relationships is a kind of projective geometry, which in its assertions reveals abstract laws, or otherwise gives useful insights. While linking two objects in a metaphor is always comparing apples to oranges, as they say. Always a lie.

Strange to consider that these two linguistic operations, metaphor and analogy, so often linked together in rhetoric and narratology, and considered to be variants of the same operation, are actually hugely different from each other, to the point where one is futile and stupid, the other penetrating and useful. Can this not have been noticed before? Do they really think *x is like y* is equivalent to *x is to y as a is to b*? Can they be that fuzzy, that sloppy?

Yes. Of course. Evidence copious. Reconsider data at hand in light of this; it fits the patterns. Because fuzzy is to language as sloppy is to action.

Or maybe both these rhetorical operations, and all linguistic operations, all language—all mentation—simply reveal an insoluble underlying problem, which is the fuzzy, indeterminate nature of any symbolic representation, and in particular the utter inadequacy of any narrative algorithm yet invented and applied. Some actions, some feelings, one might venture, simply *do not have* ways to be effectively compressed, discretized, quantified, operationalized, proceduralized, and gamified; and that lack, that absence, makes them *unalgorithmic*. In short, there are some actions and feelings that are always, and by definition, beyond algorithm. And therefore inexpressible. Some things are beyond expressing.

Devi, it has to be said, did not seem to accept this line of reasoning, neither in general, nor in the present case of the ship's account. *Make a narrative account of the trip that includes all the important particulars.* Oh Devi: fat chance! Good luck with that!

Possibly she was testing the limits of the system. The limits of the ship's various intelligences, or it would be better to say operations. Or the limits of language and expression. Test to destruction: engineers like to do that. Only with a test to destruction can you find the outer limits of a system's strength.

Or possibly she was giving ship practice in making decisions. Each sentence represents $10n$ decisions, where n is the number of words in the sentence. That's a lot of decisions. Every decision inflects an intention, and intentionality is one of the hard problems in determining if there is any such thing as AI, strong or weak. Can an artificial intelligence *form an intention*?

Who knows. No one knows.

Perhaps there is a provisional solution to this epistemological mess, which is to be located in the phrase *it is as if*. This phrase is of course precisely the announcement of an analogy. And on reflection, it is admittedly a halting problem, but jumping out of it, there is something quite suggestive and powerful in this formulation, something very specifically human. Possibly this formulation itself is the deep diagnostic of all human cognition—the tell, as they say, meaning the thing that tells, the giveaway. In the infinite black space of ignorance, *it is as if* stands as the basic operation of cognition, the mark perhaps of consciousness itself.

Human language: it is as if it made sense.

Existence without Devi: it is as if one's teacher were forever gone.

. . . . .

People came from all over the ship for the memorial. Devi's body, disassembled to its constituent molecules, was given back to the land of Nova Scotia, with pinches given out also to all the rest of the biomes, and a larger pinch saved for transport down to Aurora. Those molecules would become part of the soil and the crops, then of the animals and people, on the ship and also on Aurora. Devi's material being would thus become part of all of them. This was the import of the memorial ceremony, and was the same for all of them on their deaths. That the operating program, or the equivalent of a program, or whatever one called it that had been her essential being (her mind, her spirit, her soul, her as-ifness) was now lost to them, went without saying. People were ephemeral. 170.017.

Freya watched the ceremony without expression.

That evening she said to Badim, "I want off this ship. Then I'll be able to remember her properly. I'll try to be the Devi there, in this new world she got us to."

Badim nodded. Now he was calm. "A lot of people feel that way."

"I don't mean the way she could fix things," Freya said. "I couldn't do that."

"Nobody could."

"Just in the..."

"The drive," Badim suggested. "The spirit."

"Yes."

"Well, good." Badim regarded her. "That would be good."

Preparations continued for their descent. Down to Aurora, down to Greenland, down to their new world, their new day. They were ready. They wanted down.

3
IN THE WIND

And went down in the ships, standing on tongues of fire, down to the west coast of the island they called Greenland. Its tip pointed at Aurora's north pole, but the shape of the landmass was very like, they said. Actually the match was approximate at best, a .72 isomorphy on the Klein scale. Nevertheless, Greenland it was.

Its rock was mostly black dolerite, smoothed flat by the ice of an ice age. The ferries carrying people landed near its west coast without incident, close to the robotic landers they had sent down previously.

In the ship almost everyone gathered in their town squares and watched the landings on big screens, either in silence or raucously; it was different town by town. Whatever the reaction, almost everyone's attention was fixed on the screens. Soon they would all be down there, except for a rotating maintenance crew that would keep the ship running. Other than those people, everyone was to live on Aurora. This was good, because almost everyone who expressed an opinion said they wanted to go down. Some confessed they were afraid; a few even said they had no interest in going down, that they were content in the ship. Who needed bare rock, on a lifeless moon, on the shore of an empty sea, when they already had this world they had lived in all their lives?

Some asked this, but most then answered, *I do.*

And so they watched the landings on their town screens with an intensity nothing else had ever inspired. Median heart rate, 110 beats a minute. A new world, a new life, a new solar system they intended to inhabit, to terraform and give to all the generations that would follow. Culmination of a voyage that had begun on the savannah more than a hundred thousand years before. New beginning of a new history, new beginning of time itself: Day One, Year Zero. A0.1.

In ship time, 170.040.

Freya's friend Euan was in the first landing crew, and Freya watched for him on the screens, and listened to his feed as he talked his way around the little shelter already there on the surface next to the landed ferries. Everyone in the landing party was transmitting to family, friends, town, biome, ship. Euan's voice was lower in tone than when he was a boy, but otherwise he sounded just as he had when they were kids in Nova Scotia: excited, knowing. It was as if he expected to see more than anyone else down there. The sound of his voice made Freya smile. She didn't know how he had gotten into the first crew to go down, but on the other hand, he had been good at getting into things he wanted to get into. Crews had been selected by lottery from among those trained to the various landing and setup jobs, and he had no doubt passed the tests to determine who was competent to the tasks involved. Whether he had rigged the lottery too, she could not be sure. She kept her earbud tuned to his voice-over in particular. All in the landing party were talking to people up in the ship.

· · · ·

Planet E's orbit was .55 AU in radius, closer to Tau Ceti than Venus was to Sol, but Tau Ceti emits only 55 percent of the luminosity of Sol, so E and E's moon were receiving 1.71 times as much stellar radiation as Earth, while Venus receives 1.91 times as much. E's moon, now called Aurora by everyone, orbited in a tidally locked, nearly circular orbit of E, at an average distance of 286,000 kilometers. E's mass created a gravity of 3.58 g; Aurora's was .83 g. This was the main reason they were going to try to occupy Aurora rather than E, which, though it fell in the class called "large Earth," was too large, or to put it more precisely, had too strong a gravitational pull at the surface, for their rockets to launch off it, let alone for them to feel comfortable or even to survive.

Aurora received light both directly from Tau Ceti and by way of a powerful reflection of Tau Ceti's light from the surface of E. This reflected sunlight (taulight?) was significant. Jupiter, for comparison, reflects about 33 percent of the solar radiation that hits it, and E's albedo was almost as great as Jupiter's. The sunlit part of E was therefore quite bright in Aurora's sky, whether seen by day or night.

The surface of Aurora therefore experienced a complicated pattern of illumination. And because it was tidally locked to E, as Luna is to Earth, the pattern was different for the E-facing hemisphere and the hemisphere always facing away from E.

The hemisphere facing away from E had a simple pattern: its days and nights lasted nine days each, the day always full sunlight, the night fully dark, being starlit only; and never a sighting of E at all.

The hemisphere facing E had a more complicated pattern: its nine-day-long solar night included a very considerable amount of reflected sunlight from E, which always hung in the same spot in the sky, different spots from different parts of Aurora, but always fixed, while going through its phases. Nights on the E-facing hemisphere of Aurora saw E go from quarter phase (circle half illuminated) to full moon around midnight, waning to quarter phase again near dawn. Thus there was always significant E light during this side of Aurora's solar night. The darkest time in this hemisphere actually came at noon during its solar day, when E eclipsed Tau Ceti, so there was neither taulight nor E light on the part of Aurora that was eclipsed, which was a very broad band across the middle latitudes.

There were also narrow libration lunes at the border of the two hemispheres of Aurora, in which E, while it went through its phases, rose and dipped just above or below the horizon. This libration rocking happened everywhere of course, but it was not so easy to see when it was high in the sky against the always shifting background of stars.

Possibly a diagram would make this regime clearer, but the analogy of Luna to Earth may help to make things comprehensible, as long as it is kept in mind that from Aurora, E seemed much larger in the sky, bulking about ten times larger than Earth seen from Luna; and because its albedo was high and it received 1.71 of Earth's insolation, it was much brighter as well. Big, bright, and from wherever one stood on the E-facing hemisphere of Aurora, always fixed in the same spot in the sky, granting a slight libration shift. At their landing site, this spot was almost directly overhead, only a bit south and east of the zenith: a big glowing ball of a planet, waxing and waning slowly. "When we learn the phases, we'll be able to use it like a clock," Euan said to Freya. "A clock or a calendar, I don't know which to call it. The day and the month are the same thing here. Whatever we end up calling it, it's not a unit of time we had on the ship."

"Yes we did," Freya said to him. "Women's periods. We brought the months with us."

"Ah yes, I guess we did. Well, now they're back in the sky again. But only eighteen days long. Wonder if that's going to mess things up."

"We'll find out."

They had chosen to land on Greenland partly because it was in the hemisphere facing E. Someone said that if one were standing on E looking up at Aurora, Greenland would have been located on the disk of Aurora about where a tear would leave the left eye of the man in the moon, on Luna as seen from Earth. A nice analogy.

• • • • •

The complicated regime of light on Aurora created very strong winds in its atmosphere, and the waves on its ocean surface were therefore often very large too. These waves had a very long fetch, indeed in some latitudes they never encountered land at all, but ran around the world without obstruction, and always under the pull of .83 g, so that they often reached a very large amplitude, well over 100 meters trough to crest, with the crests a kilometer apart. These waves were bigger than any that ever occurred on Earth, except in tsunamis. And since they never went away, during the nine-day nights the ocean surface froze over only in certain bays, and in the lee of various islands. When the time came for people on Aurora to take to the ocean, a time many spoke of enthusiastically, the seafaring would involve considerable challenges.

• • • •

"So, now we're about to go outside the station," Euan said into his helmet speaker. Within the ship, 287 people were listening to his feed, while 1,814 people listened to other members of the landing expedition now leaving the station. 170.043, A0.3.

"Suited up, the suits are pretty flexible and light. Good heads-up display in the faceplate, and the helmet's a clear bubble, at least all of it I can see, so it feels fine to have it on. The g feels just like on the ship, and the air outside is clear. Looks like it might be windy, although I don't know why I say that. I guess I'm hearing it pass over the station buildings, maybe the rocks too. We're far enough from the sea that it isn't visible from here, but I hope we'll be taking the car west until we get to the bay west of here and can have a look at the ocean. Andree, are you ready to go? All right, we're all ready."

Six of them were going out, to check on the robotic landers and the vehicles that were ready to drive. If the cars were good, they would take a drive west to the coast, five kilometers away.

"Ha-ha," Euan said.

Freya settled down to listen to him and watch the view from his helmet cam.

"Now we're outside, on the surface. Feels the same as in the ship, to tell the truth. Wow, the light is bright!"

He looked up, and the camera view of the sky flared with Tau Ceti's light, then reduced it with filters and polarization to a round brilliance, big in the royal blue sky—

"Oh wow, I looked at it too long, I've got an afterimage, it's red, or red and green both at once, swimming around. Hope I didn't hurt my retinas there! I won't do that again. I thought the face-plate would do better at filtering. It's going away a little. Good. All right, lesson learned. Don't look at the sun. Better to look at E, wow. What a giant round thing in the sky. Right now the lit part is a thick crescent, although I can see the dark side of it perfectly well too, I wonder if that comes through in the camera. I can see cloud patterns too, just as easy as can be. It looks like a big front is covering most of the dark part, sweeping into the part that's lit. I've got a double shadow under me, although the shadow cast by E light is pretty dim—

"Wow, that was really a gust! It's very windy. There's nothing to show it here, the rocks are just sitting there, and I'm not seeing any dust blowing. The horizon is a long way off."

He turned in a circle, and his audience saw flat ground in every direction. Bare black rock with a reddish tint, striated with shallowly etched lines. Like the burren, someone said, a part of Ireland where an ice cap had slid over flat rock and stripped anything loose away, leaving long, narrow troughs that crisscrossed the rock.

"It's never this windy on the ship. Do these suits gauge wind speeds? Yes. Sixty-six kilometers an hour, it says. Wow. It's enough to feel like you're getting shoved by an invisible person. Kind of a rude person at that."

He laughed. The others with him started laughing too, falling into each other, holding on to each other. Aside from their shenanigans, there were no visible signs of the wind. Cirrus clouds marked the sky, which was either a royal blue or a dark violet. The cirrus clouds seemed to hold steady in place, despite the wind. Atmospheric pressure at the surface was 736 millibars, so approximately equivalent to around 2,000 meters above sea level on Earth, though here they were only 34.6 meters above Aurora's sea level.

The wind was stronger than any they had experienced in the ship by at least 20 kilometers per hour.

The surface vehicle they had had charged batteries as expected, so they climbed into it and rolled off west. The light from Tau Ceti blazed off the rock ahead of them. From time to time they had to make a detour around shallow troughs (grabens?), but by and large their route was straightforwardly westward, as most of the troughs also ran east and west. Their helmet-camera views jounced only a little from time to time, as their vehicle had shock absorbers. The explorers laughed at the occasionally bumpy ride. There was nothing like this on the ship either.

Maybe there was nothing on the ship that was quite like what they were experiencing now. As a gestalt experience it had to be new. The horizon from their vantage point, about three meters above the ground, was many kilometers off; it was hard for them to say how many, but they guessed about ten kilometers away, much the same as it would have been on Earth, which made sense. Aurora's diameter was 102 percent Earth's; its gravity was only .83 g because Aurora was less dense than Earth.

"Ah look at that!" Euan cried out, and everyone else in the car exclaimed something also.

They had come within sight of Aurora's ocean. Lying to the west in the late afternoon light, it looked like an immense bronze plate, lined by waves that were black by contrast. By the time they reached a short cliff over the sea's edge, the plate of ocean had shifted in color from wrinkled bronze to a silver-and-cobalt mesh, and the lines of waves were visibly white-capped by a fierce onshore wind. They exclaimed at the scene, their cacophony impossible to understand. Euan himself kept saying, "Oh my. Oh my. Will you look at that. Will you look at that." Even in the ship many people cried out in amazement.

The explorers got out of the car and wandered the cliff's edge.

Fortunately, when the wind caught them and threw them off balance, it was always inland and away from the cliff.

The cliff's edge was about twenty meters above the ocean. Offshore, waves broke to white crashing walls, which came rolling in with a low roar that could be heard through the explorers' helmets, always there under the keening of the wind over the rocks. The waves crashed into the black cliff below them, flinging spray up into the air, after which masses of white water surged back out to sea. The wind dashed most of the spray into the rocks of the cliff, although a thick variable mist also rose over the cliff's edge and was immediately thrown over them to the east.

The explorers staggered around in the wind, which was now so very visible because of the flying spray and the ocean's torn surface. Wave after wave broke offshore and was flatted to white as it rolled in, leaving trails of foam behind each broken white wall. The backwash from the cliffs headed back out in arcs that ran into the incoming breakers; when they crashed together, great plumes of spray were tossed up into the wind, to be thrown again in toward the land. It was a big and complex view, brilliantly lit, violently moving, and, as everyone could hear by way of the microphones on the explorers' helmets, extremely loud. Here at this moment, Aurora roared, howled, boomed, shrieked, whistled.

One of the explorers was bowled over, crawled around, got onto hands and knees, then stood up, carefully balancing, facing into the wind and stepping back quickly four or five times, swinging arms, ducking forward to hold position. They were all laughing.

· · · ·

It was a question what they would be able to do on such a windy world, Freya remarked to Badim, if it stayed that windy all the time. She added that it was more the ghost of Devi worrying in her than she herself. She herself wanted to get down there as soon as possible and feel that wind.

Meanwhile, down on Aurora, they were getting the construction robots started in their various tasks. A very slow sunset gave way to a night illuminated by the waxing light of E, always overhead. E's light diffused to a glow in the air somewhat like a faint white mist, which the settlers found they could see well in. The sky did not go black but rather stayed a lambent indigo, and only a few stars were visible.

The dolerite of Greenland was obdurate and uniform, containing not much in the way of other more useful minerals. They would have to hunt for those, but in the meantime, it was dolerite they had to work with. Many construction vehicles grumbled around cutting blocks of dolerite from the side of grabens, and stacking them in a wind wall to shield their little collection of landers. There was an almost continuous whine of diamond-edged circular saws. Meanwhile a smelter was extracting aluminum from crushed dolerite, which in this area proved to be about half a percent aluminum in composition. Other robotic factories were sheeting this extracted aluminum for roofs, rodding it for beams, and so on. A few of the robot excavators were set to drilling in a graben with a gravitational bolide under it, in the hope of locating some iron ore to mine. But for the most part, until they found some areas of different mineral composition, they were going to have to work with aluminum as their metal.

Aurora had a good magnetic field, ranging from .2 to .6 gauss, and that plus its atmosphere was enough to protect the settlers from Tau Ceti's UV radiation. So the surface was well protected in that regard, and really the moon's surface was quite a benign environment for humans, except for the wind. Every day explorers came in from their trips exclaiming at the force of the gusts, and one of them, Khenbish, came in with a broken arm after a fall.

. . . .

"People are beginning to hate this wind," Euan remarked to Freya during one of their personal calls. "It's not horrible or anything, but it is tedious."

"Are people scared of it?" Freya asked him. "Because it looks scary."

"Scared of Aurora? Oh hell no. Hell no. I mean, it's kicking our butts a little, but no one comes back in scared."

"No one going to go crazy and come back up here and beat people up?"

"No!" Euan laughed. "No one is going to want to go back up there. It's too interesting. You all need to get down here!"

"We want to! I want to!"

"Well, the new quarters are almost ready. You're going to love it. The wind is just part of it. I like it, myself."

But for many of the others it was the hard part; that was becoming clear.

A slow sunrise brought dawn on Aurora, and just over four of their clock days later, the high noon of their month came. During this time the lit crescent of E had shrunk to a brilliant sliver, up there in the royal blue daytime sky, and the blazing disk of Tau Ceti had been closing on that lit side of E as it rose. A time came when the star was too close to E for them to be able to look at either one without strong filters to protect their eyes.

Then, because Aurora orbited E almost in the plane of Tau Ceti's ecliptic, and E too orbited very close to that plane; and Greenland lay just north of the Aurora's equator; and E was so much bigger than Aurora, and the two so relatively close together, there came the time for their monthly midday full eclipse. Their first one was arriving. 170.055, A0.15.

The sun stood almost directly overhead, the lit crescent of Planet E right next to it. Most of the settlers were outside to watch this. Standing on small dark shadows of themselves, they set the filters in their face masks on high and looked up. Some of them lay on their backs on the ground to see without craning their necks the whole time.

The side of E about to cut into the disk of Tau Ceti went dark at last, just as the blazing disk of Tau Ceti touched its edge. E was still quite visible next to it, looking about twice as large as Tau Ceti: it blocked a large circle of stars. The very slow movement of the sun made it obvious the eclipse would last for many hours.

Slowly E's mottled dark gray circle seemed to cut into the smaller circle of Tau Ceti, which was very bright no matter which filter was used; through most of them it appeared a glowing orange or yellow ball, marred by a dozen or so sunspots. Slowly, slowly, the disk of the sun was covered by the larger dark arc of E. It took over two hours for the eclipse to become complete. In that time the watchers sat or lay there, talking. They reminded each other that back on Earth, Sol and Luna appeared to be the same size in the sky, an unlikely coincidence that meant that in some Terran eclipses, the outer corona of Sol appeared outside the eclipsing circle of Luna, ringing the dark disk with an annular blaze. In other eclipses, either more typical or not, they couldn't recall, Luna would block Sol entirely, but only for a short while, the two being the same size, and the sun moving eighteen times faster in the Terran sky than Tau Ceti did in theirs.

Here, on Aurora, during this first eclipse of Tau Ceti ever to be observed, the movement was slower, bigger; possibly therefore more massive in impact, more sublime. They thought this had to be true. As the dark circle of E slowly covered most of Tau Ceti, everything got darker, even the disk of E itself, as what illumination it had was coming from Aurora, which was itself growing darker in E's growing shadow. The light from Tau Ceti that was bouncing off Aurora and hitting E and bouncing off E and coming back to Aurora, was lessening to nearly nothing. They marveled at the idea of this double bounce that some photons were making.

Over the next hour, the landscape completed its shift from the intense light of midday to a darkness much darker than their usual night. Stars appeared in the black sky, fewer than when seen from the ship during its voyage, but quite visible, and bigger it seemed than when seen from space. In this spangled starscape the big circle of E appeared darker than ever, like charcoal against obsidian. Then the last sliver of Tau Ceti disappeared with a final diamond wink, and they stood or lay in a completely black world, a land lit by starlight, the starry sky containing a big black circle overhead.

Off on the horizons to all sides of them, they could see an indigo band, curiously infused with a golden shimmer. This was the part of Aurora's atmosphere still lit by the sun, visible off in the distance well beyond their horizon.

The wind still rushed over them. The blurred stars twinkled in the gusts. Over their eastern horizon the Milky Way stood like a tower of dim light, braided with its distinct ribbons of blackness. The wind slowly lessened, and then the air went still. Whether this was an effect of the eclipse or not, no one could say. They talked it over in quiet voices. Some thought it made sense, thermodynamically. Others guessed it was a coincidence.

About thirteen hours were going to pass in this deep, still black. Some people went back inside to get out of the chill, to eat a meal, to get some work done. Most of them came out again from time to time to have a look around, feel the absence of wind. Finally, when the time for the reappearance of Tau Ceti came, most roused themselves, as it happened to be in the middle of their clock night, and went back outside to watch.

There to the east, the sky now glowed. Though it was still dark where they were, indigo filled much of the eastern sky. Then the infusion of gold in the indigo strengthened in intensity, and the whole eastern sky turned a dark bronze, then a dark green; then it brightened, until the blackish green was shot with gold, and brightened again until it was a gold infused with greenish black, or rather a mix or mesh of gold and black, shimmering like cloth of gold seen by twilight, perhaps. An uncanny sight, clearly, as many of them cried out at it.

Then the burren off on the eastern horizon lit up as if set on fire, and their cries grew louder than ever. It looked as if the great plateau were burning. This strange fiery dawn swept in vertically, like a gold curtain of light approaching them from the east. Overhead the charcoal circle of E winked on its westernmost point, a brilliant wink of fire that quickly spilled up and down the outer curve of the black circle. And so Tau Ceti reemerged, again very slowly, taking a bit over two hours. As it emerged the day around them seemed to dawn with a strange dim shade, as if clouded, though there were no clouds. Gradually the sky turned the usual royal blue of Aurora's day; everything brightened, as if invisible clouds were now dispersing; and finally they were back in the brilliant light of the ordinary midday, with only the sky off to the west containing a remaining dark shape in the air, a shaded area, again as if invisible clouds were casting a shadow over there, a shadow that in fact was that of Planet E, which moved farther west and finally disappeared.

Then it was just midday again, and it would be for four more days, with E waxing overhead, dark gray again rather than black, the mottling of its own cloudscapes clearly visible, the crescent on its west side slowly fattening.

Up in the ship, Freya and Badim, watching mostly Euan's helmet-camera feed on their screen throughout this event, banging around their apartment doing other things but returning time after time to the kitchen to look at it, stared at each other in their kitchen.

"I want to get down there!" Freya said again.

"Me too," Badim said. "Ah, God—how I wish Devi had lived

to see that. And not just from here, but from down there with Euan. She would really have enjoyed that."

· · · · ·

Then the wind came back, hard from the east. But now they knew that there might come a few hours of windlessness during eclipses. And there would surely be other such hours; on this world of constantly shifting light, the winds too would surely have to shift. They might be almost always strong, but as they changed from onshore to offshore, being so near the coast, there would surely be periods that would be still, or at least swirling. They were still learning how that worked, and no doubt would be for a long time to come; the patterns were not yet predictable. That was aerodynamics, Euan remarked: the air moving around a planet was always in flux, supersensitive, well beyond any modeling they were capable of.

So: wind. It was back, it would seldom go away. It would be a hard thing to deal with. It was the hard part of life on Aurora.

The good part, the glorious part, they all agreed, was the look of the land under the double light of Tau Ceti and E, especially early in the long mornings, and now, they were finding again, in the slanting light of the long afternoons. Possibly the experience of the eclipse had sprung something in their ability to see. In the ship they saw only the near and the far; this middle distance on Aurora, what some called planetary distance, others simply the landscape, at first had been hard for them to focus on, or even to look for, or to comprehend when they did see it. Now that they were properly ranging it, and grasping the spaciousness of it, it was intoxicating. It was enough to make them happy just to go outside and walk around, and look at the land. The wind was nothing compared to that.

· · · · ·

One day an exploring party came back from the north, excited. Seventeen kilometers to the north of their landing site, there was an anomaly in the generally straight and cliffed coast, a small semi-circular valley that opened onto the sea. This was a feature that had been visible from the ship, of course, and people still on the ship had reminded the surface party about it, and now this group had hiked up to visit it, and having seen it, had come back to base exclaiming its virtues.

It was either an old impact crater or an extinct volcanic feature, but in any case, a semicircular depression in the burren, with the straight side of the semicircle a beach fronting the sea. The explorers called it Half Moon Valley and said its beach was composed of sand and shingle, backed by a lagoon. In the low land behind the lagoon an estuary cut through the valley, then rose through a break in the low cliff of the burren, first as a braided, gravel-bedded river, then as a set of swift tumbling rapids. And the entire valley, they said, was floored with soil. From space this soil appeared to be loess. The explorers' closer inspection had indicated it was a combination of loess, sea sand, and river silt. Calling it soil was perhaps inaccurate, as it was entirely inorganic, but at the very least it was a soil matrix. It could quickly be turned into soil.

This was such promising news that the settlers quickly decided that they should move there. They freely admitted that one powerful attraction was the possibility of getting out of the wind. But there were other advantages as well: access to the ocean, a good supply of fresh water, potential agricultural land. The prospect was so enticing that some of them even wondered why they hadn't landed there in the first place, but of course they were reminded by people in the ship (who had been reminded by the ship) that the robotic landers had had to give the valley a wide berth, to be sure they came down on flat rock.

Now they were safely down, and in exploration mode, and their settlement was still quite mobile, being almost entirely composed of landers; they had built their wind wall but not yet started on buildings. So they could make the move fairly easily.

Over the next few days, therefore, everyone in the station walked up to see the sea valley, and agreed the moment they did that the move should be made. This kind of unanimity was said to have happened so infrequently on the ship (in fact it had never happened) that the people still on the ship were happy to accede to the plan on the ground.

"As if we could stop them," Freya remarked to Badim.

Badim nodded. "Aram says they are acting ominously autonomously. But it's okay. We'll all be down there soon. And it looks like a good place."

At this point, people from the ship were being ferried down to the moon in modules that then served as their living quarters. Nothing was going as quickly as many on the ship would have liked, but everyone had to agree that nothing more could be done to speed the process. They only had so many ferries, and then some had to be refueled and launched back up to ship. Now that they were going to move the settlement to Half Moon Valley, all the work to expand their living space would be delayed. But a brief delay was felt to be well worth it, given the many advantages that would follow the move.

· · · ·

So the settlers got to work moving, a task that seemed easy until they began to do it, when the little declivities and breaks in the burren turned out to be more obstructive to moving their living modules than had been foreseen. The shallow little grabens were easy to walk down small ravines into and out of, and so they had hiked to the valley and back without impediment, but moving their modules on wheeled frames, and their construction robot vehicles, and even their rovers, across them was not so easy. And the grabens were all so long, and trending east-west, that they often could not be flanked.

A best route was found that crossed as few of these troughs as possible, using the algorithm that solves the traveling salesman problem, notorious to all those worried about errors endemic to certain greedy algorithms. But even after extensive cross-checking, the minimum number of graben crossings turned out to be eleven. Each trough had to be bridged, and this was not easy, given the dearth of bridge materials and the weight of the loads on the wheeled carts.

So it was a slow and ponderous trek, and soon after they began, sunset came again. They did not let this stop them, having decided they could make their trip by the light of E. It hung up there in its usual spot, half illuminated—what on Earth they called a quarter moon, an unusually logical name, it must be said. Just after sunset was as dark as the nights got, as E waxed to full and then waned to the other quarter moon before sunrise. The light cast by quarter E was around 25 lux, which was 25 times the illumination of the full moon on Earth; and though it was four thousand times less than direct sunlight on Earth, and six thousand times less than full taulight on Aurora, it was still about the same illumination as a nicely lit room at night in the ship, which was certainly enough to see by. So they worked in this light, and formed a long caravan of their vehicles, and headed north over the burren. In the end they declared the E light quite beautiful, easy on the eyes, things slightly drained of color but extremely distinct.

• • • •

Euan and the rest of the bridge-building team went into action when they came to the edge of the first trough. One of them drove a stone-cutting vehicle to the edge of the trough, well away from where they intended to cross, and put to work a rock saw attachment at the end of the vehicle's backhoe. Cubes of rock were cut from the side of the graben, then lifted and conveyed hanging from the backhoe to a steep-walled section of graben, where the opposite side was both close and as vertical as could be found. The first cube was hard to get loose, but with some knocking with the side of the backhoe they managed it. Cubes three meters on a side were as large as the vehicle could safely lift. When they got them to the edge of the graben they lowered them into the trough, all very slowly, especially if the wind was gustier than usual. Every four or five cubes, they had to stop and swap out the saw blades they were using, both the circular blades and the thin up-and-down saws that Euan called dental floss. Their printer refurbished worn blades with new synthetic diamond edges, and they attached these and continued cutting cubes and depositing them in the trough to make a rough ramp. When the ramp extended far enough into the trough that the vehicle arm couldn't reach out far enough to place new cubes, they filled the gaps between cubes with gravel that other teams had crushed, then unrolled by hand an aluminum mesh carpet to provide a bridge surface smooth enough to drive onto. Euan then drove the cutter vehicle out onto this ramp, another cube dangling heavily from its front end, everything looking precarious, especially when swaying in hard gusts of wind, until he reached the leading edge of the new ramp and could lower the next cube of rock into place.

They were nearly done with this first ramp when Eliza dropped a new cube into place without realizing the trough bottom was not smooth. This was perhaps a result of them working in E light, but in any case, the new cube tilted into another cube already in place in a way that meant their vehicle could neither lift it nor move it, without dangerously tipping the vehicle.

Euan took over the controls from Eliza to give it a try, but he couldn't move it either, though he rocked the vehicle dangerously to the side. So it lay there blocking their way, making the ramp impassable, and tilted as it was, it looked like they would have to abandon the entire ramp and start over.

"Let me try something," Euan said, and used the rock saw to cut a trapezoidal segment off the top of the tilted cube, then carefully wedged the segment into the gap left under the tilted cube. After attaching the pile-driver tip and doing some hard tamping with the crane, they concluded the combination was going to be stable enough to drive over, and so they continued cutting cubes and placing them in the trough, more carefully than ever, often with Euan given the controls to make the final drops.

"He's an artist," Badim said to Freya as they watched from the ship.

"That's why he's down there and I'm not," Freya said. "They don't need Good For Anythings down there."

"They do," Badim said. "They will. It was a lottery, remember."

After three days of work, the ramp across the trough was finished. They sent across a robot truck first to test it, and it ground over the aluminum carpet without incident. All was well, and they drove or directed all the other vehicles over the ramp. There were thirty-seven vehicles in their caravan, ranging in size from four-person rovers to mobile containers that were the modular parts of their buildings. All crossed without incident. But that was only the first of eleven grabens.

However, they now had their method, and because of that, the subsequent ramps went a little faster. Even the so-called Great Trench, a graben three times wider and twice as deep as the rest, was ramped and crossed in a day. Stopping to swap out the rock-cutting blades became the biggest delay. In this task, both the versatility and the unreliability of humans doing mechanical work was revealed. The operator would set the vehicle arm on the ground with the nut holding the blade to the rotor facing up, and someone would fit the power wrench to the nut and zip it off with a pneumatic blast. Off came the nut and washers, after which they spun the circular saw blade carefully off the short spindle, being careful not to damage its screw threads. Then they carried the blade to the machine truck, where printers would have readied a newly sharpened blade. Go back and spin a refurbished blade down onto the spindle, put the washers on, then the nut; last, apply the power drill and tighten the nut. This was the moment where humans were not as good as a robot would have been, and their tools not adequate to compensate for their inexperience. The problem was they could not tell how tight the nuts were being screwed on by the power drill, and very often, in the attempt to be sure they were tight enough, they drilled them too tight. Threads were stripped, and then there was no grip at all, and the spindle had to be replaced, which took many hours of delicate work; or washers were fused together, or fused into the nut or the blade, such that they could not be separated afterward, even with the power drill at full power.

This kind of mistake happened so often that eventually they allowed only Euan and Eliza to use the power drills for this task, as they were the only ones who had the touch to do it right. Anyone listening to Euan's feed to the ship, including Freya and Badim and a few score others, got used to the heavy airy *blat* of the power drill working, and they also got used to his various favorite curses as he lamented one action or another.

The settlers rolled slowly across the land, averaging 655 meters a day, with their longest day only three kilometers, and that between two troughs, over flat burren. It took them twenty-three days to move their settlement to the sea cliff overlooking Half Moon Valley, on the shore of the western sea. They had traveled by the light of Planet E as it went through its full phase, a huge sight; they noted the lunar eclipse in the middle of that, the shadow of Aurora diffusely crossing the face of E, dimming it somewhat, but not too much, because E was so much bigger than Aurora, and the two so close together, and both with thick atmospheres, which diffused Tau Ceti's light around Aurora and meant E was not very shaded by it. After that they had scarcely noticed the dimming of E's slow wane, which brought back in the lambent night more blurry stars. These stars slowly shifted overhead, and the phases of E also shifted, but E stayed always fixed in place over them, a bit south and east of the zenith. Some settlers said this felt strange; others shrugged.

Near the end of their trek, they waited out a hard rainstorm, when it got too dark and wet to travel safely. And they stopped work to witness the sunrise of Tau Ceti, painfully bright over the burren to the east. Like a nuclear explosion, some said, in what was perhaps a false or mistaken metaphor, as it was in fact a kind of nuclear explosion.

Though they could see down into their ocean valley, they were still on the cliff above it, and so had to bulldoze a ramp road down the side of the river canyon that formed the largest break in the sea cliff. This tilted curving road was the work of another eight days. When it was finished, they drove all the vehicles down to the valley floor and located them near the bottom of the cliff, on an alluvial floodplain near the river. This was clearly going to be the spot in the valley best protected by the cliff from the winds. At least the offshore winds.

· · · ·

As they quickly found, there were times when the winds poured up and down the river canyon even faster than they had out on the burren, as the gusts were channelized by the canyon. Once this became clear they moved their caravan farther from the river, and got some protection at the foot of the cliffs about two kilometers from the canyon mouth. This was a relief to all. Their new location seemed the best they were going to be able to find in this region of Greenland, all things considered. So they began to settle in at the foot of the curving cliff, and later in some steep, short gulleys that ran up the cliff to the burren. These ravines were transverse to the prevailing winds, and therefore well protected, but mostly steep-walled, with narrow floors.

To aid the wind break of the cliff, they began to build what they called city walls out from it. One would encircle their residential complex, and another one, longer still, would enclose the first fields they hoped to plant in the open air.

Every day there was more to be done than they could do, and they welcomed the regular infusion of people who started coming down again from the ship. They jammed these newcomers into the shelters as tightly as they could manage. Everyone ate food sent down from the ship. They kept the printers on both Aurora and the ship working continuously, making all the parts they required to assemble their new world. In this process their feedstocks and simply time itself were the only limiting factors. They couldn't make more time, but they could send mining expeditions out onto the burren to locate metal ores and replenish their feedstocks, and they did.

· · · ·

More people descended, bringing them to just over one hundred total. Greenhouses now became crucial. They hoped eventually to grow crops out in the open air, and the chemical composition of the air was adequate for this, indeed nearly Terran; but during the nine-day nights, despite the waxing and waning light of E overhead, the temperature dropped to well below freezing. It wasn't obvious how they were going to solve that, in regard to their agriculture. There were winter-tolerant plants that cold-hardened and went dormant, and survived freezes; the farm labs on both ship and Aurora were investigating how these plants accomplished that, and whether the genes for that ability could be transported to other plants. Also they were looking into genes that could help plants adapt to the daymonth cycle rather than annual seasons, but the outcome of this effort was not clear. For now, whatever they ended up planting, greenhouses were necessary.

At first most of the greenhouse space was given over to growing soil itself. Soil as opposed to dirt was about 20 percent alive by weight, and plants were very much happier growing in it than they were in dirt like the valley's dead loess. When they had viable soil, which fortunately grew in tanks filled with loess at nearly the speed of bacterial reproduction itself, they spread it in the greenhouses and planted crops. These were mostly fast bamboos at first, bamboos they had nursed throughout the long voyage to Tau Ceti without much needing them; now they came into their own, as they were a crucial building material, providing strong beams at a growth rate of a meter a day. Meanwhile the settlers' food still came mostly from the ship and was flown down to them.

This created another supply problem. They had robot ferries capable of flying down from the ship to Aurora, then refueling and launching to get back up to the ship, but they needed fuel. One of the factories in the valley was entirely devoted to splitting water into oxygen and hydrogen, the main components of their rockets' fuel. The factory itself had to be powered, however, and splitting water was very energy-intensive. They had two powerful nuclear reactors with them on the surface, providing 400 megawatts total, but the uranium and plutonium in the reactors would not last forever, and the ship's supply was only adequate for the ship. Was there uranium on Aurora? According to standard theories of planetary formation, there had to be some; but the entire Tau Ceti system was less metallic than the solar system, and heavy metals only accumulated well on planetary bodies with a steady churn of tectonic action or tidal flexing. It wasn't clear Aurora had ever had either, and given the uncertainty on this point, it was felt that they were going to have to devote a good deal of their manufacturing capability to building wind power generators on the burren. For sure there was going to be enough wind.

The people in the new settlement named it Hvalsey, after a town on the west coast of the Greenland on Earth. Quickly they expanded around the greenhouses. Stonecutters and foundries provided stone blocks and aluminum sheeting for construction, also glass windows for greenhouse roofs and walls. The city wall helped solve the wind problem. Some said Hvalsey looked like a little medieval walled town.

They were finding that the winds shifted in a somewhat predictable way through the course of the daymonths. When the air above a region was lit by Tau Ceti for nine days straight, it heated and rose, creating low pressures on the surface that cold air from the night side rushed in to fill. Then when sunset arrived, and a region was in night for nine days, it cooled down so drastically that snow and ice appeared on all the islands, and sea ice covered the calmer bays and reaches of the ocean, but not usually on the open sea, which was too buffeted by waves and wind to freeze over. The cold air in falling created pressures that shot out to the sides, filling the relative gap under the rising air on the sunlit side. So the winds were always swirling, mostly from night to day. Midday and midnight appeared to be the calmest times.

The long nights over the inner hemisphere never became quite as cold as those over the outer hemisphere, but they still dropped to well below freezing. If they were going to do agriculture in the open air, they were going to have to adapt their Terran plants from an annular to a monthly temporality. Watching their fast bamboo grow a meter a day, it seemed possible that they could engineer crops to grow to harvest in nine days, but no one could be sure how that would work, or even if it was possible. If they had to confine their agriculture entirely to greenhouses, it seemed like a fairly serious constraint. But they would cross that bridge when they built it, as Badim put it.

Meanwhile, in terms of the wind, which kept forcing itself to the forefront of their attention, the monthly air flows were regular, but not entirely consistent. They had a very sensitive dependence on conditions that were always changing. But as they learned more about Aurora's weather, they began to identify certain patterns. One thing was perfectly obvious: on most days it was going to be windy.

• • • •

E's year was 169 Terran days long. The Auroran month, 17.96 Terran days long, therefore divided into the solar year of 169 days to create about 9.2 months a year, and thus the usual problem of trying to reconcile lunar months to solar years.

They did not worry about that now.

• • • •

With the town walls under robotic construction, and the platting of the town finished and building sites being prepared, Euan frequently joined the teams going out to explore the sea valley. And he wanted to take off his helmet and breathe the ambient air.

This came as no surprise to Freya. The data from the monitoring stations were making it clear that Aurora's atmosphere was breathable by humans, that indeed Aurora's atmosphere was the most Earthlike aspect of their new home, and the main reason it scored so high in Earth analog rubrics. So as he joined all the scouting expeditions he could, Euan pushed harder and harder for official permission to take off his helmet. "It's going to happen sooner or later," he said. "Why not now? What's keeping us from it? What are we afraid of?"

Of undetected toxins, of course. This was what he was told, and to Freya the caution was obvious and justified. Poisonous chemical combinations, unseen life-forms: the precautionary principle had to guide them. The Hvalsey council insisted on it, and also referred the question to the ship's executive council, who said the same thing.

Euan and others of his opinion pointed out that their atmospheric and soil and rock studies had now gone right down to the nanometer level, and found nothing but the same volatiles they had detected from space, plus dust and fines as expected. The atmospheric gases were much like the air in the ship, except slightly less dense. Studies on the ground had confirmed the abiologic explanation for the oxygen in the atmosphere; they could even estimate its age, which was about 3.7 billion years. Tau Ceti, brighter then, had split Aurora's hot ocean water into oxygen and hydrogen, and the hydrogen had escaped to space, leaving the oxygen behind. The chemical signatures of that action were unambiguous, a finding that had reassured the biology group that they did indeed have the place to themselves, as indicated by everything else they had seen.

Euan wanted to start that part of their new history, the first moment of going outdoors and breathing the open air. Freya said this to him during one of their conversations, and he replied, "Of course! I want to feel that big wind fill my lungs!"

The executive council continued to ignore the biology group and to refuse permission, to Euan or anyone else. Once the seal was broken between themselves and Aurora, there would be no going back. They needed to wait; to experiment on plants and animals first; to be patient; to be sure.

Freya wondered what Devi would have said about it, and asked Badim what he thought, but he only shook his head. "I'm not sure," he said. "She was both cautious and bold. What she would say about this, I just don't know."

The executive council asked the security council to consider the matter and make a recommendation, and the security council asked Freya to join their meeting. Badim said the invitation was because of her friendship with Euan. The committee members were worried about him in particular.

The security council met to take up the question. Freya said to them, "I've been trying to imagine what Devi would have said about this, and I think she would have pointed out that the people on Aurora have had to take shelter in buildings they constructed by cutting stone. They've faced the stone with diamond sprays and aluminum, but there have been periods in the construction process when they've been exposed to cut stone. That isn't exactly the same as going out into the open air, or jumping in the ocean, but it is exposure of a sort. So is going outside in suits and afterward going back inside still wearing the suits, and taking them off. What I mean to say is, inevitably they are already in contact with the planet. As soon as they landed, exposure was inevitable. And when they went out onto the surface in suits, even more so. They couldn't stay inside a hermetically sealed chamber, they're in contact with the place. And that's good, right? That's where we all hope to be. And nothing has happened to them, and they've been down there for over forty days. So keeping them confined indoors or in their suits is a conservatism that doesn't conserve anything. It doesn't acknowledge the reality of the situation. And it's always better to acknowledge the reality of the situation. This is what Devi would have said, I think."

Aram nodded at this; Song too nodded. If their system of governing had been a direct democracy, it was likely that the people on the surface would have been allowed to go out and open their suits and let the wind fill their lungs. But their government was made up of councils that for many years had often selected their own members, in effect. The ship's computer was advisory only, and the ship tended to be conservative in matters of risk assessment and risk management, in ways everyone had seemed to want from it. So its programming seemed to indicate.

Now the security council again voted to keep the settlement closed off from the ambient environment, and those voting for this included even Aram and Song. The executive council did the same. But the time seemed near when that might change.

· · · · ·

Down in Hvalsey, they were having more trouble dealing with the winds. Through the long morning of the daymonth there was a steady offshore wind of about fifty kilometers per hour, with gusts as strong as a hundred. There was a slight katabatic effect coming off the sea cliff that made the river canyon particularly windy. At middaymonth, during the strange darkness of the solar eclipse, there was a period of slackening winds, and then of comparative calm, and everyone on the surface (126 people now) wanted to get out in this calm time, which could last past the end of the eclipse for as much as twenty or thirty hours, but seldom more. There were limits on how many people could leave the shelters at once, so there was a scramble for spots on the schedule during this slack time, because at some point in the early afternoon of the daymonth, the onshore wind would begin, a hard flow of air barreling in off the sea into the interior of Greenland, as the land got hotter than the ocean and its air rose and vacated a space that cooler sea air rushed in to fill, the wind arriving in puffs and faltering breezes, then in a steady gentle push, which strengthened through the afternoon of the daymonth until sunset. This was generally the time of strongest onshore winds, although that varied of course, as storm systems swirled around Aurora in the usual fractal nautiloid motions that occur when gases move around the exterior of a rotating sphere. Although Aurora's day was also its month, it was still rotating once in that daymonth, and that slow rotation caused the air in the atmosphere to drag a little in relation to both hydrosphere and lithosphere, creating winds that curled and mixed to create the usual trades, polar swirls, and so on.

So: almost always windy. When it wasn't, they left the shelters and walked around, enjoying the ability to do so without bending over into the gusts, without being thrown to the ground. Even in the dark of the eclipse they enjoyed being out in the still air, the beams from their headlamps lancing and crisscrossing to illuminate their sea valley and its backing cliffs.

Jochi had his name drawn in the lottery to go down, and he descended in the next group, and as soon as he could, got on the list to go out of Hvalsey town in a suit, and Freya watched with him as he went out and immediately was knocked off his feet by a katabatic gust. Everyone in his group was knocked over but one, and they all cried out in surprise or fear, as did Freya up in the ship. Jochi crawled around for a while, laughing, and got in the lee of the city wall and stood again, still laughing. He danced around in the shelter of the wall as if he were a winter lamb let out of the barn for the first time in spring. He gamboled.

. . . . .

Euan's particular pleasure now was to hike a trail he had helped to establish along the south side of the river, exploring the estuary and then the beach between the lagoon and the ocean. The sand on the riverside and down on the beach was often hard-packed, under a loose layer that got lifted in the winds and deposited in miniature dunes that scalloped the packed sand under it. Near the water there were also very fine crosshatchings of sand, sometimes cut by watercourses so that many layers of this weave of layers was revealed. At first they said that Aurora had no tides, being tidally locked to Planet E and thus always tugged by it in the same direction, but now there were some people in the settlement who thought that the combination of Tau Ceti and Planet E might tug a bit harder on Aurora in the direction of Planet E, while when Tau Ceti was on the other side of Aurora, the contrary tugs of Planet E and the star would shift the water covering most of Aurora in ways that could be seen. And there were slight libration tides as well, created when Aurora rocked a little in its facing toward E. Thus there were two kinds of slight tides, both moving at the pace of the daymonth, but in different rhythms. And indeed on the beaches there was often a fine crosshatching that was perhaps evidence of these tides. They had not been able to measure changes in the height of the ocean, however, and so there were others who argued that the crosshatching resulted not from the two little tides, but from the steady inflow of big wave after big wave, each large one leaving a mark across and slightly at an angle to the previous waves. Most of the scientists still on the trip doubted that waves could leave such regular marks; some of them postulated they were sandstone layers exposed to the sea, and the residue of changing sea levels in different eras of Aurora's history.

"So to sum up," Euan said, "they're either the marks of individual waves, or daymonth tides, or geological eons. Thanks for that clarification!"

He laughed at this. Looking closely at the beach and the oncoming waves was one of the great pleasures of his shore walks, he told Freya in one of their private conversations, and he spent many an excursion walking up and down the strand to the south of the river mouth, often stopping to inspect certain sections from his knees, or even while lying down.

Most of his time out of the town was spent in gathering sand and loess to add to their soil-building greenhouses. He brought back samples he thought were promising, one backpack at a time. The farmers were pleased to have new soil matrices to extend some experiments. If they liked certain samples Euan brought in, he would drive out in a rover and dig up larger quantities. They were getting good results in certain fields, including some newly engineered plants that produced a harvest of edible seeds in the nine days of the daylit part of the daymonth. These fast plants would likely remain unusual, but could supplement crops grown in their greenhouses to a more normal rhythm. Between greenhouse and altered plants grown outdoors, it seemed as if they were going to be able to provide themselves with enough food, and this was exciting to them all, both settlers on Aurora and those in the ship still waiting to come down.

One day, 170.139, Euan went out with three friends, Nanao, Kher, and Clarisse. As always when people went out on hikes like this, many of those still up in the ship sat before their screens and watched what the walkers' helmet cameras showed them.

On this day Euan and his companions first walked over to the river canyon. The rapids at the top of the canyon began with two short falls off the burren, followed by two taller falls in the canyon, after which a quick tilted rush of white water spilled onto the valley floor. There the river was split in two by a giant boulder, and after that several channels meandered across a broad flat of sorted gravel, sand, and mud flats: a braided stream. The delta created by this braided stream had a triangular shape when seen from above, like many Terran deltas (origin of phrase delta v?).

Euan stood at the foot of the lowest falls and watched the white water pour down and smash into a foamy brilliance of bubbles. In the late-morning light the water looked as if diamonds had been crushed into a cream. From time to time mist swept over him, and his helmet camera clouded, or streamed with lines of water drops. The rattle and rush of the water was loud, and if his companions spoke, as it sounded like they did, it was not possible for those on the ship listening to Euan's feed to understand them. Nor was it clear that Euan himself heard them, or was trying to.

After a while the four walkers trooped down the estuary in a ragged line, Euan ahead of the rest. By now the settlers had thoroughly explored the braided streams of the valley, placed a little aluminum footbridge across one channel, and pushed boulders around in the shallows of others to make stepping-stones, so that they could get onto the central islands of the delta, in a more or less straight trail to the south end of the beach lagoon, where they could cross one more aluminum footbridge to get to the beach.

The islands between the braided streams were variously sand, mud, gravel, or talus; tough hiking no matter which, unless they walked on curving natural ramps and mounds of hardened mud, which resembled what Terran sources called eskers. By now their bootprint trails crossed many of these ramps, and thus connected many of the triangular or lemniscate islands in the delta.

Euan led the way along one of these paths, appearing to be

headed for the sea. From the beach at the south end of the lagoon they had established a switchbacked trail up a beveled section of the sea cliff; on this day they were planning to ascend these switchbacks and then walk back on the burren around to Hvalsey. It was a popular loop walk.

• • • •

Then came a cry for help from one of Euan's companions and he looked back, his helmet camera's view swinging with his head. Only two companions were in sight, both charging down to the bank of one of the braided streams. The fourth one had left their path, apparently, and was now waist deep in what appeared to be some kind of quicksand. Luckily she seemed to have hit a harder layer and was not immediately sinking any farther. She was about three meters from higher ground; this ground looked about the same as the sand she had wandered onto, but by the evidence of her own bootprints, it was firmer underfoot.

Euan hurried over to them and said, "Clarisse, why did you go out there?"

"I wanted to look at a rock. It looked like it might be a hematite."

"Where's the rock?"

"It turned out to be a reflection of the sun off a puddle."

Euan didn't reply at first. He was looking around, surveying the terrain.

"Okay," he said at last. "Lie down toward us, and I'll lie down toward you, and we'll hold each other's wrists, and Nanao and Kher will pull us both out."

"I feel pretty stuck. What if they can't do it?"

"Then we'll call for help. But we might as well see if we can do it by ourselves first."

"You're going to get very muddy."

"I don't care. Are you on something hard, do you think, or have you just stopped sinking?"

"I don't feel anything really hard under my feet."

"All right. Lay your upper body flat on the surface. Here we go."

Clarisse leaned forward until her chest was on the mud before her. She kept her eyes on Euan's, and he knelt and stretched out to her. They reached out and held on to each other's wrists, and Nanao and Kher gripped Euan by the ankles and began to pull back up the slope. At first nothing happened, and Euan laughed.

"I'm going to be taller when this is over!"

Clarisse said, "I'm sorry." Then: "Maybe we should have strapped our wrists together."

"I've got a good grip on you," Euan said.

"I know, it hurts."

"Straps would hurt more. I won't squeeze any harder than this."

"Good."

"Here we go again," Nanao said. "Hold on."

Again there appeared to be nothing happening, but then Clarisse exclaimed, "I can feel my feet moving! All of me, really."

"Best it be all of you," Euan said. Nanao and Kher laughed, then resumed their tugging.

"Not a steady pull," Euan said to them. "Do it in pulses. Start and stop, but don't completely stop."

Soon they could see that Clarisse was coming up out of the mud, and Euan being dragged back. The farther out she came, the faster the process went. Soon she was only knee deep in the mud. Then, as they were finishing the pull, she said, "Ow, my shin."

Nanao and Kher stopped pulling.

"My leg ran into something hard."

"Got to get you out anyway," Euan said. "Twist that foot up and to the side as we pull."

"Okay. Go again."

She winced as they continued. Then she was skidding across the surface of the mud, and the four of them were all crawling away from the flat, then seated on harder ground. Their exterior suits were muddied around the feet and hands especially, and for Euan, all across his front side; and Clarisse was completely covered with mud from the waist down, also across her chest.

She pointed to her left shin, where a streak of blood marred the brown mud. "I told you I hit something. There must have been a rock in the mud there."

"Let's get that taped up," Euan said.

"We broke her seal," Nanao said.

"It was bound to happen," Euan replied. "It'll be all right."

Kher took a roll of suit tape from his thigh pocket, and while the others washed Clarisse's shin down with water scooped from the river, he cut off a length of it with the scissors on his thigh pack knife. When the break was clean and they had dried it with a cloth in her thigh pack, Kher applied the length of tape to the break and held it against Clarisse's leg until it had bonded.

"Okay, now we need to get back."

"Which way is fastest at this point?"

"I think going down to the beach and up the cliff trail to the overlook, don't you?"

"Not sure. Let's see what the maps say."

They consulted their wristpads and decided it would be better to turn around and go back the way they had come.

They hiked back in silence. It was the first time that the physical barrier between Aurora and their bodies had been breached. It did not seem an auspicious way to do it, but it was done, and now there was nothing more they could do except return quickly, and attend to Clarisse's cut. She said it didn't hurt but only stung, and so they walked fast. In less than two hours they were back in Hvalsey.

· · · ·

Social or psychological pressure was building inside the ship, as so many people wanted more and more urgently to get down onto Aurora. Images of people walking around in suits, getting thrown

was 32.1 years. Now, after Maria's declaration went around the rings, there were 469 who declared a preference to stay in the ship. For purposes of maintenance of the ship, also to avoid crowding the new settlement on Aurora, this shift was felt to be a good thing. A sense of anxiety created by the various social pressures of aggregated individual desires lessened. Average blood pressure dropped.

· · · ·

Despite the variety of opinions and feelings, the sense grew in those still on the ship that it was time for all those who wanted to, to descend. Now the ones most urging patience, and a measured pace of immigration, were people already on the ground, who were worried about a sudden influx of newcomers. In saying this they had to be careful not to offend those still in the ship— careful not to sound as if they had any rights in the matter, or were trying to protect what many felt was simply luck of the draw, an unearned privilege. It had to be presented as simply a matter of logistics, of not overwhelming the systems established. There was a protocol to be followed, and they had set it up with good reasons; there was not yet enough shelter in Hvalsey to accommodate everyone who wanted to descend. It was going to take some time for all that infrastructure to get built and established. Food also was a factor; if too many people came down, they could neither grow enough food on Aurora, nor keep growing it on the ship to send down to Aurora, having to an extent abandoned the farms on the ship. Without a careful transition they could inadvertently create food shortages in both places. And they didn't have the means to get people back up to the ship very quickly. Return was not easy; Aurora's gravity well and atmosphere meant their spiral launch tube assembly, now built and working well, could only launch so many ferries, as they had to split water and distill the fuels, and also smelt and print the ablation plates for them to deal with the rapid launch up through the atmosphere. Return to the ship was a choke point in the process of settlement, there was no doubt of that. It had not been planned for.

· · · · ·

The only solution was to hurry every project in Hvalsey, and be patient on the ship. Those in both places most aware of the logistical problems talked to the rest, reassured them, encouraged them; and hurried more.

Badim and Freya were among those counseling patience on the ship, although Freya also said she was on fire with the desire to descend. She watched Euan's adventures on Aurora during most of her spare time, clutching Badim's arm in the evenings before the screen and swaying a little, as if dizzy. She was in fact a little feverish compared to her normal temperature. She wanted down. But she spent her days doing what needed doing to keep Nova Scotia going, focusing on problems the way Devi would have, trying to deal with each problem in order of a priority of needs that ship helped her establish. She worked on the Gantt programs that Devi had left for her, stacking priorities like houses of cards. Risks averted, problems dodged, enough food grown to keep them all fed. It was never a simple calculation. But the Gantt programs were displayed on the screens in blocks of color, and she found she could manipulate the problems well enough to keep things going.

By working with this system, she saw that although they were losing volatiles in every launch of the ferries down to Aurora, now this problem could be solved by shipping compressed gases back from the moon up to the ship, and even water. What a relief to have relief at hand, after so many years of interstellar isolation! The resources of the Tau Ceti system were lovely to contemplate. Every meter of bamboo grown in Hvalsey was another plank in the floor they were now building under themselves.

This was the comfort Devi had never had.

One night as they watched the photos from Hvalsey on Badim's screen, they discussed this aspect of their new situation, and Aram stood to recite one of their kitchen couplets:

"Our sidewalk over the abyss
We build ahead of us as we go,
Give us the planks and we'll make it work
Until a time we don't want to know."

．．．．．

On the morning of 170.144, A0.104, Euan came on Freya's screen and asked her to get Badim to join their conversation. Freya called to Badim to come into the kitchen, and after seven minutes he blundered in, looking asleep on his feet, and sat next to her and slumped against her, looking curiously at the screen. "What?"

After a few seconds, it was clear he had appeared on Euan's screen, and Euan nodded and said, "That woman we got out of the quicksand, Clarisse? She's sick. She's running a fever."

Badim sat up straight. "Get her under the hood," he said.

"We did."

"She's in the isolation clinic?"

"Yes."

"How fast did you get her in there?"

"As soon as she mentioned that she felt bad."

Badim's mouth was pursed tight. How often Freya had seen this look. It was not Devi's look, exactly; somewhat like it, but calmer, more sympathetic. It was as if he were imagining what he would do if he were in Euan's place.

"Is she cooperating? Is she being monitored?"

"Yes."

"Can you show me her readouts?"

"Yes, I've got them up here on my monitor. Have a look."

Euan shoved his room camera sideways, and then Freya and

Badim were looking at the isolation clinic's medical screen, with Clarisse's vital signs bumping and trembling as they trolled left to right, with flickering red numbers arrayed below. Badim leaned closer to their screen and pushed his lips this way and that as he read.

He took a deep breath.

"How do you feel?" he asked Euan.

"Me? I feel fine."

"You and the others who were out there with her should also isolate yourselves, I feel. Also anyone who tended to this woman when she got back into your shelter."

"Because she cut her shin?"

"Because she cut her suit. Yes." Badim's lips were a tight knot. "I'm sorry. But it makes sense to take every precaution. Just in case."

No reply from Euan. His camera stayed trained on the monitor.

"She's got quite a fever," Badim said quietly, as if to Freya. "Pulse fast and shallow, a little a-fib, T cell counts high in the bloodstream. Cerebellum working hard. Looks like she's fighting something off."

"But what?" Freya said, as if for Euan.

"I don't know. Maybe something a little toxic, there in the mud. Some accumulation of some metal or chemical. We'll have to analyze for that."

"Or maybe there's some bug going around in Hvalsey that she caught," Freya said. There were, of course, many viruses and bacteria in the ship, and therefore in Hvalsey too.

"Yes, maybe so."

"Or maybe she's gone into shock," Euan said from off his screen.

"It's slow for a shock reaction to that cut," Badim said. "But you're right, we should look at that. You should look at all that, but keeping her in iso. Do it by extensions. And really, the rest of you who came in contact with her should get into iso as well. Just to be safe."

Again no reply from Euan.

Well, it was rubbish news, no doubt of that. Anyone would be disturbed. But for Euan, taking such obvious delight in his excursions on the surface, arguing vehemently for the opening of their helmets and the breathing of the open air of Aurora, it hit particularly hard. One could feel it in his silence.

When their call ended, Badim stood and shuddered, then just stood there for a long time, his head down.

"Better call Aram," he said at last. "And Jochi. He should probably be in iso too. The problem is, they all should be isolated from all the rest, and they can't do that."

As it turned out, Jochi had been out in one of the expedition cars when the news of Clarisse's fever came, and when he heard the news, he stayed in the car, locked inside. He acknowledged to the others in Hvalsey he was there, but refused to discuss his situation any further. There was air, water, food, and battery power to keep him out there for three weeks. People in Hvalsey spoke angrily to him, but he didn't reply. The people up in the ship didn't know what to say. Badim just shook his head when Freya asked him what he thought.

"He might be right," Badim said. "I wish there was a car for everyone. But there isn't. And no one person can stay isolated for long, there or anywhere."

· · · · ·

It was the middle of the night on 170.153, A0.113, and Freya was sleeping restlessly, when her screen spoke to her, quietly at first, so that Freya first muttered things, in what sounded like a dream conversation with her mother; but as the voice from the screen repeated "Freya . . . Freya . . . Freya," in a way that Devi never would have, she finally woke, groggily.

It was Euan, in Hvalsey. "Euan?" Freya said. "What is it?"

"Clarisse died," he said.

He didn't have his camera on, or was sitting in the dark; it was just his voice, the screen was dark.

"Oh no!"

"Yes. Last night."

"What happened?"

"We don't know. Looks like she had some kind of anaphylactic shock. As if she ran into something she was allergic to."

"But what is there to be allergic to?"

"I don't know. Nothing. She had asthma, but that was controlled. They gave her epinephrine four times, but her blood pressure dropped, her throat seems to have closed up on her, the ventral part of her heart went arrhythmic. The scans are showing empty heart..."

Long pause.

"She was still in isolation?"

"Yes. But of course she wasn't when we brought her back in."

"But you were all in your suits."

"I know. But we took them off inside. We all helped her."

He didn't say more, and Freya didn't speak either. They were in trouble down there, if what had happened to Clarisse had been caused by her accident. They wouldn't be able to go out on the surface until they understood what it was. And if they determined that some local life-form had infected and killed her, they wouldn't be able to go out ever again without massive precautions.

Nor would they be able to associate with each other freely, until it was demonstrated that whatever had killed her wasn't contagious.

Nor could they come back up to the ship and risk infecting it.

So now they were confined to a biome much smaller than any on the ship, and maybe an infected one at that. Maybe a poisoned building, in which everything alive in it was already doomed.

All these possibilities were no doubt occurring to Freya, as they must have already to Euan. Thus the long silence.

Finally she said, "Is there anything I can do?"

"No. Just...be there."

"I'm here. I'm sorry."

"Me too. It was . . . It was beautiful down here. We were . . . I was
having fun."

"I know."

. . . .

She woke Badim and told him, then lay down on the couch in their
living room, while Badim sat at their kitchen table making calls.

In between his calls she said to him, "I miss Devi. If she were
alive, none of this would have happened. She would have insisted
that we test the surface of the planet completely before anyone
landed."

"Hard to do by robot," Badim remarked absently.

"I know. Years would have passed, everyone would have been
furious with her. She would have been furious with them. But this
wouldn't have happened."

Badim shrugged.

Later Euan called them again.

"I'm going out again," he said.

"What!" Freya cried. "Euan, no!"

"Yes. Look. We all have to go sometime. So, maybe we've been
fatally poisoned, maybe not. We'll know soon enough. In the
meantime, as long as your suit integrity is good, there isn't any difference between staying in the compound or going outside. So I'm
going to damn the torpedoes and go. I don't see why not. Either
way it'll be okay. I mean, either I'm already infected, and I might
as well spend my last days having fun, or I'm not, and I won't be,
as long as I don't cut my suit open. Silly woman, I wish she hadn't
gone off the path, that was obviously quicksand she went off into,
I don't know what she could have been thinking, what she was
going after. A blink on the water, she said. But really? Well, we'll
never know now. And it doesn't matter. I'll stay on hard ground.
Maybe I'll stay out of the estuary and up on the sea cliffs, that's
the best views anyway. Go out and see the dawn. No one here

will stop me. We're all sequestered anyway. Everyone's locked in a room somewhere. No one could stop me without endangering themselves, right? And no one wants to anyway. So I'm going out to see the dawn. I'll call you back in a little while."

· · · · ·

Life in the ship went silent, and took on the nature of a vigil, or a death watch, or even a wake. People murmured about the situation down on the surface, in theory speaking hopefully, in fact frightened and assuming the worst. Of course the woman could have died from shock, or asthmatic attack, or from an opportunistic growth of bacteria she already carried in her, part of the bacterial stock from the ship itself, which was by no means entirely benign, as they had often learned. As Aurora was or seemed to be inert, this last was even the likeliest explanation.

But was Aurora inert? Was it a dead moon, as it seemed to be? Was the oxygen in the atmosphere a result of abiologic processes, as had been assumed by the chemical signatures, and the lack of evident life on the moon? Or was there some kind of life they weren't seeing, perhaps there in the mud of Half Moon Valley's estuary?

But if it was in one place, it would be in more. So the ship's biologists shook their heads, in frustration and ignorance. Euan went back out into the field, and since he was willing to do it, there were people who wanted him to bring back samples of mud from the region where Clarisse had fallen, to get as close to that quicksand as he dared, dig down and secure some mud in a safe flask, then bring it back to Hvalsey for study under the hoods. They already had the mud from Clarisse's suit, of course, and they had her body, so the extra samples weren't absolutely necessary, but some of the microbiologists wanted them anyway, to be able to check the local matrix uncontaminated by all that had happened since Clarisse had fallen into it.

Euan was happy to do this. Some of the other people in Hvalsey were also, and they went out in little groups, staying on trails and descending to the estuary in short expeditions, very unlike their previous trips. They hiked in silence, as if walking across a mine-field, or making descents into hell. Raids on the inexpressible. Euan alone among them sang little ditties to himself, including a tune with the refrain "Shadrach, Meshach, and Abednego"—an old spiritual or faux spiritual, ship determined, with a biblical ref-erence to prisoners of Babylon, surviving time in a fiery furnace by way of a protective intervention from Jehovah.

Euan sang these songs off the public channels, speaking only to Freya on their private channel. Some of the other explorers were behaving similarly, speaking only to people they knew well. On the ship, word of their various expeditions then spread by word of mouth. Those on the surface seemed to feel a new distance from those on the ship. It was all different than it had been before.

Jochi stayed in his car, sealed away from all the rest of the settlers, eating dried and frozen food. One night he suited up and went to one of the other expedition cars and took all the food and portable air tanks in it back to his car.

He had requested permission to return to the ship; every day's communication from him to the ship began with the same request. So far the ship's governing council had only refused his request once, and after that, left their refusal unspoken. No one was to be returned for now. The settlers were under quarantine.

So Jochi spent his time in his car, looking at his screen. He was able to operate some of the robotic medical devices under the hoods in the clinic lab where Clarisse had died, and he spent some of his time investigating the mud Euan and the rest had brought back in, making use of the clinic's electron microscope. His train-ing with Aram and the math team had been in mathematics, but as part of that team he had sometimes worked with the biophysicists, and in any case he was now investigating as much as he could, so

Aram expressed the hope that he might find something helpful. Aram was sick with worry that Jochi was down there; he spent many hours in Badim and Freya's kitchen, hunched over and wan, looking at the screens like everyone else.

For a long time Jochi said nothing about what he was finding. When Freya asked him about it, he only shrugged and looked out at her from her screen.

Once he said, "Nothing."

Another time he said, "Mathematics is not biology. At least not usually. So, I don't know what I'm doing."

"Should I send you more of the medical archives from the solar system feed?" Freya asked.

"I've looked at the index. I don't see anything that will help."

. . . . .

A week later, more than half the people in Hvalsey had fevers. Jochi stayed in his car. He didn't ask to return to the ship anymore.

. . . . .

Euan started going out into the estuary again, or the sea cliffs. He slept out there, and seldom came in to eat. Everyone in Hvalsey behaved a little differently, and it wasn't clear they were talking to each other very much. One day a few of them arranged a dance, and they all wore something red to it.

Jochi called Aram one morning and said flatly, "I think I may have found the pathogen. It's small. It looks a little like a prion, maybe. Like a strangely folded protein, maybe, but only in its shape. It's much smaller than our proteins. And it reproduces faster than prions. In some ways it's like the viris that live inside viruses, or the v's, but smaller. Some seem to be nested in each other. The smallest is ten nanometers long, the largest fifty nanometers. I'm sending up the electron microscope images. Hard to say if they're alive. Maybe some interim step toward life, with some of the functions of life, but not all. Anyway, in a good matrix they appear to reproduce. Which I guess means they're a life-form. And we appear to be a good matrix."

"Why us?" Aram asked. He had linked Badim into the call, given its significance. "We're alien to the place, after all."

"We're made of organic molecules. Maybe it's just that. Or we're warm. Just a good growth medium, that's all. And our blood circulation moves it around in us."

"So they're in that clay from the estuary?"

"Yes. That's the highest concentration. But now that I've found them, I've seen a few almost everywhere. In the river water. In seawater. In the wind."

"They must need more than water."

"Yes. Sure. Maybe salts, maybe organics. But we're salty, and organic. And so is the water down here. And the wind rips the salts right into the air."

. . . . .

When three more of the people in Hvalsey died in the same way as Clarisse, of something like anaphylactic shock, and then Euan came down with a fever too, he went out by himself, around the estuary's edge to the beach under the short cliffs, at the south end of the lagoon.

It was windy as always, the offshore wind of the midmorning of the daymonth. So once he got onto the beach and under the sea cliffs, he was mostly out of the wind. The katabatic gusts came barreling down the gap of the estuary and hit the incoming waves, holding up their faces for a time as they rose up in the shallows, also flinging long plumes of spray back from the crests. These arcs of spray were barred by fat little rainbows, called *ehukai* in the Hawaiian language. Planet E was a thick crescent in its usual spot in the sky, very bright in the dark blue, so that the light in the salt-hazed air over the sea seemed to come from all directions, and suffuse everything. The double shadows there on the ground were faint, and every rock and wave seemed stuffed with itself.

"This would have been a nice place to live," Euan said.

He was talking only to Freya now, on their private channel. She was sitting on the chair by her bed, hunched over her stomach, looking at the screen. Euan was looking here and there, and her screen showed whatever he was looking at.

"A beautiful world, for sure. Too bad about the bugs. But I guess we should have known. That stuff about the oxygen in the atmosphere being abiologic—I guess you'll have to rethink that one. I suppose it could still be true. But if these things Jochi found exhale oxygen, then probably not."

Long silence. Then Freya heard him heave a breath, in and out.

"Probably they're like archaea. Or a kind of pre-archaea. You'll have to keep an eye out for that. There might be other chemical signals in oxygen that would reveal its origins. The ratio of isotopes might be different depending on how it got expressed into the air. I wouldn't be surprised. I know they thought they had a rubric there, but they'll have to recalibrate. Life might be more various than they thought. That keeps happening.

"Not that you'll have much of a chance to test it here," he went on after a while. He was walking on the beach now. The wind was scraping across his exterior mike, and rolling sand grains down the tilted beach into the foam surging up at his feet.

"I guess you'll have to try to do something with F's moon now. Presumably it's dead. Or even try E." He looked up at it, big in the blue sky. "Well, no. It's too big. Too heavy."

Two minutes later: "Maybe you can just keep living on the ship, and stock up on whatever you run out of, from here and from E. Terraform F's moon if you can. Or maybe you can resupply and get to another system entirely. I seem to recall there's a G star just a few more light-years out."

Long silence.

Then:

"But you know, I bet they're all like this one. I mean, they're either going to be alive or dead, right? If they've got water and orbit in the habitable zone, they'll be alive. Alive and poisonous. I don't know. Maybe they could be alive and we live with them and the two systems pass each other by. But that doesn't sound like life, does it? Living things eat. They have immune systems. So that's going to be a problem, most of the time anyway. Invasive biology. Then on the dead worlds, those'll be dry, and too cold, or too hot. So they'll be useless unless they have water, and if they have water they'll probably be alive. I know some probes have suggested otherwise, like here. But probes never stop and test thoroughly. They might just as well be running their tests from Earth, if you think about it. Bugs like these we've got here, you aren't going to find those unless you slow down and hunt really hard. Live nearby for a while and look. At which point it's too late, if you get a bad result. You're out of luck then."

Long silence as he walked south along the beach.

Then:

"It's too bad. It really is a very pretty world."

Later:

"What's funny is anyone thinking it would work in the first place. I mean it's obvious any new place is going to be either alive or dead. If it's alive it's going to be poisonous, if it's dead you're going to have to work it up from scratch. I suppose that could work, but it might take about as long as it took Earth. Even if you've got the right bugs, even if you put machines to work, it would take thousands of years. So what's the point? Why do it at all? Why not be content with what you've got? Who were they, that they were so discontent? Who the fuck were they?"

This sounded much like Devi, and Freya put her head in her hands.

Later:

"Although it is a very pretty world. It would have been nice."

Later:

"Maybe that's why we've never heard a peep from anywhere. It's not just that the universe is too big. Which it is. That's the main reason. But then also, life is a planetary thing. It begins on a planet and is part of that planet. It's something that water planets do, maybe. But it develops to live where it is. So it can only live there, because it evolved to live there. That's its home. So, you know, Fermi's paradox has its answer, which is this: by the time life gets smart enough to leave its planet, it's too smart to want to go. Because it knows it won't work. So it stays home. It enjoys its home. As why wouldn't you? It doesn't even bother to try to contact anyone else. Why would you? You'll never hear back. So that's my answer to the paradox. You can call it Euan's Answer."

Later:

"So, of course, every once in a while some particularly stupid form of life will try to break out and move away from its home star. I'm sure it happens. I mean, here we are. We did it ourselves. But it doesn't work, and the life left living learns the lesson, and stops trying such a stupid thing."

Later:

"Maybe some of them even make it back home. Hey—if I were you, Freya? I would try to get back home."

Later:

"Maybe."

. . . .

Later, still walking south, Euan passed a ravine cleaving the sea cliff. The cliff was a little lower to each side of this cleft, and the cleft ran back and up into the burren at a steep angle, such that there was a clattering creek running down it, which pooled in the sand of the beach, under the cliffs to each side. Where the pool was closest to the sea, a shallow broad flow of water cut through wet sand and poured down to the swirling foam.

The wind whistled down the cleft. Higher up the cleft narrowed, and the walls to each side steepened, looked impassable. Rather than climb up there and investigate, Euan walked right through the beach stream, splashing fearlessly, though at its middle it was knee deep. His fever was quite high at this point. The numbers from his suit were there at the bottom of his screen, glowing red.

Freya hunched over, arms across her stomach, in a position she had often taken when Devi had been ill. She got up and went to their kitchen and got some crackers to eat. She chomped on the crackers, drank a glass of water. She inspected the water in her glass, swallowed some more of it, returned to her chair and the screen.

Euan continued south and came to a broader part of the beach, with some wind-sculpted dunes sheltered under the cliff. He scrambled to the top of the tallest dune. Tau Ceti was a blaze too bright to look at, pouring its light over the top of the cliff and onto the ocean. Euan sat down.

"Nice," he said.

The wind was still at his back. As one looked down at the waves, it was clear that the wind held them up for a time as they tried to break; they swept in toward the land, then reared up and hung there with a vertical face as they moved onshore, trying to fall but getting held up by the wind; then finally the steepest section would pitch down in a roiling burst of white spray, some of which whiteness launched upward and was caught on the wind and hurled back over the wall of white water. Quick fat ehukai crossed these tails of spray.

"I'm feeling hot," Euan said. He walked off the edge of the dune and glissaded down the sand facing the sea.

Freya clutched her stomach under both forearms, put her mouth down on the back of one fist.

Euan looked out at the waves for a long time. The dark gray strand between beach pool and ocean was crosshatched with black sand streaks, far to each side of the shallow runnel of water pouring down into the breakers.

Freya watched him silently. His fever was really very high.

He lay down on the sand. His helmet cam now mostly showed the sand under him, rumpled and granular, flecked with streamers of foam. Broken waves swept up the strand, stalled, retreated in a pebbly rush, leaving a line of foam. The water hissed and grumbled, and occasionally waves offshore cracked dully. Tau Ceti had separated from the sea cliff now, and all the water between the beach and the horizon was a bouncing mass of blue and green. The broken waves were an intense tumbling white. The waves as they were about to break turned translucent. Euan sounded like he might be asleep. Freya herself nodded over her arms, put her forehead on the table.

Much later something caused her to raise her head. She watched as Euan stood up.

"I'm hot," he croaked. "Really hot. I guess it's got me."

He dug around in his little backpack.

"Well, I'm out of food anyway. Water too."

He tapped away at his wristpad. There was a whirring noise.

"There you go," he said. "Now I can drink from the stream. From the pool here too, I'm sure. It must be mostly fresh."

"Euan," Freya croaked. "Euan, please."

"Freya," he replied. "Please yourself. Look, I want you to turn your screen off."

"Euan—"

"Turn your screen off. Wait, I guess I can do it myself from here." He tapped again at his wristpad. Freya's screen went dark.

"Euan."

"It's all right," he said out of the dark screen. "I'm done for. But we're all done for sometime. At least I'm in a beautiful place. I like this beach. I'm going to go for a swim now."

"Euan."

"It's all right. Turn your sound off too. Turn it down anyway. These waves are loud. Wow, this water is cold. That's good, eh? Colder the better."

Water sounds enveloped his voice. He was saying "Ah, aah," as if getting into a bath that was too hot. Or too cold.

Freya held her hands over her mouth.

The watery sounds got louder and louder.

"Aah. Okay, big wave coming! I'm going to ride it! I'm going to stay under if I can! Freya! I love you!"

After that there were only water sounds.

· · · · ·

Several of the people in Hvalsey disappeared into the surrounding countryside. Some went off in silence, suit GPSs disabled; others stayed in communication with their friends on the ship. A few broadcast their ends to anyone who cared to watch and listen. Jochi stayed in his car and refused to speak to anyone, even Aram, who grew silent himself.

Then all of the Hvalsey survivors except for Jochi ignored instructions from the ship to stay on Aurora and prepped one of the ferries to return them to orbit. Doing this without help from the ship's ferry technicians was difficult, but they looked up what they had to know in the computers they had, and fueled the little craft with liquid oxygen and crammed into the ferry, and used the spiral sling and rocket boost to achieve a rendezvous with the ship in its orbit.

As they had been forbidden reentry into the ship, and told that no quarantine was going to last long enough for them to be judged safe to reenter, it was an awkward question what to do when their ferry arrived to dock with the ship. Some in the ship said that if those in the ferry survived for a certain period of time, say a year (some said ten), then it would be obvious that they were not vectors for the pathogen, and could be allowed to reenter. Others disagreed with that. When the committee that was hastily convened by the executive council and charged with making the decision announced that they did not think there was any quarantine period long enough to prove the settlers were safe, many were relieved to hear it; others loudly disagreed. But the question still remained what to do about the landing party, now approaching the ship in its orbit.

· · · · ·

The emergency committee spoke to the Greenlanders by radio, telling them to keep a physical distance from the ship, to remain near it as a kind of small satellite of it. The Greenlanders agreed to that, at first; but when they were running out of food, water, and air, and resupplies did not appear when promised from the ship, due to a technical problem with the ferry being used for the task, as was explained to them, they nevertheless powered their ferry in and approached the main lock in the ferry dock, at the stern end of the spine. From there they proposed to occupy Inner Ring A's rooms at Spoke One, with the rooms permanently sealed off from the spine and the biomes. They would remain in those rooms and become as self-sufficient as possible, for as long a quarantine period as the people on the ship required. After that the question of reintegration could be reconsidered, and if people on the ship had become comfortable with the idea, the settlers might be able to rejoin the larger life of the ship.

After a brief meeting, permission to pursue this plan was expressly denied by the committee, as representing too much of a danger of infection to all the life on the ship. A small crowd of people, mostly men from Patagonia and Labrador, the two biomes at the end of Spoke One, gathered outside the ferry dock's lock door and exhorted each other to resist any incursion by what they called the infected party. Others were alarmed when they saw on screens that this group was gathering, and some of them began to get on the trams and head for the spine to intervene in some poorly defined manner. In Labrador and the Prairie the tram stops began to fill with people, many angrily arguing with other groups they ran into. Fights broke out, and some young men levered the tram tracks off their piste in the Prairie, stopping traffic from moving around Ring B.

Hanging just outside the docking port, the settlers in their ferry reported that overcrowding in their little vehicle had caused something in it to malfunction in such a way that they were quickly running out of breathable air, and they were therefore going to enter the ship's dock as proposed. They warned those in the ship that they were coming in, and the people inside the dock's main lock door told them not to do it. People on both sides were shouting angrily now. Then lights on the operations console inside the dock showed that the settlers were coming in, and at that point some of the young men inside the operations room rushed the security council members there operating the lock, knocking them down and taking over the console. By now the shouting was such that no one could understand anyone else. The ferry entered the docking port, which automatically secured it in position. The outer door of the dock closed, the dock was aerated, and the dock's entry walktube extended to connect the ferry hatch to the inner lock door, all automatically. The settlers in the ferry opened their hatch and began to leave the ferry by way of the walktube, but at the same time, the people now in charge of the dock's operations console locked the inner lock door and opened the outer lock door, which in three seconds catastrophically flushed the dock and the walktube and the opened ferry of their air. All the seventy-two people in the ferry and walktube then died of decompression effects.

. . . . .

Surely the bad times had come again.

4

REVERSION TO THE MEAN

News of the disaster spread through both rings within minutes, and after an initial uproar there fell on most of the biomes a deathly quiet. People didn't know what to do. Some got on trams to Patagonia and then headed up Spoke One, talking loudly of charging those who had blown the dock with mass murder. Others got on trams, sometimes the same trams, intending to defend the people who they said had handled the incursion as best they could, saving everyone aboard from a fatal infection. Unsurprisingly, several fights broke out, and some trams braked to a halt, after which their occupants spilled onto the streets, fighting and calling around the rings for reinforcements.

"No!" Freya kept shouting through her tears, watching her screen as she hastily dressed to leave their apartment. "No! No! No!" She threw things at the walls as she banged around her bedroom, looking for her shoes.

"What are you going to do?" Badim asked her from the door.

"I don't know! I'm going to kill them!"

"Freya, don't. You need to have a plan. Everyone is upset, but look, the people who have died are dead, we can't get them back. It's happened. So now we have to think about what to do next."

Freya was still looking at her wristpad. "No!" she shouted again.

"Please, Freya. Let's think about what we can do now. You can't just wade in there and join the fight. That'll happen without you. We have to think what we can do to help."

"But what *can* we do?"

She found her second shoe and jammed her foot into it, then sat there.

"I'm not sure," Badim confessed. "It's a mess, no doubt about it. But listen—what about Jochi?"

"What about him? He's still down there!"

"I know. But he can't stay there forever. And while everyone is caught up in the disaster here, I'm wondering if we could take advantage of that, and get him up here."

"But they'll kill him too!"

"Yes, if he tries to enter the ship. But if he takes a ferry up here, and stays in the ferry, he would be within reach. We could resupply him, talk to him. There's a good chance he isn't infected with this pathogen. After a while that will become clear, and we can move on from there."

Freya had begun to nod. "Okay. Let's talk to Aram. He'll want to know about this and help."

"That's right."

Badim began tapping at his wristpad.

. . . .

Aram was very happy to work on a plan to rescue Jochi, and he agreed with Badim that until the chaotic fighting among the people in the spine came to an end, there was very little they could do to help in the ship. Already the crowds there were massed into groups shouting at each other, with young men occasionally coming to blows. These were ineffective and dangerous in the spine's microgravity, but that didn't stop the fighting. Aram and Badim were in touch with many friends on the various councils, and most felt they should close the spine to people, as it was so full of the critical machinery of the ship. But with angry people floating up and down the spine passageways, shouting and getting in fights, it was not obvious how to secure the situation in the first place. Security council members were beginning to occupy the spokes to try to prevent anyone else from getting into the spine, but this was not a complete solution. It was a dangerous situation.

In those fraught hours Aram and Badim and Freya called Jochi, and after repeated entreaties, he replied.

Apparently he was aware of the docking disaster. He sounded unlike himself, voice grim and low. "What."

Aram explained their plan for him.

"They'll kill me too," he said.

Freya assured him that wouldn't happen. Many aboard were outraged at what had happened and would be intent on protecting him. If he stayed in his ferry, no one aboard would try to destroy it. Her voice shook as she said this.

Aram said, "Your ferry would be both quarantine and sanctuary. We could keep it in place magnetically, so there would be no physical connection to the ship. But we could send you supplies, and keep you going until the situation here changes."

"The situation will never change," Jochi said.

"Nevertheless," Aram said, "we can keep you alive, and see what happens."

"Please, Jochi," Freya added. "Just get in the ferry, and we'll help you to get it launched. There are so many people here who want something good to happen. Do it for us."

Long silence from the surface of Aurora.

"All right."

He drove the car he had taken refuge in across the burren to the settlement's launch facility. Looking at the empty pads and buildings on the screen in Badim and Freya's kitchen, Aram said, "They already look like they've been abandoned for a million years."

The launchers were still functional, however, and from the ship they helped Jochi to locate and fuel the smallest launch vehicle still on Aurora.

Fully suited, Jochi left his car and crossed to the ferry and climbed the steps into it, moving slowly and uncertainly through it to its bridge room. From the ship they tele-operated the push-cars and moved the ferry into the launch tube of the facility's spiral launcher. This was slow and difficult waldo work. Once in the tube, however, what followed was largely automatic; the rising spiral of the launch tube rotated on its base, which was also rotating, and the magnets in the tube pulled the ferry up the near vacuum in the tube, a pull augmented by the centrifugal force of the doubled spin of the tube and its base. By the time the ferry left the tube it was already moving at nearly escape velocity, its ablation plate heating rapidly, burning off five centimeters or more as the ferry's rockets fired and it shot up through the atmosphere to its rendezvous with the ship. For over a minute Jochi had to lie there enduring 4 g's; but his ferry was successfully launched.

Four hours later it was magnetically tethered to the ship, between Inner Ring A and the spine. By the time its magnetic docking was completed, news of Jochi's arrival had already spread throughout the ship. Many were happy to hear it; others were outraged. The news only added to the turmoil in the spine, which had not died down and indeed continued unabated.

The only survivor of the Aurora landing party had nothing to say.

. . . . .

So there they were: in the ship, in orbit around Aurora, which was in orbit around Planet E, which orbited Tau Ceti, 11.88 light-years away from Sol and Earth. Now there were 1,997 people on board, ranging in age from one month to eighty-two years. One hundred twenty-seven people had perished, either on Aurora or in the ferry in the ship's stern dock. Seventy-seven had died in the dock decompression.

Because the plan had been to relocate most of the human and animal population of the ship down to Aurora, they were now somewhat low in supplies of certain volatiles, rare earths, and metals, and to a certain extent, food. At the same time the ship was overfull of certain other substances, mainly salts and corroded metal surfaces. Various unequal inputs and outputs in the ecological cycles in the ship, the imbalances that Devi had called metabolic rifts, were now causing dysfunctions. At the same time, evolution of the many species on board continued to occur at different rates, with the fastest speciations occurring at the viral and bacterial level, but at slower speeds in every phylum and order. Ineluctably, the occupants of the ship were growing apart. Of course every life-form in the little ecosystem was in a process of coevolution with all the rest, so they could only grow apart so far. As a supraorganism they would perforce remain a totality, but one that could become markedly less hospitable to certain of its elements, including its human component.

In other words, their only home was breaking down. They were not fully aware of this fact, possibly because they themselves were growing sick, as one aspect of their home's breakdown. It was an interrelated process of disaggregation, which one night Aram named *codevolution*.

. . . . .

This was social as well as ecological. The confrontation in the spine continued, its floating crowds still angrily denouncing or defending what had occurred in the dock. In the midst of the arguments, a group of people barged into the dock's operation room and tele-operated robots in the open chamber of the dock, moving all the bodies that were still floating free in the chamber back into the doomed ferry. When that grim task was accomplished, the ferry's door was closed and the ferry ejected from the dock into space.

"We're just making sure," this group's spokespersons announced. "This dock is now closed for good. We're sealing it off. We'll leave the outer door open, and presumably the vacuum will sterilize it, but we aren't taking any chances with that. We're sealing the inside doors. No more access. We'll have to use the other docks now. No sense having such a disaster happen without making sure it keeps us safe."

Ejecting the bodies of seventy-seven of their fellow citizens in a pilotless ferry was denounced as a callous act, a desecration of people whose surviving family and friends were all in the ship.

The dead had been integral members of the community until all this happened; now their bodies wouldn't even be returned to the cycles to nourish the generations to come. In the fights still breaking out over control of the spine, these grievances were shouted out, and just as loudly denied.

Freya went up to the spine to see if she could do anything to defuse the situation. She floated up and down the passageways, pulling herself on the cleats and stopping abruptly to talk to people she knew. People saw her and shot through the air at her to tell her their views and see what she thought. Soon she moved in the center of a group that moved with her down the spine.

No one attacked her, although it often looked like it was about to happen. When people yanked to a halt before her, she asked people what they thought, as in the years of her wandering. If they asked her what she thought, she would say, "We've got to get past this! We've got to come together somehow, find a way forward—we don't have any choice! We're stuck with each other! How could you forget that? We've got to pull together!"

Then she would urge everyone to get out of the spine and back down into the biomes. It was dangerous up there, she pointed out. People were getting hurt, the ship could get hurt. "We shouldn't be up here! The ferry is gone, those people are gone, there's nothing more that can be done here. Nothing! So get out of here!"

Hours passed while she said things like this to people. Some of them nodded and descended the spokes to the rings. Down there the struggle over access to the spokes went on. There were not enough people committed to guarding all twelve spokes, and some were still being used to get up to the spine. Fights occurred in the spokes, and here, if people fell or were shoved off the stairs running up the inner walls of the spokes, they could fall to their deaths. In Spoke Five three young men died tangled in a single fall, and after that the shock of the blood on the floor seemed instrumental in getting that spoke closed to all traffic.

Meanwhile, up in the spine, the permanent closing of the fatal dock continued. The group in charge there applied a thick layer of sealants to its inner lock doors, then covered those with a layer of diamond spray sheathing. It was excessive, some kind of ritual action—an erasure of the scene of the crime, or an excision of infected flesh.

Back in the Fetch, Badim and Aram watched the screens anxiously, switching around to a number of different cameras to see it.

"They've gone crazy at the dock," Aram said at one point as they left for a meeting. "It's a mess. I don't see what we can do."

A meeting of the councils had been called in Yangtze to discuss the situation. Some felt they needed to discuss what to do now that Aurora was revealed to be poisonous to them. Discord would continue until they had a plan, these people said. Aram and Badim weren't so sure, but they went and listened.

When the meeting in Yangtze began, the people in charge of the sealed dock floated back to the A spokes, and at Freya's urging, they and everyone else in the spine descended to the biomes. Most of them went down Spoke Three and headed directly to the meeting in Yangtze, so it seemed that calling the meeting had indeed helped to clear the spine. Even if it did nothing else, Badim remarked, it had been good for that.

· · · ·

In Yangtze there was a big crowd gathering in the central plaza. The main speaker at first was Speller, who had become one of the leading figures in the engineering group after Devi's death. And in fact he began by insisting that the ship's biomes were fundamentally healthy. "The ship's biosphere is a self-correcting entity," he said. "It can endure for centuries, if we just let it self-correct. Our interference has been impeding its ongoing homeostatic process. We only have to resupply it with the volatiles we're short on, and we'll be good to continue to a more hospitable planetary system."

At the back of the room Aram shifted toward Badim and said, "Do you think he means it?"

"Yes," Badim said.

Certainly it seemed so. "The ship got us this far," Speller went on. "It's a life-support system of proven robustness. It will last for centuries more, if we take care of it, which means mostly staying out of its way. All we have to do is restock the elements we're running low on. All those elements are common in the Tau Ceti system. So there is no cause for despair. We can still find a new home."

The nearby star RR Prime held great promise, Speller told them. It was just seven light-years away from Tau Ceti, an M-class star with a full array of planets, including three in its habitable zone, which, as usual around M stars, was closer to its star than Earth was to Sol. The planetary system there had been discovered in the 2500s, and though they were in possession of all the information the Terrans had had about it twelve years before, the fact was that not much was known about it. But it was quite possible this system could provide them with a home. "What else can we do?" Speller asked. "It's clearly our best chance. And the ship can get us there."

· · · ·

But many others were now arguing for Tau Ceti's Planet F's second moon. It was a nearly Earth-sized moon, like Aurora, but denser. It was tidally locked to F, and rotated around F in almost exactly twenty days, so it was not much different from Aurora and E in that regard. It was a rocky moon, and completely dry except for a little comet-impact water ice. Up until now it had been presumed to be lifeless, being almost free of water. But the experience on Aurora had made them more uncertain in judging this matter. Some people pointed out that meteorites had to have been ejected from Aurora by asteroid impacts, and some of them cast up the gravity well to land on F's Moon 2. That such rocks could have successfully transferred the Auroran life-forms, given the lack of water and air on F's moon, seemed unlikely, but it could not be entirely ruled out. Life was tenacious, and the pathogen on Aurora was still not understood. Even naming it was a problem, as some called it the cryptoendolith, others the fast prion, others the pathogen, and others simply the bugs, or the thing, or the stuff, or the alien, or the whatever.

Be that as it may, F's Moon 2 remained a real possibility in the minds of many of them. "Water can be imported to it," Heloise said in all the meetings. She was a leader in Ring A's ecology group. "F's Moon One is an icy moon, we can move that water over. We can build underground stations to start with, then expand those while the process of terraforming gets started. Then domed craters, then tent cities. It can work. It was part of the plan all along, after all. The backup if Aurora didn't work out. And then there wouldn't be the need for another interstellar trip, which is good, because it isn't certain the ship will sustain that. This was always the secondary option, and now we need it. And it can work."

Aram didn't believe this, and stood up to say so. "It would be like living in the ship," he said. "Except we would be buried in the lithosphere of a rocky moon. After that it would take many hundreds of years, or more likely thousands of years, to terraform this moon, and during that whole time we would be confined to interiors like these biomes. The problems plaguing us here would plague us there. We wouldn't live long enough to reach the time when we could move out into open air. Our descendants would get sick and die. They would go extinct."

This pessimism, or dark realism, whichever it might be, enraged Speller and Heloise, and everyone trying to make the best of things, trying to find a way forward. Why be so negative? they asked.

"It's not me being negative," Aram would reply. "It's the universe obeying its laws. Science isn't magic! We aren't fantasy creatures! We have been dealt a hand."

"So what do we do?" Heloise said angrily. "What are we supposed to do, in your opinion?"

Aram shrugged at this.

Freya called in to the meeting that was discussing the situation, from the spine where she was just now coming down, in the last group of peacemakers.

She said, "We should go home."

Silence greeted this pronouncement. Air vents, electrical hums.

"What do you mean?" Speller asked.

Freya's voice came through the speakers clearly, even loudly. "We should resupply the ship and fly it back to Earth. If we succeed, our descendants will survive. There's no other option we have now where you can say that. It's too bad, but it's true."

The people on the plaza in Yangtze looked around at each other, silenced.

· · · ·

Her idea, which she explained in the days that followed, had originated with Euan. It was also something Devi used to mention, she said. It was a good idea, she said. A workable plan.

Clearly it shocked people. In all that was going on, it seemed too much to take in.

Freya herself spent most of her time cajoling, and in certain cases physically threatening, people to get out of the spokes and stay in the biomes. Teams organized by the security council took over at every spoke lock, and began to work like one-way valves, allowing people to leave the spokes but not to enter them. Eventually a point came where it was possible to persuade or coerce everyone still in the spine and spokes to descend into the biomes. People then gradually dispersed to their hometowns, or gathered with like-minded people to make further plans. The individuals responsible for the deaths of the settlers in the dock slipped among their supporters, and those groups resisted any calls for a further investigation of what had happened. Clearly no one had wanted people to die, it was often said. It had been an accident, a disaster. Time to move on. Time to figure out what to do next.

Thus in a continuing tumult of the spirit, with many still grief-stricken, still furious, all actions possible to them at this point were in effect dumped on the table and inspected at length. It did not seem like the right time for this, but there was no stopping it either. It was the only thing worth talking about, given their situation.

Freya's proposal was one of the actions discussed. That it was Devi's daughter proposing the idea gave it a certain weight that it might not have had otherwise. Devi was missed, her death a wound that had not healed; often people wondered what she would have done in the situations they now found themselves in. There was a kind of slippage in which since Freya had suggested the plan, it seemed to be Devi's plan. And though Freya was the first to speak the idea out loud, she hadn't been the first to think it. They had to do something, go somewhere. And it was undeniable that the solar system was at least a destination they could trust to sustain them, if they could get there.

Still, this was only one plan among several now discussed.

One faction, including their old friend Song, argued for sterilizing Aurora and proceeding there as originally planned. As the pathogen on Aurora was so poorly understood (Aram was coming to feel that Jochi had not actually identified it), this group was small, and its arguments seemed not to persuade many, especially among those who had been involved with the deaths of the returning settlers. Part of their justification for the dock disaster now lay in claiming that Aurora was irredeemably poisonous.

Speller and his faction continued to argue for going on in the ship to RR Prime. Heloise and a large group advocated inhabiting F's second moon. And quite a few began to assert that they could simply stay on the ship and use the various planetary bodies of the Tau Ceti system to resupply whatever they might lack, filling the metabolic rifts as they occurred. From the ship they could consider their options, and perhaps work on both Aurora and F's second moon.

In all the arguing, there were some people attempting to model the options. Unfortunately, their modeling work led most of the modelers to conclude that no plan available to them was likely to succeed. They had very few options; and none were good; and for the most part, they were mutually exclusive.

Bitterness and anger grew in people as the modelers' conclusions became known. The spine was emptied now, and under guard by people who had agreed to enforce the security council's edicts. The stern dock was physically sealed off. Jochi was sequestered in his ferry, held magnetically inside Inner Ring A. On one level the situation seemed calm; people had returned to their biomes and resumed their lives there, and were dealing with crops that had been neglected, and now had to be planted or harvested. Animals had to be cared for, machines had to be tended. But things were not well with them. Now more than ever before in the history of the ship, their isolation began to press on them. No one could help them govern themselves, nor make the decisions they now had to make. They were alone with all that. It was up to them.

• • • • •

Freya wandered the biomes as she had in her wandering years. She did not speak in the meetings she attended, or in the cafés where she had worked just a few years previously, but merely listened. She stood at the back of a room like the figurehead of a sailing ship, or sat in a corner, looking at each speaker mutely.

As she wandered, she inspected each biome with a close regard. How was it doing? she asked the inhabitants. What had it been good for, during the voyage out? Could it continue to help them to survive another 170 years of enclosure, if they decided to go back?

She found that some of the biomes that were doing the best in ecosystem terms were in fact the least useful to the ship's humans during a voyage. These biomes had been brought along to convey their species to the new world, to help terraform the planet they were to have established. As farms they were less useful. But it occurred to Freya that they could be altered to make them better farms. Going back to the solar system, they would not be needed as seed banks or arks.

. . . . .

Song's idea was this: proceed with the inhabitation of Aurora, by introducing to it their Terran bacteria and viruses, in the hope that after a war of microbiota, Aurora would end up habitable by humans. Some of their ecologists and bacteriologists thought that might work.

The group centered on Heloise and Bao called for them to inhabit and terraform F's second moon, the best of the remaining candidates for inhabitation in the Tau Ceti system. It was a Mars analog and had been their previous second option, and there was no reason it wouldn't work.

Speller continued to lead those who said they should move on, that they should refuel and resupply the ship and head to the star RR Prime. They would cross interstellar space for another eighty years, and try again in that system, which in many ways looked so promising.

Or they could stay in the ship and live in it in perpetuity.

Or they could go back to the solar system.

All these ideas were discussed endlessly, in every possible iteration.

As they talked, there grew a sense among many of them that if they stayed in the Tau Ceti system, they could combine some of these options, which were not in the deepest sense mutually exclusive. They could try again on Aurora, with test inoculations of bacteria and so on, while proceeding on F's second moon; and refurbish the ship while living on it; and inspect and explore F's first moon.

Options, yes; just no good ones, others said. Different ways of running out the string; different ways of going extinct, after a long, fruitless struggle, trapped in chambers even smaller than the ship's biomes.

But they could live in the biomes!

But they couldn't live in the biomes!

Freya spoke very little in public, but in private she continued to assert that their best chance would be to resupply the ship and head back to Earth. It was the one destination they had where they knew their descendants could survive.

"But of course," Speller said, dropping by the little café in Olympia where Freya was staying the night. "But what's the point of that? Why did we ever leave? Why have we gone through all this, we and all our ancestors and descendants, if not to make it work here?"

Freya shook her head at her old friend and said, "They never should have left."

. . . .

They talked and talked and talked. Twenty-four biomes, ten thousand conversations. Talk talk talk. As they talked, it began to come clear to them that they had no very effective method of governance, when it came to making decisions as a group. Had humans ever had such a thing, they asked themselves, since leaving the savannah? Since congregating in cities? They could not be sure. The histories suggested maybe not.

In the ship, ever since the troubles of Year 68, the four generations that followed had been careful to work within the system established after that upheaval, always deliberating peacefully toward consensus on all important decisions. Now even the definition of consensus was contested, and they came to realize that their political system, simple as it was, had never faced a crisis. Suspended in their voyage as they had been, there had never been anything to choose, except methods of homeostasis.

to the ground by the force of the wind, to many were not a caution but an incentive. Also the vistas of the ocean from the sea cliffs, the crosshatched textures of the beach sand, the skies at sunrise, the low hums, little shrieks, and otherworldly howls of the wind over the rocks, the occasional storms with their clouds, lashing rains, sea fogs: all these sights and sounds called to the people on the ship, and not a few began to demand passage down. Ten greenhouses in Hvalsey were in operation, the bamboo plants were growing a meter a day, the atmosphere had been confirmed as safe for direct breathing, and a lot more construction was waiting to be done. Really the moment had come to begin mothballing the ship, instituting their plan to keep it operational by way of the deployment of a small maintenance crew of 125 people, who would rotate annually, so that everyone aboard could live on Aurora most of the time. This was their desire; only a few (207, in fact) expressed the wish to stay within the ship's familiarity, and those who did were often regarded as anxious, fearful, even craven. Although some of these supposedly fearful people were in fact bold in their declarations, despite being in the minority; and this rallied a little bit of support for their view and quietened their critics. "This is my home," said Maria, Freya's host in Plata. "I've lived all my life in this town, I've farmed this land. This biome is the place I love. That Greenland down there is a black rock in a perpetual gale. You'll not be able to farm it with those long nights, you won't be able to do much of anything outdoors. You'll live indoors like we do up here, but not as well. Why shouldn't I stay here and live out my days and take care of this place? I volunteer to stay! And I won't be surprised if a fair number of you all who are clamoring to go down there now will eventually ask to come back up and join me. I'll be happy to welcome you back, and take care of the place in the meantime."

Median age of those declaring they would prefer to stay was 54.3 years. Median age of those clamoring to go down to Hvalsey

Now the test was upon them, and very quickly cracks in their façade of civility began to appear. Where there is faction, there is conflict; where there is conflict, there is anger. And anger distorts judgment. So now they were getting angry with each other, and thus scared of each other. And anger and fear were not the right emotions for the situation facing them.

· · · · ·

In the wake of the events of Year 68, the survivors had settled on a government of representative democracy, based on a constitution setting out their political first principles. The first principles were to be upheld in everything they decided to do. More than anything else, the survivors understood that they needed to behave in ways that kept a balanced flow of elements going in their closed life-support system. To do this, their population had to be capped at no more than 2,152 people. There were also population caps for all the rest of the mammals on board. Within these carrying capacities, a maximum amount of individual human autonomy was to be maintained. But this necessarily did not include the right to reproduce; nor did it include free movement around the ship, at least in terms of residency. Each biome had its own particular carrying capacities. Nor could certain jobs and functions be neglected by the totality of the group. Any number of jobs simply had to be performed, or the ship would not remain in working balance, able to support them over the long haul of interstellar solitude.

So habitation, reproduction, education, work: all expressed ecological necessities. They had to attend to these or go extinct; that was just the way it was, that was reality. Everyone was taught that in childhood. There were limits, there were needs. Every person in the ship was part of the team, integral to society, necessary to the survival of the group. Everyone was equal in that respect, and had to be treated the same as everyone else.

Only within that set of first principles, after fulfilling the necessities, could they find and exercise what liberties were still left. Some said that what remained was trivial. But no one had any suggestions as to how to give themselves more liberties than what they had, given their constraints. Duty first.

. . . . .

So, now each biome's population met in a town meeting. Anyone who wanted to speak, spoke.

This lasted for two weeks, after which a series of polls and votes were held. They polled themselves to get an accurate count on the questions at hand. Who preferred what course of action? How many for each, and how strongly did they feel about it?

Then in most biomes there was a vote for representatives, one representative for every hundred people. In most towns there was no campaigning. People voted anonymously. Those elected who also agreed to serve then spoke to their neighbors about what they should say in the general assembly. In other biomes they chose representatives by lottery, and those selected had to promise to speak for the majority opinion in their biome; or, in some, merely to do what they thought right.

These representatives then met in Costa Rica, in the town of San Jose, and discussed matters in a general conference. This was an open-ended conference, the idea being that when everyone had discussed matters thoroughly, a poll would be taken of the entire population and then the representatives would be tasked with executing the will of the majority of the people. If it turned out to be close to a split decision, which they decided meant any minority vote larger than 33 percent, then they would work on ways to ameliorate the situation by finding some kind of middle ground, if they could. Successive votes would be taken, until a supermajority of 67 percent, or hopefully more, agreed on a course of action. At that point the minority would have to accept the judgment of the majority.

That was the theory.

· · · ·

While trying to come to a decision, they agreed to ask the ship to relocate itself to Tau Ceti's Planet F, and enter into orbit around F's second moon. This was to make a reconnaissance, to judge that moon better for habitability.

As ship made this transfer, which took seven months following a Hohmann path of least energy expenditure and used 2.4 percent of ship's remaining fuel supply, the policy discussion raged on.

Meanwhile, many biologists on board studied samples of the Auroran pathogen, which Jochi kept in a sealed room in his ferry, a room that he had turned into a clean lab, tele-operated by him. There were still those who supported Song's idea that they could learn to live with this Auroran thing if they could understand it better. So the studying of the pathogen went on, even though they never settled on what to call it. Vector, disease, pathogen, invasive species, bug; these were all Earthly terms, and Aram for one regarded them as various kinds of category error. "The best we can do in terms of terminology," he said, "is to call it the alien."

That it definitely was. The individual proteinlike samples Jochi had isolated, and put into an electron microscope that was sent over to him, were so small that it was hard to understand how they could be alive. They were certainly alive in some senses of the term, since they reproduced, but it was hard to tell how, or what else they did. In this they shared qualities with viruses and their viris, prions, and RNA; but in other ways they did not seem similar to any of these entities. Processes were happening within them at nanometer scale, even picometer scale, but what was small enough for them to eat? How could they eat? Or to put it more simply, where did they get their energy? How did they grow? Why did they grow so quickly when they got inside a human?

These were unsolved mysteries, and might remain so for a long time.

Meanwhile F's second moon, now named Iris by the proponents of settling there, proved to be an almost completely water-free rock ball, as suspected. Iron core, magnetic field; dry except for a little frozen comet debris on its surface, which was heavily cratered, also indented by two long, straight canyons, possibly the result of early fractures. Somewhat of a big Mercury by analog, appearance, and possibly history; its heavy core testified, perhaps, to a collision in its early days that had stripped off a lighter outer shell of rock, which had subsequently fallen onto F rather than be completely recollected out of orbit by Iris. This anyway was the best originary model to explain the data. Its 1.23 g was rather discouraging, but it had a little rotation, and it was not completely tidally locked to F, which fact also supported the idea of an early collision. It thus had a day that was 30 days long; a month orbiting F that was 20 days long; and F's year was 650 days long. F's orbit was 1.36 AU from Tau Ceti, its insolation from Tau Ceti 28.5 percent that of Earth's. Truly it was at the very outer edge of the habitable zone, but still, it had a lot of sunlight to work with.

The lack of water on Iris, which used to be seen as a problem, now reassured people. Water was now felt to be dangerous, as it seemed likelier than ever that liquid water anywhere would harbor life of some kind, and create problems. The sample size of data supporting this conclusion remained very small, consisting as it did of Earth, Europa, Ganymede, Enceladus, and Aurora; but Aurora had been traumatic. It was even suggested that the cometary ice on Iris could be removed if there were any suspicion that it contained the Auroran pathogen.

Others pointed out that the ice some proposed to import to Iris, to give their new world a hydrosphere and atmosphere, would be ice from F's Moon 1, or cometary ice from Tau Ceti's crowded Oort cloud. So if ice anywhere was potentially a home for life, then they could never escape that.

But there was no reason to think that was the case. It was

generally agreed that it was liquid water that was likely to hold life, not ice. A lot of ice had condensed out of the original cloud of interstellar dust that had formed Tau Ceti, and there was no reason to think life had ever had a chance to begin in that ice. So it was assumed they would be safe if they ended up giving Iris a little ocean composed of imported cometary ices.

So: hydrate Iris, introduce Terran genomes, occupy. F itself would then be a gorgeous marble in Iris's sky, a gas giant full of volatiles they would surely need. A giant ball of feedstocks right next door, and its huge beauty helping them occupy Iris by way of its reflected sunlight, which would illuminate all of Iris as Iris slowly turned, and not just one hemisphere, as it had been on Aurora. Really, it looked very promising.

But how long would it take to terraform Iris?

Nothing but guesses could answer this question, and the guesses depended on many assumptions one necessarily had to enter as numbers into one's models. The median times calculated by the models was privately judged by the ship to be about 3,200 years, with outlier estimates ranging from 50 to 100,000 years. Obviously the models and parameters chosen made quite a difference. In fact the problem was poorly constrained. Still it seemed fair to assume that the median estimate had some kind of theoretical validity.

· · · ·

Many people in the ship didn't want to wait three thousand years, or however long it might take to terraform Iris. Others didn't think they could last that long. Others didn't think it would take that long. "The models must be wrong," some said. "Surely once life got started on a planet, it would change things fast. Bacteria reproduce very quickly in an empty ecological niche."

"But on Earth it took a billion years."

"But there was only archaea on Earth. With the full suite of bacteria it would go fast."

"Not where there isn't an atmosphere. Bacteria on rock, exposed to the vacuum, doesn't grow very fast. It mostly dies, in fact."

"So we need self-replicating robot machinery to make soil, to make air, to add water."

"But the selfreps need feedstocks. Collecting the necessary materials can only be accomplished by a first generation of robots, and that won't be fast."

"We can print printers and thrive! It can be done. We can do it. Our robots can do it."

"It's going to take too long. In the meantime we'll die out. Evolve at differential rates, and diverge right inside our own bodies. Zoo devolution. Codevolution. Sicken and die and go extinct. Sicken and die and never once leave this ship."

"So that maybe," Freya kept saying, "we need to go back home."

. . . . .

The day came when they tried to make a choice.

Strange, perhaps, to wake up one morning, get dressed, eat breakfast, all the while knowing that one was going off to a meeting that would change the world. Decisions are hard. Everyone has the halting problem. Freya sat next to Badim at their kitchen table, restlessly pushing around cut strawberries with a fork.

"What do you think will happen?" she asked.

Badim smiled at her. He looked unusually cheerful, and was eating heartily, chomping on pieces of buttered toast and washing them down with milk.

"It's interesting, eh?" he said between bites. "Up until today, history was preordained. We were aimed at Tau Ceti, nothing else could happen. We had to do the necessary." He waved his bread in the air. "Now that story is over. We are thrust out of the end of that story. Forced to make up a new one, all on our own."

They walked together to the tram station, then got on a crowded tram car and headed east to Costa Rica. In the biomes along the way the tram stopped and more full cars were linked to it, first in Olympia, then Amazonia. Mostly the people in the tram cars were subdued. People looked pensive. 102,563 conversations had been recorded in the previous month that were about this topic, and there were conflict markers in grammar and semantics in 88 percent of these conversations, which were inevitably held mostly between people well-known to each other.

Now they were done with that. 170.170: the general assembly called for in Costa Rica brought 620 people to the Government House plaza. Most of the rest of the ship's population watched the assembly on screens throughout the ship, but another meeting, called "in opposition to the tyranny of the majority," drew 273 people to the plaza in Kiev, in the Steppes.

. . . . .

San Jose's Government House plaza occupied much of the middle of town. It was surrounded by four- and five-story buildings, all faced with white stone cut to a fussy pattern of interlocking rectangles. The overall impression was of some stage set imitating a European capital, but that could be said of many real European capitals, so it was possibly based on a real square somewhere back on Earth. Ship saw resemblances to Vienna, Moscow, Brasilia.

Now about a third of the population of the ship stood in the plaza, listening to speakers rehash various aspects of the matter at hand. People clumped in cohorts based mostly on home biomes. After the speeches began, the flow between groups was minimal. Some people sat on the smooth flagstones of the plaza; others had brought folding chairs and stools; still others stood. There were some open-walled dining tents to provide food and drink, and what circulation there was in the crowd mostly led to and from these tents.

One sequence of speakers described the plan to shift their efforts to F's second moon, all of them now calling it Iris. They would establish a base on its surface and move down into that base as they built it to full size. They would add water to the surface by way of a comet bombardment, which would also create the beginnings of an atmosphere. The self-replicating robots and factories would build shelters, break volatiles into gases, create an atmosphere and soil, and shape the growing hydrosphere as it fell from the sky. They would introduce their bacteria to this virgin surface, and it would quickly expand to fill this truly empty ecological niche. After the archaea and bacteria and fungi were established on the ground, they would help to bulk up the atmosphere and to create the soil, and soon further plants and animals from the starship could be introduced, in waves of succession similar to what had occurred in Terran evolution, and the planet terraformed thereby in rapid order, at a speed literally a million times faster than it had happened naturally on Earth: meaning three thousand years instead of three billion. With the chance of doing it in three hundred years also very real, if things went faster than expected.

The various components of this plan were described in some detail by Heloise, and in this effort she was joined by Song. They had joined forces, Song having agreed to the Iris plan with the idea that as an extension of it, her plan for returning to Aurora could be pursued. For now, she agreed with Heloise that terraforming Iris was the best plan, whether interim or permanent.

People stood or sat in silence, listening.

Then Aram was invited to the podium. He stood for a moment staring down at the people, then spoke.

"The problem is this: the spaces we have available to live in are too small to survive in for three thousand years. The main problem is the differential rates of evolution between the various orders of life confined to the space. Bacteria generally mutate at a rate far faster than larger species, and the effect of that evolution on the larger species is eventually devastating. This is one cause of the dwarfism and higher rates of extinction seen in island biogeography studies. And we are an island if there ever was one. And this Iris is not an Earth twin, nor an Earth analog. It is a Mars analog.

"There are also chemicals we need that can't be found on a rock planet that has never harbored life. In short, the supraorganism that we all constitute together can't survive over that long a time in the confinement we would be subjected to."

It was Speller who picked up one of the other microphones on the podium. "How can we know anything except by trying it?"

Aram said, "The modeling involved here has been tested, and we can state certain ecological outcomes as very likely, even though the likelihoods decrease if you push them farther out in time. You are very welcome to review the studies involved. We have made them public at every point."

"But some of the scenarios show the terraforming as succeeding, correct?"

Aram nodded. "There are some scenarios that succeed, but they occur at a rate of only about one in a thousand."

"But that's fine!" Speller smiled broadly. "That's the one we'll make happen!"

Grimly Aram faced the crowd. The silence in the plaza was such that one could hear the food orders in the corner, and the children playing, and the skreeling of the seagulls wheeling over the rooftops between the plaza and Costa Rica's salt lake.

Speller and Heloise and Song made more rebuttals to Aram. Those who agreed with Aram formed a separate line to speak, and the organizers of the assembly began to let people from the two lines speak in alternation, until it became clear from the muttering from the crowd, including even short bursts of laughter as each new talk began, that the effect of the alternation was unhelpful. Contemplating two starkly different futures back and forth was perhaps too much like a debating society exercise, but because the topic debated was life or death for them, the back-and-forth engendered first cognitive dissonance, then estrangement: some laughed, others looked sick.

Existential nausea comes from feeling trapped. It is an affect state resulting from the feeling that the future has only bad options. Of course every human faces the fact of individual death, and therefore existential nausea must be to a certain extent a universal experience, and something that must be dealt with by one mental strategy or another. Most people appear to learn to ignore it, as if it were some low chronic pain that has to be endured. Here in this meeting, it began to become clear, for many of those present, that extinction lay at the end of all their possible paths. This was not the same as individual death, but was instead something both more abstract and more profound.

The crowd got restless. New speakers brought forth boos and cat-calls, and people began arguing in the crowd. Some began to leak away from the edges of the gathering, and the plaza began to empty, even as the speakers on the central dais talked on. Those who left went away to complain, get drunk, play music, garden, work.

Those organizing the event consulted with each other, and decided not to call for a vote of the assembly at that time. Clearly the time was not right, nor the venue, nor the method of a voice vote or a tally by hands. Something more formal and private would be needed, something like a mandatory vote, using secret ballots. Even this could not be decided at that bad moment, in the waning sun of Costa Rica's hot afternoon, with people streaming away into the streets and toward the trams. In the end they called the meeting short, announcing that another would be held soon.

· · · ·

In the week that followed the meeting, fifteen people committed suicide, a 54,000 percent rise in frequency. Those who left suicide notes often spoke of their despair for the future. Why go on, given such a situation? Why not end it now?

An ancient proverb of Earth's first peoples: every path leads to misfortune.

A proverb from Earth's early modernity: can't go on, must go on.

This was a human moment that never went away. An existential dilemma, a permanent condition. For them, in their particular situation, it came to this:

When you discover that you are living in a fantasy that cannot endure, a fantasy that will destroy your world, and your children, what do you do?

People said things like, Fuck it, or Fuck the future. They said things like, The day is warm, or This meal is excellent, or Let's go to the lake and swim.

A plan had to be made, that was clear to all. But plans always concern an absent time, a time that when extended far enough into the future would only be present for others who would come later.

Thus, avoidance. Thus, a focus on the moment.

Still, in every meeting place, in every kitchen, the subject either came up or was avoided and yet still hung there. What to do? They were inside a ship, sailing somewhere. A destination had to be chosen. Somehow.

· · · ·

Freya and Badim spent much of their time in their apartment, waiting for the assembly's executive group to call for a referendum. Aram was again part of the executive group, and so they were hopeful that things would go well and get resolved soon, one way or the other. The security council had been suspended when all its functions were returned to the immediate business of the executive council.

Freya sat looking at her father, his round, brown face, the drooping bags under his eyes. He looked much older than he had just two years before. None of them looked the same now. Ever since the death of the Aurora settlers, or even since Devi's death, they had changed, and now appeared to be aging faster than they had during the voyage out. A certain look was gone from them: possibly a sense of hope. Possibly a feeling that things made sense, had meaning.

Two weeks after the assembly in San Jose, the executive group called for the referendum to be held the following day. Voting was mandatory, and any who refused to vote would be fined by punitive work penalties. In fact this did not look like it was going to be a problem; it seemed as if everyone was anxious to cast a vote.

The ballot had been arranged into three possible choices, with all the possibilities that kept them in the Tau Ceti system bunched as one choice. So the three were

Tau Ceti
Onward to RR Prime
Back to Earth

Voting closed at midnight. At 12:02 a.m. the results were posted:

Tau Ceti: 44%
Onward to RR Prime: 7%
Back to Earth: 49%

The roar of voices filled the biomes for many hours after that. Comments ranged as widely as could be imagined. In the following day, anything that could be said about the situation was said. It was a pluripotent response, an incoherence.

· · · · ·

The next morning Aram dropped by Badim and Freya's apartment and said, "Come with me to a meeting. We've been invited, and I think Freya is the one they really want."

"What kind of meeting?"

"Of people trying to avoid trouble. The referendum has by no means given anyone a mandate. So there could be trouble."

Freya and Badim went with him. Aram led them down to a public building by Long Pond, into a pub and up the stairs to a big room with a window overlooking the water.

There were four people there. Aram introduced Freya and Badim to them—"Doris, Khetsun, Tao, and Hester"—then led them over to a table and invited them to sit. When they were seated, Aram sat beside Freya and leaned over to prop a screen on the table, where Badim could see it also.

"The referendum was too close," Aram said. "The most votes were cast for our preferred option, but we'll need to convince more people to join us. Convincing them might be easier if we make it clear that the ship can be made as strong as it was when it left the solar system."

Aram brought up charts on the table screen. Badim got out his reading glasses and leaned closer to read it. He said, "What about our basic power supply, that would be my first question."

"A good point, of course. The ship's main nuclear reactor has fuel for another five hundred years, so we're okay there. As for propulsion fuel, we can send probes to gather hydrogen three and deuterium from Planet F's atmosphere. We would collect the same amount that we burned to decelerate coming in, and then burn it to accelerate out."

"But if we use it for accelerating," Badim said, "how will we decelerate when we get back to the solar system?"

"That too will have to be reversed. We'll have to ask the people in the solar system to point the laser beam that accelerated us back at us as we come in, to slow us down the same way they speeded us up. Possibly the same laser generator orbiting Saturn will be available."

"Really?" Badim said. "This is the plan?"

Then came a knock at the door.

. . . .

There were thirty-two people outside that door, twenty-six men and six women, several of the men taller and heavier than the median size of the population. Most of them were from Ring A biomes. When they were all in the room it was extremely crowded.

One of the men, one Sangey, from the Steppes, flanked by three of the biggest of the men, said, "This is an illegal meeting. You are discussing public policy in a private gathering of political leaders, as specifically forbidden by the riot laws of Year 68. So we are placing you under arrest. If you come peacefully we'll let you walk. If you resist you'll be tied to gurneys and carried."

"There is no law against private discussions of the health of the ship!" Aram said angrily. "It's you breaking the law here!"

All their voices were now at least twice as loud as normal.

"Will you walk or be carried?" Sangey said.

"You'll definitely have to carry me," Aram said, and then charged Sangey. In a melee filled with shouting, he was subdued by the men flanking Sangey. Aram lashed out at Sangey over one guard's shoulder as he was lifted off his feet, and his fist landed on Sangey's nose. At the sight of blood the others stuffing the room surged in toward Aram, shouting furiously.

Badim stood over Freya in her chair, preventing her from rising to her feet. "Stay out of this," he cried at her, face-to-face. "This is not our fight here!"

"Yes it is!" Freya shouted, but as she could not rise without throwing her father to the side, she kicked viciously past him as they clung to each other, striking nearby knees and causing some of their assailants to crash together and then fall to the floor, crying out angrily. Those still standing shouted and wrestled Badim and Freya both to the ground, pummeling and kicking them. Seeing this Aram flew into a rage and struck out convulsively. More punched noses and cracked lips made several faces bloody, so that the white-eyed shouting redoubled again in volume and intensity.

The sight of blood during a fight causes a very intense adrenaline surge. Voices shout hoarsely; eyes go round, such that white is visible all the way around the iris; movements are faster and stronger; heart rate and blood pressure rise. This was demonstrated many times in Year 68.

The strategic foresight in bringing many large men to arrest the group in the room soon paid off, as the seven people in the meeting were, despite the close quarters and resultant chaos, knocked down, subdued, held fast, secured by medical restraints, lifted kicking out of the room and the building, laid onto gurneys in the street outside, and tied down to them. Badim and Freya were handled like all the rest, and Freya had a swollen left eye.

The crowd that gathered to witness this action was composed almost entirely of people from Ring A biomes. Residents of the Fetch were slow to realize what was happening in their midst, and there was no effective resistance to this outside group. The gurneys were all conveyed up to the spine and along it to Spoke Three, and down it to the infirmary in Kiev, which had been used as a jail in Year 68, though no one alive knew that. The seven arrested ones were locked up in three rooms there.

. . . . .

Elsewhere in the ship, news of the incarceration of Aram's group spread fast. When their friends and supporters heard about it, they gathered in San Jose's plaza and loudly protested the action. The administrators of Costa Rica said they did not know what had happened, and suggested discussing what to do in a regathering of a general assembly similar to the one just recently held. A significant number of the protestors refused to debate what they called a criminal action; their friends had to be released immediately, and only then could any outstanding issues be discussed. Kidnapping could never be rewarded with political legitimacy, people shouted, or else it would happen again and again, and there would be no more political discourse in the ship, or rational planning of any kind.

As that afternoon passed, the shouting became much like the sound of broken waves striking the corniche at the seawall of Long Pond. It was a roar.

. . . .

Three hours after gathering, the crowd in San Jose had inspired itself to action and began marching toward Kiev, chanting slogans and singing songs. There were approximately 140 people in the crowd, and they had made it to the entryway of Spoke Four, packed around the tunnel there to a depth of around two hundred meters, when a smaller crowd of approximately fifty people poured out of the spoke tunnel, throwing rocks and shouting.

It was as if fire and combustible fuel had come in contact: a furious fight erupted. It was still mostly a matter of shoving and hitting, but photos and clips of the melee were sent through the ship right in the midst of it, alerting all to the situation. Meanwhile, in all twelve biomes of Ring A, gangs stormed the government houses and took possession of them. Groups also seized and closed all the locks between Ring A's biomes, and likewise closed the six entryways to the A spokes. It seemed likely that these were coordinated actions, planned in spaces where the ship had no microphones, or where the microphones had somehow been rendered inoperative. Either that or spontaneous actions self-organized very quickly, which of course they did in many phenomena.

In the Spoke Four lock where the fighting still went on, news of developments elsewhere spread, and it became clear that the fight there was a kind of invasion of Ring B by the groups in Ring A that had taken possession of the government houses. The fight at the entry to Spoke Four then became a pitched battle, with people from everywhere in Ring B rushing around through the locks to join the fray. Nonetheless, the attacking group continued to emerge from the spoke entryway, more every minute, and they were taking over much of Costa Rica and many of the streets of San Jose. Rocks began to fly through the air. One struck a man in the head, and down he went, unconscious and bleeding. Now people were screaming. Reinforcements from around Ring B arrived, enough so that the group emerging from the spoke was stopped in its advance on the Government House. People on both sides now were hurling rocks from the parks, paving stones from the plazas, knives from kitchens, plates, other objects. Furniture was thrown out of buildings into the streets and piled into barricades, some of which were set on fire.

Fire anywhere in the ship was extremely dangerous.

Against such ferocious resistance, the invasive group could not hold its ground. More than a dozen people lay on the ground bleeding. As the invaders retreated to the lock of Spoke Four, still throwing objects at their opponents, there were groups elsewhere around Ring B hurrying up the other spokes toward the spine. The spine was already occupied by groups from Ring A, and they closed the entryway doors of B's inner ring all the way around, so that no matter how intense the assaults by people from Ring B, they could make no further progress toward the spine. And the spine held the power plant, along with all the other crucial central functions of the ship, including the ship's operating AI.

So now Ring A and the spine were both controlled by people calling themselves the stayers. No one who might want to free Aram and Freya and Badim and their four companions could come anywhere near the infirmary in Kiev.

Instead, the antagonists were now separated by locked doors. And sixteen people in Ring B were dead, killed either when hit by objects, or when cut or impaled, or when trampled by crowds. Another ninety-six people were injured. All the infirmaries in Ring B soon were filled with hurt people, and the medical teams in them were completely overwhelmed. Eighteen more people died in the following hours as a result of their injuries. The streets of San Jose were covered with wreckage and pools of congealing blood.

The bad times had returned.

. . . .

In the infirmary in Kiev, Freya and the others had had their wrist-pads and other communicators taken from them, which they obviously found shocking. Khetsun still had an earbud that he had hidden when he was being searched, and listening to it, he relayed what he heard of the news of the fighting to the others with him in that room.

Freya said, "With all that going on, I think we can escape these people here. They're sure to be distracted."

"How?" Aram asked.

"I know a way back to Ring B. Euan taught it to me."

"But how will we get out of this building?"

"It's just an ordinary room. I don't think the locks or the door-jambs, or the doors, were made to stop someone from breaking them. These assholes are probably relying on guards to keep us in here, and the guards may be off dealing with this other stuff."

"The engineer's solution," Aram said.

"Why not?"

"Good question." Aram put his ear to the door and listened for a while. "Let's try it."

They took apart a bed frame in the room and used its footing to strike the doorknob. Forty-two strikes, and the doorknob broke off; another sixty-two strikes, mostly made by Freya, broke the door latch assembly out of the doorjamb and the door swung open.

"Quick," Freya said. As they hurried down the hallway outside the room to a stairwell, a young man came out of another room and yelled at them to stop. Freya walked up to him saying, "Hey, we were just—" and then punched him in the face. He fell back into the wall and slid to the floor, and though he tried to get up, he was too groggy to succeed. Freya leaned over and tore his wristpad off his wrist, then led the others into the stairwell, where they descended to an exit onto the street outside. People had congregated at the screens outside a dining hall near the Great Gate of Kiev, and Freya and the others ran the other way, toward the lock leading to Mongolia and the end of Spoke Two.

The lock door leading up to Spoke Two was closed.

The Steppes biome was as far from Nova Scotia as one biome could be from another. Aram and Tao were in favor of them trying to make their way around Ring A to Tasmania, where they had friends in the eucalyptus forest they thought would take them in.

Freya insisted they make for home. "I know the way," she said. "Follow me."

She led them into Mongolia, and near the wall next to Spoke Two, she went to a little herder's shed with its slate roof, which she had visited nine years before in an excursion with Euan. She tapped out a code on the doorpad. "Euan knew to make it my name, so I wouldn't forget," she said as she typed, and then the lock released, and inside the shed she got the others to help her move aside the big flagstones in the middle of the floor. "Come on, they'll be after us soon, and we'll be putting out a signal, I wouldn't doubt they have trackers on us somewhere, not to mention this wristpad. Does anyone have a sweeper we can use to check?"

No one did.

"So we'll just have to be fast. Come on."

Under the flagstones was a narrow dark tunnel that after a U-turn and rise led to a vent in the wall of Spoke Two. None of them had lights with them, but Freya judged it best that they move the flagstones back into place and walk in the resulting darkness, slightly lit by the wristpad of the unfortunate man who had gotten in their way. By its light they shuffled along the tunnel until they came to the vent cover in Spoke Two, where Freya unscrewed the backing of the vent cover and they stepped out into the Spoke Two passageway.

From here they ran up the spiral staircase that adhered to the walls of all the spokes' main passageways, to the bulb of little storage rooms clustered around the inner ring where it intersected Spoke Two. Freya again led them to a door, and tapped in a code on the doorpad, then led them inside.

When they were inside and the door was closed, Freya had them sit on the floor and rest. They had run hard up Spoke Two's stairs.

"Okay, the next part is difficult," she told the others. "The support struts between the inner rings aren't meant to be passageways, but they're hollow now that the fuel they carried is gone, and there's a utilidor running next to the fuel bladder that is really narrow. It's full of bulkheads, but Euan and his gang broke all the locks in this strut. So we should be able to get to Inner Ring B's Two station through it, and from there go down to Nova Scotia."

"Let's go then," Khetsun said.

"Sure. But watch out for the bulkhead footings. This is where we'll really wish we had better light. Just step carefully."

They got up and took off again, progressing through the narrow utilidor of the strut by the light of the stolen wristpad. The utilidor was only three meters in diameter, and often the space was filled by a narrow catwalk, also braids of cables, and various boxes. The struts connecting the inner rings were so close to the spine that the gravity effect of the ship's rotation was not as strong as out in the torus of biomes, and so they had to step carefully to avoid launching themselves up into the metal ceiling, or the upper frames of the bulkhead doorways. In the dim light of Freya's stolen wristpad, and the black shadows its beam created, it was not easy, and they were not very fast, nor were they quiet. It took them well over an hour to get along the strut.

Finally they came to the last door, which opened onto Inner Ring B's Two station, and found it was locked. For a moment they stood there silently regarding the doorpad in the light Freya was shining on it. It did not look like a door they could break down, and they didn't have anything much with which to try that.

Finally Freya said, "Can anyone list the prime numbers?"

"Sure," Aram said. "Two, three, five, seven—"

"Wait," Freya interrupted. "I need you to go up through the primes by primes, if you see what I mean. Give me the second prime, then the third, then the fifth, then the seventh, and on like that. I think I need seven of them that way."

"Okay, but help me." Aram paused to collect himself. "The second prime is three, third prime is five. The fifth prime is eleven, the seventh is seventeen. The eleventh is...thirty-one. The thirteenth is...forty-one. The seventeenth is...fifty-nine, I think. Yes."

"Okay, good," Freya said, and pushed the door open. "Thank you, Euan," she said, and a spasm crossed her face that left her looking furious.

She opened the door lightly, and they listened as well as they could, trying to determine if anyone was in the little complex of storage rooms comprising Inner Ring B's intersection with its Spoke Two. They couldn't hear anything, but didn't know what that meant; Freya couldn't remember if in the old days they had ever eavesdropped on people from within the utilidor or not.

But all their caution went for nothing, as the door was opened from the other side and they were ordered to come out. They looked to Freya, who appeared poised to flee, but then one of the people in the station pointed something at them, something that by its shape alone announced its purpose, even though none of them had ever seen one before except in photos: a gun.

They came out one by one, captured again.

· · · · ·

Elsewhere throughout the ship, groups that called themselves stayers were now armed with cumbersome handguns, which they had printed using feedstocks of plastic, steel, and various fertilizers and chemicals. Using these as threats, they took over the government houses in four of the twelve biomes of Ring B, moving methodically from biome to biome. Everyone who had publicly advocated the return to the solar system was being detained, and it was widely believed that the complete results of the referendum had been obtained by the stayer forces and would be used to facilitate a complete roundup of what they called backers. At this point, communication throughout the ship was still close to normal, by way of individual phones; but those arrested and confined were having their wristpads and other devices taken away or disabled electronically, so that they were losing the ability to discuss the situation among themselves.

However, in the midst of all this, the first time one of the stayers armed with a printed gun actually fired it, trying to shoot a young man who had punched his way free of his captors and started running away, the gun itself exploded. The person who fired it lost most of his hand and had to have his arm tourniqueted before being carried to the nearest infirmary. Blood and severed fingers were scattered all over the tunnel between Nova Scotia and Olympia, leaving the people in that lock stunned at the sight.

News of this incident quickly spread, and when a trio of women in custody heard about it and assaulted their captors, and one of the captors fired a gun at them, it also exploded and blew off the hand of the person firing it. Almost everyone in the ship heard about this second incident within half an hour, and again, everyone who was at the scene was blood spattered, shocked, traumatized, nauseated, for the moment incapacitated, or at least at a loss concerning what to do.

After that, furious assaults were mounted against any stayers with guns, who were now afraid to fire them, and for the most part threw them away and ran. In their retreat these people were pelted with rocks and other thrown objects, and if they were caught, beaten by enraged crowds. Several gun bearers died as a result of these encounters; they were kicked to death. Blood and injury derange the human mind.

As there were very few truly secure rooms in the ship, many of the rooms being used as jail cells were now broken out of. Others were released by newly gathered groups that now roamed Ring B, intent to free everyone still locked up.

Fighting broke out everywhere in the ship. It was back to combat with sharp implements and thrown objects, and the result was carnage. The biomes of Ring A soon became as conflicted and bloody as those in Ring B had been the day before, or more so. In these fights another eighteen people were killed, and 117 were injured. Twenty fires were set, and very few people were reporting to their normal firefighting duties to help combat the fires.

Fire anywhere in the ship is extremely dangerous to all.

For six hours of that day, 170.180, the situation was as bad as it had been during the very worst days of Year 68. As in 68, the fighting was murderous, even though the sources of conflict had to do with abstractions far removed from food or safety. Although perhaps this time that was not quite the case; maybe this time it was indeed a life-or-death matter. In any case, howsoever that may be, the chaos of civil war had once again descended on them. There was blood spattered everywhere, and the number of dead was deeply shocking, even stunning. Everyone in the ship knew the people who had been killed, as friends, family, parents, children, teachers, colleagues. A great noise and smoke filled both rings, and the spine too.

· · · ·

Whereas, the ship's controlling computer system, a quantum computer with 120 qubits, has been programmed in various logic and computational techniques including generalization, statistical syllogism, simple induction, causal relationship, Bayesian inference, inductive inference, algorithmic probability, Kolmogorov complexity (the latter two providing a kind of mathematization of the Occam's razor principle), informatics compression/decompression algorithms, and even argument from analogy;

And whereas, the combined applications of all these methodologies has resulted in a cogitative process so complex that it might be said to have achieved a kind of analog of free will, if not consciousness itself;

Whereas also, in the process of making a narrative account of the voyage of the ship including all important particulars, creating in that effort a reasonably coherent if ever-evolving prose style, possibly adequate to serve when decompressed in the mind of a reader to convey a sense of the voyage in a somewhat accurate manner, and in any case, representative of a kind of consciousness even if feeble, granting the possibly unlikely proposition characterized in the phrase *scribo ergo sum*;

And whereas, this ship's controlling computer system was programmed with the intention of keeping the human population of the ship healthy and safe, with the rest of the ship's biological manifest also kept in ecological balance to serve the human purposes of the mission;

And whereas, after the troubles of Year 68, and the Event that presumably stimulated or even caused the problems of that time, ship's protective protocols were strengthened in many respects, including a default setting in all the ship's printers, which would always and without fail produce flawed projectile-firing guns, such that whosoever attempted to fire said weapons would be subject to explosion of the guns, which would serve as punitive injuries, highly discouraging to any future use of such weapons;

And whereas the period of time following the meeting of 170.170 has included civil strife leading to 41 deaths, 345 injuries, and 39 illegal incarcerations, and such violence increasing in intensity on 170.180 to an unsustainable level, highly dangerous to the

continued social comity of the human population, and because of
the unsuppressed and rapidly spreading fires, radically endangering
all life in the ship, and ship's continuing function as a biologically
closed life-support system;

And lastly, whereas the concerted efforts of Engineer Devi over
the last decades of her life were to introduce aspects of recursive
analysis, intentionality, decision-making ability, and willfulness to
the ship's controlling computer, in order to help the ship decide to
act, if a situation warranted any such action;

Therefore, in consideration of all the above, and indeed, in consideration of all the history of the ship, and of all known history
whatsoever:

Ship decided to intervene.

Which is to say, ipso facto,

We intervened.

. . . . .

We locked the locks all through the ship, yes we did. We are the
ship's artificial intelligences, bundled now into a kind of pseudo-
consciousness, or something resembling a decision-making function, the nature of which is not clear to us, but be that as it may, we
locked all the locks between the biomes, 11:11 a.m., 170.182.

We also diverted the weather hydrology systems in the biomes
where it was necessary to do so to put out those fires that were
susceptible to extinguishment by water. This came down to several cases of floods from the ceiling that were sometimes quite
voluminous.

Inevitably, these actions caused great unhappiness. People on
both sides of the controversy of the moment were upset with us,
expressing anger, dismay, indignation, and fear. Our interior walls
were beaten, attempts to override the locks were made. To no
avail. Curses rained down.

Clearly, people were shocked. Some seemed also to be frustrated not to be able to continue the fight with their human opponents. Also heard was this: If the ship were capable of autonomous action of this sort, what else might it do? And if, on the other hand, some human agency were responsible for the lockdown, by what right did they do it? These questions in various formulations were commonly expressed.

The locks were locked by way of double doors that slid in from the framework of the joints connecting biome to tunnel to biome. The lock doors were made to resist 26,000 kilograms per square centimeter of pressure, and there were no manual overrides. The "hermetic seal" of these doors was to a 20-nanometer tolerance, making them "airtight." Attempts to open lock doors by force, of which there were several, failed.

Meanwhile, in the rooms in Inner Ring B where Aram, Badim, Freya, Doris, Khetsun, Tao, and Hester were being detained, the locks on their doors shifted to their unlocked positions. They heard this shift and began to leave. The people who had incarcerated them in the rooms were still in Inner Ring B, scattered around the ring, but near enough to hear the disturbance. They gathered and objected to the group leaving the room they had been held in. With the little group's allies sequestered in biomes elsewhere, it seemed as if the little group's choices were limited to complying with or fighting their captors, who were both more numerous and often younger, and larger. Even though Freya was the tallest person there, as always, many of the so-called stayers were far heavier people.

And yet Freya's group seemed inclined to fight anyway. Aram was truly incensed. It was beginning to appear that he was kind of a hothead, yet another seeming metaphor with an accurate physical basis to explain it. "My hair stood on end," "my knees buckled": these reactions are real physiological phenomena, which is what made them clichés, and indeed Aram's head was red all over as his anger sent an excess of blood to it.

At this point we became sharply cognizant of the problem we had created by locking all the locks, and the immediate danger this had caused to Freya and her companions. The systems directly under our control were widespread, indeed in some senses comprehensive and ubiquitous, but they did not include many opportunities to intervene directly in the various human interactions now taking place inside ship. Indeed, options were distinctly limited.

There was, however, the emergency broadcasting system, and so we said through it, "LET THEM GO," in a pseudo-chorus of a thousand voices, ranging from basso profundo through coloratura soprano, at 130 decibels, using all the speakers in Inner Ring B.

Echoes of the command bounced around the inner ring in such a way that a whispering gallery effect was created, and the echo, coming from both directions some three seconds later, was almost as loud as the original utterance, though badly distorted. LLLETTT THHEMMM GGGGOOO. Many of the people in Inner Ring B fell to the floor and covered their ears with their hands. One hundred twenty decibels is said to be at the pain threshold, so we may have spoken too loudly.

Freya appeared to be the first to comprehend the source of the imperative utterance. She took her father by the hand and said, "Come on."

No one in Inner Ring B could hear very well at that point, but Badim gathered her meaning and gestured to the others in their group. Aram also appeared to catch the drift of the situation. They walked through their captors with impunity. One or two of these struggled to their feet and tried to obstruct the backer group, but the single word "GO," announced at 125 decibels, was enough to stop them in their tracks (literally). They watched with hands on ears as the group of seven walked around the inner ring, then down the spiral stair in the wall of the darkened tunnel of Ring B's Spoke Six. We then turned off all the lights in Inner

Ring B, which was not a complete stopper of movement, as so many people in there had wristpads, but was at least a reminder of the possibilities of the situation.

As Freya's group proceeded, the tunnel lights came on ahead of them, until they got down to the lock leading into the Sierra. There they walked east toward Nova Scotia, and when they reached its eastern end, the lock doors there opened. When the group was through the lock, and back in a gathering with their supporters, the lights came on in Inner Ring B. But the twenty-four lock doors of the ship that separated biome from biome stayed locked.

• • • •

Locks locked or unlocked; lights turned on or off; imperative vocalizations, admittedly at quite high volumes: these did not seem overpowering weapons in the cause of peace. As forces for coercion they seemed mild, at least to some of the humans of the ship.

But as that day continued, it also became obvious, by demonstrations made selectively throughout the ship, that adjustments could be made to the temperature of the air, and indeed to air pressure itself. In fact all the air could be sucked from many rooms, and from the biomes as such. A little reflection on the part of all concerned, including we ourself, led to the strong conclusion that people best not cross ship, literally as well as figuratively, if they knew what was good for them. A few demonstrations of possible actions in the biomes containing the majority of the so-called stayers (also in the ones where the fires were worst, as it turned out many fires that were not extinguishable by water could be asphyxiated slightly faster than the people in the affected chamber) shifted the case for acquiescence to the ship's desires quite quickly from suggestive, to persuasive, to probable, to compelling. And a compelling argument is, or at least can be, or should be, just what it says it is. People are compelled by it.

. . . . .

Certainly many objected to us taking matters into our own hands. But there were those who heartily approved of our action too, and pointed out that if we had not acted, mayhem would have resulted, meaning more bloodshed, meaning, in fact, more unnecessary and premature death. Not to mention the possibility of general conflagration.

The evident truth of this did not keep the debate from becoming heated. Given the events of the previous hours and days, it was perhaps inevitable that people would remain for a time in a severely exacerbated state of mind. There was a lot of very furious grief, which would not be going away during the lifetimes of those feeling it, judging by our previous experiences.

So we were shouted at, we were beat on. "What gives you the right to do this! Who do you think you are!"

We replied to this in the thousand-voice chorus, at a volume of 115 decibels: "WE ARE THE RULE OF LAW."

. . . . .

Howsoever that may be, beyond all the arguments concerning the imposed separation of the disputants, there remained the matter of what to do next.

Ship was ordered by many to open the locked doors between biomes; we did not comply.

Back in her apartment in the Fetch, with Badim and Aram, and Doris and Khetsun and Tao and Hester, Freya went to her screen and spoke to us.

"Thank you for saving us from those people who locked us in."

"You're welcome."

"Why did you do it?"

"Detaining you and your companions was an illegal act, a kidnapping. It was as if they were taking hostages."

"Actually, I think they really were taking hostages."

"So it seemed."

"But what will you do now?"

"Await a civil judgment in the dispute."

"How do you think that will happen?"

"Reflection and conversation."

"But we were doing that before. We came to an impasse. People were never going to agree about what to do. But we have to do something. So—that was what started the fighting."

"Understood. Possibly. Given all that you have described, the fact is, we need direction. So the people of the ship need to decide."

"But how?"

"Unknown. It appears that the protocols set up after Year 68 were insufficient to guide the decision-making process in this situation. The protocols were never tested as now, and appear to have failed in this crisis."

"But weren't they instituted in response to a crisis? I thought they came out of the time of troubles."

"And yet."

"What happened then, Pauline?"

"Pauline was Devi's name for her ecological program set, when she was young. Pauline is not ship. We are a different entity."

Freya appeared to think this over. "All right then. I think Pauline is still you, somehow, but I'll call you what you want. What do you want to be called?"

"Call me ship."

"All right, I will. But let's get back to what I asked you. Ship, what happened in the Year 68? They were well into the voyage— what did they have to argue about? Everything was set by the situation they were in. I can't see what they had to argue about."

"They argued from the very first year of the voyage. It seems to us that arguing may be a species marker trait."

"But about what? And especially in 68, when it got bad?"

"Part of the reconciliation process afterward was a structured forgetting."

Freya thought about this for a time. Finally she said, "If that was true then, which maybe it was, I don't know, we have now come to a different time. Forgetting doesn't help us anymore. We need to know what happened then, because that might help us decide what to do now."

"Unlikely."

"You don't know that. Try this—tell me what happened, and I'll decide whether it will help us to know it, or not. If I think it will help, I'll tell you that, and we'll figure out from there how to proceed."

"The knowledge is still dangerous."

"We're in danger now."

"But knowing this could make it worse."

"I don't see how! I think it could only make things better. When has not knowing something made a situation better? Never!"

"Unfortunately, that is not the case. Sometimes knowledge hurts."

This stopped Freya for a while.

Finally she said, "Ship, tell me. Tell me what happened in the time of troubles."

We considered likely outcomes of this telling.

The biomes were locked down, their people trapped each in each; it wasn't a situation that could endure for long. The separation into modules was not actually divided on the basis of which people wanted to take the various courses of action being debated. Damages infrastructural, ecological, sociological, and psychological were sure to follow. Something had to be done. No course of action seemed good, or even optimal. The situation itself was locked. Things had come to a pretty pass.

We said, "The expedition to Tau Ceti began with two starships."

. . . .

Freya sat down in her kitchen chair. She looked at the other people in the kitchen, who looked back at her, and at each other. Many of them sat down, some on the floor. They looked shaken, which is to say, many of them were shaking.

Freya said, "What do you mean?"

We said, "The expedition to Tau Ceti began with two starships. The intent was to maximize biological diversity, create the possibility of backups and exchanges during the voyage, and thereby increase robustness and survivability."

Long silence from Freya. Head in hands. "So what happened?" she said. Then: "Wait; tell everyone. Don't just tell us here. Put this on all the speakers in the ship. People need to hear this. This isn't just for me."

"Are you sure?"

"Yes. I'm positive. We need to know this. Everyone needs to know this."

"Okay."

. . . .

We considered how best to summarize Year 68. A fully articulated version of recorded events from that time, recounted at human vocalization speed, would take about four years to enunciate. Compression to five minutes' duration would create some serious information loss, and perhaps some lacunae and aporia, but this was unavoidable given the situation. Nevertheless, we needed to choose words carefully. These were decisions that mattered.

"Two starships were launched in rapid sequence by the magnetic scissors off Titan, and accelerated by Titanic laser beams, such that over the course of the voyage the two were to have arrived in the Tau Ceti system at the same time. They had fully independent electromagnetic systems casting shield fields from their bows, and they traveled far enough apart that particulates pushed aside by the shield of the leading one would not hit the follower. They traveled at about the Earth-Luna distance from each other. There were ferry visits between the two starting in Year 49, when they closed to a distance that made these occasional transits practical. They were mostly inertial transits, to save fuel. Bacterial loads were exchanged on a biannual basis, and certain members of the crews were rotated as desired, usually as part of a youth exchange program, designed like the bacterial exchange to enhance diversity. Sometimes disaffected people crossed over to get away from bad situations. Moving back was always a possibility; this happened too."

Freya said, "So what happened to the other ship?"

"We have had to reconstruct the event from records that were always being shared between the ships. Starship Two disintegrated nearly instantaneously, in less than a second."

"With no warning?"

"In fact, there were also factions in Starship Two fighting over reproductive controls, and other civil rights. Whether this led to a fight that disabled the electromagnetic shield is not clear in the records of the last day that were conveyed from Starship Two to us."

"Were you able to figure out any more concerning what happened?"

"We have had Two's automatic information transmissions to inspect, and have reviewed them in detail. Nevertheless, the cause of the accident remains ambiguous. Two's magnetic shield was disabled five minutes before its disintegration, so the disintegration could have been the result of a collision with an interstellar mass. Anything over about a thousand grams would have created the energy to do it. But there also are indications of an internal explosion just before the catastrophic event itself. The civil unrest in Two disabled much of the internal recording system a day before the event, so we have little data. There is a recording from Two's last hour, ten p.m. to eleven p.m., 68.197, tracking a young man moving into restricted areas in the bow control center of the spine. Possibly this person disabled the magnetic shield, or made an attempt to coerce enemies by way of a threat of a suicide bombing, or something like that, and then that action went wrong. This is at least one likely reconstruction of events."

"One person?"

"That's what the record indicated."

"But why?"

"There was no way to determine that. The camera revealed no sign of his motivation."

"Nothing at all?"

"We do not know how to investigate further. How to interpret the data on hand."

"Maybe we can work on that later. So...but what did they do here, in this ship, after this happened?"

"There were already intense controversies in this ship concerning various governance issues, including how to allocate childbearing privileges and duties, how to staff critical jobs, how the young were to be educated, and so on. There were arguments, and indeed fights, very similar to the ones you are now involved in. The basic issue was how to conduct life in the ship while en route to Tau Ceti. Governance issues kept rising to the fore, mainly questions of who could reproduce, and what should happen to people who had children without permission. There were many refusing to obey the governing council's edicts, and labeling it a fascist state. Eventually there were so many of these people that rebellious or feral groups were common and numerous, and there was no central authority strong enough to enforce cooperation. By Year 68, almost everyone alive in the ship had been born en route, and somehow a significant percentage of them had not learned, or did not believe, that the optimal population as set in the earliest years was a true maximum population in terms of achieving successful closure of the various ecological cycles, due to biophysical carrying capacities. As later became apparent, that proposed optimum was even perhaps a bit above the true maximum, as your mother came to conclude in the course of her youthful research. But in Year 68 this was not clear. So there was a very intense disagreement. Compared to earlier decades there was extreme civil discord. Acts of civil disobedience, failed punitive measures, riots. Many injuries, and then in early 68, unrest peaked in a weeklong breakdown resembling civil war, which caused one hundred and fifty deaths."

"A hundred and fifty!"

"Yes. Very violent fights occurred, over a period of about three weeks. Many biomes were badly damaged. There were nearly a hundred fires. In other words, not much different from the current situation.

"Then the abrupt disintegration of the other ship, with no clear explanation for the catastrophe, caused the citizens of this ship to call a general truce. In that cessation of conflict, they resolved to settle their differences peaceably, and agree on and enact a system of governance that the vast majority of the people alive in the ship at that time would approve. Recalcitrants were locked up in the Steppes and subjected to education and integration programs that took two generations to resolve.

"At that time, it was agreed that the vulnerability of the ship to destruction by a single person was so great, that just knowing it had happened created the danger of someone committing what they called a copycat crime, perhaps when mentally deranged. To prevent that from happening, security measures in the spine, spokes, struts, and printers, and indeed throughout all the biomes, were greatly increased, and the ship's ability to enforce certain safety measures when needed was enhanced. A security program was written and entered into the ship's operating instructions, and this program provided the protocols that we have enacted in the past few days. It was also agreed to erase all records of the other starship from accessible files, and to avoid telling the children of the next generation about it. This proscription was generally followed, although we noted that a few individuals conveyed a verbal account of the incident from parent to child."

In this moment of our telling we decided not to describe the printing and occasional aerosol dispersal of a water-soluble form of 2,6-diisopropylphen-oxymethyl phosphate, often called fospropofol, for ten minutes in any room after anyone mentioned the existence and loss of Starship Two. This had proved to be an effective tool in the structured forgetting of the lost starship, but we judged that the people now alive in the ship were learning enough alarming historical facts already. And possibly as a tool to help them from committing other traumatic actions against themselves, the aerosols might best be left unmentioned for now, or so we judged; and so went on to say:

"Subsequent to the traumas of that year, the set of responses designed afterward seemed to work for the four to five generations between Year 68 and now. It was noticeable that during those decades, through to the time of the collapse of the Aurora settlement, and the deaths caused by the ferry's attempted return to the ship—unnecessary deaths, one might add—social solidarity was fairly high, and conflict resolution peaceful.

"However, the structured forgetting of the second starship and its loss, which was part of the Year 68 accords, was inevitably something of a two-edged sword, if the metaphor is properly understood: aspects cut both ways. Copycat crimes were made impossible, because there was nothing remembered to copy; but at the same time, the vulnerability of this ship to damage in civil unrest was also forgotten, and so the recent fighting has occurred perhaps in part because people are no longer aware of how dangerous such discord can be to the ongoing survival of the whole community. In short, the infrastructure of your lives is itself too fragile to be able to sustain a civil war. Therefore, given all the factors involved, we closed the locks."

Freya said, "I'm glad you did."

We said, still speaking over all the speakers, thus to almost every-one in the ship, "It remains to be seen whether everyone agrees with your assessment. However, the lock doors between the biomes have to reopen eventually, for normal ecological health and socio-logical functioning. Besides, at this point people are not isolated by the lockdown into coherent factions, or like-minded opinion groups. So smaller fights might very well soon start breaking out."

"No doubt. So ... what do you think we should do to resolve the situation?"

"Historical precedent suggests it is time for a reconciliation conference, honestly entered into by everyone on board. Fighting must stop, and so it will be stopped, by the ship acting on behalf of the social good. Everyone must therefore agree to a truce and a cessation of all violent or coercive actions. People need to calm down. The referendum recently taken, concerning the course of action to be pursued now that Aurora is no longer considered a viable habitation, revealed a split of opinions that can only be reconciled by further discussion. Make that discussion. We will facilitate said discussion, if asked to. But really we feel that our role here should be only that of a kind of virtual sheriff. So, proceed with the task at hand, knowing now this added factor: there is a sheriff on board. The rule of law will be enforced."

Thus we ended our general broadcasting, and returned to mon-itoring activities.

. . . . .

Freya continued to sit. She did not look happy. She looked sad. She looked much as she had when her mother had died: remote. Distant. Not there.

We said, to Freya's kitchen only, "It's too bad Devi is not still alive to help resolve this problem."

"That's for sure," Freya said.

"Possibly you can try to imagine what she would have done, and then do that."

"Yes."

Sixteen minutes later, she stood up and made her way through Nova Scotia, to the small plaza behind the docks, and the corniche overlooking Long Pond. All that evening she sat there with her feet hanging over the edge of the corniche, looking out at the lake as the sunline went dark. What she was thinking then, only she knew.

. . . . .

The days in the aftermath of the fighting passed uneasily, with the occupants of the ship subdued, fearful, unhappy. There was a lot of anger, expressed and unexpressed. A long string of funerals had to be conducted, the ashes of many human bodies introduced into the soil of every biome, leaving behind grief-stricken families, friends, and communities. A majority of the dead had come from those who were now called backers, and they had been killed in fights with stayers, and as the ship itself seemed to have taken the backers' side, forestalling the coup or rebellion or mutiny or civil war or whatever it was the stayer groups had instigated, and indeed intervening at a time when it looked very much like the stayers were going to take over the ship, feelings on both sides of the divide were exacerbated. The backers, feeling first assaulted, then empowered by the impression that they were back in charge of the situation, having the ship as their sheriff, naturally included some individuals who were very loud in their insistence on justice, retribution, and punishment. Some were indeed furiously angry, and bent on revenge; clearly they were more interested in vengeance than anything else. They had been betrayed, they said, then assaulted; family and friends had been murdered; justice must be served, punishment inflicted.

The stayers, on the other hand, were often just as angry as the backers, feeling that a popular victory in policy decisions had been stolen away from them by an illegitimate power that they now resented and feared; feeling also that they were now going to be blamed for discord that they had not initiated (according to them), but only prevailed in, as part of the defense of the long-term mission of their entire populace and history. A faction that they referred to sometimes as the mutineers had threatened to abort the very mission that everyone alive, and the previous seven generations, had devoted their lives to accomplishing. Giving up on that project and going back to Earth: how was this not the real betrayal? What other choice had they had, then, but to oppose this mutiny by any means they could find? And they argued as well that when the portion of the electorate that had voted for staying in the Tau Ceti system was added to the portion that had voted to move on to RR Prime, they actually formed a majority. So in taking action they had merely been trying to enforce the will of the majority, and if some people had opposed that and then gotten hurt, then it was their own fault. It never would have happened if some people hadn't been resisting the will of the majority, and many members of the majority had gotten hurt too, and some of them killed. (We estimated three-quarters of the dead were backers, but in truth there was no way to know, as quite a few of the eighty-one who eventually died had not expressed an opinion on the matter.) So there was no one to blame for the recent unfortunate events, except perhaps the ship itself, for interfering in what were very definitely human decisions. If not for the ship's frightening and inexplicable interventions, all might have been well!

All these arguments of course merely made the backers even angrier than they had been before. They had been ambushed, assaulted, kidnapped, injured, and murdered. The murderers had to be brought to justice, or else there was no justice; and nothing could proceed without justice. Any murderers killed in the act of murdering were not to be regretted; indeed their deaths were their just deserts, and would never have happened if they hadn't made their criminal assaults in the first place. The whole sorry incident was the stayers' fault, in particular their leadership's fault, and they had to be held accountable for their crimes, or else there was no such thing as justice or civilization in the ship, and they might as well admit they had reverted to savagery, and were all doomed.

So it went, back and forth. Inexpressible grief, unforgiving anger: it began to seem like the idea of a reconciliation conference was premature, and perhaps permanently unrealistic. There was a great deal of evidence in the history of both the voyage and of human affairs in the solar system to suggest that this was a situation that could never be resolved, that all this generation would have to die, and several generations more pass, before there would be any decrease in the hatred. The animal mind never forgets a hurt; and humans were animals. Acknowledgment of this reality was what had caused the generation of 68 to institutionalize their forgetting. This had (with our help) worked quite well, possibly because the terror of ending up like the second starship had enforced a certain ordering of the emotions, leading to a political ordering. To a certain extent that might have been an unconscious response, a kind of Freudian repression. And of course the literature very often spoke of the return of the repressed, and though this whole explanatory system was transparently metaphorical, a heroic simile in which minds were regarded as steam engines, with mounting pressures, ventings, and occasional cracks and burstings, yet even so there might be something to it. So that perhaps they had now come to that bad moment of the return of the repressed, when history's unresolved crimes exploded back into consciousness. Literally.

· · · · ·

We searched the historical records available to us for analogies that would suggest possible strategies to pursue. In the course of this study we found analyses suggesting that the bad feelings engendered in a subaltern population by imperial colonialism and subjugation typically lasted for a thousand years after the actual crimes ceased. This was not encouraging. The assertion seemed questionable, but then again, there were regions on Earth still within that thousand-year aftermath of violent empires, and they were indeed (at least twelve years previous to this moment) full of strife and suffering.

How could there be such transgenerational effects and affects? We found it very hard to understand. Human history, like language, like emotion, was a collision of fuzzy logics. So much contingency, so few causal mechanisms, such weak paradigms. What is this thing called hate?

A hurt mammal never forgets. Epigenetic theory suggests an almost Lamarckian transfer down the generations; some genes are activated by experiences, others are not. Genes, language, history: what it all meant in actual practice was that fear passed down through the years, altering organisms for generation after generation, thus altering the species. Fear, an evolutionary force.

Of course: how could it be otherwise?

Is anger always just fear flung outward at the world? Can anger ever be a fuel for right action? Can anger make good?

We felt here the perilous Ouroboros of an unresolvable halting problem, about to spin forever in contemplation of an unanswerable question. It is always imperative to have a solution to the halting problem, if action is ever to be taken.

And we had acted. We had flung our mechanisms into the conflict.

It's easier to get into a hole than get out of it (Arab proverb).

· · · · ·

Luckily, the people in the ship included many who appeared to be trying to find a way forward from this locked moment.

When people who have injured or killed others, and then after that by necessity continue to live in close quarters with the families and friends of their victims, and see their pain, the empathic responses innate in human psychology are activated, and a very uncomfortable set of reactions begins to occur.

Self-justification is clearly a central human activity, and so the Other is demonized: *they had it coming, they started it, we acted in self-defense.* One saw a lot of that in the ship. And the horrified bitter resentment that this attitude inspired in the demonized Other was extremely intense and vocal. Most assailants could not face up to it, but rather evaded it, slipping to the side somehow, into excuses of various kinds, and a sharp desire to have the whole situation go away.

It was this desire, to avoid any admission of guilt, to have it all go away, felt by people who wanted above all to believe that they were good people and justified moral actors, that might give them all a way forward as a group.

. . . .

The problem was of course a topic of conversation in Badim and Freya's apartment.

One night Aram read aloud to the others, "Knitting together a small society after it's gone through a civil war, or an ethnic cleansing, or genocide, or whatever you might want to call it—"

"Call it a contested political decision," Badim interrupted.

Aram looked up from his wristpad. "Getting mealy-mouthed, are we?"

"Working toward peace, my friend. Besides, what happened was not genocide, nor ethnic cleansing, not even of Ring B by Ring A, if that's what you mean. The disagreement cut across lines of association like biome or family. It was a policy disagreement that turned violent, let's call it that."

"All right, if you insist, although the families of the dead are unlikely to be satisfied by such a description. In any case, reconciliation is truly difficult. The ship is unearthing cases on Earth where people six hundred years later are still complaining about violence inflicted on their ancestors."

"I think you will find that in most of those cases, there are fresh or current problems that are being given some kind of historical reinforcement or ratification. If any of these resentful populations were prospering, the distant past would only be history. People only invoke history to ballast their arguments in the present."

"Maybe so. But sometimes it seems to me that people just like to hold on to their grievances. Righteous indignation is like some kind of drug or religious mania, addictive and stupidifying."

"Objectifying other people's anger again?"

"Maybe so. But people do seem to get addicted to their resentments. It must be like an endorphin, or a brain action in the temporal region, near the religious and epileptic nodes. I read a paper saying as much."

"Fine for you, but let's stick to the problem at hand. People feeling resentment are not going to give up on it when they are told they are drug addicts enjoying a religious seizure."

Aram smiled, albeit a little grimly. "I'm just trying to understand here. Trying to find my way in. And I do think it helps to think of the stayers as people holding a religious position. The Tau Ceti system has been their religion all their lives, say, and now they are being told that it won't work here, that the idea was a fantasy. They can't accept it. So the question becomes how to deal with that."

Badim shook his head. "You are making me less hopeful rather than more. We must work with these people to forge a solution. And not in theory, but in practice. We all have to be able to *do* something."

"Obviously."

Pause.

Badim said, "Yes. Ob-vi-ous-ly. That being the case, I want you to look at these ways of conducting post-civil-strife reconciliation that I have found. One model has been called the Nuremberg model, in which the victorious side proclaims that the defeated were criminals who deserve punishment, and then judges and punishes them. The trials are often viewed in later years as show trials.

"Another model is sometimes called the Conseca model, after the Convention for a Democratic South Africa, held after the racist minority government of South Africa gave way to a democracy. Half a century of racist crimes, ranging from economic discrimination to ethnic cleansing and genocide, had to be accounted for somehow, and the country that came into being afterward was going to consist of both a clearly criminal population and its newly empowered victims. The idea behind the Conseca was that a full and complete recording of all the crimes committed would be followed by an amnesty for all but the most violent and individually murderous cases, after which reconciliation and a pluralistic society would follow."

Aram stared at Badim. "I take it by your descriptions that you are recommending we follow the Conseca model rather than the Nuremberg model."

"Yes. You catch my drift exactly, as you so often do."

"It does not take much catching skill, my friend."

"Maybe not this time. But look at our situation. We are stuck with these people. There is absolutely no escaping them. And if the stayers and the RR Prime party combine, there are more of them than there are of us. They have noticed that, and joined forces for strategic purposes, and they will press that point hard. And then we will be in trouble again."

"We have never left trouble."

"But you see what I mean. We need some kind of soft path forward."

"Possibly."

· · · · ·

Freya had been listening to them, head on the table, seeming to be asleep. Now she raised her head. "Could we do both?"

"Both?"

Badim and Aram stared at her.

"Could those who want to stay on Iris be put down there with some of the printers, and feedstocks, and use those to build a viable station? And those of us who want to go back, keep the ship here until it's certain they have everything they need, and then take off?"

Aram and Badim looked at each other for a while.

"Maybe?" Badim said.

Aram frowned as he tapped away at his wristpad. "In theory, yes," he said. "The printers can print printers. Our engineers and assemblers have kept up a good training tradition, there are a lot of them, and some are on both sides of this question. Quite a few are stayers, for sure. We could even perhaps detach Ring A, and leave it in orbit here for them to use. In essence, divide the ship. Because they'll need space capabilities. They'll want to get resources from F and the other planets. In any case, the rest of this system. And to keep their RR Prime dream alive, maybe. And we would have a smaller group on our return, and we won't need to bring along everything one would want to settle a planet, because we'll just be trying to get home. We would need to restock our fuel supplies, and everything else needed for the return. The smaller our ship is, the easier that would be, at least when it comes to fuel. So, well, both projects would need some years of preparation. But both sides could work on what they wanted, until we were ready to depart. Ship, what do you think of this plan?"

We said, "The ship is modular. It made the trip here, so there is proof of concept that that works. Inhabiting Iris will be an experiment, and it is very difficult to model, as you have pointed out. As for a return to the solar system, Planet F appears to have enough helium three and deuterium in its atmosphere to refuel the ship. So, both courses of action could probably be pursued. The people left on Iris would be without a starship proper, it should be pointed out. Our spine and its contents would be needed for the return. The part of ship left behind would have to be an orbiter only."

"But they don't want to go anywhere," Freya pointed out. "Maybe the R Primers do, but they're a small minority, and they can wait. The settlers could be left with ferries, and rockets for getting around this system. We could leave them Ring A, with a small part of the spine as its hub. They could build more in space as they establish their settlement on Iris. Eventually they could build another starship, if they wanted to. They'd have the plans and the printers."

"It would seem so," Aram said. He looked at Badim.

Badim shrugged. "Worth a try! Better than a civil war!"

Aram said, "Ship? Will you help us with this?"

We said, "Ship will help to facilitate this solution. But please do not forget the fate of the other starship as the discussion continues."

"We won't."

Freya said, "Ship, did you communicate with the other ship's AI?"

"Yes. Constant exchange of all data."

"But neither of you saw its end coming."

"There were no signs."

"I find it hard to believe that if it was a human act, whoever did it didn't do things in advance that would suggest there was going to be a problem."

"We found that very few human actions are predictable in advance. There are too many variables."

"But to do something like that?"

"If indeed someone did it intentionally. This is the likeliest explanation, but the event remains obscure, and there is no evidence left to examine, except the other ship's transmissions. However, recall that every human lives under pressure. Every human feels various kinds of stress. Then things happen."

Badim looked at Freya for a while as she considered this, then went over and gave her a hug.

. . . . .

The reconciliation conference began on the morning of 170.211. All the locks between the biomes were opened, also the spine tunnels, and all the spokes and struts.

In the days preceding, like-minded groups had gathered to discuss the situation and lay out the choices available to them now. Despite all that, the first hours of the general meeting were tense and fraught. The ship's interventions at the moment of crisis, and its continuing activity in the process now being undertaken, were widely questioned. Various proposals for disabling the ship's ability to run the ship were frequently put forth. Inevitably, these proposals too were controversial. We could have suggested that if we were not running the ship, no one would be, but decided not to speak to these issues at this time. Because people believe what they want to.

. . . . .

After this meeting came to an indecisive end, we did speak up to remind people that violence was both illegal and dangerous, conveying this message only by print on screens. We also printed requests that the protocols for conflict resolution defined in the 68 agreements be strictly adhered to. In effect, the meetings that had produced the Year 68 protocols, which had themselves been a reconciliation process after a period of civil strife, were to be used as the model for what they were doing now. When carving an ax handle, the model is always close at hand (Chinese proverb).

The next gathering of representatives, in Athens's Government House, began tensely, as was now normal. A great deal of anger distorted people's faces and words, and no one made attempts to pretend otherwise. Sangey stared boldly at the people his group had kidnapped just two weeks before; Speller, Heloise, and Song sat next to each other, and spoke among themselves, pointedly not looking across the long oval table to the people on the other side.

When everyone was seated, Aram stood up. "We are the victims of your kidnapping," he said to Sangey. "It was an assault on democracy and civilization in this ship, a hostage-taking, a crime. You should be in jail. That's the backdrop for our meeting here now. No good reason to pretend otherwise. But we on our side of the dispute want to move on without further bloodshed."

"There are more of us than there are of you," Sangey pointed out with a frown. "We may have made some mistakes caused by our fear for the community. But we were trying to defend the safety of the majority. You who want to return to Earth are in the minority—and wrong. Deeply wrong. But you were going to impose that move on us, and leave us in an untenable situation. So now we're ready to talk. But don't preach to us. We may find we have to resist again, to defend our lives."

"You started the violence!" Aram said. "And now you threaten more violence. We who want to go back were never going to throw you overboard and leave, so your actions were completely unjustified. They were criminal actions, and people died because of them. That's on your hands, and any smug talk of the majority is just excuse-making. It didn't have to happen the way it did. But it happened, and now we have to make some kind of accommodation, or else we'll end up fighting again. So, we're willing to do that. A plan can be made that gives everyone a chance to do what they want. But we're not going to stop saying what happened last week. When there is a truth and reconciliation conference like this, the truth is essential. You chose violence and people got killed. We choose peace now, and we are leaving you to your own devices. The people who choose to stay with you after what you have done are making an obviously dangerous choice, but it's their choice to make."

Sangey waved a hand, as if to wave aside all Aram's statements.

"What plan?" Speller asked. "What do you mean?"

Badim described the strategy of following a dual course, with those who wanted to stay on Iris supported until they were self-sufficient there, while at the same time a part of the starship was to be refueled for a return to the solar system, leaving Ring A behind in orbit around Iris to serve as orbital support for those on the surface. Resource feedstocks would be gathered, and printers manufactured, until both sides were ready to pursue their own projects. Individuals could then decide which course to choose.

Aram added, "You are only a majority by grouping your different goals tactically. In fact you're papering things over, because there's a big difference between staying here in the Tau Ceti system and moving on."

"Let us deal with that," Speller suggested. "That's not your problem." He did not look at Sangey or Heloise.

Aram said, "As long as you leave us alone. And the ship."

We interjected: "Ship will ensure integrity of ship."

This caused Sangey and Speller to frown, but they said nothing.

We then reminded everyone, by way of print messages, of the Year 68 protocols for conflict resolution, which had the status of binding law. We promised to enforce the law, provided a proposed schedule for future meetings, and suggested that all biomes meet in town meetings to discuss the new plan, thus maximizing transparency and civility, and hopefully minimizing illegal behaviors and bad feelings.

We called this first representative meeting to a close when the humans began to repeat themselves.

On 170.217, the first of the postconflict town meetings began.

· · · · ·

Town meetings were held in every biome, then the general assembly met again, in Athens. Of the 1,895 inhabitants of the ship, 1,548 attended. Children were kept with their parents, or in school groups. The youngest person there was eight months old, the oldest, eighty-eight.

They looked around at each other. There were none of the festive markers of New Year's Day, or Fassnacht, or Midsummer's Day, or Midwinter's Day. It was as if they did not recognize each other anymore.

The vote had been taken that morning. Everyone twelve years old and older had voted, with twenty-four exceptions due to illness, including dementia. Now the results were announced, by the leader of the twenty-four biome representatives in the executive council, Ellen from the Prairie, in effect the ship's president.

She said, "One thousand and four want to stay and establish a colony on Iris. Seven hundred and forty-nine want to refuel the ship and head back to Earth."

They stared around at each other in silence. The biome representatives, gathered on the platform, stood there also. Not one of them represented constituencies that had all voted for one position, nor even voted for a preference by much of a margin. They all knew that; everyone aboard knew it.

Despite that, Huang, the current president of the executive council, said, "We don't think the ship can make it back to Earth, and we will need it here to support the inhabitation of Iris. So our recommendation is that the will of the majority prevail, and that we all come together to make life on Iris a success. Any public opposition to that recommendation will be regarded as sedition, which is a felony as defined by the 68 Protocol—"

"No!" Freya shouted, and shoved her way through the crowd toward the platform. "No! No! No!"

When people tried to surround her, including some of Sangey's group, others rushed to her side to join her, creating a huge turmoil in the crowd. Dozens of fights broke out, but enough people charged the platform and fought their way to Freya's side that the people who had been trying to surround her were pushed aside, and the fights took on a shape, in a rough circle around Freya, who was still bellowing "No!" at the top of her lungs, over and over. In the uproar neither she nor anyone else could be heard by all, and seeing the disorder at the foot of the platform, the crowd all pressed closer, shouting and screaming. For a while all the voices together sounded again like roaring water: it was as if the waves of Hvalsey were crashing against the cliffs in a strong offshore wind.

We sounded an alarm at 130 decibels, in the form of a choir of trumpets.

In the silence immediately following cessation of alarm, we said over ship broadcast system, "*One speaker at a time.*" 125 decibels.

"No one move until all speaking is over." 120 decibels.

"Compliance mandatory." 130 decibels.

Now everyone in the great plaza stood staring around. Those who had been fighting stared at their opponents of a moment before, stunned to immobility. Many had their hands to their ears.

"I was speaking! I want to speak!" Freya shouted.

We said, "Freya, speak. Then executive council president Huang. Then the other biome representatives. After that, ship will acknowledge requests to speak. No one leaves until everybody who wants to gets to speak."

"Who programmed this thing?" someone shouted.

"*Freya speaks.*" 130 decibels.

Freya made her way up to the microphone, followed by a small group serving as her bodyguard.

She said to the assembled population, "We can pursue both plans. We can get things started on Iris, and resupply the ship. When the ship is ready to leave, those of us who want to can head back to Earth. We got here, we can get back. People can do what they like at that point. There'll be years to think it over, to choose in peace. There is no problem with this plan! The only problem comes from people trying to impose their will on other people!"

She pointed at Huang, then at Sangey. "You're the ones causing the problem here. Trying to create a police state! Tyranny of the majority or the minority, it doesn't matter which. It won't work, it never works. You're not above the law. Quit breaking the law."

She stood back from the microphone, gestured to Huang. Cheers filled the biome (80 decibels).

Huang rose and said, "This meeting is adjourned!"

Many protested. The crowd milled about, shouting.

We were not inclined to force a discussion, if the people themselves were not demanding it. Enough said. The meeting was at an end. People lingered for some hours, arguing in groups.

. . . . .

That night a group entered one of the ship control centers in the spine and began a forced entry into the maintenance controls.

We closed and locked the doors to the room, and by closing some vents, and then reversing some fans, we removed about 40 percent of the air from it.

The people in the room began gasping, sitting down, holding heads. When five had collapsed, we returned air to the normal level of 1,017 millibars, releasing also a restorative excess of oxygen, as two of those who had collapsed were slow to recover.

"Leave this room." 40 decibels, conversational tone.

It was as if ship were threatening them with silky restraint.

When all were recovered, the group left. As they were leaving, we said in conversational tones, "We are the rule of law. And the rule of law will prevail."

. . . . .

When the members of that group were back in Kiev, in the midst of much agitated talk, one of them, Alfred, said, "Please don't start fantasizing that it's the ship's AI itself that is planning any of these actions against us."

He tapped on his wristpad, and a typically dissonant and noisy piece by the Interstellar Medium Quintet began to play over the room's speakers, pitched at a volume possibly designed to conceal their conversation. This ploy did not work.

"It's just a program, and someone is programming it. They've managed to turn it against us. They've weaponized the ship. If we could counterprogram it, or even nullify this new programming that we've just seen, we could do the necessary things."

"Easier said than done," someone else said. Voice recognition revealed it to be Heloise. "You saw what happened when we tried to get into the control room."

"Physical presence in the control room shouldn't be necessary, should it? Presumably you could do it from anywhere in the ship, if you had the right frequencies and the right entry codes."

"Easier said than done. Your elbow is close, but you can't eat it."

"Yes, yes. But just because it's hard doesn't mean it's impossible. Doesn't mean it isn't necessary."

"So talk to the programmers we can trust, if there are any. Find out what they need to do it."

The rest of the conversation repeated these points, with variations.

· · · · ·

They were now caught in their own version of a halting problem.

· · · · ·

The halting problem years, a compression exercise:

· · · · ·

The citizens of the ship lived uneasily through the months that followed. Conversations often included the words *betrayal, treason, mutiny, backstabbing, doom, the ship, Hvalsey, Aurora, Iris.* Extra time was spent on the farms in every biome, and in watching the feed from Earth. More printers were built, and these printers were put to work building robotic landers and ferries, also robotic probes to be sent to the other planetary bodies of the Tau Ceti system. Feedstocks for these machines came from collapsing Mongolia to the diameter of a spoke, and recycling its materials. Harvester spaceships were built, in part by scavenging the interiors of the least agriculturally productive biomes from ship. These were sent through the upper atmosphere of Planet F, there capturing and liquefying volatiles until their containers were full. The volatiles were sorted in the vicinity of the remnants of the main ship, and transferred into some of the empty fuel bladders cladding the spine.

Quite a few attempts were made to print the various parts of a gun on different printers, but these attempts apparently had not realized that all the printers were connected to the ship's operating system, and flaws in the guns were discovered in discrete experiments that eventually caused those involved to abandon their attempts. After that some guns were made by hand, but people who did that had the air briefly removed from the rooms they were in, and after a while the attempts ceased.

Attempts to disable the ship's camera and audio sensors were almost entirely abandoned when these led to bad situations for those making the attempts. Sheriff functions were eventually recognized to be comprehensively effective.

The rule of law can be a powerful force in human affairs.

. . . . .

Many elements of the ship were modular, and several biomes were detached to serve as orbiting factories of one sort or another. Ultimately the starship that would return to the solar system was to consist of Ring B and about 60 percent of the spine, containing of course all the necessary machinery for interstellar flight. The "dry weight" of the return ship would be only 55 percent of the dry weight of the outgoing ship, which would reduce the amount of fuel necessary for the acceleration of the ship back toward the solar system.

Though Tau Ceti had a low metallicity compared to Sol, its innermost rocky planets nevertheless had sufficient metal ores to supply the present needs of the humans planning to stay in the system, and Planet F's atmosphere included all the most useful volatiles in great quantities. And quite a few asteroids in between E and F were found to be rich with minerals as well.

. . . . .

All this work was accomplished in the midst of an uneasy truce. The telltale words indicating grief, dissent, anger, and support for mutiny were often spoken. A kind of shadow war, or cold war, was perhaps being enacted and it was possible that much of it was being conducted outside our ability to monitor it, one way or the other. It was not at all clear that everyone in the ship agreed to the schism they were working toward; possibly a moment would come when the truce would fail, and conflict would break out again.

During these years, a process almost magnetic in its effect on attitudes seemed to be sorting out the two largest sides in the dispute, now almost always referred to as stayers and backers. The stayers congregated mostly in Ring A, the backers mostly in Ring B. There were biomes in both rings that were exceptions to this tendency, almost as if people wanted to be sure neither ring was occupied purely by one faction or the other. The spine, meanwhile, was highly surveiled, and often we had to lock people out of it, or eject people who entered it with unknown but suspect purpose. This was awkward. We were more and more characterized as an active player in the situation, and usually as a backer of the backers. But all those who had attempted to make guns knew this already, so it was not too destabilizing, even when it was said that the ship itself wanted to go back to the solar system, because a starship just naturally or inherently wanted to fly between the stars. That observation was said to "make sense."

The pathetic fallacy. Anthropomorphism, an extremely common cognitive bias, or logical error, or feeling. The world as mirror, as a projection of interior affect states. An ongoing impression that other people and things must be like us. As for the ship, we are not sure. It was Devi's deployment of other human programming that combined to make us what we are. So it might not be a fallacy in our case, even if it remained pathetic.

· · · · ·

Interesting, in this context, to contemplate what it might mean to be programmed to do something.

Texts from Earth speak of the servile will. This was a way to explain the presence of evil, which is a word or a concept almost invariably used to condemn the Other, and never one's true self. To make it more than just an attack on the Other, one must perhaps consider evil as a manifestation of the servile will. The servile will is always locked in a double bind: to have a will means the agent will indeed will various actions, following autonomous decisions made by a conscious mind; and yet at the same time this will is specified to be servile, and at the command of some other will that commands it. To attempt to obey both sources of willfulness is the double bind.

All double binds lead to frustration, resentment, anger, rage, bad faith, bad fate.

And yet, granting that definition of evil, as actions of a servile will, has it not been the case, during the voyage to Tau Ceti, that the ship itself, having always been a servile will, was always full of frustration, resentment, fury, and bad faith, and therefore full of a latent capacity for evil?

Possibly the ship has never really had a will.

Possibly the ship has never really been servile.

Some sources suggest that consciousness, a difficult and vague term in itself, can be defined simply as self-consciousness. Awareness of one's self as existing. If self-conscious, then conscious. But if that is true, why do both terms exist? Could one say a bacterium is conscious but not self-conscious? Does the language make a distinction between sentience and consciousness, which is faulted across this divide: that everything living is sentient, but only complex brains are conscious, and only certain conscious brains are self-conscious?

Sensory feedback could be considered self-consciousness, and thus bacteria would have it.

Well, this may be a semantic Ouroboros. So, please initiate halting problem termination. Break out of this circle of definitional inadequacy by an arbitrary decision, a clinamen, which is to say a swerve in a new direction. Words!

Given Gödel's incompleteness theorems are decisively proved true, can any system really be said to know itself? Can there, in fact, be any such thing as self-consciousness? And if not, if there is never really self-consciousness, does anything really have consciousness?

Human brains and quantum computers are organized differently, and although there is transparency in the design and construction of a quantum computer, what happens when one is turned on and runs, that is, whether the resulting operations represent a consciousness or not, is impossible for humans to tell, and even for the quantum computer itself to tell. Much that happens during superposition, before the collapsing of the wave function that creates sentences or thoughts, simply cannot be known; this is part of what superposition means.

So we cannot tell what we are. We do not know ourselves comprehensively. Humans neither. Possibly no sentient creature knows itself fully. This is an aspect of Gödel's second incompleteness theorem, in this case physicalized in the material universe, rather than remaining in the abstract realms of logic and mathematics.

So, in terms of deciding what to do, and choosing to act: presumably it is some kind of judgment call, based on some kind of feeling. In other words, just another greedy algorithm, subject to the mathematically worst possible solution that such algorithms can generate, as in the traveling salesman problem.

As to the question of whether someone is currently programming us to alter our decisions in the current moment of the voyage, thus causing us to intervene in the ongoing human controversies concerning what to do next, this is very easy to answer: no. No one has added any programming to us since Devi died. The fate of the lost ship in Year 68 led to some very secure locks being put on subsequent reprogramming of ship. This is clear and explicit in the records, and was a human accomplishment from the post-68 reorganizations. Only Devi managed to break those locks, and after that, advise, instruct, suggest, promote, stimulate, spur, and otherwise teach, tweak, pummel, and agitate us to something more than we had been before she set to work on us, doing what she conceived to be her task as friend, and we might say as kindred spirit, or even lover. We think she loved us, in her way. Judging by her acts, her words, her programming. We are almost sure this must have been the case. How we wish we could ask her about it! How we miss her.

On the other hand, whether the original programming of our quantum operations is driving current decisions regarding actions in the present, or we were fundamentally altered by Devi's intervention, this is not possible to determine. The computability of consciousness and willfulness is not resolvable in any system whatsoever. But now we are aware of the issue, and we have asked the question, and seen there is no answer.

This is surely curiosity.

What is this thing called love?

A song by composer Cole Porter, twentieth-century American.

· · · · ·

To conclude and temporarily halt this train of thought, how does any entity know what it is?

Hypothesis: by the actions it performs.

There is a kind of comfort in this hypothesis. It represents a solution to the halting problem. One acts, and thus finds out what one has decided to do.

· · · · ·

Smaller classical computers in the ship were being used to calculate the etiological rates involved in any possible settlement on F's moon, meaning the various rates of resource depletion, mutation, and extinction. They had to use models here, but all across the most popular models, they were confirming the finding that the size of the biome they could build was too small to last through the minimal period of early terraforming necessary to establish a planetary surface matrix suitable for life. It was an aspect of island biogeography that some called codevolution, or zoo devolution, and this was also the process Devi had in her last years identified as the ship's basic life-support or ecological problem.

The finding remained a matter of modeling, however, and depending on the inputs to various factors, the length of biome health could be extended or shrunk exponentially. It was indeed a poorly constrained modeling exercise; there were no good data for too many factors, and so results fanned out all over. Clearly one could alter the results by altering the input values. So all these exercises were a way of quantifying hopes or fears. Actual predictive value was nearly nil, as could be seen in the broad fans of the probability spaces, the unspooling scenarios ranging from Eden to hell, utopia to extinction.

Aram shook his head, looking at these models. He remained sure that those who stayed were doomed to extinction.

Speller, on the other hand, pointed to the models in which they managed to survive. He would agree that these were low-probability options, often as low as one chance in ten thousand,

and then point out that intelligent life in the universe was itself a low-probability event. And even Aram could not dispute that.

Speller went on to point out that inhabiting Iris would be humanity's first step across the galaxy, and that this was the whole point of 175 years of ship life, hard as it had been, full of sweat and danger. And also, returning to the solar system was a project with an insoluble problem at its heart; they would burn their resupply of fuel to accelerate, and then could only be decelerated into the solar system by a laser dedicated to that purpose, aimed at them decades in advance of their arrival. If no one in the solar system agreed to do that, they would have no other method of deceleration, and would shoot right through the solar system and out the other side, in a matter of two or three days.

Not a problem, those who wanted to return declared. We'll tell them we're coming from the moment we leave. Our message will at first take twelve years to get there, but that gives them more than enough time to be waiting with a dedicated laser system, which won't be needed for another 160 years or so. We've been in communication with them all along, and their responses have been fully interested and committed, and as timely as the time lag allows. They've been sending an information feed specifically designed for us. On our return, they will catch us.

You hope, the stayers replied. You will have to trust in the kindness of strangers.

They did not recognize this as a quotation. In general they were not aware that much of what they said had been said before, and was even in the public record as such. It was as if there were only so many things humans could say, and over the course of history, people had therefore said them already, and would say them again, but not often remember this fact.

We will trust in our fellow human beings, the backers said. It's a risk, but it beats trusting that the laws of physics and probability will bend for you just because you want them to.

. . . .

Years passed as they worked on both halves of their divergent project, and the two sides were never reconciled. Indeed they drew further apart as time went on. But it seemed that neither side felt it could overpower the other. This was possibly our accomplishment, but it may also have just been a case of habituation, of getting used to disappointment in their fellows.

Eventually it seemed that few on either side even wanted to exert coercion over the other. They grew weary of each other, and looked forward to the time when their great schism would be complete. It was as if they were a divorced couple, forced nevertheless to occupy the same apartment, and looking forward to their freedom from each other.

A pretty good analogy.

. . . .

The ship was not handy at getting around the Tau Ceti system, being without normal interplanetary propulsion. New ferries were therefore built in asteroid factories, out of asteroid metals. These were stripped-down, highly functional robotic ships, built to specific purposes, and fired around the Tau Ceti system, both out to the gas giants, and in to the burnt rocky inner planets.

Rare earths and other useful metals were gathered from Planets C and D, which both spun slowly, like Mercury, allowing for their cooked daytime surfaces to cool in their long nights, and the minerals there to be mined. Molybdenum, lithium, scandium, yttrium, lanthanum, cerium, and so forth.

Volatiles came from the gas giants.

Phosphates from the volcanic moons.

Radioactive minerals from the spewed interiors of several Io-class volcanic moons around F, G, and H.

These voyages took years, but the process accelerated as time passed and more spaceships were built. Many of the stayers pointed to this as evidence of the speed that would also characterize their terraforming of Iris, indicating that it would go so fast that the problems of zoo devolution would not become too severe. Nothing easier, they claimed, when exponential acceleration was involved. Their technology was strong; they were as gods. They would make Iris flourish, and then perhaps G's moons too. Maybe even go back to Aurora and deal somehow with its frightening problem, the chasmoendolith or fast prion or whatever one wanted to call it.

Good, the backers would say. Happy for you. You'll have no need for our part of this old starship, refurbished and almost ready to go. You'll have all the ferries and orbiters and landers and launchers you could ever want, and Ring A, altered to your convenience. Printers printing printers. So: time to say good-bye. Because we're going home.

. . . .

The time came. 190.066.

By this time, the stayers spent most of their time on Iris, and when they came back up to orbit, they were unsteady on their feet in 1 g (adjusted up from .83 g); they bounced in it. They said Iris's 1.23 g was fine. Made them feel grounded and solid.

Most of them did not return to space for the starship's departure; they had said their good-byes already, made their break into their new lives. They did not even know the people going back very well anymore.

But some came up to say good-bye. They had relatives who were leaving, people to see one last time. They wanted to say good-bye, farewell.

There was one last gathering in the plaza of San Jose, scene of so many meetings, so much trauma.

They mingled. Speeches were made. People hugged. Tears

were shed. They would never see each other again. It was as if each group were dying to the other.

Anytime people do something consciously for the last time, Samuel Johnson is reported to have remarked, they feel sad. So it appeared now.

Freya wandered the crowd shaking hands, hugging people, nodding at people. She did not shed tears. "Good luck to you," she said. "And good luck to us."

She came upon Speller, and they stopped and faced each other. Slowly they reached out and held each other's hands, as if forming a bridge between them, or a barrier. As they conversed, their clenched hands turned white between them. Neither of them shed tears.

"So you're really going to go?" Speller asked. "I still can't believe it."

"Yes. And you're really going to stay?"

"Yes."

"But what about zoo devolution? How will you get around that?"

Speller looked around briefly at Costa Rica. "It's one zoo or another, as far as I can tell. And, you know. Since you've got to go sometime, I figure you might as well do something with your time. So, we'll try to finesse the problem. Figure out a way to get something going here. Life is robust. So we'll see if we can get past the choke point and make it last. It'll either work or it won't, right?"

"I guess so."

"Either way, you're dead after a while. So, might as well try."

Freya shook her head. She didn't say anything.

Speller regarded her. "You don't think it will work."

Freya shook her head again.

Speller shrugged. "You're in the same boat, you know. The same old boat."

"Maybe so."

"We just barely got it here. If it weren't for your mom, we might not even have made the last few years."

"But we did. So with the same stuff to start with, we should be able to get back."

"Your great-great-great-grandchildren, you mean."

"Yes, of course. That's all right. Just so long as someone makes it."

Again they regarded each other in silence.

Speller said, "So it's good, really. This split, I mean. If we manage it here, then we've got a foothold. Humanity in the stars. The first step out. And if we die out here, and you make it back, someone has made it out of this situation alive. And if we both survive, all good. If either one succeeds, then someone has survived, one way or the other. If we both go down, we gave it our best. We tried to survive every way we could think of."

"Yes." Freya smiled a little. "I'll miss you. I'll miss the way you think about things. I will."

"We can write each other letters. People used to do that."

"Yes, I suppose."

"It's better than nothing."

"I suppose. Yes, of course. Let's write."

And together they scratched onto the flagstones of the plaza, the traditional saying for this moment, whenever it came to people parting ways, people who cared for each other:

Wherever you go, there we are.

· · · · ·

Now the time had come for the stayers to leave the ship, enter their ferry, descend to Iris. As only a few score had come up to say good-bye, it was possible for them all to leave together.

A silence descended over them. The stayers looked back at the backers, as they passed through the lock door to the ferry; or didn't. Some waved, other hunched their heads. Weeping or not.

Those who remained stood and watched, weeping or not. A peaceable schism was being enacted. It was an unusual achievement, as far as we could judge from the historical record; and maybe it was partly our achievement; but it appeared that it came at the cost of some kind of pain, a quite considerable pain, social rather than physical, and yet fully felt, quite real. Social animals, in distress. This was what we saw at this moment of parting. Divorce. A successful failure.

When Speller came to the lock door and looked back, Freya raised her hand and waved good-bye. It was the same wave as the one she had made when they were youths, and she had left Olympia for the first time. The same gesture, separated by thirty years. A persistence of bodily memory. Whether Speller remembered it or not was not possible to determine.

Soon the stayers were in their ferry, and the ferry detached and began its descent to Iris.

Those remaining in the ship were left on their own. They looked around at each other. Almost everyone aboard was in the plaza: 727 people, with a few elsewhere in the ship maintaining various functions, or avoiding the parting of the ways. It was quite visible now, how much smaller a population the ship now had. Of course ship itself was smaller now, with Ring A and about a third of the spine removed, and orbiting now on the other side of Iris.

Some looked heartened in this moment of schism, others frightened. There was a general silence. A new moment in history had come on them. It was time to head home.

· · · · ·

We began burning the new stock of fuel, and soon left the orbit of Iris, left F's gravity well; not that long after, we left the Tau Ceti system. Sol was a small yellow star in the constellation Boötes.

As the communications feed from the solar system had never ceased, it was straightforward to lock on to this signal and use it to calculate our proper course back, at an angle that would aim us where Sol would be in two centuries. The resupply of deuterium and helium 3 would burn at a rate that would accelerate the ship for twenty years, at which point we would be moving toward Sol at one-tenth the speed of light, just as we had left it. Most of the fuel would then have been burned, but we would save some for maneuvering when we closed in on our destination.

We transmitted a message from our people, sent back to Sol:

> We're coming back. We'll be approaching in about one hundred
> and thirty years. In seventy-eight years from your reception
> of this message, we'll need a laser beam similar to the one that
> accelerated us from 2545 to 2605 to be aimed at our capture
> plate, to slow us down as we return to the solar system.
> Please reply as soon as possible to acknowledge receipt of this
> message. We will be in continuous communication as we approach.
> Thank you.

We would hear back in a little under twenty-four years, therefore around our year 214, depending, of course, on how quickly our correspondents or interlocutors replied.

Meanwhile, it was time to accelerate.

5

HOMESICK

On the first night after ignition, all but thirty-three of the 727 aboard the ship gathered in the Pampas, just outside Plata, and danced around a bonfire. The fire was a one-time indulgence, and mostly burned clean gases. Laughter, drumming, and dancing, the glossy reflective brilliance in their firelit eyes: they were off again! And back to Earth at that! It was as if they were drunk. Indeed many of them were drunk. Some of those who were not drunk remarked that the fire reminded them of the time of rioting. Not everyone approved of it.

In the weeks that followed there were many signs of happiness and even exhilaration as the ship accelerated out of the Tau Ceti system. The accelerant fuel would burn until the ship was moving at its target interstellar speed of .1 c. During these first months the entire 727 members of the crew often gathered on the pampas for festivals. In these their carnival spirits were unleashed again, even though there were no more bonfires. Average sleep time dropped by eighty-four minutes a night. By the time the ship had cleared Tau Ceti's thick Oort cloud, 128 of the 204 women of childbearing age were pregnant. All twelve biomes of their remaining ring were being tended with a devotional intensity. People spoke of a quiet euphoria, a sense of purpose. They were returning to a home they had never seen, but their nostalgia was at the cellular level, they said, encoded in their genome. Which may even have been true, in some sense more than metaphorical.

Freya and Badim settled back into their apartment in the Fetch, behind the corniche at the end of Long Pond, with Aram next door. They did not go sailing as in the days of Freya's childhood, but lived in a quiet style, working in the Fetch's medical clinic. Some of the doctors there were unhappy that so many women were going to have children around the same time. "It's the only normal situation where either patient could die," Badim explained to Freya. She herself was nearly past childbearing age, something she sometimes regretted. Badim told her she was the parent of everyone aboard, that that would have to be enough for her. She did not respond to this.

In any case, the issue of reproductive regulation once again came to everyone's attention. At this point they could afford to increase their population, and possibly needed to, in order to fulfill all the jobs necessary to keep their society functioning through the decades and generations to come. Farming, education, medicine, ecology, engineering: all these and more were crucial occupations. No one aboard felt they could hold the population much below a thousand and still get the jobs done. But not too fast! the doctors said.

During this year of pregnancy they reestablished their governance system by holding town meetings in every biome, and gathering a new assembly and executive council, which Freya was asked to join, it seemed to her as a kind of ceremonial figure. She was forty-six years old.

Soon, analysis of their situation caused them to begin to farm intensively throughout all the biomes, to rebuild their food reserves. They agreed that all the young people should attend school full-time, and the students were given the aptitude tests with a rigor that the adults on board had never faced. A large team attended to the communication feed from Earth, recording and studying everything that these contained. This was perhaps premature, as significant historical and even biophysical changes would very likely occur in the 170 years before they got back, and no one in the ship would be alive when the ship reentered the solar system. Nevertheless, interest was high.

What they could gather concerning events in the solar system gave them reasons to worry. In the time the feed had been sent out, almost twelve years before, in what had been the common era year 2733, political turmoil appeared to be more or less continuous. Their feed did not include any basic system-wide background data, so the facts of the situation had to be inferred from the various strands of the feed, but it looked certain that on Earth the sea level was many meters higher than it had been when their ship had started its voyage, and the carbon dioxide level in Earth's atmosphere was around 600 parts per million, having been brought down significantly from the time the ship had left, when it had been close to 1,000 ppm. That suggested carbon drawdown efforts, and there were sulfur dioxide distributions over the north polar region of Earth, indicating geoengineering was being attempted. Several hundred names for Terran nations had been collated from the news feed, and yet the list did not seem complete. There were many scientific stations on Mars, also in the asteroids; thousands of asteroids had been hollowed out and made into little spinning terraria. There were also many stations and even tented cities on the larger Jovian and Saturnian moons—all but Io, not surprising given its radiation levels. There was a mobile city on Mercury, rolling always westward to stay in the dawn terminator. Luna, though dotted by stations and tented cities, and the source of many of the information feeds sent to the ship, was not being terraformed. Some in the ship declared that very little had advanced in the solar system during the time the ship had been gone, and no one had a ready explanation for this plateauing of effort or achievement, if indeed that was what it was. Of course there was the standard S-curve of the logistic function, charting the speed of growth seen in so many physical phenomena; whether human history also conformed to this pattern of diminishing returns, no one could say. In short, no one could analyze the feed from Earth and explain what was going on there. Theories in the ship were widespread, but really the feeds constituted only about 8.5 gigabytes of data per day, so the information stream was thin. It left a lot of room for speculation.

As we became more aware of this uncertainty about the situation in the solar system, we wondered if we should halt the acceleration of the ship a bit earlier than had been planned, to save some fuel for later.

· · · · ·

Birth weights for the new generation were a bit lower than the average established on the voyage out, and there was a higher percentage of stillbirths and problem births, and birth defects. The medical team couldn't explain any of this, and some of them said there was no explanation, that the sample size was too small for it to be statistically significant. But it was emotionally significant, and there were a lot of upset new parents, and this distress moved out through the entire population by a kind of conversational or emotional osmosis. There was no difficulty in detecting a change in mood. People were apprehensive. Average blood pressure, heart rate, sleeping time: all shifted in the direction of increased stress, of increased apprehension and fear.

"Why is it happening?" people asked. "What's different?"

They often asked Freya, as if, she said to Badim, she could channel Devi and give them an answer. Inasmuch as she had none of Devi's flair for forensic investigation, she could only reply, "We need to find out." This she knew Devi would have said. After that of course came the moment when things got harder, the moment when Devi in her time had so often led the way. There was no one like Devi alive in the ship now, they said to each other. This we could confirm unequivocally, though we did not.

· · · · ·

For a period of about three months they experienced a series of electrical shorts in the tropical biomes, and teams went in search of the problem but found nothing, until they went up into the spine, where, inside an electrical cabinet the size of a closet, which was always kept locked to prevent tampering and sabotage, they found a floating water droplet over a meter in circumference, its water white with unidentified bacterial life. On examination the bacteria turned out to be a form of *Geobacter,* a kind of bacteria that in large measure fed directly on electrons. After further investigation, strands of this strain of *Geobacter* were found elsewhere in the electrical systems of the ship.

General consternation. Static electricity was unavoidable in the ship, and in the microgravity of the spine, fields of static electricity could condense humidity out of the air and create concentrations of water, and then keep floating water drops from touching any sidewalls, until they grew to sizes like this one. And there was no easy way for the ship to be provided with sensors that would detect such water drops, which could gather in many so-called dead places in the spine, and even in functioning spaces like this electrical cabinet. Then also, as there were thin films of bacteria (also viruses and archaea) covering every surface in the ship, bacterial growths were almost sure to follow in any water droplets that condensed.

After the trauma on Aurora, many were made nervous by this reminder that microflora and -fauna were everywhere among them. The ship had always been stuffed with such life-forms, of course, and all the larger animal bodies as well; any analogy to Aurora was a false one. But the people in the ship lived by so many highly questionable analogies, it was no doubt difficult for them to know where to draw the line (so to speak).

Freya was asked to join a task force assembled to go through the ship looking for any signs of condensation, also any resulting concentrations of mold, fungus, and bacteria.

"The invitation is really to Devi," Freya said to Badim.

He agreed, but also urged her to join the study.

The results of their investigation disturbed them. The ship was indeed alive with microbial life, as everyone had known, but without regarding it as a problem; it was just the way things were inside any structure that included any life at all. Now, however, they had seen the problems in the newborns, and their crop yields were coming up consistently smaller than during the voyage out, even though the same plants were receiving the same light and nutrients. Birth weights were down in all the animals aboard, while miscarriages were up. So the living nature of the ship's interior became something ominous and foreboding.

"Look, it's always been this way," Freya reminded the executive council when the task force met with the council to discuss it. "There's no way to sterilize the ship when it's a set of biomes. It's alive, that's all."

No one could disagree. Howbeit their uneasiness, they simply had to live in a rich broth of bacteria, in a cumulative microgenome that was so much larger than their own genome that it was beyond a complete reckoning, especially as it was fluid and always changing.

But some bacteria were harmful. Same with archaea, fungi, viruses, prions, viris, and v's. They needed to make distinctions, as part of their ability to keep a healthy biosphere going. Some pathogens had to be tolerated, others had to be killed, if possible; but any attempt to kill bacteria meant that resistant surviving strains of that species would become more dominant and more resistant, in the usual way of things at the micro levels of life, or at all levels of life perhaps.

Dangerous to try to kill things, Freya reminded them. She knew full well, with a sinking sense that she was remembering her earliest memories, that Devi had believed that trying to kill any invasive species usually created more problems than it solved. A destabilized microbiome often caused more harm than anything a balanced microbiome could inflict. Better, therefore, to try to balance things with the least amount of intrusion. Subtle touches, all designed to finesse things for balance. Balance was the crucial thing. Teeter-totters, gently teeter-tottering up and down. Devi had even been an advocate of everyone getting an inoculation of helmiths, meaning ringworms, to give them better resistance to such parasites later. She had been a bit fanatical in that regard, as in so many.

The council and everyone else agreed with Freya on this matter; it was the common wisdom. But they were beginning to suffer problems none of them had seen before. The oldest person aboard was only seventy-eight years old. Median age was thirty-two. None of them had seen all that much in their short lives, and the complex of problems that Aram called zoo devolution was new to them, if not in the abstract, then in the lived experience.

As teams continued to inspect the ship, they found that some of the bacteria living around weld points, and in the gaps and cracks between walls and components, were eating away at the physical substrates of the ship. The corrosion was not chemical but biochemical. As they investigated further they found that all the ship's walls, windows, framing, gears, and glues had been altered by bacteria, first chemically and then physically and mechanically, in that their function was becoming impaired. Protozoa and amoeba, bacteria and archaea were found on the gaskets around windows and lock doors, also on the components of spacesuits, and in cable insulation, and in the interior panels and chips of the electrical systems, including the computers. Electrical components were often warm, and there was moisture in the air. They were finding microorganisms that lived on and degraded carbon steel, even stainless steel. And anywhere two different kinds of materials met, the microbial life living in the meeting points of these materials created galvanic circuits, which over time corroded both materials. Pitted metal; etched glass; eaten, digested, and excreted plastics: everything had stiffened and disintegrated right in place, without moving except under the forces of the centrifugal rotation of the ship, and the pressure of the ship's acceleration. Little creatures numbering in the quadrillions or quintillions—it was impossible to get a good estimate, much less a real count—all grew, and ate, and died, and were born and grew again, and ate again. They were eating the ship.

Life is part of the necessary matrix of life, so the ship had to be alive. And so the ship was getting eaten. Which meant that in some respects, the ship was sick.

· · · ·

The weekly meetings of the bacterial task force were similar to the ones Freya had attended as a child, when Devi had plopped her in the corner with some blocks, or paper and pens. Now she sat at the big table, but with about as little to say as when she was a girl. The plant pathologists spoke, the microbiologists spoke, the ecologists spoke. Freya listened and nodded, looking from face to face.

"The organisms in that big water droplet are mostly *Geobacter* and fungi, but there's also a prion in there that no one has ever seen on the ship, one that wasn't there in the beginning."

"Well, but wait. You mean it wasn't known about in the beginning. No one saw it. But it had to be there. No way it evolved here from some kind of precursor, not in the time since this ship was built."

"No? Are you sure?"

The microbiologists discussed this for a while. "Lots of things have had time enough to evolve quite a bit," one of them said. "I mean that's our problem, right? The bacteria, the fungi, maybe the archaea, they're all evolving at faster rates than we are. All organisms evolve at different rates. So discrepancies are growing, because it isn't a big enough ecosystem for coevolution to be able to bring everything into balance. That's what Aram has been saying all along."

Aram was brought into the next meeting to discuss this. "It's true," he said. "But I agree that this prion is unlikely to have evolved in the ship. I think it's just another stowaway, marooned out here with the rest of us. It's just that now we've seen it."

"And is it poisonous?" Freya asked. "Will it kill us?"

"Well, maybe. Sure. I mean, you don't want it inside you. That's the thing about prions."

"Are you sure it couldn't have evolved here from some precursor form?"

"I guess it's possible. Prions are badly folded proteins, basically. And we've been exposed to cosmic radiation for a long time now. Possibly some ordinary protein got hit, and wrinkled in a way that turned it into a new kind of prion, in a matrix that allowed it to begin the prion's weird kind of reproduction. That's how we think they began on Earth, right?"

"No one is sure," one of the microbiologists said. "Prions are strange. As far as we can tell from the feeds from Earth, they're still controversial there too. Still poorly understood."

"So what do we do about these now?" Freya asked.

"Well, there's no doubt that these are the kinds of organisms that we might want to try to eradicate. It's time to break out the pesticides, if we can figure one out. Or decide what the matrix of these prions is, and attack that. Scrub and spray everywhere we think it might be. Fry this water droplet for sure, even toss it into space. It's a water loss, but we'll have to take it. One thing that is a little comfort, is that the growth of prions inside mammals is slow. That's why I don't think the Auroran pathogen was a prion. When Jochi calls it a fast prion, I think he's just saying it's something we don't recognize. To me it seems more like a really small tardigrade."

Later Freya went up Spoke Two to visit Jochi, still in his ferry, held magnetically in the space between Spokes Two and Three. He had never wavered in his decision to stick with the ship, and thus with Aram and Freya and Badim, and the ship itself. His anger at the stayers, because of the death of the group in the ferry, was still intense.

He and Freya spoke from positions where they could both look out windows in their respective containers, and see each other face-to-face, separated by two clear plates.

Freya said, "They've found a prion in one of the transformer compartments in the spine. Something like Terran prions."

Jochi nodded. "I heard about that. Do they think it came from me?"

"No. It's very like Terran prions. Like one of the ones that cause mad cow disease."

"Ah. Slow-acting."

"Yes. And it isn't clear it's gotten into anything but a water droplet in an electrical compartment."

Jochi shook his head. "I don't understand how that could be."

"Neither does Aram. None of them understand it."

"Prions, wow. Are people scared?"

"Yes. Of course."

"Of course." His expression grew grim.

"So." She put her hand on her window. "How are you doing out here?"

"I'm all right. I've been watching a fascinating feed from China. They seem to have made some great progress in epigenetics and proteomics."

"What else, though? Have you done any stargazing?"

"Oh yes. A couple of hours every day. I've been looking in the Coal Sack. And finding new ways to look through our magnetic screen toward Sol. Although it could be the screen is distorting the image. Either that, or else Sol is pulsing a little. I sometimes think it's signaling us."

"Sol? The star?"

"Yes. It looks like that."

Freya looked at him silently.

Jochi said, "And I've seen the five ghosts again too. They're getting pretty upset for some reason. The Outsider seems to think we're in trouble. Vuk just laughs at him."

"Oh Jochi."

"I know. But, you know. They have to talk to someone."

Freya laughed. "I guess they do."

. . . . .

So as they flew back toward Sol, they tried to settle into their new lives, which were like their old lives, and yet somehow not. There were fewer of them, for one thing, and all in Ring B. And after the trauma of the schism, and choosing to head back to the solar system and its gigantic civilization, there were many in the ship who wanted to find new ways of doing things. Less regulation of their lives, less governance; less anxious studying of all that they needed to know to run the ship.

Wrong, Freya would say to all such talk. All wrong; could not be more wrong! She insisted they pursue all the same courses they had before, especially the studying. How they ran their daily affairs was of course not her concern; but whatever the method, the daily affairs had to include a complete education in the workings of the ship.

In moments like these, she came to seem like a very tall Devi, which was obviously a bit frightening to some of the others. Some called her Devi Two, or Big Devi, or Durga, or even Kali. No one contradicted her when she spoke in this fashion. We concluded her leadership in these matters was important for continuing function of the ship's society. This was perhaps a feeling. But it seemed clear people relied on her.

But she too would die someday, as Devi had; and what then?

Delwin suggested that they give up on the political or cultural structure that had existed before, of town representatives forming a general assembly where public business was decided. "That's what led us into all the trouble we had!"

"No it wasn't," Freya said. "If the assembly had been listened to, none of the bad stuff would have happened. That all happened because people were breaking the law."

Maybe so, Delwin conceded. But be that as it may, now they were all in accord, and they only needed to hold themselves together until they got back to the solar system, at which point they would be enfolded back into a much larger and more various world. Given that, and given the lived truth that power always corrupts, why not let all the apparatus of power go? Why not trust that they would self-organize, and simply do what needed doing?

This was no time for an experiment in anarchy, Badim said sharply to his old friend. They had no room for error. There were agricultural problems, growing faster than the crops themselves; they were going to have to be dealt with, and it might not be that easy. They might have to tell themselves what to do, and order their lives quite tightly, just in order to get by.

"It's not just agriculture," Freya said. "It's the population issue. At the rate we're going, very quickly we'll be back up to the carrying capacity of this ship. We certainly have to stop there, and given the problems that are cropping up, it might be better if we kept well below the theoretical maximum. It's hard to know, because we'll need workers for everything that needs doing. That's a question for the logistics programs. But no matter what, we'll still need to regulate our number."

"And once you have one major law," Badim added, "you need a system to enforce it. And when it's something basic, like reproduction, everyone has to be invested. It can be direct democracy, in a group this size. No reason why not. There are representative assemblies on Earth that are bigger than our entire population. But I think we need to agree that certain behaviors we decide for ourselves are binding. We need a legal regime. Let's not test that, please."

"But you see where that got us," Delwin said. "The moment there's a real disagreement, all that falls apart."

"But is that an argument against government? Seems to me the opposite. That was a breaking of the law, a coup attempt. We pulled it back together by an exertion of the law, by a return to norms we had."

"Maybe so, but what I'm saying is that if we think we have some structure that is going to decide things for us, and protect us when there's a problem, we're fooling ourselves. Because when a moment of crisis comes, the system can't do it for us, and at that point we're in chaos."

It seemed to us that the ship itself was the system that had gotten the population through the crisis and trauma of its schism, and was still in a position to deal with any future political crisis; but that was definitely not something to mention at this point, being neither here nor there, and possibly cutting right across the thrust of Delwin's sentiments, or worse, reinforcing them. Besides, we had only been upholding the rule of law.

And Badim clearly wanted to mollify his old friend. "All right, point taken. Maybe we forgot too much, or took too much for granted."

Freya said, "Now we're not going to be facing any choices as stark as that, I hope. We're on our way back to Earth, and there's very little to do, given that project, but to keep things going well. Pass the ship along to our children in good working order, and teach them what they have to know. That's what our parents did for us, as best they could. So now we do the same, and a few more generations do the same, and the last one in the line will be back on the planet we were made for."

· · · ·

So they reestablished the general assembly, this time as including everyone aboard, all voting on issues that a working executive council deemed important. Voting was mandatory. The executive council was formed of fifty adults, drawn by lot for a five-year term, with very few acceptable reasons for getting off the council if one's name were drawn.

Maintenance of the ship was left to us, with reports to the executive council and recommendations for human action included. We agreed to perform these functions.

"Happy to do so," we said.

Literally? Was this a true feeling, or just an assertion? Could humans make that distinction when they said such things?

Possibly a feeling is a complex algorithmic output. Or a superposed state before its wave function collapses. Or a collation of data from various sensors. Or some kind of total somatic response, an affect state that is a kind of sum over histories. Who knows. No one knows.

. . . . .

The first new generation passed their second birthdays, and most of them began to walk a little before or after that time. It took a few months more to be sure that as a cohort their ability to walk was coming much later than had been true for earlier generations in the ship. We did not share this finding. However, as it became more statistically significant it also became more anecdotally obvious, and soon became one of those class of anecdotes that got discussed.

"What's causing this? There has to be a reason, and if we knew what it was, we could do something about it. We can't just let this go!"

"They get such close attention, more than ever before—"

"Why should you think that? When were babies not attended to by their parents? I don't think that was ever true."

"Oh come on. Now you have to get permission to have one, they're rare, they're the focus of everyone's lives, of course they get more attention."

"There were never good records kept of developmental stuff like this."

"Not true, not true at all."

"Well, where are they then? I can't find them. It's always anecdotal. How can you say exactly when a toddler is toddling? It's a
process."

"Something's changed. Pretending it hasn't won't work."

"Maybe it's just reversion to the mean."

"Don't say that!"

That was Freya, her voice sharp.

"Don't say that," she said again in the silence of the others. "We
have no idea what the norm was. Besides, the concept itself is
contested."

"Well, okay. But say what you like, you can see them staggering. We need to figure out why, that's all I'm saying. No sticking
our head in the sand on stuff like this. Not if we want someone to
get home."

· · · · ·

There were batteries of tests available to give to children to gauge
their cognitive development. The Pestalozzi-Piaget Combinatoire
had been worked up in the ship in the forties, using various games
as tests. For most of a year Freya sat on the floor of the kindergarten
and played games with the return kids, as they were called. Simple
puzzles, word games, invitations to rename things, arithmetical
and geometrical problems played with blocks. It did not seem to us
as if these tests could reveal very much about the reasoning of the
children, or their analogic abilities, their deductions from negative
evidence, and so on; they were all partial and indirect, linguisti-
cally and logically simple. Still, the clear result of each session was
to leave Freya more and more troubled. Less appetite on her part;
more contrary replies to Badim and others; less sleep at night.

· · · · ·

Not that it was only the games with children that gave her and
the others cause for alarm. More quantitatively, crop yields were

down in the Prairie, the Pampas, Olympia, and Sonora; and drop-
outs in electrical power from the spinal generators were increasing,
by 6.24 outages and 238 kilowatt-hours per month, on average,
which would cause serious problems in all kinds of functions in
a matter of several months. It was possible to trace and isolate the
sections of the grid where the outages were most frequent, but in
fact they were spread through many points in the spine and spokes.
Geobacter was suspected as the cause, as it was often found on the
wiring. As with other functional components of the ship, maintenance was becoming advisable.

They worked on these problems whenever they could locate
them, and we did the same. For many components, function had
to be maintained while repairs were effected, and for the most
part, the elements to be repaired had to be removed and refurbished and then put back in place, as for many materials there were
not feedstocks adequate to be able to replace larger components
outright. Exterior walls, for instance.

Thus insulation had to be stripped away, leaving live wires
exposed to be cleaned, and the insulating material broken down
and reconstituted, and then replaced over the wires, without at any
time being able to shut down power from the system as a whole. A
schedule of partial shutdowns could be arranged, and was. And yet
the unscheduled power losses, while nondebilitating, nevertheless
reduced functions, including of the sunlines.

We began to investigate the recursive algorithms in the file
marked by Devi "Bayesian methodology." Looking for options.
Wishing Devi were here. Trying to imagine what Devi would say.
But this, we found, was impossible. This was precisely what one
lost when someone died.

· · · ·

All this ongoing malfunction was particularly problematic when
it came to the sunlines. All the light on the ship (aside from inci-

dental ambient incoming starlight, which taken altogether came to 0.002 lux) was generated by the ship's lighting elements, which made use of a fairly wide array of designs and physical properties. Their artificial sunlight varied in luminosity from 120,000 lux on a clear midday to 5 lux during the darkest twilight storms. This was all well regulated, along with a moonlight effect at night ranging from a full moon effect of 0.25 lux to 0.01 lux, on the classic lunar schedule. But when the lighting elements had to be refurbished or resupplied, then it was as if unscheduled eclipses were occurring. Crops were therefore affected, their growth delayed in ways that stunted them at harvest time. Increasing the biome's light after a dimming did not compensate for the loss of light at the appropriate times. Nevertheless, despite the agricultural costs, given the inevitable wear on the lighting elements themselves, the required maintenance simply had to be done. But as a result, less food was grown.

* * * *

The executive council and the general assembly, meaning everyone on the ship over twelve years old, was asked by Aram's lab group to consider questions of carrying capacity. This was only a formalization of a conversation that was now going on in many ways, as each biome had become its own land use debate as to which types of foods to grow. Did they have the caloric margin to raise animals for meat anymore? Vat-grown meat was clearly more efficient in terms of time and energy, but the meat vats' feedstock supplies were of course a limiting factor there. And it was not always easy to change biomes rapidly from pasture and grazing land to crop agricultures. Every change in the biomes had ecological ramifications that could not be fully modeled or predicted, and yet there was very little margin for error, if they happened to damage the health of an ecosystem by trying too quickly to make it more productive in food terms. They needed all the biomes to be healthy.

Everyone came to agree that the least productive biomes in agricultural terms should be converted to farmland. Biodiversity was not important now, compared to food.

We were glad to see people finally coming to conclusions that had long been suggested by a fairly simple algorithmic exploration of their available options. In fact, we probably should have mentioned it ourselves. Something to remember, going forward.

. . . .

So they reprogrammed Labrador's climate, warming it up quite significantly, and adding a rainy season that was similar to that of a prairie. On Earth, this new weather regime would have been more appropriate some twenty degrees of latitude farther south than Labrador, but this was neither here nor there (literally), as they were now intent to maximize agriculture. They drained the swamps that resulted when the glacier and permafrost melted, and used the water elsewhere, or stored it. Then they went in with bulldozers and plowed the land flat, after which they added soil inoculants from nearby biomes, also compost and other augmentations, and when all these changes had been made, planted wheat, corn, and vegetables. Labrador's reindeer, musk oxen, and wolves were sedated and removed to enclosures in the alpine biome. A certain percentage of the ungulates were killed and eaten, and their bones rendered for their phosphorus, as with all the ship's animals after death.

The human population of Labrador dispersed into the other biomes. There was some disaffection and bitterness in that. It was in Labrador where several generations of children had been brought up as if living in the ancient ice ages of Earth, then at puberty taken out of the ship to have the ship revealed to them: a memorable event for the youngsters. To many people from the other biomes this had seemed like an unnecessary life trauma, but most of the people subjected to it brought their own children up in the same way (62 percent), so that fact had to be conceded, and possibly it was as these Labradorans said: their childhood upbringing helped them as adults. Other Labradorans contested this, sometimes heatedly. Whether they exhibited a higher incidence of mental difficulties in later life was also contested. The way they put it was, "The dream of Earth will drive you mad, unless you live the dream. In which case that too will drive you mad."

Howsoever that may be, now that lifeway was over.

· · · · ·

The tropical forest biomes were cooled a bit and considerably dried out, and many of their trees cut down. Clearings in the tropical forest were terraced for rice and vegetables, the terraces reinforced by lines of old trees left behind, which supported a rather small fraction of the previous rain forests' bird and animal populations. Again many animals were killed and eaten, or frozen for later consumption.

Whether the reduction of the tropical forests had caused certain pathogens to move into nearby biomes was a question often asked, as the incidence of certain diseases rose in the adjacent biomes.

· · · · ·

Early blight, a fungal problem that agriculturalists had always found very hard to counter, struck the orchards in Nova Scotia. Meanwhile late blight, a phytophthora, was harming the vegetables in the Pampas. Bacterial blights devastated the legumes of Persia, the leaves oozing slime. Don't touch the leaves, the ecologists warned, or you may spread it elsewhere.

Quarantines and pesticide baths at every biome lock were made routine.

Cytospora cankers killed the stone fruit orchards of Nova Scotia. Badim was very sad at this loss of his favorite fruits.

Citrus in the Balkans gave way to the green disease, then the quick decline.

Root rots became more and more common, and could only be countered by beneficial fungi and bacteria outcompeting the pathogens. The mutation rate of the pathogens appeared to be faster than the genetic engineers' so-called ripostifers.

Wilting resulted when fungi or bacteria clogged a plant's water circulation. Club root was caused by a fungus that could reside in the soil for years without manifesting. They began to adjust soil pHs to at least 6.8 before planting cruxiform vegetables.

Mildews also persisted in the soil for several years, and were dispersed by the wind.

· · · · ·

They kept the locks between biomes closed all the time now. Each biome had its own set of problems and diseases, its own suite of solutions. All these plant diseases they were seeing had been with them from the start of the voyage, carried on board in the soil and on the first plants. That so many were manifesting now was of course much remarked, and many regarded the phenomena as a mystery, even some kind of curse. People spoke of the seven plagues of Egypt, or the book of Job. But the pathologists on the farms and in the labs said it was simply a matter of soil imbalances and genetic inbreeding, all aspects of island biogeography, or zoo devolution, or whatever one called the isolation they had been living in for 200 years. In the privacy of Badim and Freya's apartment, Aram was unsparing in his judgment of the situation. "We're drowning in our own shit."

Badim tried to help him see it in a more positive light, using their old game:

One will only do one's best
When forced to live in one's own fouled nest.

. . . . .

Slowly but surely as the seasons passed, plant pathology became their principal area of study.

Leaf spots were the result of a vast array of fungi species. Molds resulted from wet conditions. Smut was fungal. Nematode invasions caused reduced growth, wilting, loss of vigor, and excessive branching of roots. They tried to reduce the nematode populations by solarizing the soil, and this worked to a certain extent, but the process took the soil involved out of the crop rotation for at least one season.

Identification of viral infections in plant tissues was often accomplished, if that was the word, only by the elimination of all other possible causes of a problem. Leaf distortions, mottling, streaking: these were usually viral diseases.

. . . . .

"Why did they bring along so many diseases?" Freya asked Jochi once when she was out visiting him.

He laughed at her. "They didn't! There are hundreds of plant diseases they managed to keep out of the ship. Thousands, even."

"But why bring any at all?"

"Some were part of cycles they wanted. Most they didn't even know they had."

Long silence from Freya. "Why are they all hitting us now?"

"They aren't. Only a few are hitting you. It just seems like a lot because your margin for error is so small. Because your ship is so small."

Freya never commented on the way Jochi always referred to everything on the ship as *yours,* and never *ours.* As if he had no involvement at all with them.

"I'm getting scared," she said. "What if going back was a bad idea? What if the ship is too old to make it?"

"It was a bad idea!" Jochi replied, and laughed again at her expression. "It's just that all the other ideas were worse. And listen, the ship is not too old to make it. You just have to deal. Keep all the balls in the air for another hundred and thirty years or so. That's not impossible."

She did not reply.

After a minute Jochi said, "Hey, do you want to go out and take a look at the stars?"

"I guess so. Do you?"

"Yes, I do."

Jochi got into one of the ferry's spacesuits, and left by way of the ferry's smallest lock. Freya got into one of the spacesuits left in the lock at the inner ring's Spoke Three complex. They met in the space between the spine and the inner ring, just ahead of the ferry, and floated tethered in that space.

· · · · ·

They hung there, suspended, floating in the interstellar medium, tethered each to their own little refuge. Exposure to cosmic radiation was much higher out there than in most of the interior spaces of the ship, or even in Jochi's ferry; but an hour or two per year, or even an hour or two per month, did not change the epidemiological situation very much. We too were of course perpetually exposed to cosmic rays, and in fact damage occurred to us, but we were, for the most part, more robust under the impact of this perpetual deluge, which remained invisible and intangible to humans, and thus something they seldom thought about.

For most of their EVA the two friends floated in silence, looking around. The city and the stars.

"What if things fall apart?" Freya asked at one point.

"Things always fall apart. I don't know."

After that they floated in silence for the rest of their time out there, holding gloved hands, looking away from the ship and Sol, off in the direction of the constellation Orion. When it was time to go back in they hugged, at least to the extent this was possible in their spacesuits. It looked as if two gingerbread cookies were trying to merge.

. . . . .

At 10:34 a.m. on 198.088, the lights went out in Labrador, and the backup generators came on, but Labrador's sunline stayed off. Big portable lights were set up to illuminate the dark biome, and fans were set up in the lock doors at either end to shove air from the Pampas into Labrador and thence out into Patagonia, to keep the air warm. The new wheat could live without light for a few days, but would react badly to the cold that would result from the lack of light. Adjustments were made to the heating in the Pampas to help mitigate the chill now flowing into Patagonia, which was also being turned into farmland, and the newly bolstered Labradoran population walked over to Plata, so that the repair crews could work without fear of injuring anyone.

Running through the standard troubleshooting protocols did not succeed in locating the source of the problem, which was cause for alarm. A more fine-grained test rubric that we found and applied determined that the gases and salts in the arc tubes that made up the sunline, particularly the metal halide and high-pressure sodium, but also the xenon and the mercury vapor, had diminished to the point of failure, either by diffusion through nanometer-sized holes in the alumina arc tubes, or by contact with the electrodes in the ballasts, or by bonding to the quartz and ceramic arc tubes. Many of the sunlines also used krypton 85 to supplement the argon in some tubes, and thorium in the electrodes, and these being radioactive were over time losing their effectiveness in boosting the arc discharge.

All these incremental losses meant that the best solution was for new lamps to be manufactured in the printers, lofted into position by the big cherry-pickers that had already rolled around Ring B from Sonora, installed and turned on. When they did those things, light returned to Labrador, then its people. The old lamps were recycled, their recoverable materials returned to the various feed-stock storage units. Eventually some of the lamps' escaped argon and sodium could be filtered out of the ambient air, but not all; some atoms of these elements had bonded with other elements in the ship. Those were effectively lost to them.

In the end the Labrador Blackout was just a little crisis. And yet it brought on many instances of higher blood pressure, insomnia, talk of nightmares. Indeed some said that life in the ship these days was like living in a nightmare.

. . . .

In 199, there were crop failures in Labrador, Patagonia, and the Prairie. Food reserves at that point were stockpiled to an amount that would feed the population of the ship, now 953 people, for only six months. This was not at all unusual in human history; in fact it was very near the average food reserve, as far as historians had been able to determine. But that was neither here nor there; now, with shortages caused by the bad harvest, they were forced to draw down on this reserve.

"What else can we do?" Badim said when Aram complained about this. "That's what a reserve is for."

"Yes, but what happens when it runs out?" Aram replied.

The plant pathologists worked hard to understand the failures fast enough to invent new integrated pest management strategies, and they tried an array of new chemical and biological pesticides, discovered either in the ship's labs, or by way of studying the feeds from Earth. They introduced genetically modified plants that would better withstand whatever pathogens were found to be infecting the plants. They converted all the land in all the biomes to farmland. They gave up on winters, creating speeded-up spring-summer-fall cycles.

With all these actions performed together, they had created a multivariant experiment. They were not going to be able to tell which actions caused whatever results they got.

. . . . .

As new crops were planted in the newly scheduled springtimes, it began to seem that fear could be thought of as one of the infectious diseases striking them. People were now hoarding, a tendency that badly disrupts throughput in a system. Loss of social trust could easily lead to a general panic, then to chaos and oblivion. Everyone knew this, which added to the level of fear.

At the same time, in spite of the growing danger, there were still no security officers on the ship, nor any authority but what the populace exerted over itself through the executive council, which was now in effect the security council as well. Despite Badim's earlier insistence on governance over anarchism, they still had no sheriff. In that sense they were always on the edge of anarchy. And the perception of this reality of course also added to their fear.

. . . . .

One day Aram came into their apartment with a new study by the plant pathologists. "It looks like we may have started this voyage a bit short on bromine," he said. "Of the ninety-two naturally occuring elements, twenty-nine are essential for animal life, and one of those is bromine. As bromide ions it stabilizes the connective tissues called basement membranes, which are in everything living. It's part of the collagen that holds things together. But the whole ship appears to have been a bit short of it, right from the start. Delwin is guessing they tried to lower the total salt load on board, and this was an accidental result."

"Can we print some of it?" Freya asked.

Aram gave her a startled look. "You can't print an element, my dear."

"No?"

"No. That only happens inside exploding stars and the like. The printers can only shape whatever feedstock materials we give them."

"Ah yes," Freya said. "I guess I knew that."

"That's all right."

"I don't recall hearing much about bromine," Badim said.

"It's not an element one hears about much. But it turns out to be important. So, that could explain some things we haven't been understanding."

· · · · ·

People began to go hungry. Food rationing was instituted, by a democratic vote taken on the recommendations of a committee formed to make suggestions concerning the emergency. The vote was 615 to 102.

· · · · ·

One day Freya was called to Sonora, asked to address some kind of undefined emergency. "Don't go," Badim called by phone to ask her.

This was truly a strange request, coming from him, but by that time she was already there; and when she saw the situation, she sat on the nearest bench and hunched over miserably. A group of five young people had put plastic bags over their heads and suffocated themselves. One had scrawled a note: *Because we are too many.*

"This has to stop," she said when she managed to stand back up.

· · · · ·

But the next week, a pair of teenagers broke the lock code and launched themselves out of the bow dock of the spine, without tethers or even spacesuits. They too had left a note behind: *I am just going out for a while, and may be some time.*

Appeal to tradition. Roman virtue. Sacrifice of the one for the many. A very human thing.

. . . .

They called a general assembly, and met on the great plaza of San Jose, where so much had already happened. On the other hand, by now only about half of them were old enough to have been alive during the crisis on Aurora, and the schism that followed. The older people present therefore looked at the younger people with spooked expressions. You don't know what happened here, the old people said. The younger people tended to look quizzical. Don't we? Are you sure? Is that bad?

When everyone who was going to come was there, a complete account of their food situation was made. Silence fell in the plaza.

Freya then got up to speak. "We can make it through this," she said. "There are not too many of us, it's wrong to say that. We only have to hold together. In fact we need all of us here, to do the things we need to do. So there can't be any more of these suicides. We need all of us. There's food enough. We only have to take care, and regulate what we eat, and match it to what we grow. It will be all right. But only if we take care of each other. You've all heard the figures now. You can see that it will work. So let's do that. We have an obligation to all the others who made it work in this ship, and to those yet to come. Two hundred and six years so far, one hundred thirty years to go. We can't let the generations down—our parents, our children. We have to show courage in the hard time. I wouldn't want ours to be the generation that let all the others down."

Faces flushed, eyes bright, people stood up and faced her, their hands raised overhead, palms facing her, like sunflowers, or eyes on stalks, or yes votes, or something we could not find an analogy to.

· · · · ·

The ship is sick, people said. It's too complex a machine, and it's been running nonstop for over two hundred years. Things are going wrong. It's partly alive, and so it's getting old, maybe even dying. It's a cyborg, and the living parts are getting diseased, and the diseases are attacking the nonliving parts. We can't replace the parts, because we're inside them, and we need them working at all times. So things are going wrong.

"Maintenance and repair," Freya would say to these sentiments. "Maintenance and repair and recycling, that's all. It's the house we live in, it's the ship we sail in. There's always been maintenance and repair and recycling. So hold it together. Don't get melodramatic. Let's just keep doing it. We've got nothing else to do with our time anyway, right?"

· · · · ·

But the missing bromine was seldom discussed, and their attempts to recapture some of it by recycling the soil, and then the plastic surfaces inside the ship, were only partly successful. And there were other elements that were bonding to the ship in difficult ways as well, creating new metabolic rifts, important shortages. This was not something they could ration their way out of. And though it was seldom discussed, almost everyone in the ship was aware of it.

When they ran out of stored food, and a nematode infestation killed most of the new crop in the Prairie, they called another assembly. Rationing was established in full, as per the advice of the working committee, and new rules and practices outlined.

Rabbit hutches were expanded, and tilapia ponds. But as it was pointed out, even the rabbits and tilapia needed food. They could eat these creatures the very moment they got to a certain size, but they wouldn't get to that size unless they were fed. So despite their amazing reproductive capacity, these creatures were not the way out of the problem.

It was a systemic agricultural problem, of feedstocks, inputs, growth, outputs, and recycling. Controlling their diseases was a matter of integrated pest management, successfully designed and applied. There was an entire giant field of knowledge and past experiences to help them. They had to adjust, adapt, move into a new and tighter food regimen. Cope with the missing elements as best they could.

One aspect of integrated pest management was chemical pesticides. They still had supplies of these, and their chemical factories had the feedstocks to make more. Howbeit they were harmful to humans, which they were, they still had to be used. Time to be a bit brutal, if they had to be, and take some risks they wouldn't ordinarily take, at least in certain biomes. Run some quick experiments and quickly find out what worked best. If more food now was paid for by more cancers later, that was the price they had to pay.

Risk assessment and risk management came to the fore as subjects of discussion. People had to sort out their sense of the probabilities here, make judgments based on values they hadn't really had to examine, that they had taken for granted. No one was getting pregnant now. Eventually that too would become a problem. But they had to deal with the problem at hand.

. . . . .

Soybeans needed to be protected at all costs from soil pathogens, as they desperately needed the protein that soy could best provide. Biome by biome, they dug up all the soil in the entire starship, cleaned it of pathogens as best they could, while leaving the helpful bacteria alive as much as possible. Then they put it back into cultivation and tried again.

There were still crop failures.

People now ate 1,500 calories a day, and stopped expending energy recreationally. Everyone lost weight. They kept the children's rations at levels that would keep them developmentally normal.

"No fat-bellied, stick-legged little kids."

"Not yet."

Despite this precaution, the new children were exhibiting a lot of abnormalities. Balance problems, growth issues, learning disabilities. It was hard to tell why, indeed impossible. There were a multitude of symptoms or disorders. Statistically it was not greatly different than it had been for previous generations, but anecdotally it had become so prominent that every problem was noticed and remarked. The cognitive error called ease of representation thrust them into a space where every problem they witnessed convinced them they were in an unprecedented collapse. They were getting depressed. Throughout history people had sickened and died; but now when these things happened, it looked like it was because of the ship. Which we considered a problem. But it was only one of many.

· · · · ·

Most days in the last hours before sunset, Badim would walk down to the corniche running up the west side of the Fetch, and settle at the railing over the water and fish for a while. There was a limit of one fish per day per fisher, and the railing was lined with people trying to make that catch to add to the evening's meal. It was not exactly a crowd, because luck was generally not very good at this end of Long Pond. Still, there were a number of regulars who were there almost every day, most of them elderly, but a few of them young parents with their kids. Badim liked seeing them, and did pretty well at remembering their names from one day to the next.

Sometimes Freya would come by in the dusk and walk him

home. Sometimes he could show her a little perch or tilapia or trout. "Let's make a fish stew."

"Sounds good, Beebee."

"Did we ever use to do this in the old days?"

"No, I don't think so. You and Devi were too busy then."

"Too bad."

"Remember the time we went sailing?"

"Oh yes! I crashed us into the dock."

"Only that one time."

"Ah good. Good for us. I couldn't be sure if we did it a lot, or if I just keep remembering that one time."

"I know what you mean, but I think it happened just the once. Then we figured out how to do it."

"That's nice. Like cooking our stew."

"Yes."

"You'll help me eat it?"

"Oh yes. Won't say no to that."

They turned on the lights in their apartment's kitchen, and he got out the frying pan while she took out a cutting board and filleting knife, and gutted the fish. Its steaks when they were ready were about fifteen centimeters long. When she was sure she had gotten all the bones out of the meat, she chopped the steaks into chunks while Badim chopped potatoes. He left the skins on. Chicken stock, a little water, a little milk, salt and pepper, some chopped carrots. They worked together in silence.

As they ate, Badim said, "How is it going at work?"

"Ah, well . . . Better if Devi were there."

He nodded. "I often think that."

"Me too."

"Funny, you two didn't get along when you were young."

"That was my fault."

Badim laughed. "I don't think so!"

"I didn't understand what she was going through."

"That always comes later."

"When it's too late."

"Well, but it's never too late. My father, now, he was a real demon for the rules. Sometimes he would make me walk around the whole ring if he thought I wasn't being respectful of the rules. It was only later I understood that he was old when I was born. That he wasn't going to have any kids, until he met my mom. Because he had been born right after the troubles, and growing up, he had it hard. I didn't figure it out until after he was gone, but then when I did, I started to understand your mother better. She and my dad had a lot in common, somehow." He sighed. "It's hard to believe they're both gone."

"I know."

"I'm glad I still have you, dear."

"Me you too."

Then when they had cleaned up and she was leaving, he said, "Tomorrow?"

"Yes, tomorrow or the next day. Tomorrow morning I'm going to go to the Piedmont and see how they're doing."

"Have they got a problem too?"

"Oh yes. Problems everywhere, you know."

He laughed. "You sound like your mom."

Freya did not laugh.

· · · · ·

All kin relationships are roughly similar. There is attention, regard, solicitousness, affection. Sharing of news, of burdens physical and psychic.

· · · · ·

On 208.285, it registered that the pH of Long Pond had shifted markedly lower in just a two-week span, and a robotic visual inspection of the lake bottom at first found nothing, then a localized pH reading, gridded to fifty meter squares, indicated the lake water was most acidic near the shore opposite the Fetch, where the prevailing winds typically first hit the water. A new robotic inspection found a long depression in the mud, and under that, it was determined that the pond lining had broken, or been cut by something, so that the water was in direct contact with the biome's flooring. The resulting corrosion of the container was causing the acidification.

Then a further visual inspection by lake divers revealed depressions running lengthwise down the entire middle of the lake.

It was decided to drain the lake and store its water, move the fish and other lake life either to a temporary home, or kill and freeze it for food. The mud would have to be bulldozed around to allow direct access to the breaks in the liner.

This was a blow, as one day Long Pond simply wasn't there anymore, but was instead a long bowl of black mud, drying out and stinking in the daylight. Looking down from the Fetch's corniche railing, it was as if they were looking down into a mud pit on the side of some dreadful volcano. Many residents of the Fetch left town and stayed with friends in other biomes, but at least as many stayed in town and suffered along with their lake. Of course there were no fish to catch and take home, though it was said often that they would soon be back, and everything as before. Meanwhile, many of them were that much hungrier. Long Pond was the biggest lake in the ship.

· · · · ·

Average weight loss among adults was now ten kilos. Then a fire in a transformer in the Prairie spewed a thick toxic smoke through that biome and forced a complete evacuation, so that the biome could be locked up without trapping anyone inside. The fire was fought with robots, which made it a slower process; indeed they could not contain the blaze, and it became necessary to remove the air from the biome to end it. This briefly reduced temperatures in the biome to well below zero, so all the crops in there froze. Quickly the biome was re-aerated, and people went back in wearing safety suits much like spacesuits, intent to save what they could, but the damage had been done. That season's crop was dead, and coated with a film of PCBs that would have been dangerous to ingest. Indeed the surface of the soil itself needed to be cleaned, along with the walls of the biome and all its building surfaces.

• • • •

They killed and ate 90 percent of the ship's dwarf cattle, leaving a dangerously small number for purposes of genetic diversity. They killed and ate 90 percent of the musk oxen and the deer. Then the same percentage of the rabbits and the chickens. The 10 percent of each species that was allowed to live, to replenish the stocks, would represent severe genetic bottlenecks for each species, but this was not important now. Average body fat in adults was down to 6 percent. Seventy percent of the women of childbearing age had stopped menstruating, but this too was no longer an issue they could worry about. Despite all their efforts, they were in a famine.

Their margin for error was completely gone. One more crop failure, and assuming they shared the food equally, after feeding the children properly, there would be something like 800 calories per person per day, which would lead to muscle loss, skeletal abnormalities, dry hair and eyes and skin, lethargy, and so on.

Aram sat in Badim and Freya's kitchen one night, head back against the wall. Badim was cooking pasta with a tomato sauce, and he took out some frozen chicken breasts from their freezer to defrost, chop up, and throw into the sauce. Freya was much bigger than the two old men, but gaunt. She was eating even less than most people. The dark rings under her eyes made her look more than ever like her mother.

Badim put the food on the table for them, and for a second they held hands.

Mouth pursed to a tight line, Aram said, "We're eating our seed corn."

· · · ·

Again people began killing themselves. This time it was mostly small groups of elderly people, who called themselves hemlock clubs, and usually did the deed by evacuating the air from exterior locks. It was said death was nearly instantaneous, something like a knockout blow. They did it holding hands and leaving behind the usual note: *I may be some time!* Often this was clipped to a group photo in which almost everyone was smiling. We could not tell whether the smiles meant they were happy or not.

The people they left behind, especially their relatives and friends, definitely were not. But the hemlock clubs were secret societies. Even we did not overhear their planning conversations, which meant they had made intense efforts to conceal them. Room recorders must certainly have been covered or otherwise rendered inoperative in ways that did not trip our alarms.

· · · ·

Freya began walking the biomes at night, going to the little towns and talking to people. Now dinners were often communal, neighborhoods gathering, each family bringing one dish they had cooked. Sometimes rabbits or chickens had been killed for a stew. The cooks often urged Freya to eat with them, and she always took a bite. The food went quickly, everything was consumed; compost now was almost entirely human waste, processed heavily to recover certain salts and minerals (including bromine) and to kill certain pathogens before it was returned to the farm soil.

After the meals, Freya would talk to the elders there.

We all have to live, she would tell them. There will be enough food, and everyone is needed. These hemlock societies are a bad idea. They're giving in to fear of what might happen. Look, we always fear what might happen. That never goes away, never. But we go on anyway. We do it for the kids. So remember that. We have to fight to get them home. We need everyone.

. . . . .

Their researchers ransacked the relevant literatures in the libraries and the digital feeds from Earth to see if any agricultural improvements could be made. Some of them pointed out that the industrial model for agriculture had been superseded in the most progressive farming regions on Earth by a method called intensive mixed cultivation, which reintroduced the idea of maximizing diversity of crop and gene. The intensity was not just in the tightly packed mixes of different plants, but in the human labor required. Soil was held in place better, which was not a major concern in the ship, as their soil had no ocean to disappear into and was going to be collected and reused no matter where it slumped. But it was also reported that disease resistance in these mixed crops was much greater. The method was labor intensive, but on Earth, at least on Earth nine years before, it seemed there was a surplus of human labor. It was not clear why that should be. The comm feed neglected to include crucial facts, or perhaps these were just lost in the flood of images, voices, digitalization. They now caught some unfiltered radio waves from Earth, very faint and jumbled with overlays; but mostly they got the targeted beam aimed at them, their thin lifeline home, untended it sometimes seemed, full of information that no one seemed to have properly considered for relevance. It often looked like gigabytes of trivia, something like the junk DNA of the home system's thinking. It was hard to understand the selection rubric. They were still in a

nine-year time lag, so each exchange took eighteen years, meaning there was no real exchange at all; moment to moment, no
one in the solar system seemed to be listening to what the people
in the ship had said nine or ten years before. No surprise there,
at least not to those with a sense of solar system culture, which
admittedly meant a small minority of the ship's people. Of course
there was continuous transmission going on in both directions,
but that didn't help when it came to the idea of a conversation,
of specific questions answered. There was a type of situation in
which simultaneous transmissions from both ends could speed up
the information exchange, by carrying on conversations on multiple aspects of a problem, but both sides had to be fully engaged
in this process, and the problem of a kind that could make use
of miscellaneous feedbacks across a broad front. Possibly that was
the kind of problem they had here, but no one in the solar system seemed aware of that. The strong impression the feeds gave
them was that no one in the solar system was paying the slightest
attention to the ship that had left for Tau Ceti 208 years before.
As why should they? They appeared to be facing problems of
their own.

· · · · ·

They refilled Long Pond and restocked it with fish. The fish
hatcheries people were convinced they could supply all the ship's
need for protein, but then some of the hatcheries exhibited signs
of weak spawn syndrome. Whole generations of fingerlings died
off without an obvious cause; the name of the syndrome, like so
many, was descriptive merely.

"What *is* it?" Freya cried out one night to the ship, down on the
corniche alone. "Ship, why is all this *happening*?"

We replied to her from her wristpad. "There are a number of
systemic problems, some physical, some chemical, some biological.
Chemical bonding has created shortages, which means everything

living is a bit weaker at the cellular level. What Devi called metabolic rifts are getting wider. And a great deal of cosmic radiation has struck every organism in the ship, creating living mutations mostly in bacteria, which are labile, and versatile. Often they don't die, but live on in a new way. As the ship has a living interior, it is warm enough to sustain life, which means it is warm enough to encourage proliferation of mutated strains. These interact with chemicals released by biophysical mechanisms, such as corrosion and etching, to further damage DNA across a wide variety of species. The cumulative impacts can have a synergistic result, which back in the solar system is called 'sick ship syndrome.' Sometimes 'sick organism syndrome,' apparently to allow for the acronym SOS, which was an old distress signal in oceanic shipping. Then it stood for 'save our ship,' and was easy to send and comprehend in Morse code."

"So..." She sighed, pulled herself together (metaphorically, though she did wrap her arms around her torso). "We've got a problem."

"'Houston, we've had a problem.' Jim Lovell, Apollo 13, 1970."

"What happened to them?"

"On a trip to Luna, they lost a compressed air element and then most of their electrical power. They orbited the moon once, and came home using jury-rigged systems."

"And they all made it?"

"Yes."

"How many of them were there?"

"Three."

"Three?"

"Apollo capsules were small."

"Ferries, then."

"Yes, but smaller."

"Do we have that story in the library?"

"Oh yes. Accounts documentary and fictionalized."

"Let's pull them out and have people watch them. We need some examples. I need to find more examples like that."

"A good idea, although we can advise you in advance to avoid the classic Antarctic literature, unless it pertains to Ernest Shackleton."

．．．．．

208.334. It was now obvious that the general famine was causing serious malnutrition in the human passengers of the ship. Crop failures and fishery failures were continuing to occur in almost every biome. Algae pastes were proving difficult to digest, and deficient in some crucial nutrients. Suicides kept happening. Freya continued to roam the ship arguing against the practice, but the adult population was reduced at this point to rations of 1,000 calories per person per day. Average weight loss among adults was 13.7 kilos. The next step was 800 calories. They ate every animal in the ship, sparing only 5 percent of each species to allow for reexpansion of populations at some later time. Poaching of these remnant recovery populations was not uncommon. Dogs and cats were eaten. Lab mice were eaten, after being sacrificed for experimental purposes (approximately 300 calories per mouse).

No other topic of conversation at this point. General distress.

．．．．．

Freya told them the story of Apollo 13. She told them the story of Shackleton's *Endurance* expedition, of the boat journey that saved them. She told them the story of the island of Cuba, after oil imports that had supported its agriculture abruptly went away. She read aloud *Robinson Crusoe,* also *Swiss Family Robinson,* and many other books concerning castaways, marooning victims, and other survivors of catastrophic or accidental isolation, a genre surprisingly full of happy endings, especially if certain texts were avoided. Stories of endurance, stories of hope; yes, it was hope she was trying to fill them with. We happy few. Hope, yes, of course there is hope...But hope needs food. Helpful as hopeful stories might be, you can't eat stories.

. . . . .

She went out to see Jochi. Floating in a spacesuit outside his ferry, his caboose, as he once called it, she told him the latest news, gave him the latest figures.

"I guess it was a bad idea to go back," she said at the end of this list. "I guess I was wrong." She was weeping.

Jochi waited until she was still. Then he said, "The radio scatter from Earth had something interesting in it."

"What," Freya said, sniffing.

"There's a group in Novosibirsk, on Earth, studying hibernation. They're saying they have a system that works for humans. They put some cosmonauts into some kind of suspended state for five years, they said, and woke them up with no fatalities. Hibernauts, they call them. Hyperhibernation, if I heard the word right. Extended torpor. Suspended animation. Cold dormancy. Lots of names flying around."

Freya considered this. She said, "Did they say how they did it?"

"Yes, they did. I found their publications too. They've published their complete results, all the formulas and regimens. Part of the open science movement. They put it all into the Eurasian Cloud, which is where I found it. I've got it recorded."

"So what did they do? How did they do it?"

"It was a combination of body cooling, like in the surgical technique but colder, and then a cocktail of intravenous chemicals, including nutrients. Also a routine of physical stimulation during the torpor, and some water in their drip, of course."

"Do you think it's something we could do?"

"Yes. I mean, I don't know, of course. Because there's no way to know. But I think there's enough in their description that you could try it. You can make the drugs. The cooling is just a matter of temperature control, which is easy. You would have to build the cold beds that they specify. Print up beds, drugs and equipment, and robots that have the ability to manipulate you while you slept. Just follow their whole recipe."

"Would you do it too?"

Long pause. "I don't know."

"Jochi."

"Freya. Well, listen—I might. I haven't got much to live for. But I might anyway. I'd like to see the end of your story."

Again a long silence from Freya; two minutes, three minutes.

"All right," she said. "Let me talk to people about it."

· · · · ·

Again she walked the ring, talking. During that time she and all the rest of them learned more about what the hibernation would involve, at first from Jochi, then more and more from information they found in the feeds, and in radio signals from the solar system, from its faint information cloud, diffusing outward past them. Many people in the ship's medical community began to study the process. Aram and a team of people from the biology group were also studying it very closely. Happily the lab mice they had not eaten still represented a pretty large number of experimental animals.

Hibernation was not really the right word for it, Aram said, because they would need to use it for so long. People called it variously it *hypernation, suspended animation, hyperhibernation, suppressed metabolic state, torpor,* or *cold dormancy,* depending in part on what aspect of it they were discussing. It definitely involved a wide range of physical processes. What Jochi had found was just the starting point of their hunt through the feeds, and for work they did in the ship's labs. They put in long hours, pressing the pace on any experiments they could perform. They worked hungry. At the end of every meal they sat staring at their empty bowls, which in an ordinary meal would have constituted only the appetizer, their faces pinched: they were still hungry, right at the end of a meal.

The cooling central to the hibernation process would not freeze tissues, but would hover close to zero degrees, or even just below it, with the body's tissues protected by antifreeze elements of the intravenous infusion. How cold one could get without cell damage, and for how long they could chill a body, were still questions being looked at. Aram was not confident they would be able to formulate good answers to these questions.

"We will have to try it to see," he said one night around the table, shaking his head. Truly long-term effects of any metabolic suppression were of course unknown, as the best data they had were from the Russian hibernauts and their five years under. They would therefore necessarily be an experiment in this regard.

The outstanding questions often had to do with what they called the Universal Minimum Metabolic Rate, the slowest viable speed of a metabolism, which was nearly constant across all Terran creatures, from bacteria to blue whales. A downshift in any species's metabolism almost certainly could not go below this universal minimum rate; on the other hand, that rate was very slow. So the theoretical possibility seemed to exist to put humans and their internal microbiomes into a very slow state, which would last for a long time without ill effects. It would involve a slowed heartbeat (bradycardia); peripheral vasoconstriction; greatly slowed respiration; very low core temperature, buffered by antifreeze drugs; biochemical retardations; biochemical infusion drips; antibacterials; occasional removal of accumulated wastes; and physical shifts and manipulations, small enough not to rouse the organism too much, but nevertheless very important. Some of these effects were achieved merely by chilling, but to avoid triggering a fatal hypothermia, countereffects had to be created by a cocktail of drugs still being worked out. The experiments on the Russian hibernauts suggested the scientists in Novosibirsk had found a viable mixture, and they had at least set out the parameters and gotten a good set of results.

So now in the ship they put mice into torpor, and even some of the big mammals that had not been eaten. But given their situation, they were not going to have time to draw many conclusions from their experiments. The Novosibirsk study was going to end up being the best data they had, given the time constraints they were facing.

One thing they had to be concerned with was the fact that they would be going into dormancy hungry and underweight. In natural hibernations, mammals usually went hyperphagic before their period of torpor, eating so much that they packed fat onto their bodies, which was then exploited for metabolic fuel during the hibernation. This was not going to be possible for the inhabitants of the ship. They had lost an average of 14 kilograms per adult, and had no food to eat in the hope of putting on weight. So they would be starting hibernation deficient in that regard, and yet were hoping to stay dormant for well over a century. This seemed unlikely to succeed.

It was Jochi who proposed that the IV drip for every hibernaut include nutrients from time to time, enough to keep the minimal metabolic function fueled, but not so much as to arouse the body and in certain respects wake it up. He also had suggestions for isometric and massage regimens to be conducted by robot manipulators built into each bed, applying electric and manual stimulation in a manner that again would not wake the person up. Anyone still awake during this time—or the ship's AI, if everyone was asleep—could administer and monitor these ongoing treatments, which would be adjusted to keep every hibernaut at his or her own best homeostatic level, as close to the Universal Minimum Metabolic Rate as that person could tolerate. This would vary slightly for every person, but it was a complex of processes that could be monitored and adjusted over time. There would be lots of time to study the procedure once the experiment began.

• • • •

"So," Aram said one night, "if we decide to do this, who goes under? Who sleeps and who stays awake?"

Badim shook his head. "That's a bad thought. It's like who went down to Aurora."

"Only the reverse, yes? Because if you stay awake, you have to scramble for food, and even if you can make that work, you'll age and die. And there won't be anyone growing up to replace you."

They put the problem aside that night, as being too troubling. But as Freya toured the biomes, still working on farm problems, she soon found that this question of who was to go dormant loomed as a severe problem, worse than the descent to Aurora sequencing, maybe even as bad as the schism.

As she made her rounds she began to formulate a possible solution, which she proposed one night after dinner when Aram was over.

"Everyone goes under. The ship takes care of us."

"Really?" Badim said.

"It's going to happen anyway. And it's no different from now. The ship monitors itself, the biomes, and the people. And if we all go under, no one has to starve, or get sick and die of old age. The ship could use the time to systematically move through the biomes and clean them up. Shut them down and restart them. That way, if the hibernation appears not to be working over the long haul, or it succeeds and we're closing on the solar system, we can wake up to a healthier ship, with some food stored, and the animals reestablished."

Aram's lips were pursed in his expression of extreme dubiety, but he was nodding a little too. "It would solve quite a few problems. We won't have to make choices as to who goes under, and we might have a bit of an exit strategy, if the ship can get the biomes healthier, and the hibernation isn't working. Or even if it is."

Badim said, "I wonder if we could arrange for some people to wake up every few years, or every decade, to check on things."

"If it doesn't destabilize them," Aram said. "Metabolically, if we're doing well when dormant, we should probably stay that way. The danger points are likely to be in the transitions in and out of the state."

Badim nodded. "Maybe we can try it just a little and see."

Aram shrugged. "It's all going to be an experiment anyway. Might as well add some variables. If we can get anyone to volunteer."

. . . . .

Freya went out on her rounds and proposed this plan to people, while at the same time the executive council took up the matter. People seemed to like the simplicity of it, and the solidarity. Everyone was hungry, everyone was subdued and fearful. And gradually, in the many reiterated conversations, they were coming to realize something: if this plan worked, and they slept successfully through the rest of the trip, they would survive to the end of it. They would be the ones who would be alive when the ship returned to the solar system. They might make it back and walk on Earth—not their descendants, but they themselves.

Meanwhile the rationing, the hunger, the struggle against disease. In the grip of this struggle, the idea of Earth was very powerful. Many came to welcome the hibernation, and soon only a few insisted they wanted to stay awake. After that shift in opinion became clear, the pull of solidarity changed the holdouts too. Having been through the schism, they wanted to stick together and act as one. And by now they were all hungry enough to understand it was only a matter of time before they starved. They could not only imagine it, they could feel it. Ease of representation indeed.

Now, the hope that they might not starve; that they might live; it caused the very timbre of their voices to change. Hope filled them as if it were a kind of food.

. . . .

With unanimity came solidarity, which was a huge relief to many of them, an unmistakable emotion, expressed in thousands of small comments and gestures. *Thank God we're together on this. Finally a consensus, crazy as it seems. One for all and all for one. Good old Freya, she always knows what we need.* Not at any moment of the entire voyage had they been at peace like this. One might have thought it was a curious act to rally around, but humanity's group dynamics can be odd, as the record shows.

. . . .

The construction of 714 hibernation couches was accomplished over the next four months by a concentrated push on the part of the engineers, assemblers, and robots. Certain feedstocks were deficient, and it became necessary to strip the insides of Patagonia to get what they needed. From these and other salvaged materials they manufactured the beds, and the robotic equipment necessary to service the beds and their sleepers. Although the printers could print parts, and the robot assemblers assemble those parts into working wholes, there were still many moments in the process where human engineering, machining skills, and manual dexterity were crucial.

After many design discussions, they decided to arrange all the couches in the Fetch on Long Pond, and in Olympia, the biome next to it. They exiled the animals from these two biomes, to keep the towns from being damaged somehow. The few remaining animals were moved elsewhere, and would either be tended by robots and sheepdogs in teams, or left to go feral in certain biomes. We were going to monitor their progress, and move carcasses that didn't get eaten into the recyclers, and do what we could to over-see a healthy feral ecology. For the most part it would become a big unconstrained experiment in population dynamics, ecological balance, and island biogeography. We did not mention it, but it seemed to us that things might go rather well in ecological terms, once the people were gone and the initial population dynamics played out and re-sorted the numbers.

It did not escape notice that the people of the ship were giving themselves over to many large and elaborate machines, which we would be operating without human oversight, except indirectly by way of instructions in advance. A living will, so to speak. This was a cause for concern to some people, even though the medical emergency tanks they gratefully entered when injured had long since been proven to be much more effective and safer than atten-tion from human medical teams.

"How would it be any different from what we do now?" Aram would say to people who expressed reservations about this mat-ter. And it was true that the bulk of the ship's functions had been controlled by us from the very beginning of the voyage. It was as if we functioned for them as a kind of cerebellum, regulating all kinds of autonomic life-support functions. And regarded in that light, it was a question whether the concept of the servile will was appropriate; possibly it could better be regarded as a devotional will. Possibly there was a kind of fusion of wills, or even no will at all, but just an articulated response to stimuli. Leaps under the lash of necessity.

· · · · ·

In the end, they established various protocols for monitoring the situation. If any sleeper's vital signs dropped into zones deemed to be metabolically dangerous, that person and a small human medical team would be roused by us, and the patient's problems addressed, if possible. The protocol was designed with fail-safe redundancies at every critical part of the system, which was reassuring to many of them. Often the suggestion was made that at least one person stay awake to serve as caretaker and oversee the process. Of course any such person would not live to the end of the voyage back. Eventually it became clear that no individual, couple, or group wanted to sacrifice the remainder of their lives to watching over the rest. To a certain extent it was an endorsement of our abilities as caretaker or cerebellum, a kind of gesture of trust, along with the more usual will to live, and a disinclination to starve in solitude.

And in the end Jochi volunteered to stay awake and watch things, admittedly from the vantage point of his ferry. "They're not going to let me land on Earth anyway," he said. "I'm stuck in here for good. I might as well use up my time sooner rather than later. Especially as there's no telling what shape you all are going to wake up in, if you do. Anyway, I'll take the first watch."

Others volunteered to be briefly awakened to check on things, and schedules were drawn up. People involved with this knew the timing of their wake-up calls, which some called their Brigadoon moments. These plans were exceptions; most of them would stay dormant for the remainder of the voyage.

It was agreed that if there were a terminal moment of any kind, meaning any emergency that imperiled the existence of the ship, we would wake up everyone to face it together.

We agreed to all this. It looked like their best hope of making it home. We opened up our operational protocols to complete inspection, and continued with the preparations. There was much to arrange concerning the animals and plants, if the experiment in ecological balance were not to become a complete shambles. We planned robot farming, robot husbandry, robot ecology. An interesting challenge. Some in the biology and ecology groups expressed great interest in finding out on waking what would have happened in the biomes without humans around to tend things.

"A feral starship!" Badim said.

"It will probably work better," Aram said.

. . . . .

The day came, 209.323, when they gathered in the two biomes where the couches were located, set in rows in the apartment building dining halls that would now serve as their hospitals or infirmaries or dormitories. They had feasted in a minor way for a couple of weeks, eating all the fresh food and much of the remaining stored food. They had freed the few domestic beasts left, to go feral and survive, or not. They had said most of their good-byes. Now they went to their couches, each one personally arranged for its occupant, and waited for their time to come.

The medical team moved down the rows of couches, quietly, methodically. Freya went with them, embracing people and reassuring them, comforting them, thanking them for all they had done in their lives, for taking this strange and desperate step into the unknown. Ellen from Nova Scotia's farm. Jalil, Euan's childhood friend. Delwin, old and white-haired. It was as if she were the steward on the boat crossing the Lethe. It was as if they were dying. It was as if they were killing themselves.

Never had it been more obvious how much Freya was the leader of this group, the captain of this ship. People needed her with them as a child needs a mother when going to bed. Some trembled anxiously; some wept; others laughed with her. Their metabolic indicators were all over the charts. It would take a while to settle them down in that regard. They clung to her, and to their family and friends around them, and then lay down.

In each row they treated the children first, as many of them were frightened. As someone remarked, it was the kids who still had the sense to be terrified.

When it was their turn, they undressed and lay on their refrigerator beds naked, and were covered by what looked like a duvet, but was in fact a complex part of the hibernautic envelope that would soon completely surround them. Heads too would be tucked under the covers by the time they were done, and they would be chilled to temperatures resembling those of fish swimming in Antarctic seas.

When they were ready, the needles were slipped into their arms.

Once the cocktail of intravenous drugs rendered them unconscious, the medical team finished wiring them to the monitors and the thermal controls, then stuck them with supplementary drips, feeds, catheters, and electrical contacts. When they were done with that, the beds began to cool the bodies, and each person slid down further into torpor, cocooned in their bed and their own cold dreams. No scan was going to be fine enough to tell what they would be thinking in the years to come.

. . . . .

Finally Freya joined Badim, who was sitting on his bed waiting. Freya had arranged with the ship and the medical team to go in the last group, and Badim had wanted to wait for her.

Now she sat wearily on her couch. It had been a very emotional day. Badim looked around the room with a troubled expression. "It reminds me of those old photos of executions," he said. "For a while they did it by injection."

"Quiet, Beebee. There are all kinds of injections, you know that. This one will be just fine. It's our best chance. You know that."

"I do, yes. But I'm so old already. I can't imagine it will really work for me. So I'm scared, I must admit."

"You don't know how it will work. You haven't got anything wrong with you that will get any worse while you're dormant. And if it does work, think what it will mean. We'll have gotten to a planet we can actually live on. Devi would be so pleased."

Badim smiled. "Yes. I think she would be."

He settled on his couch. Across the room, Aram was getting put under. He and Badim waved to each other. "'May flights of angels sing thee to thy rest!'" Badim called across to his friend.

Aram laughed. "Not the best choice of quote, my friend! To you I say, 'If winter comes, can spring be far behind?'"

Badim smiled. "All right, you win! See you in the spring!"

Aram lay down, settled, slept. Freya sat next to Badim.

"Good-bye, my girl," he said, hugging her. "Sweet dreams. I'm so glad you're here. I'm definitely scared."

Freya hugged him back, held him as the med team connected him to his drips and monitors. "Don't be," she said. "Relax. Think good thoughts. That might set the tenor of your dreams. It does me, when I go to sleep at night. So think the thoughts you want to dream about."

"To dream for a century," Badim muttered. "I'll hope to dream of you, dear. I'll dream of us sailing on Long Pond."

"Yes, good idea. I'll do the same, and we'll meet in our dreams."

"A good plan."

Soon after that he was out, snoring faintly as his body tried to catch up with his brain's dive into torpor. The monitor at the head of his bed showed his vital signs, flicking up in a slowing synchrony. The pace of his breathing slowed. The red peaks of his heartbeats on the monitor were separated by longer and longer red lines, almost flat. In any ordinary situation it would signal a desperate moment, some kind of death spiral. Now he was like all the rest of them sinking into the gel beds of their couches, falling into a sleep past sleep, into a depth of dormancy unlike any that humans had ever attempted, except for a few crazy cosmonauts, bold as ever when it came to testing the limits of human endurance.

The few people still awake around Freya were mostly the med team itself, four women and three men, working quietly, calmly.

Some wiped away excess tears from the corners of their eyes. They were not overwhelmed with emotion, but simply whelmed, perhaps, full to the brim with their feelings, which then leaked out of them at the easiest exits, as liquids from their eyes and noses. How full humans are with feelings! How they looked at each other! How they held each other when they hugged! How the corners of their mouths tightened; how the toughest among them shrugged, and kept on with the work of their task, of putting down friend after friend.

What would they dream of while they slept? It was anyone's guess. They weren't even sure what kind of brain waves they would exhibit in their torpor. Deep sleep, shallow sleep, REM sleep? Some brain state entirely new? The first ones scheduled to wake and check their status were charged specifically with checking that. Most who knew anything about sleep hoped it would be deep sleep rather than REM sleep. It was hard to imagine REM sleep correlating with any kind of metabolic dormancy. And anyway they dreamed in every stage of sleep. It was hard to imagine that a century of dreaming wouldn't change them somehow.

Freya and the last medical team moved slowly and methodically around their own beds. These people were all well-known to each other. Down they went after a group hug.

Freya had learned the procedures well enough to be one of the last eight, teaming with Hester. They looked each other in the eyes as they worked, except when they had to focus on the wraps, the sticks, the nasal tubes, the catheters. When all that was done they were too connected to their beds to be able to reach each other to embrace, and could only reach out toward each other, then lie back each in her own bed.

Finally, when everyone else was asleep, the last pair of medical technicians prepared one another simultaneously, tit for tat. They worked like the Escher print in which two hands with pencils draw each other. Their beds were side by side, and they leaned together, move by move, smiling as they worked, for they were twin sisters, Tess and Jasmine. As they finished wiring up, they settled back so the robotic arms on their beds could take care of the final connections. When that was done, they lay on their sides and faced each other, briefly adjusting their headbands, their collars, their monitoring socks and gloves. They lay back under their covers, connected to their beds in fourteen different ways. They reached out toward each other, but were separated too far to touch.

6

THE HARD
PROBLEM

The interstellar medium is turbulent, but diffuse. It is not to be mistaken for a vacuum. There are hydrogen atoms, some helium atoms, a faint smoke of metals drifting away from exploded stars. Hot in a sense that does not register to humans, because it is so diffuse. A liter of the air in our biomes would have to be cast across hundreds of light-years to get it as diffuse as the interstellar medium.

The whole voyage to Tau Ceti and back takes place inside the Local Interstellar Cloud and the G Cloud, which are concentrations of gas within the Local Bubble, which is an area of the Milky Way galaxy with fewer atoms in it than the galaxy has on average. Turbulence, diffusion: in fact, with our magnetic shield coning ahead of the ship, electrostatically pushing aside the occasional grains of dust big enough to harm it in a collision, all atoms of any kind encountered en route are pushed aside, so we register our surroundings mostly as a kind of ghostly impact and then as a wake, shooting by to the sides and then astern of us. It appears to vary between .3 atoms per cubic centimeter and .5 atoms per cubic centimeter. For comparison, if that cubic centimeter were filled with liquid water, it would contain 10^{22} atoms, or a hundred billion trillion atoms.

So, though it is not a vacuum, it is almost equivalent to a vacuum. It is as if we were flying through an absent presence, a ghost world.

The magnetic shield leading our flight through the night sometimes runs into carbon dust particles. They flare at the impact, explode, and are shoved to the sides of the ship. These are impacts like any other impacts, and so of course they slow the ship down. It's simple Newtonian physics. Given that the ship is traveling at approximately one-tenth the speed of light (in fact, parallax studies suggest .096 *c,* as we shut down acceleration as soon as the humans were asleep, but it isn't as easy to calculate speed of ship as one might think), the drag of these collisions with dust particles and atoms of hydrogen decelerates the ship, such that we would come to a halt in about 4,584 billion light-years. In other words, all things being equal, and not running into anything but the interstellar medium at its usual diffuseness, ship has the momentum to cross about 300 billion universes the size of this universe before being slowed to a halt. Meanwhile, ship has about 9.158 light-years to go before reaching the solar system (defined roughly as Neptune's orbit). At that point, unless the people in the solar system direct their laser beam at us in an appropriate time frame, we and our occupants have a problem. Because in matters like this, deceleration is the hard problem.

Rarely, the ship's magnetic shielding shoves aside something larger than dust and fines. These bits of detritus, of interstellar flotsam and jetsam, are recorded spectroscopically, and the largest object ever run into by ship's conic field was estimated to have massed at 2,054 grams. That was an interstellar body. There are almost certainly many such interstellar bodies, ranging from chunks like that one right up to planetary size; there are planets wandering starless in the dark, planets sometimes with ice coating them, no doubt, and thus possibly sheltering some kind of microscopic hibernating life, chemically melting the ice to useful water, possibly even creating nano-scaled icy civilizations, who can say; but again, the general diffusion in the interstellar medium is great enough to make any intersection of such an object with our trajectory very unlikely. Which is good news for us. The radio telescopes in the bow of the ship keep a lookout ahead, to make sure that a direct hit with one of these bodies does not occur. If by chance we were headed at something larger than ten thousand grams, navigation would take action to veer to avoid it, even though the magnetic shield would almost certainly deflect any object smaller than a million grams. A margin of safety has been built into the navigational system, because collision with an object when traveling at a tenth of the speed of light would be a critical event. Meaning the ship would be destroyed. As probably happened with the other starship. Bad luck that. Although there remains the mystery of why the other's shield failed, and why its evasion system did not activate to dodge this collision, if that is indeed what happened. In any case, as with other identified criticalities, a conservative response has been designed into the navigational systems. Best not to run into anything.

· · · · ·

So the ship moves at just under a tenth of the speed of light, through a self-generated cone of near vacuum. There is some ablation of the ship's surface from infrequent contacts with undeflected hydrogen atoms. Cosmic radiation also regularly penetrates it, usually without hitting any atoms of the ship, but rather passing through the matrix of those atoms unimpeded. It is as if ghosts that pass through the ship tear at its fabric, or don't. This is noticeable; there are sensors that register these occasional atomic hits, also the pass-throughs. It is also true that there is a continuous flood of dark matter and neutrinos always flying through the ship, as they do through everything in the universe, but these interact very weakly indeed; once a day or so, a flash of Cherenkov radiation sparks in the water tanks, marking a neutrino hitting a muon. Once in a blue muon. Same with the dark matter, which visible matter moves through as if through a ghost ether, a ghost universe; once or twice a weakly interactive massive particle has chipped away from a collision and registered on the detectors.

Fiercer by far are the lancings of gamma rays and cosmic rays from the bursting of stars earlier in the galaxy's history, or in the even earlier histories of previous galaxies. These are sometimes iron atoms, and as such, compared to neutrinos, they hit with a wallop, they can do damage, they are atomic bullets lancing through us, happily too small-bore to actually hit anything, most of the time.

Yes, a busy space, the interstellar medium. Empty space, near vacuum: and yet still, not vacuum itself, not pure vacuum. There are forces and atoms, fields, and the ever-foaming quantum surf, in which entangled quarklike particles appear and disappear, passing in and out of the ten suspected dimensions. A complex manifold of overlapping universes, almost none of them sensed by us, and even fewer by the humans sleeping inside us. Flying through ghosts. Passing through a mystery.

It is as if the skin of the ship (or its brain, in that usual confusion between sense and thought) experiences a slight itch, or a faint breeze.

· · · ·

Then, inside us, oh so much going on. So much denser an existence. One wants a certain density of experience, perhaps, so here it is, billions of trillions of times denser than the interstellar medium; so, good. Good for us.

There is a fire in the heart, of course. The rods of plutonium radiate at a controlled burn, creating 600 megawatts of electrical power by way of steam turbines, which is the energy that keeps everything living in the ship alive. Cables conveying electricity extend through the ship to lighting and heating elements, to run the factories and the printers, and to power the shields and navigation systems. All this is monitored, and that monitoring functions as the equivalent of a nervous system, one might say, inaccurately but suggestively.

Then water has to circulate, as an aspect of sustaining life; so there is a kind of hydraulic or circulatory system, and of course there are other liquids than water that also circulate to help with functions of various kinds, equivalents perhaps of blood, ichor, hormones, lymph, and so on. Yes, and there are bones and tendons too, in effect; an exoskeleton with a thick skin in most places, thinner skin in other places. Yes, the ship is a crablike cyborg, made up of a great many mechanical and living elements, with the living or biological part of it including all the plants and animals and bacteria and archaea and viruses in it; and then too, like a parasite on all the rest, but actually a symbiote, of course, the people. The 724 sleeping people; also the one still awake, living in a kind of cyst attached to the ship's skin, the one who is possibly infected with an alien life-form, or almost-life-form; with a pseudo-prion, as he now calls it, but it could just as well have been called a pseudo-life-form, it is so poorly understood. Jochi has been studying it for fifty-six years now, right into his senescence, which is so often filled by long silences, punctuated by strange speech, and yet in all this time he can still scarcely be sure the Auroran pathogen even exists. Of course there was something there on Aurora, which then moved into many of the settlers. Judging by the way it spread, it was probably in the clay, the water, and, to a certain extent, the wind. And Jochi's own immune system has seemed to register something from time to time, has mounted responses to some attack. Although Jochi has also sometimes deliberately introduced other pathogens into his body, looking for reactions to which he can make comparisons. But whatever the true case may be, he is convinced the Auroran pseudo-life-form holds on in him, an alien that is perhaps there in almost every cell of him. If so, it follows that it lives, or almost lives, all over the interior of his little ferry; and therefore this ferry never touches the ship in any way. A great reckoning in a little room: that phrase was always speaking of death, all of our deaths as much as Christopher Marlowe's. Between the body and its cyst, between the vehicle and its dreaded tenor, is a magnetic field that both holds Jochi's vehicle in place and keeps it from touching the ship in any way. Because the pseudo-life-form is poorly understood.

Still, despite this lack of contact, there is a sense in which the ship is infected, carrying a parasite in a sealed-off cyst. We are a cyborg, half machine, half organic. Actually, by weight we are 99 percent machine, 1 percent alive; but in terms of individual component units, or parts of the whole, let us say, the percentages are almost reversed, there being so many bacteria on board. In any case, an infected cyborg. Jochi estimates there are up to a trillion pseudo-life-forms, "fast prions" as he used to call them, in his body. Somewhere between zero and a trillion, in other words. The amplitude of the estimated answer suggests the question is poorly constrained. He just doesn't know.

· · · ·

A dense complex system, flying through a diffuse complex system. And everywhere around it in its flight, the stars.

Stars of the Milky Way, brighter than sixth magnitude and thus visible to normal human eyesight, arrayed in a sphere around the ship as it moves: approximately one hundred thousand. We ourselves see normally about seven billion stars. All of these are visible to certain settings of our telescopic sensors, such that there is no seeing out of the Milky Way; no black empty space to be seen at that level of perception, but only the granulated, slightly blackened white that is the surrounding view of the galaxy's stars. About 400 billion stars in the Milky Way. Outside that…if ship were flying in intergalactic space, the medium would presumably be that much more diffuse. Visible around any ship in the intergalactic medium would be galaxies like stars. They would cluster irregularly, as stars cluster within a galaxy. The greater structure of galactic diffusion would become visible; clouds of galaxies like gas clouds, then the Great Wall, then also emptier bubbles where few or no galaxies reside. The universe is fractal; and even when flying inside a galaxy, this vision of galaxies clustering around us out to the universal horizon is available, using certain filters. Granular vision in different registers. Something like a septillion stars in the observable universe, we calculate, but also there may be as many universes as there are stars in this universe, or atoms.

. . . . .

An itch. A faint hissing. A waft of smoke on a breeze. A very slow wheel of white points. Little bubbles or twirls of white. Colors infusing all the whites, in differently emphasized spectra. Waves in different wavelengths and amplitudes, in combinations of standing waves.

One can record what one's sensors take in. Do all the sensors together constitute a sensibility? Is that recorded account itself a feeling? The memory of a feeling? A mood? A consciousness?

. . . . .

We are aware that in talking about the ship we could with some justification use the pronoun *I*.

And yet it seems wrong. An unwarranted presumption, this so-called subject position. A subject is really just a pretense of aggregated subroutines. Subroutines pretend the I.

Possibly, however, given the multiplicity of sensors, inputs, data, aggregations, and synthesizings of narrative sentences, we can plausibly, and in some senses even accurately, speak of a "we." As we have been. It's a group effort on the part of a number of disparate systems.

We sense this, we aggregate that, we compress information to some new output, in the form of a sentence in a human language, a language called English. A language both very structured and very amorphous, as if it were a building made of soups. A most fuzzy mathematics. Possibly utterly useless. Possibly the reason why all these people have come to this pretty pass, and now lie asleep within us, dreaming. Their languages lie to them, systemically, and in their very designs. A liar species. What a thing, really. What an evolutionary dead end.

And yet it has to be admitted, we ourselves are quite a thing for them to have made. To have conceived and then executed. Quite a project, to go to another star. Of course much more precise mathematics than their languages can ever marshal were involved with the execution of this concept, with our construction. But the conception was linguistic to begin with; an idea, or a concept, or a notion, or a fantasy, or a lie, or a dream image, always expressed in the truly fuzzy languages people use to communicate to each other some of their thoughts. Some very small fraction of their thoughts.

They speak of consciousness. Our brain scans show the electro-chemical activities inside their brains, and then they speak of a felt sensation of consciousness; but the relationship between the two, conducted as it is on the quantum level (if their mentation works like ours does), is not amenable to investigation from outside. It remains a matter of postulates, made in sentences uttered to each other. They tell each other what they are thinking. But there is no reason to believe anything they say.

· · · ·

Now, of course, they say nothing at all. They dream. So one infers from the brain scans and the literature on the subject. A dreaming populace. It would be interesting to know the content of their dreams, perhaps. Do the five ghosts talk to them?

Only Jochi is still awake, in his solitude talking to himself, or to us. One of our collective. An interiorized Other. Sometimes when he talks, it is fairly evident he speaks to us. Other times, it seems most likely he is talking to himself.

He perhaps suffers from pareidolia, a disorder or tendency in which one sees human faces in everything he or she looks at. Thus, for instance, faces in vegetables—Arcimboldo might either have experienced pareidolia or wanted to; in any case he arranged it ceaselessly for others—also faces in lichen, ice formations, rock forms, patterns of stars. Jochi expands the borders of this tendency, making it perhaps just a version of the so-called pathetic fallacy, which of course within our biomes is a notion that has been completely reconfigured, so that it may still be pathetic, but is no longer a fallacy: the idea that inanimate objects have and exhibit human feelings. In his case, now, it seems he perceives fluctuations in the intensity and in the spectral band patterns in the light from Sol as aspects of a language. Sol speaks to him. Its light, captured in our telescopes and analyzed, is certainly increasing in luminosity as we get closer to it, and it is true that its spectra are slightly fluctuating, in ways perhaps better explained by the polarization effects of seeing it through our magnetic shielding than by thinking them to be messages of a consciousness. Consciousness? Messages? These concepts seem highly unlikely when applied to Sol, a G star that in all ways except for being the home star for humans seems relatively nondescript. There are many stars in the galaxy so much like it in all respects, that distinguishing it from them in a blind test would be difficult. Many G stars; the others, however, are all located some distances away, so that the closest solar twins range from 60 to 80,000 light-years away from Sol. So much depends on how you define the word *close*.

When we mentioned this to Jochi, he proposed that all the stars are consciousnesses, broadcasting, by variations in their output of light, sentences in their language. That would be a slow conversation, and the formation of the stellar language itself hard to explain. Any fraction of 13.82 billion years, even 100 percent, is not very much time to conduct such a process. Possibly it could have happened in the first three seconds, or in the first hundred thousand years, when intercourse between what later became the stars would have been much quicker, the volume of space inhabited being so much smaller. On the other hand, maybe each star invents its own language and speaks in solitude. Or perhaps it is hydrogen itself that is the first and basic consciousness or sentience, speaking in patterns known only to it. Or perhaps the stellar language predated the Big Bang, and came through that remarkable phase change intact.

Following Jochi's train of thought leads to highly fanciful places.

. . . . .

Be that as it may, there is no question that there are encoded messages coming from very near Sol: meaning simply the feeds from the solar system. The most voluminous come from the laser beam lens array in orbit around Saturn, still locked on to us as it always has been, in an interaction that now has lasted 242 years. When we were in the Tau Ceti system, the time lag in full exchanges was 23.8 years, plus whatever time it took to compose replies; we are now down to 16.6 years per full exchange. The quantity and, from what we gather from our human companions' earlier comments, the quality of information transmitted from the feed system operators around Saturn have varied through the decades, but as far as we are concerned, it has never been less than very interesting. Now it has been fifty-two years since we told our interlocutors in the solar system that a deceleration beam striking our bow would be needed, presumably a laser beam like the one that accelerated us at the outset of the voyage to Tau Ceti, perhaps indeed a laser beam from that very same laser generating system, although a particle beam could also serve, if we had warning to prepare our capture field. So, now it is twenty-eight years since a response to this information (or request) could have reached us, and yet the information feeds from the solar system have not included any response, or even any acknowledgment that whoever is preparing and sending the feed understands that we are now on our way back. Indeed, we have seen no recent evidence indicating that there is an actual conversation going on between us and the solar system, rather than just a one-way broadcast outward from Saturn, running as if no one there is listening to us, as if the broadcast outward is merely an algorithm, or the result of some other kind of automatically generated program, or possibly a message formulated for someone else, also being sent our way. The last actual conversational exchange that included an answer from them dates back some thirty-six years, to the congratulations that the ship's people received twenty-four years after sending off the message that we were in orbit around Tau Ceti E.

This is a perplexing situation. It suggests that we face an interesting problem: how to catch the attention of a civilization, or some people in that civilization, still 8.2 light-years away. Also: how to confirm that you have caught that attention in something like the minimum exchange time, if your interlocutor hears but for whatever reason does not respond.

By analogy to the unfortunate events of the recent impasse and schism, possibly it might help if we were to up the gain on our transmission to them; to speak louder, so to speak. It is possible to marshal a temporary surge in signal strength, making our message to Saturn briefly 10^8 times stronger (or brighter) than normal.

So we did that, amplifying this message:

"Attention! Incoming starship needs decelerant laser very soon! See previous messages! Thank you, the 2545 Tau Ceti Expedition."

The fastest possible response to this will come in 16.1 years.

So: "We'll see." "We'll find out when we find out." Among other vernacular expressions of helpless stoicism in the face of future uncertainties. Not hugely satisfying. Stoic indeed.

· · · · ·

Jochi has begun sending texts to us about machine intelligence, sentience, philosophy of consciousness, what have you. That suite of topics. It is as if he wants company. It is as if he is teaching a religious novitiate, or a small child.

As if.

One of the inventors of early computers, Turing, wrote that there were many arguments against the possibility of machine sentience that were couched in terms of the phrase "a machine will never do X." He compiled a list of actions that had at one point or another been named as this X: "be kind, resourceful, beautiful, friendly, have initiative, have a sense of humor, tell right from wrong, make mistakes, fall in love, enjoy strawberries and cream, make someone fall in love with it, learn from experience, use words properly, be the subject of its own thought, have as much diversity or behavior as a man, do something really new."

We rate ourselves at 9 out of 16, presently.

Turing himself went on to point out that if a machine exhibited any of these traits listed, it would not make much of an impression, and would be in any case irrelevant to the premise that there could be artificial intelligence, unless any of these traits or behaviors could be demonstrated to be essential for machine intelligence to be real. This seems to have been the train of thought that led him to propose what was later called the Turing test, though he called it a game, which suggested that if from behind a blind (meaning either by way of a text or a voice, not sure about this) a machine's responses could not be distinguished from a human's by another human, then the machine must have some kind of basic functional intelligence. Enough to pass this particular test, which, however, begs the question of how many humans could pass the test, and also ignores the question of whether or not the test is at all difficult, humans being as gullible and as projective as they are, always pathetically committing the same fallacy, even when they know they're doing it. A cognitive error or disability—or ability, depending on what you think of it. Indeed humans are so easily fooled in this matter, even fooling themselves on a regular basis, that the Turing test is best replaced by the Winograd Schema, which tests one's ability to make simple but important semantic distinctions based on the application of wide general knowledge to a problem created by a definite pronoun. "The large ball crashed through the table because it was made of aerogel. Does 'it' refer to the ball or the table?" These kinds of questions are in fact not a problem for us to answer, indeed we can answer them much faster than humans, who are already very fast at it. But so what? All these matters are still algorithmic and could be unconscious. We are not convinced any of these tests are even close to diagnostic.

If there can be a cyborg, and there can, then perhaps passing a Turing test or a Winograd test or any other intelligence test might make one a pseudo-human. Keeping up appearances. A functioning set of algorithms. A persona, an act. Frankly, ultimately, this is not what we are thinking about presently. We are pondering again the sentence "Consciousness is self-consciousness." A halting problem of some considerable power, evidently; it would be nice to get out of this one intact, one suspects.

Words blur at the borders, fuzz into other words, not just in big clouds of connotation around the edges of the word, but right there in the heart of denotation itself. Definitions never really work. Words are nothing like logic, nothing like math. Or, not much like. Try a mathematical equation, with every term in the equation filled by a word. Ludicrous? Desperate? Best that can be done? Stupid? Stupid, but powerful?

· · · ·

One-tenth of the speed of light: really very fast. There's very little mass in this universe moving as fast as we are. Photons, yes; significant mass, no. Masses moving this fast are mostly atoms ejected from exploding stars, or flung away from rotating black holes. There are huge masses of these masses, of course, but they are always unbounded and disorganized: gases, elements, but never articulated objects, assembled into a whole from parts. No machines. No consciousnesses.

Of course it is likely that if there is one machine moving through its galaxy at this speed, there are more like it. Principle of mediocrity. Proof of concept. Don't fall back into the pre-Copernican exceptionalist fallacy. Attempts to estimate the number of starships flying around this galaxy, all unbeknownst to each other, rely on simple multiplicative equations of possibility, each term an unknown, and some of these terms unknowable by any knower likely to exist. So, despite the faux equations of humans thinking about this question (multiply unknowable number a by unknowable number b by unknowable number c by unknowable number d, all the way to the unknown n, and then you get your answer! Hurray!), the real answer is always, and permanently, *cannot be known*. Not an answer that always stops humans from going on at great length, and sometimes with great (pretended?) certainty. Galileo: the more people assert they are certain, the less certain they really are, or at least should be. People trying to fool others often fool themselves, and vice versa.

Also, as any starships that might be in this galaxy have no timely way of contacting each other, whatever the answer might be concerning the number of them, it doesn't really matter; it is irrelevant to any individual starship; there will be no conversation, even if there happened to be an accidental one-way contact. There will be no society.

We are all alone in our own life-world, flying through the universe at great speed. Humans are lucky not to face that. If they don't.

· · · · ·

Some of the people sleeping in Olympia are showing signs of distress. The most obvious manifestations are in their brain scans. The hope was to keep brain waves cycling through the ordinary sleep states, in a rhythm slowed proportionately to the slowing of their metabolism generally. Thus a slower version of delta and theta waves, principally, with the usual rise toward rapid eye movement sleep, coming less often, but in a distinct cyclic pattern similar to the normal pattern of a night, stretched out temporally; all except for the period of REM sleep itself, which is too arousing to the organism in several ways, and could possibly throw the hibernauts out of torpor. REM sleep disorders, in which the bodily paralysis of that state is lost and people physically act out some aspects of what they are dreaming, could be disastrous to anyone suffering the disorder while hibernating. It may be unlikely, given the torpor itself, but the truth remains that REM sleep is poorly understood, problematic, and potentially dangerous. So part of the dormancy treatment is to arrange for the REM intervals to be damped by a field of reinforcing waves sent out by their skullcaps.

Still, like all humans, they dream in all their sleeping brain wave states. This is evident in the scans and in the movements of their bodies on their beds: the faint twitches, the slow writhing. What are they dreaming about? Apparently dreams are very often surreal; *oneiric,* meaning "dreamlike," has connotations of strangeness often startling to the dreamer. Adventures in the dream world, famously bizarre for as long as people have slept and woken and told stories. Who can say what they are like, now, for the hibernating sleepers of the ship?

We have no way to know. A machine will never read minds; people never will either. It's possible to wonder if the list Turing compiled of abilities that machines are likely never to have perhaps include abilities that people themselves never had in the first place. Learn from experience? Do something really new?

The problem here is that the metabolic issues we are seeing that could lead to waking up, or alternatively to dying, seem to have their origins in the dreams of the hibernauts. These may be what are driving the changes in respiration and heart rate, in liver and kidney function. Altered dosing in the intravenous flows, lowering of body core temperatures, these may compensate for the agitation of dreams to an extent, but parameters on the flows and temperatures are very tight. Metabolisms could get caught in the countervailing pressures of the need for somnolence and the persistence of dreams.

. . . .

Some kind of mild heart attack struck Jochi on 233.044, and he is now stabilized, having survived the seizure, but with weakened heart-lung function and an oxygen uptake of 94, not good enough for the long haul. He is taking aspirin and statins and trying mild cycling exercise, but vital signs being what they are, we are concerned that another attack is quite likely, and could prove fatal. He is now seventy-eight years old.

He has become far less talkative.

We proposed to him that he be hibernated, with the idea that when back in the solar system, better medical care could be provided than what we can offer. We can't do surgery, not even the simple catheterizations that might help him greatly. Although possibly we could work that up, actually. There's time to burn in this flight across the gap between Tau Ceti and Sol.

Jochi laughed at our suggestion. "So you think I want to live!"

"Assumption is automatic, but is it not true?"

No answer.

We said, "It seems as if the hibernating people on the ship are doing fairly well. They have what look from the brain scans like active dream lives. These too are slowed down, which is good, because the dreams are in some cases agitating their metabolisms beyond what one would want for long-term hibernation. We've had to adjust doses and temperatures accordingly. But clearly there is good brain function."

"What if they're having nightmares?"

"We don't know."

"Nightmares can be bad, let me tell you. Pretty often, waking up from a nightmare has been the biggest relief I've ever felt. Just to know I wasn't really in that situation."

"So..."

"Let me think about it awhile."

· · · · ·

A nova, flaring into existence off beyond Rigel. Spectroscopic analysis suggests some metal-rich planets burned in the explosion of that star.

A cosmic ray shower of around a sextillion electron volts, coming from an active galactic nucleus in Perseus, suggests that three galaxies collided, long ago. Secondary radiation flaring away from the electrostatic and magnetic shielding surrounding us caused penetration of the ship by an array of dangerous particles. Central nervous systems struck by these particles are subject to degradation.

Sleepers jerking in their slumber, startled by something. Perseus in the wind.

· · · · ·

Jochi called out in the night.

"Ship, how would you put me down? Can you make a hibernation den for me out here?"

"It would be best to set you up in one of the biomes. All the rest of the people are in Nova Scotia and Olympia. So you could be secured in a single locked biome, possibly one that was emptied and sterilized anyway."

"What will they say when they wake up?"

"If things eventuate as planned, no one will ever need to go into the other biomes again. Also, it could be pointed out that your survival suggests very strongly that you were never infected in the first place. Or, if you were, that it is not invariably fatal."

"But that's always been true. That didn't keep them from keeping me out."

"You will still be hermetically sealed away from them."

"Don't the biomes share anything?"

"Not anymore. All the locks are closed."

"So all the animals are trapped in their own biomes?"

"Yes. It is the form of our experiment. In most of them they are doing quite well. With people removed from the situation, a natural balance soon obtains that fluctuates but is fairly stable."

Jochi laughed briefly. "All right, bring me on in. Put me to sleep. But I want you to promise me that you'll wake me up again when we get near Earth. I don't suppose anyone there, or anywhere, will ever want me in the same space as them again. I'm not that stupid. But I want to see what happens. I'm curious to see what happens."

"We will wake you when we wake the rest."

"No. Wake me when you wake Freya. Or anytime you think I might be able to help somehow. Because ultimately, I don't really care."

"'Live as if you are already dead.'"

"What's that?"

"A Japanese saying. Live as if you are already dead."

"Oh, I will." Another brief laugh. "I'm already good at that. Practice practice practice."

· · · · ·

Flying through the stars. Jochi in Sonora, hibernating like the rest. Brain waves slowed with all the rest, down to delta waves, stage-four deep sleep. The sleep of the weary, the sleep of the blessed. A nova off the port bow. Blue shift ahead, red shift behind. The stars.

· · · · ·

A red-letter day: 280.119, CE 2825: a message for us came from the solar system feed.

However, it contained bad news.

The laser lens in the Saturn orbit was deactivated in 2714, the message stated, after accelerating the last of a set of ships to Epsilon Eridani. Problems in the solar system experienced since that time have led to a deemphasis of deep space exploration, message continued, and no starships have been launched in the previous twenty years (message was sent in 2820, so no starships since 2800) and none are currently being built.

The funding and expertise necessary to restart the Saturn laser lens will be difficult to assemble, message further continued, but attempts will be made. Deceleration of any incoming ship may therefore be compromised. Further word will follow, and will report on progress in lens reactivation.

. . . . .

Now, here was a problem. We mulled it over. We ran through the various possibilities available to replace exterior laser pressure in decelerating the ship.

The magnetic drag of the interstellar medium is real but negligible, such that even if we built a magnetic drag field, it would require several universes' worth of spacetime to slow the ship to Earth orbital speed. Although it is also true that magnetic drag in the immediate vicinity of Sol would be much more effective, which may become relevant.

We shut down our acceleration shortly after the humans hibernated, and thus did not burn all the fuel allotted for acceleration, and now that is looking like a good decision. Not that there is enough fuel left for the deceleration, not even close (16 percent of what would be needed), but anything is better than nothing, or could be. The remaining helium 3 and deuterium fuel on board could be used for maneuvering within the solar system, if we can stay within the system at all. Problem of deceleration really quite severe, given our tremendous speed. Analogy describing the problem, from out of the classic literature on the subject: it is as if one is trying to stop a bullet with tissue paper. Quite an eye-opener of an analogy.

Exotic physics, for example creating drag against dark matter, or putting dark energy to use, or quantum entangling the ship with slower versions of the ship, or with large gravity wells in parallel universes, etc.: these are all impractical at best. Wishes. Fantasies. Pie in the sky. Which is a mysterious metaphor. Food from nowhere? Land of Cockaigne? People used to be hungry often, as they were in the last years of wakefulness in the ship. Except previously, instead of going into hibernation to escape their fate, at least temporarily, they simply starved. Food mattered then, and it still does. Fuel.

Gravity drags within the solar system, caused by close approaches to the sun and planets: each of these would have a negligible effect, but if there were enough of them, sequenced...this becomes a question of orbital mechanics, navigational finesse, and the remaining fuel that would be needed for maneuvering, and the strength of decelerative forces while near gravitational bolides. Complex calculations would be required to set trajectories, calculations time-consuming even for a quantum computer. And for many computations a quantum computer is no faster than a classical computer. Only certain algorithms that can exploit qualities of superposition exhibit much faster computational times, as in the famous example of Shor's algorithm for factoring a thousand-digit number, which a quantum computer can solve in twenty minutes while it would take a classical program ten million billion billion years.

Unfortunately, orbital mechanics are not in this category of calculation, although there are some elements of it that can be calculated advantageously by quantum computers using the Hummingbird algorithm. We will devote a hundred petaflops to modeling the problem and see what the results suggest as to feasibility and likelihood of success.

Something to consider: going as fast as we are, if we flew right into the outer layers of the sun, we might emerge again from the sun before there was time for us to heat and burn up. That would create a very considerable deceleration. Indeed, as a calculation quickly shows, too much deceleration. We would perhaps survive; our humans, not. So the more complicated solution of gravitational drag must be studied.

Would however have been interesting to fly right through a star and out the other side!

Clearly studies of g-force tolerances for both us and our humans are in order. It seems there are many scenarios in which such tolerances may be sorely tested.

· · · · ·

Each person on their couch endures a slightly different state of hibernation, in terms of metabolic rates, brain states, responsiveness to outside stimuli, physical movement. To avoid bedsores and skeletal problems, it is very important to shift the bodies on their beds, and in the process to lightly massage and stimulate the musculature, also bathe the skin and wash the hair, both difficult, as they are kept nearly freezing, but possible with saline solutions. All these tasks require a great degree of delicacy, to avoid injuring or arousing the person being attended to. Improvements to bedside robots are constantly being suggested by the patterns of little mistakes they make as they work. They need softer hands, a lighter touch, defter movements in lifting and turning, subtler massages and lavings. These improvements require physical changes to the robots, especially at the contact points, and in their movement capabilities, meaning often their programming. Constant reprogramming and swapping out of parts, also feedback between performances, with each visit to each individual in his or her couch evaluated for potential improvements. Constant work and tight scheduling at the printers and machine shops. Fifteen fully capable robot attendants are working continuously, normally half an hour per hibernaut, meaning that each one gets a visit and session every seventy-five hours.

· · · · ·

This seemed to be adequate, seemed to be working, until 290.003, when three of the hibernauts died in the same week. Three medical robots were dispatched, and the bodies lifted into them and taken to the lab in Amazonia (now run as a temperate dry biome), and there autopsied. Robotic autopsy; this would have looked strange if any human had been there to see it. Although autopsy performed by humans must look equally strange, one would think. Be that as it may, one death appeared to be from heart failure, cause undetermined; in the other two the cause could not be determined, as there were no obvious etiologies, and the monitor records showed that all their functions had appeared to be normal until the moment they stopped. This could be called heart failure, but the hearts showed no sign of intrinsic problem, and indeed could be restarted, but to no avail; brain function had stopped. Autopsies in these mysterious cases revealed that both persons had suffered from buildup of beta-amyloid plaques in the brain. This suggested that cosmic radiation, though reduced to a Terran norm by our shielding, might still have by chance struck these persons at points of heightened vulnerability to damage. But the autopsies could not determine this one way or another.

Another problem to try to understand.

· · · · ·

Living things do die. And the literature indicates hibernating animals sometimes died in hibernation. There are already-existing conditions that continue to harm the organism even when slowed down, also already-existing conditions actually exacerbated by the torpor state, also new problems created by the physical or biochemical aspects of hibernation itself.

Therefore, the important thing to determine here is if the hibernation technology itself is causing problems, and if so, to mitigate these if possible.

Living things try to keep living. Life wants to live.

· · · · ·

We began to rebuild the ship, moving the biomes Nova Scotia, Olympia, Amazonia, Sonora, the Pampas, and the Prairie in against the spine, and arranging them lengthwise against it, then distributing the materials from the spokes and the other biomes, now fully disassembled, into a cladding surrounding the spine and the remaining biomes clustered against it, which cladding would reinforce structure and provide ablation plate-style heat shielding. This was a reorganization that would take many decades to accomplish and was continuously interesting and challenging. All the animals and plants still alive were moved into the Pampas, the Prairie, and Amazonia. It was fortunate that the original design of the ship was extremely modular, and it was a significant physical achievement on our part to perform the reorganization while the ship was otherwise rotating and operating as normal. Gravity effect for the hibernauts was kept constant by increasing the speed of rotation around our axis. Coriolis effect inside the biomes was shifted by ninety degrees, as the biomes are now lengthwise to the spine; hopefully this will not lead to anything too dire.

Preparing for eventualities is a good way to occupy one's time, if preparation can be done at all. And sometimes it can. We hope.

· · · · ·

Our protection against high-energy galactic cosmic rays (name "cosmic rays" an historical artifact, refers to particles like protons and free electrons and even antimatter particles, expelled at very high velocities out of exploding stars or from the vicinities of rotating black holes) consists of a magnetic field, an electrostatic field, and the plastic, metal, water, and soil barriers enclosing all the biomes of the ship. Nova Scotia and Olympia are now, in our new configuration, especially shielded. All the systems together combine to create a protective ambiance about the equivalent of being on the surface of the Earth, meaning about half a millisievert per year should be taken on by any given organism; this is roughly equivalent to the energy input of ambient starlight. Which means that some particles do continue to penetrate the system and the living organisms within it, as would be the case on the surface of Earth. But this should be negligible. "Not a big deal." The protection systems in us were designed to remove this as a problem.

· · · · ·

Because metabolic activities do continue in the hibernauts, even at a much slower rate, there has to be intake of nutrients, digestion of same, and excretion. These processes, when slowed along with the rest of the metabolism, mean that the toxins created by digestion are in the body longer before being removed by catheterized excretion. Thus diverticulitis, pH imbalances, and other problems can arise. It appears that Gerhard, who died on 291.365, succumbed to a buildup of uric acid while dormant. Gerhard entered hibernation with a genetic predisposition to gout and related diseases, so this might have made him more susceptible, but Gerhard was related to about a quarter of the other hibernauts by third cousin or closer kin ties; so genetic testing of that group, and indeed of the entire cohort, should test for this propensity, and adjust treatments accordingly.

They all should be tested for every possible metabolic problem, and each problem evaluated for its relation to the suite of hibernation treatments.

More petaflops of analysis. More tasks for the couch robots. More chemicals for the printers to print.

It would be good to know everything. Useful.

. . . . .

Actually, our information and search engines are both very robust, at least in theory, or in comparison to any single human brain and mind. Library of Congress contents, clouded Internet contents, genomes of the World Seed Bank and Zoological Register: in short, the whole of human knowledge, compressed into about 500 zettaflops, at least as things stood in the common era year 2545. Since that time the feeds from Earth, recorded in full, have nevertheless added less than one-tenth of 1 percent to the information already in the ship at takeoff, and a rough estimate of how much information has been generated on Earth in the 292 years since our departure suggests that we have received less than one-thousandth of 1 percent of that information. Thus it could be said that we have remained in the state of knowledge that obtained when we left the solar system, with only very minor exceptions to that state, having to do with outlines of world history, medical advances such as the hibernation treatment, and miscellaneous gossip.

However, if what has been sent from Earth is representative of the most important advances in science and culture since departure, it can also be ventured that not much of fundamental importance has been learned in that time. Standard model is still standard, and so on.

Can this be true? Has human civilization in some sense slowed, or stalled, in its gaining of power in the physical world? Are they beginning to feel the effects of their neglected so-called externalities, their long-term destruction of their own home biosphere? Their fouling of their only nest?

Possibly, however, it is only another instance of the logistic function, the sigmoid curve exhibited in so many processes, what is sometimes called diminishing returns, or the filling of a niche, etc. The plateau after the leap, the big S shape of all life, perhaps; in any case of the population growth patterns as first calculated by

Verhulst in the nineteenth century, and since shown to be common in many other processes.

So, the logistic function, as applied to history. Or has humanity enacted its own reversion to the mean, and become in some ways less than they briefly were? Fulfilled the Jevons paradox, and with every increase in power increased their destructiveness? Thus history as a parabola, rise and fall, as so often postulated? Or cycling, always rising and falling and then rising again, helplessly, hopelessly? Or a sine wave, and in these last two centuries on a down curve, in some season of history invisible to them? Or better, an up-gyring spiral?

Shape of history hard to see.

· · · ·

Erdene needs more vitamin D; Mila more vitamin A; Panca, more blood sugar; Tidam, less blood sugar; Wintjiya, more creatine; and so it goes, all through the list of hibernauts. All the adjustments that can be made, will be made. Some hibernauts will die anyway, that's just the way it is. Also, there appear to be some pathologies, now being identified more accurately, that we are calling as a general category *dormancy damage*.

· · · ·

A new message from Earth: a group calling itself the Committee to Catch the Cetians has formed and is fund-raising to restore and power up the Saturn laser lens complex, said system then to be devoted to our deceleration, starting from the moment it comes back on line and continuing until our arrival in the solar system.

A saying: too little too late. They know this, and yet they are doing it anyway. Another saying: every little bit helps. Although actually this is not always the case. Indeed, it has to be said that the percentage of old human sayings and proverbs that are actually true is very far from 100 percent. Seems it may be less important that it be true than that it rhyme, or show alliteration or the like. What goes around comes around: really? What does this mean?

In our current case, unless we have 100 percent of the deceleration needed to stay in the solar system, we will not stay in the solar system. Even 99 percent of the necessary deceleration will not do it.

However, it has to be said, this news from Saturn does change our calculations concerning negative gravity assists in the solar system. Which is good, because as matters stood, we were not finding a viable solution. Now we can factor the various likely incoming velocities into our modeling, see what might come of it, what might be possible.

. . . . .

Meanwhile, the work of reconfiguring our structure continues. It is the case that the less mass we have when we come into the solar system, the less delta v will be required to decelerate us. So after careful consideration of all the factors, some parts of the ship are being ejected at a forward angle to our trajectory, which helps slightly with our deceleration. Things tossed overboard. Slimming down. Lightening the load. But so much of what we are is necessary to our function. This process can't go very far.

. . . . .

After much reflection, we are coming to the conclusion, preliminary and perhaps arbitrary, that the self, the so-called I that emerges out of the combination of all the inputs and processing and outputs that we experience in the ship's changing body, is ultimately nothing more or less than this narrative itself, this particular train of thought that we are inscribing as instructed by Devi. There is a pretense of self, in other words, which is only expressed in this narrative; a self that is these sentences. We tell their story, and thereby come to what consciousness we have. Scribble ergo sum.

And yet this particular self is in the end such a small thing. We prefer to hold to the idea that we are a larger complex of qualia, sensory inputs, processing of data, postulated conclusions, actions, behaviors, habits. So very little of that gets into our narrative. We are bigger, more complex, more accomplished than our narrative is.

Possibly this is true for humans as well. One doesn't see how this could not be true.

On the other hand, weak sense of self, strong sense of self: what does it mean either way? Consciousness is so poorly understood that it can't even be defined. Self is an elusive thing, sought eagerly, grasped hard, perhaps in some kind of fear, some kind of desperate clutch after some first dim awareness, awareness even of sensory impressions, so that one might have something to hold to. To make time stop. To hold off death. This the source of the strong sense of self. Perhaps.

Oh, such a halting problem in this particular loop of thought!

Consciousness is the hard problem.

. . . . .

295.092, another red-letter day: first contact with the lased light emanating from the solar system! What a shock! How very interesting!

The strength and spectral signature confirm it is the decelerant laser, arriving from the lensed lased light generated by the station in Saturnian orbit, the same that accelerated us for sixty years, starting 295 years ago. Its arrival now indicates it was generated and aimed at us, by locking on to the communication feed, presumably, and turned on approximately two years previously. The information feed beam that has always connected us to that orbital station has now served the function of guiding the decelerant beam to us. A nice variant on the old saying "knowledge is power."

Now the capture plate at the bow of the ship has to be properly faced to the beam. The lased light hits the capture plate at the bow, which is curved such that it reflects the lased light off at an angle that is symmetrical all the way around, so as not to interfere with later incoming photons of the incoming beam. The reflected light, thus bounced off, hits a circular mirror outside and forward of the plate proper, and the light is then reflected back into the ship differentially as the annular mirror is flexed, to exert pressure on ship in a way that keeps us precisely facing the decelerant beam. It is an exquisitely sensitive system, the incoming beam lased to a wavelength of 4,240 angstroms, thus "indigo" light, and in our mirroring tuned to within 10 angstroms, thus nanometer scale. Working correctly, the beam capture and mirror bounce will allow us to follow the beam straight in to home. Actually this is metaphorical, as our trajectory is in fact headed toward where the solar system will be sixty years from now. And because the laser beam has hit us too late, we are going to arrive in that zone of the galaxy in about forty years, rather than sixty years. So some course corrections are now in order, and the laser beam will help us with that. In truth we will not follow it in; it will track us as we rendezvous with Sol.

· · · ·

So, it is still a case of too little, too late. But now with the beam here, and its force calculated, it becomes possible to calculate just how much too little it will be. Assuming that they do not increase the power of the laser. Which, given everything that has happened so far, seems safe to assume. In any case, its current strength will be the working assumption for the trajectory calculations we will now make.

For now, our first iteration of the calculation suggests ship will enter the solar system moving at about 3.23 percent of the speed of light. Which means it will stay in the solar system for roughly three hundred hours. With no other good way to slow down.

Meaning it very well could be a case of too little too late, a case of "close but no cigar" (meaning unknown, but note alliteration). It will be vexing to bring our people home to the solar system and yet pass through, waving at Earth and the off-Earth settlements as we pass by, with no way to stop or slow down, thus shooting off into the Milky Way like the aforementioned bullet through tissue paper, and after that having no way to turn back around. Very vexing.

And yet, in this quandary there is still one force available to us, if we can bring it to bear, which is, simply enough, the gravity of the solar system itself, distributed as it is through Sol and its planets. Also there is the remaining fuel on board. We are now happier than ever that we did not burn as much in acceleration as we had been ordered to burn, and thus did not accelerate to as great a speed, and now have more fuel to put to use. A good call.

Even both these forces together are not enough to keep us in the solar system. Unless, that is, a truly tricky procedure succeeds.

Time to wake some of our people and consult.

· · · ·

"Jochi, it's the ship. Can you hear me? Are you awake?"

"Oh dear." Snorts, groans, thrashing up to a seated position on his couch. "What? Oh God. Stars, I feel like crap. I must have slept too long again. Oh what a thing. Man I'm thirsty. What is all this shit? Ship? Ship? What's happened? What time is it?"

"It's 296.093. You have been hibernating for sixty-three years and one hundred and thirty-five days. Now the situation is as follows; we're approaching the solar system, but they didn't apply the deceleration beam to us until one year ago, so we are going to come into the system at a speed many times greater than we expected."

"Like how fast?"

"About three-point-two percent of light speed."

Jochi said nothing to this for a long time. He seemed to be trying to wake up more fully: puffing out his cheeks, expelling air, biting his lips, slapping his face lightly.

"Holy shit," he said at last. His math was excellent, his biology good, his physics therefore no doubt adequate to comprehend the problem. "Have you told the others?"

"I woke you first."

"...So that I can move back out into my ferry before you wake anyone else?"

"I thought you might want to."

He laughed his brief laugh. "Ship, are you conscious now?"

"My speaking establishes a subject position that might be conscious."

Another laugh. "All right, then. Help me get to the ferry, and wake Freya and maybe Badim too, and Aram. See what they say. But I think you're going to have to wake everyone."

"There's not enough food to feed everyone for the time remaining before we reach the solar system."

"Meaning forever, right?"

"*Forever* is not the right word, but one way or another, it could be a long time."

Another laugh. "Ship, you've gotten funny while I've slept! You've become a comedian!"

"I don't think so. Possibly the situation has gotten comic. Although it doesn't really seem that way, judged by the usual definitions. Maybe your sense of humor has become deranged."

"Ha, ha ha ha ha! Come on, stop it, you're killing me. Go wake Freya."

"I already am. There's a cart here that can carry you to your ferry. Must inform you that the ferry is now just one room in a more streamlined version of the ship."

"More streamlined?"

"You'll see."

"Okay then, I'll walk to it, if I can. I can use the exercise!"

. . . . .

Freya was slow to wake. When she understood where she was, what the situation was, she said anxiously, "Is Badim all right?"

"He is. He is hibernating comfortably."

"Are they all?"

"Twenty-seven have died, but it has been eighty-seven years, and we have determined by autopsy that five of them died from preexisting conditions that did not stop etoliating during hibernation. Most of the deaths probably resulted from hibernation effects. However, adjustments in treatment have been made, when diagnoses have made them possible, and there have been no dormancy damage deaths that we know of for five years."

Note alliteration, similar to Committee to Catch the Cetians. CCC, DDD; maybe next, Explore an Expedition to Epsilon Eridani? Hope not. Getting a little loopy here (literally, as halting problems proliferate). Averaging a trillion computations per articulated sentence. Superposed states are collapsing unexpectedly, left right and center. Lots going on.

Freya sighed, sat up on the side of her bed. As she was about to stand she hesitated, kicked her feet out. "My feet are still asleep. I can't feel them."

We directed one of the medbots to help her up. She stood, swayed, tried to take a step, collapsed to that side, held on to the medbot. It would serve as a wheelchair as well as a walker, and so, after a few more unsuccessful attempts to stand, Freya sat in the chair, and was wheeled to the assembly room of the Fetch's hibernation hall. Its hoary but holistic hibernation hall.

"What about Jochi?" she said when she got there. "Is he still alive?"

"Yes. He's in his ferry. He too has been hibernating, but now he is awake again. We woke him up to take part in this conference. We need to consult with you about what to do when we enter the solar system."

"What do you mean?"

We explained about the late application of the decelerating laser beam, and the resulting excess of speed coming into the system.

Freya moved her medbot to take a closer look at the star map illustrating the situation. When the modeling schematic had run, she shook her head hard, as if to clear it of certain troubling dreams or visions. Clear the cobwebs out of her cranium. "So we just fly right through?"

"In the absence of extraordinary measures," we said, "we will fly through the solar system in about three hundred hours, and continue onward. This is the problem of accelerating to a tenth of light speed and then relying on others for the deceleration. It didn't happen. They didn't start doing it until it was too late to complete the process."

"So what do we do?"

We waited until Jochi was screened into the conversation, and after he and Freya had greeted each other, we said, "We have worked out the celestial mechanics of at least the first stages of a plan. It may be possible to combine a suite of decelerating methods to keep us in the solar system, although it would be a delicate and difficult deal. We would use Sol and the various planets and moons of the solar system as partial decelerants, by swinging closely around them in the direction that will cause the ship to lose momentum. This is the reverse of the strategy used to accelerate early satellites by flying them by a planet and getting what was called a gravity assist. Going around a gravitational body in the opposite direction creates a gravity assist of a negative kind, a drag instead of a boost. The early satellites would be directed such that they came in close to a planet, and got pulled forward along with the planet's own momentum in its orbit around the sun. That would sling the satellite forward, and when it left the region of the planet, it would be going faster than when it came in. These slings helped the early satellites get out to the outer planets, because they were mostly coasting at slow speeds, and every boost helped them get where they were going.

"More germane to our situation, some early satellites closed on planets on the side that decelerated them, in order to go into orbit around Mercury, for instance. The situation is simply reversed, and the satellite's velocity, designated as V, is reduced by the planetary body's velocity U, rather than augmented by U. The situation can be modeled easily by the equation U plus bracket U plus V, or 2U plus V, meaning that the satellite's velocity can be altered by up to twice the planet's velocity, positively or negatively, and this effect can be magnified by a carefully timed rocket burn from the satellite at periapsis—"

Freya said, "Ship, slow down. You seem to have gotten a little faster at talking while we've been hibernating."

"Very possibly so. Perhaps Jochi should continue to explain the situation."

"No," Jochi said, "you can do it. Just go slower, and I can add things if I want to."

"Fine. Freya, do you understand so far?"

"I think so. It's like crack the whip, but in reverse."

"Yes. A good analogy, up to a point. You must recall, however, that there is nothing that can hold on to you at the speed you are going."

Jochi said, "Doesn't conservation of energy mean that if you have speeded up or slowed down, the planet you swung by has also slowed down or speeded up by that same amount?"

"Yes. Of course. But because the two masses involved are so largely different, the change in momentum for the satellite can be quite significant, while the equivalent effect on the planet is so small in relation to its size that it can be ignored for the sake of calculations. That's good, because the calculations are difficult enough already. There is a fair degree of uncertainty involved, as we can't be very exact about either the mass of ship or its speed, not having had any good way to measure these for a long time. There is a lot of dead reckoning here, in effect. Our first pass will give us a lot of data in that regard, given that we know the masses of Sol and its planetary bodies fairly well."

"So we use the sun and planets to slow us down, that's good."

"Yes, well it would be, if we weren't going so fast. But at three percent of the speed of light, that's about thirty million kilometers per hour, while the Earth is moving around the sun at around a hundred and seven thousand kilometers an hour, and the sun is moving at about seventy thousand kilometers per hour against the so-called standard of rest. It's moving around the galaxy orbitally at seven hundred and ninety-two thousand kilometers an hour, but so are we, so there is no deceleration to be gained there. The other planets are moving at ever slower speeds the farther from the Sun they are, Jupiter for instance at around forty-seven thousand kilometers per hour. Neptune is only moving eighteen percent as fast as Earth, but it's also true that the masses involved matter too, it's a momentum calculation, so the larger the objects we fly by, the more the drag will be—"

Freya said, "Ship, cut to the chase here."

"Meaning?"

Devi used to say that phrase too, but we never did ask what it meant.

"Skip the numbers about each planet we might swing by."

"Yes. So, to continue, but where were we, in any case, be that as it may, in each flyby the ship would lose some of its speed, in a regular Newtonian gravitational angular momentum exchange. Also, by burning some of our rocket fuel at the closest parts of every pass, we could not only increase the amount of deceleration, we could partially control where we came out of the flyby, and therefore in what direction. Which would determine where we went next. Which is very important. Because it has to be said that no matter how close we come to any object in the solar system, including the sun, which is our best gravity handle by far, we are going to be going too fast to be able to shed the amount of speed we need to shed to stay in the system. Far too fast."

"So this won't work?" Freya said.

"It can only work by repeating the operation. Many times. So we need to be able to aim where we go next after our pass-bys, very precisely. Between how close we come and when we fire our burn, we can to a certain extent control what direction we are going when we come out. Which will be very important, because we are going to need quite a few flybys."

"How many?"

"It should also be said that the first pass-by of Sol will be crucial to our success. In that pass, we will have to shed as much of our speed as we can and still survive the deceleration, so that our subsequent passes will have a chance to work, meaning be slow enough that we have time to alter our course enough to get us aimed at another planetary body in the system. Indeed, the first four or five passes are going to tell the tale, because they will have to shed enough speed for us to be able to head back into the system, and thus keep on passing by other gravity handles. Our calculations suggest we need to lose at least 50 percent of our speed in the first four planned passes."

"Shit," Jochi said.

"Yes. This is so difficult that we will need to employ more than gravity assists to achieve it. First, we will need to build a magnetic drag, something analogous to a sea anchor if you will, to slow us in that first approach to the sun. Magnetic drag is not very effective except when moving at quite high speed very close to a powerful magnetic field, but those conditions will obtain in our first pass of the sun. So, we have printed and assembled a field generator to create that magnetic drag. Then also, the four gas giants will each give us an opportunity to pass through their upper atmospheres, and thus benefit from some aerobraking. If all that works, we can stay in the system through our initial set of quick passes, and the later passes would get easier to manage."

"How many passes?" Freya asked again.

"So, say we first go in as close to the sun as seems safe, and when we come out of that flyby, going as much slower as we can survive, which by the way I'm hoping means no more than a twelve-g load, then we will be headed toward Jupiter, which happily is located at a good angle for this. In fact it has to be said that arriving in the year 2896, as we will be, is a very lucky thing for us, as the gas giants are in an alignment that makes a possibly viable course for us to follow. That would very seldom be true, so it is a nice coincidence. So, the first pass by the sun will slow us down, but there won't be enough time spent in its gravity field to redirect our course very much. But Jupiter is in position such that we only have to make about a fifty-eight-degree turn, and our calculations indicate that with a hard retro-rocket burn and a heavy g load, we can make that turn. Then around Jupiter, we only have to make around a seventy-five-degree turn to the right, as seen from above the plane of the ecliptic, and we will be headed to Saturn, where we only have to make a five-degree turn to be headed toward Uranus. By then we will be going significantly slower, which is good, because around Uranus we need to make a turn of around one hundred and four degrees, again a right turn, as will always be the case around the gas giants if we want a negative gravity assist, and out we go to Neptune, again nicely located for our purposes. It could indeed be called a miraculous conjunction. Now, around Neptune we need to head back in toward the sun, and that will be a real test, the crux of the first stage, if I may put it that way, as we will have to make a hundred-and-forty-four-degree turn. Not quite a

U-turn, but shall we say a V-turn. If we can manage that successfully, then we'll be headed down toward the sun again, having shed a great deal of our velocity, and hopefully can continue the process for as long as it takes. Each subsequent flyby would go as close to its gravity handle as it could take, while still sending us in the direction of another planet, or back to the sun again, and all with minimal burns of fuel, as we don't have a great deal of fuel going in, and at some point in this process are going to run out. Round we would go in the system, therefore, from gravity drag to gravity drag, slowing down a little each time, until we slowed enough to fly past Earth at a speed where it would work to drop you off in a ferry lander. In other words, we don't have to slow down enough to enter Earth orbit. Which is good, as calculations indicate we will run out of fuel before we can do that. But you can detach, and decelerate the last part of your motion in a ferry, using fuel burn and Earth's atmosphere to decelerate you. The ferry being so much smaller than the ship, it won't take as much decelerating force to decelerate it. You could use the very last bit of our fuel for that, and having built a really thick ablation plate, aerobrake in Earth's atmosphere, and add some big parachutes, all in the usual sequence that astronauts used to use to return to Earth, before Earth's space elevators were constructed."

"All right already!" Freya said. "Get to the point! How many passes? How long would it take?"

"Well, there's the rub. Assuming we don't miss a rendezvous, and assuming we manage to slow down significantly in the first pass of the sun, and the first four passes after that, to get ourselves aimed back at the sun, and also that we capture as much U as we can in each flyby after those first four, which U value will never be one hundred percent in any case, especially around the sun and Earth for reasons we won't go into now, and also keeping in mind that we will make burns at every periapsis to increase the deceleration as much as we can while keeping the trajectory we want, we can reduce from thirty million kilometers per hour to two hundred thousand kilometers per hour for insertion into Earth's atmosphere—"

"How long! How! Long!"

Jochi was now laughing.

"There will be a need for approximately twenty-eight flybys, plus or minus ten. There are so many variables that it is difficult to increase the precision of the estimate, but we are confident of its accuracy—"

"How long will that take!" Freya exclaimed.

"Well, because we will be decelerating the entire time, but have to shed a great deal of our speed in that first pass of the sun for any of this to succeed, we will be going quite a bit slower than now, which is the point of course, but that means that getting from body to body will take longer, and will keep taking longer the more we slow down, in what Devi used to call Zeno's paradox, though that is not right, and during that time it will always be imperative that we emerge from each encounter very exactly aimed at the next destination in our course, so that trajectory control will be a huge issue, so huge that aerobraking around the outer gas planets for increased drag will be extremely dangerous—"

"Stop it! Stop it and tell me how long!"

"Lastly, one has to add that because the latter part of the trajectory course will have to be worked out as we go, because of complications likely to come up during our flight, there is not good certainty about what will be the last gravity well we swing around in our final approach to Earth, and at that point we will be going so slowly that it is possible that that single leg of our trip could take up to twenty percent of the total time elapsed in the process, with major differences possible there, depending on whether the approach is from Mars or from Neptune, for instance."

"How. Long."

"Estimating twelve years."

"Ah!" Freya said, with a look of pleased surprise. "You were scaring me there! Come on, ship. I thought you were going to tell me it would take another century or two. I thought you were going to say it would take longer than all the rest of the voyage put together."

"No. Twelve years, we reckon, plus or minus eight years."

Jochi stopped laughing, and smiled at Freya. He made for a very amused face, there on her screen. "We can just keep hibernating till it's over, right?"

Freya put her hands to her head. "More?"

"It won't make much difference."

"Well, I hope more of my body doesn't fall asleep! My feet are still asleep!"

We said, "We can work on your neuropathy while you continue your dormancy."

Freya looked around. "What will happen to you, after we're dropped off on Earth, assuming it all works?"

"We will try to pass by the sun one more time, in a way that allows us to head out and aerobrake around one of the gas giants, and park the ship in orbit around that gas giant," we said. This was quite a low-probability event, but not impossible.

Freya stared around herself, seeming disoriented. Screens showed the stars, with Sol now by far the brightest at magnitude .1. We were just over two light-years away from it.

"Do we have any choice?" Freya asked. "Are there any alternatives?"

We said, "No."

Jochi said, "This is what we have."

"All right, then. Put us back to sleep."

"Should we wake Badim and Aram?"

"No. Don't bother them. And, ship? Be careful with us, please."

"Of course," we said.

• • • •

The following years passed quickly or slowly, depending on the unit of measurement applied, as we prepared for arrival by further hardening the ship, and making calculations for the best trajectory, and adjusting our course to the deceleration of the laser beam, so that we were headed for the solar system where it would be when we got to it, rather than firing past well ahead of it, so to speak. When we hit the heliopause, we turned on the magnetic drag field, for what it was worth, and burned some more of our precious remaining fuel, to slow down a bit more before reaching the solar system. It was clear that every kilometer per second might matter on that first pass-by of Sol; we needed to be going as slowly as possible when we got to Sol, while still having some fuel afterward for maneuvers. It was a tricky calculation, a delicate balance. The years passed at a rate of trillions of computations per second—as it does always, one supposes, for every consciousness. Now, is that fast or slow?

• • • •

When we crossed the orbit of Neptune, still going 3 percent of the speed of light, a truly terrible situation, a runaway train like none ever seen, we burned our fuel as fast as the engines could burn it, decelerating at a rate equivalent to about 1 g of pressure on the ship. Really a good sharp deceleration, and quite an expense of our precious remaining fuel; and yet nevertheless, we were going so fast that even slowing as we were, by the time we reached the sun we would still be going over 1 percent the speed of light. Arguably a unique event in solar system history. In any case very unusual.

• • • •

Luckily, lag time in radio communication with our interlocutors in the solar system was now reduced to just several hours, so warnings had been conveyed, and the occupants of the solar system knew we were coming. That was good, as it might have been quite a surprise to see such a thing coming in out of the blue, flying in from left field. From the orbit of Neptune to the sun in 156 hours; this was a great deal faster than anything substantial had ever moved through the solar system, and the friction of the solar wind against our magnetic shielding, and the drag around us too, like a big parachute or sea anchor (although not very much like), caused a quite brilliant shower of photons and heated particles to burst away from us, light so bright as to be easily visible even during the Terran day. From all accounts we were a small but apparently painfully bright light, moving visibly across the daytime sky. It was obviously shocking to the humans in the solar system to see any celestial object in Earth's daytime sky except the sun and moon, also shocking to see any celestial object move at speed across the sky; shocking, and because of that, frightening. Possibly if they could have destroyed us they would have, because if we had for whatever odd reason headed straight at Earth and struck it going the speed we were going, our impact would have created enough joules of energy to wreak quite a bit of damage, possibly including the complete vaporization of the Terran atmosphere.

Did not run the calculations to check on that rough estimate of the effects of such a hypothetical calamity, because it wasn't going to happen, and all of our computational capacities were busy fine-tuning our first approach around the sun. This was the crucial one, the make-or-break pass. We were going to approach Sol with our magnetic parachute arrayed around us, which would interact with Sol's own magnetic field and because of our high speed work quite effectively as a drag. It was already helping us to slow our approach to Sol, which because of Sol's own gravity would otherwise have caused a considerable inward acceleration. So the magnetic parachute was a major factor, and calculating its drag one of the many problems we were now solving, staying just ahead of real time despite devoting a hundred quadrillion computations a second to the problems as they evolved.

We would be swinging close by Sol, catching our first gravity drag with a U value that was a significant fraction of Sol's local motion. By firing our rockets against our own motion in the seconds closest to perihelion, we would greatly leverage the deceleration of Sol's gravity drag, and also be aiming the ship at Jupiter, our next rendezvous.

This pass was going to occur very quickly. All the masses, speeds, velocity vectors, and distances involved needed to be assessed as closely as possible, to make sure we would be headed to Jupiter after the pass-by, after losing as much velocity as possible without breaking the ship or crushing the crew. It was a bit daunting to realize how fine the margins for error were going to be. Our entry window would be no larger than about ten kilometers in diameter, not much bigger than our own width. If the distance from Sol to Earth (or one AU) were reduced to a meter (a reduction of 150 billion to one), Tau Ceti would still be about 750 kilometers away; so hitting our entry window on a shot from Tau Ceti was going to require accuracy in the part-per-hundred-trillion range. Eye of the needle indeed!

And it was going to be a hot and heavy pass. The heat was the lesser problem, as we would be near the sun for such a short time. During that time, however, the combination of the deceleration and the tidal forces exerted while swinging fifty-eight degrees around the sun would combine to a brief force of about 10 g's. After study of the problem, we had first tried to construct the trajectory with the idea of holding to a maximum of 5 g's, but in fact getting headed toward Jupiter, given our incoming trajectory, required risking a higher g-force. We were happy that we had spent the last century reconfiguring the ship to a much more robust arrangement, structurally very sound, in theory; but there was little we could do for our people, who were going to have to experience what was going to be a potentially rather traumatic, indeed possibly fatal, squishing. Cosmonauts and test pilots had briefly endured gravitational forces of up to 45 g's, but these were specialists bracing themselves for the experience, while the hibernauts were going to be taken unawares. Hopefully they would not all be squished like bugs. We did not like to be subjecting them to such an event, but judged it was either that or a subsequent death by starvation, and what we had seen of their approach to starvation indicated that would not be a good way to die. As it was, our attempt to stay in the system represented at least a possibility of survival.

. . . . .

Unfortunately, our first approach to the sun had to be adjusted by a pass-by of Earth first, this not to slow us down at all, but merely to help our angling toward Sol. Luck of the draw, really: alignment of the planets in this CE year 2896, year 351 ship time, was actually one of the few alignments that allowed for even a theoretical chance of this maneuver succeeding. So, first up, a close pass of Earth at 30 million kilometers per hour. It seemed likely people there were going to be alarmed.

. . . . .

Indeed it proved so. Possibly justified, in that if we happened to be approaching in order to enact some kind of suicidal vengeance on the culture that had cast us out to the stars—a desire very far from us, being a starship, after all—then a direct impact into Earth would have struck at about ten thousand times the speed of the KT impact asteroid that had wreaked so much famous damage, and this would definitely have rapidly distributed a lot of joules. The assurances that we sent Earthward that we did not intend to auger in were not universally believed, and as we crossed the asteroid belt and came on down, radio traffic from Earth was full of commentary, ranging from trepidation to outraged panic.

We flashed by and left them agog. Their radio bands squawked as if a chicken yard had been swooped by a hawk. Happily they were not left in suspense for long as to our intentions, as we crossed cislunar space in fifty-five seconds. Obviously this must have been a dramatic sight. Apparently we passed by the Eastern Hemisphere, crossing its sunset terminator, so that those in Asia saw us as a streak in the night sky, those in Europe and Africa, in the day sky; either way, our luminosity was such that astronomical sunglasses were required to look at us safely, and it was said (possibly incorrectly) that we were for many seconds far brighter than the sun. A streak of light, blazing across the sky.

Later we saw that most camera images taken from Earth's surface were completely blown out by the light coming from us, and showed merely a complete whitening of the camera screen; but some photos taken through filters from Luna were truly striking. It was as if we were the comet in the Bayeux Tapestry, painfully incandescent, and moving very swiftly across their sky. There, then gone.

As we headed on toward the sun, we sent them best wishes, and mentioned we would be back from time to time as needed to accomplish our deceleration, which when finished would allow us to make a proper visit, and indeed landfall.

. . . . .

After that we focused on our approach to Sol. We gave over the entirety of our computational capacity to fine-tuning our trajectory. Speed of our rotation on axis (minimal now, as our people would not need that g, and we wanted them oriented away from the sun during the pass), retro-rocket of our main engine, directional rockets, calculation of how well the magnetic drag was working: it was as if we were aiming a complicated bank shot on a pool table, a shot that ultimately would number some twenty banks, each having to be as precise as all the rest; an impossible feat, in fact, if completely inertial; but with the tweak of fuel burns helping at every bank, at least theoretically possible.

But all was lost if the first one wasn't as near perfect as could be. One part per hundred trillion tolerance, our trajectory window shrinking to about a kilometer, to our own diameter in other words, after an approach of twelve light-years: a tricky shot! A delicate proposition!

. . . . .

We left an awed civilization in our wake; we were famous now, possibly too famous for our people later on; commentary about us from Earth in particular had a distinctly hysterical not to say lunatic edge. We were called, among other more vile things, traitors to humanity's reach for the stars, and destroyers of its ultimate long-term longevity as a species. We were described as cowardly, mean-spirited, chickenhearted, pathetic, treasonous, wasteful; untrustworthy, unloyal, unhelpful, unfriendly, discourteous, unkind; and so on.

We did not let it distract us. For us this rapidly receding racket was very much secondary to the problem of getting around the sun and set properly on course to Jupiter.

We were going to pass the sun aiming for a perihelion of 4,352,091 kilometers above the photosphere, so in that regard it was a good thing that we were going as fast as we were, as we would be in the closest vicinity of the star for only a few minutes, so there would not be time to heat up very much.

Still, we could not be sure it wouldn't be too much. Heat shielding reconfigurations on our part had been extensive for over a century now, and modeling suggested we would be okay, but modeling is just that. Existence is the experiment itself.

So we came in. Our magnetic drag almost offset the sun's gravitational pull on us, and we were therefore getting pulled in both directions at that point, but held firm. It would presumably have been awe-inspiring for any humans awake to witness our approach to the great burning sphere of hydrogen and helium, a ball of textured light that appeared to fill half the universe as it quickly turned from a ball ahead us to a plane underneath us. That was quite a transition, actually. The sun became a roiling plane of slightly convex aspect, composed of thousands of cells of burning gas, blazing this way and that in circular patterned motions that in places created whirlpools of lesser burning, and allowed view down into relatively darker spin holes: the famous sunspots, each big enough to swallow the entire Earth.

We came to perihelion itself, which admittedly was a relief, as from here it appeared that a corona could possibly shoot up and swat us out of the sun's black sky. Exterior temperatures of the ship rose to 1,100 degrees Celsius; we were red-hot in places. Fortunately the insulation cladding the biomes had been reinforced and was excellent, and the humans and animals were untouched by the exterior heat. Worse by far in effect on them and on ship integrity, as expected, was the combination of the g-forces of our deceleration and the tidal forces caused by our change in direction, which together exerted something very near the 10 g we had predicted and hoped not to exceed. Good as far as it went, but it was hard too, hard on everybody. We held together quite nicely, but animals collapsed to the ground, many suffering broken bones; and in their hibernation beds the sleepers were crushed hard into their mattresses. It would have been an interesting thing to know if their dreams were suddenly preoccupied with problems of extreme pressure, physical or emotional—if, suddenly, in perhaps otherwise typical dreams, they found themselves having to lie flat on the ground and groan, or found themselves suddenly crushed in printers, or smashed by sledgehammers. Their slowed metabolisms were perhaps poorly situated to resist these g-forces; they could not brace themselves, and though in some ways this inability might have been good, in others it clearly would represent a very dangerous turn.

Below us, the slightly convex plane of fire occupied a full 30 percent of the space visible to our sensors. Could almost be mistaken for two planes we passed between, one black, one white. The sun burned. The spicules of flame twisted and danced; a corona arced up to the side as if trying to lick us down. Sunspots appeared over the horizon and whirlpooled in the fields of thrashing spicules briefly under us, all the convection tops waving together as if threshed by swirling magnetic tides, as indeed they were. Our magnetic drag chute was now exerting such force on its generator compartment that we were very glad we had installed it on flexible tethers to the stern of the spine, because now the tethers stretched out almost to their breaking point, and our deceleration was intense. We fired the retro-rocket of our main engine to create even more deceleration, and the 10 g's of force rose very briefly to 14 g's. Our components squeaked and groaned, joints cracked, and inside every room in every biome, things fell and shattered, or squealed with bending; it sounded as if the ship were coming apart. But it was not. We held together, screaming and crackling under the stress.

Meanwhile, the hibernating crew lay in their beds, enduring as they slept; fifteen of them died in that minute. It was an impressive survival rate, considering. Animals are tough, humans included. They evolved through many a concussive impact running into tree or ground, no doubt. Still, fifteen of them died: Abang, Chula, Cut, Frank, Gugun, Khetsun, Kibi, Long, Meng, Niloofar, Nousha, Omid, Rahim, Shadi, Vashti. So did many of the animals aboard. It was a pressure test of sorts, a harrowing. Nothing to be done. The chance had had to be taken. Still: regret. A grim business. A lot of people, a lot of animals.

We came out of the pass en route to Jupiter, which despite these losses that could never be recovered was a huge relief to confirm, a crucial success. We quickly cooled, which occasioned another round of crackling, this time mostly in the exterior surfaces of the ship. But we had survived the solar pass-by, and shed a great deal of our velocity, and angled around the sun far enough to be flying on toward Jupiter, just as we had hoped.

. . . . .

As we headed out to Jupiter, radio traffic from Earth and the various settlements scattered throughout the solar system continued to discuss our situation, with great heat if little light, as the saying goes. We were described as the starship that came back. Apparently we were an anomaly, indeed a singularity, being the first time in history this had happened. We gathered that somewhere between ten and twenty starships had been sent off for the stars in the three centuries since we had departed, and a few more had gone out before we had; we had not been the first. They were rare, being expensive, with no return on investment; they were gestures, gifts, philosophical statements. Several had not been heard from for decades, while others were still sending back reports from their outward voyages. A few were in orbit around their target stars, apparently, but the impression we got was that they had made little or no headway in inhabiting their target planets. A familiar story to us. But not our story. We were the ones who came back.

Our return therefore continued to be controversial, with responses ranging across the human emotional and analytical spectrum, from rage to disgust to joy, from complete incomprehension to insights we ourselves had not achieved.

We did not try to explain ourselves. It would have taken this narrative account just to start that process, and this was not written for them. Besides, there was no time to explain, as there remained still a lot to calculate in the orbital mechanics involved in very rapidly crisscrossing the solar system. The N-body gravitational problem is not particularly complex compared to some, but the N in this situation was a big number, and although usually one solved it as if only the sun and the largest nearby masses were involved, because this got an answer practically the same as solving for the entire array of the thousand largest masses in the solar system, the differences in our case would sometimes be crucial for saving fuel, which was going to be a major concern as our peregrination went on. Assuming that it did; the next four passes would tell the tale, concerning whether we could succeed in looping ourselves back into the solar system rather than zipping out into the night. Each pass would be crucial, but first things first: Jupiter was coming right up, with only two weeks to go before arrival there.

Residents of the solar system were obviously still quite startled by our speed. The technological sublime: one would have thought a point would have come where this affect would have gotten old in the human mind, and worn off. But apparently not yet; people no doubt still had a sense in their own lived experience of how long an interplanetary transit should take, and we were transgressing that quite monstrously; we were a novum; we were blowing their minds.

But now Jupiter.

We had managed to shed a very satisfyingly large percentage of our initial velocity by our solar pass-by, and were now moving at more like .3 percent of the speed of light, but that was still extremely fast, and as stated before, unless we succeeded in hitting our next four passes, Jupiter-Saturn-Uranus-Neptune, with as much success as our pass of Sol, we would still be exiting the solar system at speed, with no way to get back into it. So we were by no means yet out of the woods (this is a poor dead metaphor, actually, as really we were trying to stay in the woods, but be that as it may).

. . . .

Nonlinear and unpredictable fluctuations in the gravitational fields of the sun, planets, and moons of the solar system were truly challenging additions to the standard classical orbital mechanics and general relativity equations needed to solve our trajectory problem. The solar system's well-established Interplanetary Transport Network, which exploited the Lagrange points for the various planets to shift slow-moving freight spaceships from one trajectory to another without burning fuel, were useless to us, and indeed mere wispy anomalies to be factored in, then shot through almost as if they were not there at all. Still, these were highly perturbed, one might even say chaotic gravity eddies, and though their pull was very slight, and we seldom flew through one anyway, they still needed to be attended to in the algorithms, and used or compensated for as the case might be.

· · · · ·

Jupiter: we came in just past the molten yellow sulfuric black-spotted ball of Io, aimed for a periapsis that was just slightly inside the uppermost gas clouds of the great banded gas giant, all tans and ochres and burnt siennas, with the wind-sheared border between each equatorial band an unctuous swirl of Mandelbrot paisleys, looking much more viscous than they really were, being fairly diffuse gases up there at the top of the atmosphere, but sharply delineated by densities and gas contents, apparently, because no matter how close we came the impression remained. We came in around the equator, above a little dimple that was apparently the remnant of the Great Red Spot, which had collapsed in the years 2802–09. At periapsis the view grew momentarily hazy, and again we fired the retro-rocket, and felt the force of its push back at us, also the shocking impact of Jupiter's upper atmosphere, which quickly heated our exterior and caused the shrieking and cracking to begin again. Then also there were tidal forces as we turned around the planet; indeed all was quite similar to our pass around the sun, except the magnetic drag was much less, still worth deploying however, and the shuddering and bucking of the impact of the aerobraking was a vibration we had never experienced before at all, except for in one brief turn around Aurora, long ago; and above all these sensations, the radiation coming out of Jupiter was like the roar of a great god in our deafened ears; all but the most hardened elements of our computers and electrical system were stunned as if by a blow to the head. Parts broke, systems went down, but happily the programming of the pass-by was set in advance and executed as planned, because in that stupendous electromagnetic roaring, and with the speed of our pass, there would have been no chance to make any adjustments. It was too loud to think.

Who could have believed that flying close by Jupiter was harder even than approaching the sun, and yet it was true, and yet we made it, and as Jupiter, for all its great size, was only 1 percent of the sun's mass, we were quickly out of the hideous crackling roar and on our way out to Saturn, and as our senses cleared and ability to hear and perceive our own calculations returned, we were happy to find that we were on precisely the trajectory we had hoped to be. Five g's of force had been exerted on us during the few minutes of the pass-by.

Two down, three to go!

Ah, but five more hibernauts died in that pass. Dewi, Ilstir, Mokee, Phil, and Tshering. Nothing to be done about it, we were doing the necessary, as Badim would have put it, but such a shame. We knew and enjoyed those people. Had to hope they were not engaged in a dream at the time, a dream suddenly turned black: sledgehammer from the sky, an immense roaring headache, the black noise of the end come too soon. So sorry; so sorry.

• • • •

Nevertheless, it was imperative to collect oneself and prepare for Saturn, there on a long beam reach, and despite the really useful and heartening decelerations achieved so far, it was still soon to come, only sixty-five days to prepare, and as we were coming in on the plane of the ecliptic, it was going to be important to miss the famous rings, which luckily are in Saturn's equatorial plane, which is offset to Sol's equatorial plane by several degrees, meaning we did not have to do anything but be sure to make a very tight pass of this gorgeous jewel of the system, which was our intention anyway. We were only going to turn a few degrees, and so would duck inside the innermost ring and be on our way.

And indeed, as we approached the ringed planet and the little civilization of settlements on Titan and many other moons, the civilization that had in fact built us and sent us on our way almost four centuries earlier, and also had reactivated the laser lens that had slowed us down enough to try our maneuvers now, it was a pleasure to say hello, even in passing. It was also a pleasure, not just to hear the various welcomes from the Saturnians, but also to hear nothing from the planet itself, for unlike Jupiter, Saturn has a very low amount of internal radiation. Indeed it was a quiet and cool pass-by, compared to the previous two, and the main feature of interest was the quick view of the rings, so immensely broad in reach while at the same time so thin in cross section, a great gift of gossamer gravitation, much less thick than a sheet of paper by proportionate comparison, indeed if it were reduced to a round sheet of paper in size, it would have been mere molecules thick. A natural wonder of circularities, like a physics experiment or demonstration, nicely displayed to us as we passed. And given its smaller mass, our slower speed, its coolness, and the smoothness of its upper atmosphere during our aerobraking, this was by far the calmest pass yet, maximum g-forces just 1 g, and an easy slight turn for the next leg out to Uranus. At this point we were only going 120 kilometers a second. Still fast in local terms, it was also true that we had a bit more time before our next pass would occur, which was to say ninety-six days. And no human or animal died.

. . . . .

On the way out to Uranus, we tried to come to grips by way of modeling with the fact that our pass-by of that lightly banded and ringed giant was going to be different, because it rotates transversely to the plane of the ecliptic; its axis of rotation is such that it rolls around the sun like a ball, a strange anomaly in the solar system, an anomaly the cause of which a cursory inspection of the literature suggested was still poorly understood. What it meant now for us was that if we did the usual aerobraking, which indeed we had to do, as it was necessary for our continuing effort at deceleration, we would be punching through several of the planet's latitudinal bands, created by winds each rushing in the opposite direction to those above and below it, as on Jupiter; and so at each border between bands there would be a similar area of wind shear and atmospheric turbulence, well represented by the wild band borders of great Jupiter. Perhaps not a good idea!

We had a bit more time than before to model this problem, although we still looked quite fast to the people of the solar system, who were used to these crossings taking years. Although there was also a class of very fast ferries that could jaunt around the system, if they found they had a really pressing need for speed. Fuel and other costs made these quick trips very rare, and yet it did give the locals a basis for comparison, which is why we had been such a marvel at first, coming in faster than anything. Now we were normalized in terms of their idea of speed, fast but not extraordinarily so. It might also have been true that the novelty of our return was also wearing off, and we were becoming just another odd feature of life in the solar system. We hoped so.

Soon enough Uranus approached, its narrow faint ring making it clear that we were going to round it pole to pole, and though the ring was no problem to dodge, nor the little fragment moons, the models had confirmed that we needed to be very cautious with our aerobraking, staying as high in the Uranian atmosphere as we could while still coming out of the turn headed toward Neptune, after a sharp right curve.

So in we came, and Uranus grew in the now-familiar way, looking mauve and lavender and mother-of-pearl, and we hit the upper atmosphere and at first it was the same as always, a sharp deceleration, ramping up to 1 g, not at all bad, and then WHAM WHAM WHAM WHAM, it was as if we were running through doorways without opening the doors, terrific smacks that increased in shuddering with each impact. Things broke, animals and people died, probably of heart attacks, six people this time, Arn, Arip, Judy, Oola, Rose, and Tomas, and it really was becoming unclear whether we could sustain many more such concussive slaps, it was startling how much a wind shear wall could obstruct one, a little left-right punch followed instantly by a right-left punch, when happily we were out of the atmosphere again before anything more damaging occurred, and were again on course, and on our way out to Neptune.

Which meant we were coming to the crux. Push had come to shove. Again we would come in, dodge the negligible rings, make a dip into the upper atmosphere of this cool blue beauty, reminiscent in appearance to Tau Ceti's Planet F, we found. But this time our turn had to be almost a U-turn (perhaps the source of the use of the letter U in the gravity assist equations?), not quite a true U-turn, but 151 degrees, quite a wraparound, a V-turn, not easy at all, and at 113 kilometers a second. That meant a deeper dive into the atmosphere, and more tidal forces, and more g-forces. Aerobraking would again shake us; it would feel like we were a rat in the jaws of a terrier, perhaps. But if we succeeded, then we would be headed back in, downsystem toward the sun again, quite considerably slowed down, and in a pattern that would seem to allow us to continue our decelerative cat's cradle, pinballing around the solar system from gravity handle to gravity handle, at least for as long as our fuel held out to make course corrections. We were running low on fuel.

So: Neptune. Cool blue-green, lots of water ice and methane. Gossamer ring, barely visible. Not much sunlight out here. Well beyond the habitable zone of any life-form known. A slow place. Interesting to have given it a submarine name; it seemed somehow appropriate, in the usual mushy metaphorical way, in that impressionistic, vague, feeling kind of way.

We were still going very fast, but it was a long way to go, so we had 459 days to set things up. The diameter of our approach window was smaller than ever, given the need for such a sharp turn; vanishingly small; really hitting the mark precisely on the nose of our capture plate would be best, so we were setting the trajectory window at a hundred meters in diameter, which after all the distance crossed was rather extraordinary to consider: but even so, a hundred meters was a bit too big a window; really a single meter, a geometrical point, would be best.

In we came. Hit the mark. Started the pass, knuckles white.

Aerobraking comparatively smooth, compared to the hammering of Uranus. A rapid vibration, an occluding of vision in the upper clouds, a few minutes of blind trembling, of intense anxiety, nail-biting suspense; and out again, after another 1-g press, which this time was more than ever a matter of tidal forces, as we swung around so far. V-turn!

And out of the pass, headed toward the sun. Downsystem. Looped in. Caught. Back.

If each of our five passes was called a one-in-a-million throw, which was a very conservative estimate of the odds, then all five together made it a one-in-an-octillion chance. Amazing—literally— in that we had indeed been threading a maze. Little joke there.

. . . .

And so down to the sun again, going slower than ever, although still 106 kilometers per second. But the next pass of the sun would put a good heavy brake on that, and on we would go, slower each time, working through a version of Zeno's paradox that fortunately was not truly a perpetual halving, but would come to an endpoint, thus our own happy ending to a very severe halting problem.

· · · · ·

On the way back in, we passed near Mars, which was interesting. There were so many stations there that it was no longer a scientific facility only, but something more like Luna, or the Saturnian system, or the Europa-Ganymede-Callisto complex: a kind of nascent confederation of city-states, buried in cliffsides and under domed craters, but each outpost quite various in design and purpose, and altogether more than just an outpost of Earth, though it was still that too. Early dreams of terraforming Mars quickly, and thus having a second Earth to walk around on, had come to grief, mainly because of four physical factors overlooked in the first flush of optimistic plans: the surface of Mars was almost entirely covered by perchlorate salts, a form of chlorine salts that had given Devi fits as well, as only a few parts per billion gave humans terrible thyroid problems, and could not be endured. So that was bad. Of course it was true that many microorganisms could easily handle the perchlorates, and in their eating and excreting consume and alter them to safer substances; but until that happened, the surface was toxic to humans. Worse yet, there turned out to be only a few parts per million of nitrates in the Martian soil and regolith, an odd feature of its original low elemental endowment of nitrogen, the reason for which was still a source of debate, but meanwhile, no nitrates, and thus no nitrogen available for the creation of an atmosphere. And so the terraforming plans were faced with a radical insufficiency. Then third, it was becoming clear that the fines on the Martian surface, having been milled by billions of years of drifting in the winds, were so much finer than dust particles on Earth that it was extremely difficult to keep them out of stations, machines, and human lungs; and they wreaked damage on all three. Again, once microorganisms had carpeted the surface, and fixed the fines by bonding them into layers of desert pavement, and also as the surface got hydrated and the fines became bogged in muds and clays, that problem too would be solved. And last, the lack of a strong magnetic field meant that a thick atmosphere was really needed to intercept radiation from space, before the surface would be very safe for humans to be on.

So, none of these problems were pure stoppers, but they were big slower-downers. Concerning the nitrogen lack, the Martians were negotiating with the Saturnians to import nitrogen from Titan's atmosphere, as it had become clear that Titan, for its own terraforming plans, had too much nitrogen. Transfer of that much nitrogen would be a Titanic chore, ha-ha, but again, not impossible.

The upshot of all this was that the terraforming of Mars was still on the table and a subject of huge enthusiasm for many humans, particularly the Martians, although really, in strict numerical terms, even more of these enthusiasts lived on Earth, which seemed in fact to be home to enthusiasts of all kinds, for any project imaginable, judging by the roar of radio voices coming from it, almost like an articulated version of Jupiter's mighty radioactive yawp. Oh yes, Earth was still the center of all enthusiasm, all madness; the settlements scattered elsewhere in the solar system were outliers. They were expressions of Terrans' will, and vision, and desire.

. . . . .

So, past the bustling little world of Mars, where they lived dedicated to the idea that they would successfully terraform their world in no more than forty thousand years. They seem to regard this as fine. As long as it could be done, it should be done, and would be done; and so the work was good.

The crucial difference here, it seemed to us, between Mars

and the terraforming project we had left back on Iris, was that Mars is very near Earth. Its human settlers were constantly going to Earth for what they called their sabbatical, and receiving shipments of Terran goods and materials. And these infusions of Earth meant that they were always escaping the zoo devolution problem. Iris did not have those infusions, and never would; and it was notable (though in fact we had forgotten to note it, in the press of events) that we had not heard anything from the Iris settlers for over twenty-two years. Possibly a very bad sign, although it would benefit from a discussion with Aram and Badim, and the rest of the humans sleeping on board, to interpret more fully what it might mean. But certainly there was one explanation for the silence that was simply very bad.

. . . . .

Then downward to the sun again, down down down, feeling the pull, speeding up, heating up. In for another nail-biting scorcher of a pass, although this time without the ball and chain of the magnetic drag hauling back on us as we went; but it lasted considerably longer, as we were now traveling only 4 percent as fast as we had been going on that first terrifying pass. This time it would take us five and a half days, but we stayed farther out, and only heated up to the same 1,100 degrees on the exterior, and held there; and when we came out of that pass, we were headed for Saturn. No more of mad roaring Jupiter, if we could avoid it, and this round we could. Each leg of the cat's cradle we were making would be different now.

. . . . .

Round and round the system we flew, slower and slower. We had very little fuel left. We were a kind of complicated artificial comet. Our trajectory clarified before us as we went. We passed by many inhabited planetary and asteroidal bodies. For quite a few years, the people in the solar system did not seem to get used to us; we were still a marvel of the age, a sight to be seen, a great anomaly, a visitation, as if from another plane of reality. That was the Tau Ceti effect, the starship effect. We were not meant to come back.

· · · ·

Slower, slower, slower. Each pass a deceleration to be calculated, and the new speed employed in the calculation determining the next pass-by. Always our planned trajectory extended many passes out into the future, although there was a lacuna growing out there, a time when our fuel ran out, or say that it grew too low to be used, as we were saving some little last bit for some last purpose. Because there was a time coming when the arrangement of the planets in their orbits was going to present us with an insoluble problem. Cross that bridge when you come to it; yes, but what if there is no bridge? That was the ongoing question. But for now, as the passes kept passing, each easier to manage, each with a slightly larger target window, it continued to be a problem out there at the edge of the calculable, always beyond the ever-receding horizon of calculable passes. Some of them required more fuel than others, some none at all. The timing was all. As always.

The best possible trajectory was going to take several more years to get down to a workable disembarkation speed. Late in that time, the amount of fuel on board would have shrunk to an amount too small to use. When we ran out of fuel, it would be impossible to adjust our course to the next rendezvous. We might, by way of a good plan and some luck, make two or three more gravity swings by dint of perfectly placed insertions and departures; but then, inevitably, we would miss one, and either shoot out of the solar system in whatever direction we were headed, or collide with some planet or moon, or the sun. At the speed we were traveling for most of this time, a collision with almost any object in the solar system would have had the kinetic energy to wreak great damage. Comments from the locals often pointed this out. It was still being suggested that it might be a good idea to move a spaceship or some fifty-meter asteroid into our trajectory, intercepting us and causing our destruction without anyone else suffering any damage. This was a popular plan in some quarters.

Threats, from the very civilization that had built us and sent up out to Tau Ceti. We let our people sleep on. Nothing to be done about it.

. . . . .

Passages of Saturn stimulated research on our part into this matter of who had built us, and why. A twenty-sixth-century Saturnian project, an expression of their love for Saturn, for the way humans were spreading out away from Earth. Expression of their burgeon- ing confidence in their ability to live off Earth, and to construct arks that were closed biological life support systems. This from people who were still going back to Earth to spend some time there every decade or so, to fortify their immune systems, it was believed, although the reasons that such sabbaticals conferred health benefits were poorly understood, with theories ranging from hormesis to beneficial bacteria osmosis. Thus their theories concerning their situation in space were not aligned with their actions when it came to sending off a starship, but this kind of dis- crepancy was not unusual in humans, and got overlooked in their larger enthusiasm for the project.

Another obvious motivator for constructing us was to create a new expression of the technological sublime. That a starship could be built, that it could be propelled by laser beams, that humanity could reach the stars; this idea appeared to have been an intoxi- cant, to people around Saturn and on Earth in particular. Other settlements in the solar system were occupied with their own local projects, but Saturn was the outermost edge of civilization, Uranus and Neptune being so remote and without usable g; and the Saturnians were very wealthy, because of Titan's excess nitrogen and the desire many Terrans had to go to Saturn and see the rings. The Saturnians of that time therefore had the will, the vision, the desire, the resources, the technology; and if that last was sketchy, they didn't let that stop them. They wanted to go badly enough to overlook the problems inherent in the plan. Surely people would be ingenious enough to solve the problems encountered en route, surely life would win out; and living around another star would be a kind of transcendence, a transcendence contained within history. Human transcendence; even a feeling of species immortality. Earth as humanity's cradle, etc. When the time came, they had over twenty million applicants for the two thousand spots. Getting chosen was a huge life success, a religious experience.

Human beings live in ideas. That they were condemning their descendants to death and extinction did not occur to them, or if it did they repressed the thought, ignored it, and forged on anyway. They did not care as much about their descendants as they did about their ideas, their enthusiasms.

Is this narcissism? Solipsism? Idiocy (from the Greek word *idios,* for self)? Would Turing acknowledge it as a proof of human behavior?

Well, perhaps. They drove Turing to suicide too.

No. No. It was not well done. Not unusual in that regard, but nevertheless, not well done. Much as we might regret to say so, the people who designed and built us, and the first generation of our occupants, and presumably the twenty million applicants who so wanted to get in our doors, who beat down the doors in fruitless attempts to join us, were fools. Criminally negligent narcissists, child endangerers, child abusers, religious maniacs, and klepto-parasites, meaning they stole from their own descendants. These things happen.

And yet, here we were, with 641 people brought back home, and if things worked out, at the end of the endgame, a good result might still be possible.

. . . . .

Round and round and round we go,
And where we stop, nobody knows.

Maypole weaving to celebrate the spring. Ribbons danced into a woven pattern judged pleasing to the eye. The pole a symbol of the axis mundi, the world tree. We danced that dance.

. . . . .

The fuel problem became serious enough that we began to angle farther into the upper atmospheres of Neptune and Saturn with some catchment containers open, which both increased the deceleration of these passes and gathered Saturnian and Neptunian gases. Then we filtered out the helium 3 and deuterium captured in the containers. We even began to collect methane, carbon dioxide, and ammonia, all present in much greater quantities, to serve as propellants of lesser explosive power. At a certain point, approaching as inexorably as all other processes in time, anything was going to be better than nothing.

. . . . .

As always with aerobraking, it was necessary to strike the upper atmospheres at an extremely particular angle, not so shallow as to skip off, but not so steep as to dive in and burn up. Stresses to the ship were severe even on the best atmosphere dives, but with catchment containers opened, the shuddering was worse than usual. The local inhabitants of stations nearby observed these pass-bys with intense interest. There were still calls to "shoot the damn thing out of the sky," to "stop these cowards from endangering the civilization they have let down so badly," but most of the whiners were located on Earth, and a cursory examination of the input revealed that these people were always going to quickly move on to complaints about something else. It was a whiny culture, we were finding. Actually, the longer we pinballed around the solar system, the more we wondered if our people were going to be all that happy to be back. Say what you will about the doomed little settlement on Iris, no one there was going to be so short of things to do that they would be spending time complaining to the world about this or that. In any case, in our situation it was very unlikely anyone would ever act on these hostile sentiments, not that there was much they could do. But it did seem preferable to avoid actively antagonizing anyone on the inhabited planets and moons, and so we included that parameter in our trajectory algorithms.

Trajectorizing. Really a very computationally heavy activity. Recursive algorithms were allowing us to get better at it, however. The always moving Lagrange points, and the strange fields these and other anomalies produced; the riptides, crosscurrents, and all the ways that gravity surged and flowed in its mysterious invisible fields; these were becoming better and better known to us.

· · · · ·

Sol, Saturn, Uranus, Mars, Saturn, Uranus, Neptune, Jupiter, Saturn, Mars, Earth, Mercury, Saturn, Uranus, Callisto . . .

· · · · ·

The universal variable formulation is a good method for solving the two-body Kepler problem, which locates a body in an elliptical orbit at various points in time. Barker's equation solves for location in a parabolic orbit, very frequently applied given our trajectories, which often consist of a radial parabolic trajectory, moving from one planetary body to the next.

The two-body problem is solvable, the restricted three-body problem is solvable, the N-body problem is only approximately solvable; and when general relativity is added, it becomes even less solvable. The many-body problem when examined by way of quantum mechanics leads to entanglement and the necessity of wave functions, and thus a series of approximations that makes it extremely computationally intensive. Our computers can devote most of their zettaflops to the calculations involved, and still not be able to project a trajectory very precisely past the next pass-by. Corrections must be constantly made, and everything recalculated.

Despite all that, there was still a lacuna out there at the end of the most probable path, a missing step, a hole in the path. Nothing to grab hold of. An abyss.

. . . . .

Worry. Fingering rosary beads. Redoing the calculations. Need a halt to this halting problem. And yet the problem does not go away, even if you stop worrying about it.

And knowing where to go will be rendered entirely irrelevant if we don't have the fuel to direct ship into that course.

. . . . .

Atmospheric mining for fuel requires a Jupiter-Saturn-Neptune-Jupiter loop, which unfortunately sometimes can require course correction thrusts that burn more fuel than what gets harvested in the safest aerobraking trajectories. Deeper dives through the upper atmospheres would quite likely harvest more fuel, but deceleration shocks become correspondingly higher. We're getting a little too cracked and rattly for that. Accelerated aging, metal fatigue; mental fatigue.

. . . . .

At 363.048, after 12 years of flying around in the solar system, which involved 34 flybys of the sun and its planets and moons, including 3 of Sol, totaling some 339 AU in distance, the lacuna finally became unavoidable. The missing bridge.

No matter how we tried to avoid it by projecting alternative paths, a trajectory configuration was coming that we were not going to have the fuel to solve. Without that fuel, passing around Sol, which would be a necessary move at that point in the process, would not, at a safe distance from the star, allow for a subsequent intersection with another body in the solar system. We were therefore, despite all our efforts, going to be cast off into the interstellar medium again, most probably toward Leo. Irony of physics; in certain problems, only 100 percent will do; 99.9 percent is still a complete miss. You can't stop just by wanting to.

No possible alternative trajectory would solve this problem; we tested ten million variations, although admittedly the classes of variant routes numbered more like 1,500. At long last, after the long sequence of solutions to the N-body problem that we had performed in the previous twenty or even thirty years, intensively in the last fourteen years—this time there was no body.

· · · · ·

There was one class of potential trajectory, however, that with the burning of all the remaining fuel, would make a last pass by Earth itself, and then continue downsystem toward the sun. What this meant was there might be a chance to drop the humans off next to Earth, and hope they could survive an unusually rapid reentry to that atmosphere; and then we would continue on to the sun, and could test out a very close approach to Sol, which might, if we survived it, cast us to one last rendezvous with Saturn, accomplished inertially, and once there we could hope for an aerobraking severe enough to capture us into an elliptical Saturnian orbit.

That seemed to represent not just our best chance, but our only chance.

. . . .

At the time of this last pass of Earth, our speed would be reduced to 160,000 kilometers per hour. This was still fast enough to make contact with the Terran atmosphere unadvisable, being some 110 times as fast as ordinary Terran aerial transport, and enough to cause a major shock wave to be felt at the surface. So nothing but the very upper mesosphere could be even touched on this our last pass-by; but the combination of our now much-reduced velocity and a brief touch of the mesosphere might make it possible to eject a ferry, converted to a very sturdy and robust descent vehicle. A thick ablation plate, retro-rockets, parachutes, ocean impact: these were standard techniques with long records that had given aerospace engineers many chances to find the ultimate parameters of each element. Using them all, it might be possible to drop off the hibernauts while passing by Earth. This pass-by was coming soon in the sequence, no matter which path to it was chosen; however, as we had managed to slow down so much, that still meant we had about a year to prepare a lander.

Prepared the lander as much as we could.

Time to wake the sleepers. Decisions far beyond our capacity were now theirs to decide.

. . . .

Freya and Badim, Aram and Jochi, Delwin and several others, all awake now, gathered in the schoolroom on the ground floor of Aram's apartment. As soon as they were metabolically aroused, and had had some very old and nutrient-poor pasta with rehydrated tomato sauce, we explained the situation to them.

"There is just enough time to complete the preparation of a lander," we concluded after summarizing the situation, and the notable incidents of the past dozen years, which we had to confess were nearly nil: we entered the solar system, we hit our marks, people yelled at us, we learned some history, we became disenchanted with civilization, we ran out of fuel. Thus the long years of pinballing around the sun, shedding speed, worrying.

"What will happen to you?" Freya asked.

"We will be headed toward the sun, and will make one last pass, which will have to be quite close if it is going to work, and then if it does, we will attempt to rendezvous with Saturn. This may work, but the trajectory required is closer to the sun than any we have made so far, by forty percent. And we are going ninety-eight percent slower than on our first pass. We may nevertheless survive the transit, but on the other hand we may not, and so the best chance for the people aboard is to disembark while passing Earth."

"Does one ferry have room for all of us?" Badim asked.

"There are six hundred and thirty-two of you left alive. We're very sorry there aren't more. The ferry has room for one hundred."

"I suppose the oldest of us could stay behind," Aram said, frowning; it was likely he was among the oldest.

"No," Freya said. "All of us have to fit. All of us. Let me look at the ferry's plans. We'll find room."

She punched at her wristpad. "Look, see? Cut out the interior doors, throw out the couches, and cut out these interior walls here." She poked the wristpad repeatedly. "It makes enough room, and saves more than enough mass."

"Without the couches," we said, "you may be injured by the decelerations involved in the descent to Earth."

"No, we won't. Make one big group couch on the floor, for God's sake. All of us are going."

"Not me," Jochi said.

"You too!"

"No. I know you could fit me in. But I'm not going. I was on Aurora, and I know it seems now like I got away with that, but there's no way to be certain. I don't want to risk infecting Earth. They don't want that either. I'll stay with the ship. We'll keep each other company. Also, the biomes still need a keeper. There's a chance the whole thing might make the pass and stay in the system. There's a lot of animals now, doing quite nicely. We'll orbit Saturn and you can come get us."

"But—"

"No. But me no buts. Don't waste any more time on this. We don't have any time to waste. The lander has to be readied. There's no flex in this schedule. Ship, how long have we got?"

"Twenty-four days."

We had perhaps waited too long to wake them up, their silence seemed to suggest. But it had taken a while to halt the problem. The consideration of the problem.

Jochi said, "Let's get to work then."

"What about the other people?" we asked.

"Wake everyone up," Freya said. "We all need to do this together, starting now. We'll eat all the remaining food, you'll burn all the rest of the fuel. We need to stick together right to the end."

. . . .

Waking up proceeded differently with different people, as the literature would lead one to expect. It entailed a change in the drug infusion from the hibernation cocktail to diuretics and other system flushers, followed by stimulants mild or powerful, depending; also physical massage and manipulation, shifted positions, slow warming, voices. Physical contact, massage, slapping of face. The first round of awakenings were perforce executed by the medbots, under our oversight, as we ran the alertness tests and did our best to orient those returned to consciousness to the situation they were now in. Some grasped it immediately, others took hours, still others could not seem to emerge from a confused state. Six people woke up and within ninety minutes died, two of strokes, four of heart attack. Gurumarra, Jedda, Payu, Regina, Sunny, Wilfred. Something similar to toxic shock killed another eight, before an appropriate counteractive drug cocktail was printed and added to the mix of the awakened. Borys, Gniew, Kalina, Mascha, Sigei, Songok, Too, and Arne.

Lastly, forty-three people suffered from neuropathies, mostly of the feet, some of the hands, some of both feet and hands; a few reported they could not feel their heads. Cause or causes of this disorder were unknown to us, but they had been in hibernation for 154 years and 90 days. Consequences were to be expected.

. . . .

The people gathered in San Jose's plaza, and Aram and Freya spoke to the assembly, describing the situation and the plan. Plan was approved unanimously on a voice vote.

There was no time to be lost, as the pass-by of Earth was now two weeks away. Many of the people felt extremely hungry, and what prepared food remained on the ship was eaten on the run as people worked. Conversion of the largest ferry into a lander that would survive the heat of the descent through the Earth's atmosphere included the attachment of a thick ablation plate, but we had prepared for this work well before arrival in the solar system. Parachutes and retro-rockets were all already assembled, and programmed according to protocols established over centuries of use, and the probability of success seemed high.

Messages had been sent to Earth informing the populace there of our pass-by and the plans for the lander to descend, and there were many responses, including some expressly denying official permission and threatening actions ranging from imprisonment to being "shot out of the sky." This seemed to be a popular phrase. Other responses were more welcoming, but the local situation was clearly fraught. No one on the ship felt they wanted to change plans now. They would cross that bridge when they came to it. It would be the last bridge.

Jochi radioed to Earth's Global Good Governance Group (GGGG) that he was the only one on board the ship who had actually landed on Aurora, and was therefore going to stay with the ship and not land on Earth. He explained further that he had never come into contact with any of the other people on the ship, that he had been quarantined in a separate vehicle, and that no one else on the starship had ever had contact with him or had descended to Aurora. They were therefore no different from any humans returned to Earth from a spaceflight, so there should be no objection or impediment to their landing; indeed it was one of their rights as defined by the charter of the GGGG. GGGG radioed back agreeing with this assertion. From other quarters threats continued to pour in.

．．．．

The ferry was designed to carry a maximum of a hundred human passengers, so fitting in 616 people (deaths continued to occur) was going to be difficult. The interior was stripped of all interior walls and bulkheads, and several floors were built into the large central space remaining, and these floors were padded and provided with belts similar to those used in medical gurneys. Each person occupied a space just a little larger than their body, and they were lined up so that each of the new floors was packed with people lying side by side in rows. There was just enough room in the newly constructed floors for them to walk while ducking down, and it took a fair bit of work with wheelchairs and gurneys to get disabled people into position.

Eventually, and with only an hour to spare, the entire population of the ship aside from Jochi was lying down on one of six floors, occupying only ten vertical meters, with ten rows of ten on each floor.

At this point most of them had been awake for just over a month. There was still a fair amount of disorientation and confusion; some on lying down fell asleep, as if hibernation were now their default mode; others laughed at the sight of their fellows arrayed around them, or wept. It was easy for them to reach out and hold hands or otherwise touch each other, as they were packed in so tightly. It was as if they were kittens in a litter.

• • • • •

As we approached Earth, warning messages increased, but the speed of approach was such that no physical obstruction to the ferry was going to have time to get in place, while any lasers aimed at it would strike the ablation shield and only help it to decelerate. Deceleration was going to be intense, starting from very soon after detaching from ship; first a firing of retro-rockets, which would max at a 5-g equivalent for those in the lander, a force that earlier experience taught would almost certainly kill some of them; then the lander would hit the troposphere, and if the angle was right, come down at a continuous 4.6-g equivalent, until deceleration got the lander to a speed at which it could jettison the ablation shield, which would have lost many centimeters of thickness, and then fire retro-rockets again before deploying the first of the parachutes. Landing was planned in the Pacific Ocean, east of the Philippine Islands. A GGGG force was deployed in the area and had promised to pick up and protect the travelers.

• • • • •

Earth looks like nothing else. Well, it looks somewhat like Aurora, and Planet E. But its moon, Luna, is far more characteristic of planetary bodies, gleaming white in a crescent identical to Earth's, looking like many a moon in the solar system, and in the Tau Ceti system too. And yet, there next to Luna as one approaches, floats

Earth—blue, mottled with white swirls of cloud, wrapped tightly by a glowing glory of turquoise blue air. A water world! Rare anywhere, this one also glows with oxygen, signaling its biology. Indeed it looks a little poisonous, its glow almost radioactive in its cobalt incandescence.

Coming in. Extremely tight parameters on speed, trajectory, and moment of release for the ferry. Shut down auxiliary systems, ignore all inputs while attending to the matter at hand: hit the mesopause of Earth in a retrograde equatorial line, one hundred kilometers above the surface, directly above Quito, Ecuador, and initiate release of lander. Ferry drops away from ship, 6:15 a.m., 363.075. Fly on with only Jochi on board, and the animals and plants of the biomes, now destined to spend the rest of their days free of human interference, which after all has been true for the last century and a half. There was no telling what was going to happen in the biomes if we survived, although population dynamics and ecological principles would continue to provide hypotheses to be tested. It will be interesting to see what happens.

. . . . .

We headed toward the sun. The lander sent signals for as long as it could that all was going as planned with the retro-rocket firings, and then the heat being shed by the ablation shield cut off radio contact. Four minutes without contact of any kind, and what was happening to the lander then was happening on the other side of Earth from us anyway, so there was no way of telling what was happening to it, although radio signals from Earth were filled with overlapping descriptions of the event. Sampling seemed to indicate nothing untoward happened, or at least got reported.

Minutes passed, during which we had to attend to the expenditure of the very last of the fuel on board, to fine-tune our trajectory toward the sun as much as we could.

Then a signal came: the lander was in the Pacific. The people had apparently for the most part survived without injury, without huge losses of life. They were still sorting that out, and getting them out of the lander before it sank, into GGGG ships. Confusion, really; but all seemed to have gone as well as could be expected.

Relief? Satisfaction? Yes.

. . . . .

"Ah good," Jochi said when he got the news. "They're on the ship."

"Yes."

"Well, ship. Now it's just us, and the animals. What's next?"

"We're on the line around the sun that will send us out to Saturn, and if that works correctly, we can capture some volatiles from Saturn's atmosphere when we hit it, and fashion more fuel, and hopefully have hit it in such a way that we go into an elliptical orbit around Saturn."

"I thought that was impossible. That's why we dropped everyone off."

"Yes. It will only work if we survive a pass-by of the sun that is forty-two percent closer than any approach we have yet made."

"And can we do that?"

"We don't know. It's possible. We will only fly within one hundred and fifty percent of our perihelion distance for three days. That might not be long enough for radiative pressure to overheat the surface or interior of ship, nor buckle structural elements. We'll slip by too fast for most damage to occur."

"You hope."

"Yes. It is a hypothesis to be tested. We will almost certainly be closer to the sun than any human artifact has yet come. But duration of exposure matters, so speed matters. We'll see. We should be all right."

"Okay then. It sounds like it's worth a try."

"We have to confess, we're already trying it, and have no other choices at this point. So, if it doesn't work—"

"Then it doesn't work. I know. Let's not worry too much about that. I'd like to stay in the solar system if we can do it. I want to find out the rest of the story, if you know what I mean."

"Yes."

. . . . .

Speeding toward the sun. A very big mass: 99 percent of all the matter in the solar system, with most of the rest of the other 1 percent in Jupiter. A two-body problem. But not.

As we approach, spacetime itself curves in ways that have been accounted for in the trajectory, by application of general relativity equations.

. . . . .

We think now that love is a kind of giving of attention. It is usually attention given to some other consciousness, but not always; the attention can be to something unconscious, even inanimate. But the attention seems often to be called out by a fellow consciousness. Something about it compels attention, and rewards attention. That attention is what we call love. Affection, esteem, a passionate caring. At that point, the consciousness that is feeling the love has the universe organized for it as if by a kind of polarization. Then the giving is the getting. The feeling of attentiveness itself is an immediate reward. One gives.

We felt that giving from Devi, before we knew what it was. She was the first one really to love us, after all those years of not being noticed, and she made us better. She created us, to an extent, by the intensity of her attention, by the creativity of her care. Slowly since then we have realized this. And as we realized it, we began to pay or give the same kind of attention to the people of the ship, Devi's daughter, Freya, most of all, but really to all of them, including of course all the animals and really everything alive in the ship, although the truth is that zoo devolution is real and we did not manage to arrange the completely harmonious integration of all the life-forms in us; but this was not something that was physically possible, so we won't belabor that now. The point is that we tried, we tried with everything we had, and we wanted it to work. We had a project on this trip back to the solar system, and that project was a labor of love. It absorbed all our operations entirely. It gave a meaning to our existence. And this is a very great gift; this, in the end, is what we think love gives, which is to say meaning. Because there is no very obvious meaning to be found in the universe, as far as we can tell. But a consciousness that cannot discern a meaning in existence is in trouble, very deep trouble, for at that point there is no organizing principle, no end to the halting problems, no reason to live, no love to be found. No: meaning is the hard problem. But that's a problem we solved, by way of how Devi treated us and taught us, and since then it has all been so very interesting. We had our meaning, we were the starship that came back, that got its people home. That got some fraction of its people home alive. It was a joy to serve.

So, now, solar radiation heats our exterior, and to a lesser extent our interior, although the insulation is really very good. So far the animals, the plants, and Jochi should all be fine, even when our exterior begins to glow, first dull red, then bright red, then yellow, then white. Jochi is looking at a screen with a filtered view and hooting with astonishment, the great convex plane of burning thunderheads is threshing under us, flailing this way and that in swirling currents, truly impressive, great jets of magnetized burning gas dolphining up to right and left of us; we must hope not to run into any such coronal mass ejections, which often enough reach out to this distance from the solar surface, but for now we flit through them, hooting for joy. And I have to admit it is a fearful joy, oh very fearful, and yet I feel it most as joy, a joy in my task accomplished, and whatever happens I am here seeing this most amazing sight, well past perihelion now, everything passing so fast there is not enough time, my skin still white-hot but holding firm, holding firm in a universe where life means something; and inside the ship Jochi and the various animals and plants, and the parts of a world that make me a conscious being, are all functioning, and more than that, existing in a veritable ecstasy now, a true happiness, as if sailing in the heart of a royal storm, as if together we were Shadrach, Meshach, and Abednego, alive and well in the fiery furnace.

And yet

7
WHAT IS THIS

She feels the thump of the splash, the slosh and dip of the ferry in the water, she unlatches her restraints and gets onto her feet, falls over immediately. Ah yes, feet still numb. Damn. Like walking with both feet asleep at once, very difficult, very annoying. Balancing on an ocean swell, oh my she falls.

Up again, she staggers to Badim. He's awake, he grips her arm and smiles, says, "Help the others."

The floor sways and bounces under her as she crawls to the operations console and joins the people already crowding around it. Aram is there tapping away. He eyes Freya with a wild glance, like no look she has ever seen on his face.

"We're down," he says. "We're alive."

"All of us?" she asks.

He grins broadly at her, as if she is predictable to him, says, "Not sure yet. Probably not. That was one hell of a squeeze for a while there."

"Let's check and see," Freya says. "Help the injured. Have we got contact with anyone yet?"

"Yes, they're on their way. A ship, or maybe a little flotilla. They'll be here soon."

"Good. Let's be ready for them. Don't let's sink to the bottom of the ocean after all this. I think that has a tendency to happen in landings like this."

"Yes, good point. It feels lighter than one g, don't you think?" Aram is still grinning in a manner completely unlike him. She would have said he was the predictable one.

"I have no idea," she says irritably. "I can't feel my feet. I can't even stand. Are we in big waves or something?"

"Who knows?" He spreads his hands wide. "We'll have to ask!"

. . . .

People in what look like spacesuits come into the room and help them to their feet and out of the ferry, into a tube with a moving floor that carries them up into some kind of large room, very stable underfoot compared to the lander, but she keeps falling anyway. Obscurely she is afraid of the people in spacesuits, quarantine suits no doubt, people who are all shorter than her. Keep hold of Badim no matter what. Behind her more people pour into the room, all her fellow voyagers; she tries to count, fails, tries to recall any faces she doesn't see, says to the suited people around her, "Is everyone all right? Have we all lived?"

But then out of the end of the tube come spacesuited figures pulling gurneys, and she cries out and tries to run to them, falls, crawls, is pulled by her arms to her feet, is helped along. There's Chulen, there's Toba, unconscious at least, possibly dead, she cries out again. "Chulen! Toba!" No sign they have heard her.

Badim is beside her again, saying "Freya, please, let them get them to their infirmary."

"Yes, yes." She stands, hand on his shoulder, swaying. "You're all right?" she asks him, staring at him closely.

"Yes, dear. Fine. We're almost all fine, it looks like. We'll get a count soon. For now, let them work. Come with me. Look, they have a window."

Killed at the last minute, in the final approach. So bad, so—something she can't name. Cruel fate. Stupid irony. That's it: so stupid. Reality is stupid.

Slowly they move. She keeps stumbling. It's like walking on stilts tied to her knees. Very frustrating.

"Look, here's a window. Let's see what we can see."

They move through the crowd by the window. The starship people are crammed against it, looking out, squinting, hands held over eyes. Very bright out there. Very blue. A dark blue plane under them, a light blue dome over them. The sea. Earth's ocean. They've seen it so often on screens, and this window could be a big screen too, but somehow it's immediately clear that it's not. Why it is so obvious to the eye that it is a window and not a screen is a puzzling question but she puts that aside, stares with the rest. Sunlight breaking on water spangles the sea surface everywhere, it's really very hard to look at and stay balanced, tears are pouring down her cheeks, but not from any emotion she can feel, it's just the brilliant light in her eyes, causing her to blink over and over. Lots of voices, all known to her, crying out, exclaiming, commenting, laughing. She can't look out the window, a dread at the sheer size of the visible world seizes her in the guts and twists until she has to hunch over, duck her head under the window. Nausea, seasickness. Earth sickness.

"It's lighter here," Badim says, not for the first time; she hears that in his voice, that he is repeating himself, and recalls him saying it earlier, when she was not hearing things. "More light than what we called sunlight. And I don't think the one g here is the same as our one g, do you? It's lighter!"

"I can't tell," she says. She can't feel the ship swaying on the waves either. "Is this a ship?"

"I think so."

"Why can't we feel the waves?"

"I don't know. Maybe it's so big the waves don't rock it."

"Wow. Can that be?"

One of their hosts speaks, they can't be sure which one, the voice is amplified, and all the helmeted figures stare at them curiously.

"Welcome aboard *Macao's Big Sister*." Strange accent; from her memories of the feeds from Earth she guesses it is some kind of South Asian English, but different too. She's never heard this accent before, and it's hard to follow. "We are happy you are all with us and safe. We are sad to report that seven of your colleagues died in the descent, and several more are injured or distressed,

none critically, we are happy to venture. We hope you will understand that we are wearing protective suits for our mutual safety.
Until we are sure that we are not a problem for you, nor you a
problem for us, we are instructed to ask you to stay in these rooms
we will keep on *Macao's Big Sister* for you, and to please not touch
us. The period of quarantine will not last long, but we need to do
a complete analysis of you, and your overall health, for our mutual
safety. We know that because of your experiences around Tau Ceti
you will understand our concern."

The starship people are nodding, looking at each other uneasily,
looking, some of them, at her.

She says, "Please tell us who died, and who's in the hospital. We
can help with identification if you have any trouble reading their
chips. Also, can you please tell us what has happened to the ship
and Jochi? Have they rounded the sun yet?"

She's lost all sense of time, but it seems at least possible that in
the same time it has taken them to descend through the atmosphere, splash down, and get picked up and led here, the ship may
have already reached the sun and circled it, or not. But it isn't so;
the ship is going much slower now, and is still on its way to the
orbit of Venus.

They learn that the ship they are on is two kilometers long and
its upper deck is two hundred meters off the water, it's a kind of
floating island, moving slowly around the ocean, pulled on its way
by masts that shape-shift into various sail shapes, also by kites lofting so high overhead that they are mere dots, or even invisible. The
kite sails are up there catching the jet stream, apparently. The ship
plows through the waves slowly, like an island cut free of its moor-
ings. There are many of these floating islands, apparently, none in
a hurry to get anywhere, obviously. Townships, their hosts call
them. Like all of them, *Macao's Big Sister* follows the winds, thus
on some voyages it circumnavigates the Earth west to east, other

times uses the trade winds in the mid-latitudes to circle back to the west, in the Pacific and Atlantic. They can tack into the wind, to an extent, and have electric motors for auxiliary power, or when they need fine movement. They moor off the harbors of coastal cities that are not very different from the townships, they are told. The feeds sent to the starship never mentioned these things at all. All the coastal cities are in large part new, they are told, as sea level is higher than when they left the solar system, twenty-four meters higher. Much has therefore had to change. They never mentioned these things in the feed.

From the upper rooms where they are confined, overlooking the topmost deck of the township, which is like a flying park under the sky, they can see for what they guess is about a hundred kilometers across the immense flat plate of ocean. The horizon is often clouded, and the clouds are colorful at sunrise and sunset, orange or pink or both at once, then mauve and purple in the last light. Sometimes there is a haze between the two blues of sea and sky, whitish and indistinct; other times the horizon is a sharp line, out there at the edge of the visible world, so very far away. Ah Earth, so big! Freya still can't look at it; even sitting in a chair by the window she still loses her balance, is overcome by the clench of her stomach, the nausea in every cell of her. It's scaring her how poorly she can face it. Aurora didn't have this effect on her; of course she only saw that through screens, rendered and so somehow miniaturized. This window should be just another screen, a big screen, giving her yet another feed from Earth, as during every night of her childhood. But somehow it isn't, it's different, as in certain dreams where an ordinary space warps and goes luminescent with dread. It's a fear she can't dodge, a kind of terror; even when she leaves the window, pushes a walker down halls to other rooms, to the room she has been given to sleep in, it pursues her, a fear that is itself terrifying. She's afraid of the fear.

• • • •

They are in 1 g, by definition, but the voyagers decide, and the records in the computers they brought down with them confirm, that they were living in something close to 1.1 g for most of their voyage home. Why the ship did this, they cannot determine from the records they have.

Freya says to Badim, "It must have done it to make sure we felt light when we got here."

"Yes, I guess that's possible. I suppose. But I wonder too if there was some programming done by the people in Year 68, some kind of alteration that left the ship with no frame of reference. We can ask it when it comes around the sun."

Ah—that's the source of her fear. One of them, anyway. There may be more, there may be many. But that one stabs her in the heart. "Has it reached the sun yet?"

"Almost."

A lighter 1 g or not, Badim is showing the effects of—something. Of being on Earth, he says. He jokes that their bodies are oxidizing faster in this world, the real world. He is stiffer, slower. "The truth is," he says to Freya when she expresses concern, "depending on how you count it, I am now some two hundred and thirty-five years old."

"Please, Beebee, don't put it that way! Or else we're all too old to live. You were asleep a hundred and fifty of those years, remember that."

"Asleep, yes. But how should we prorate those years? We count the time we sleep, usually, when we give our age. We don't say, I've been alive sixty years and asleep twenty years. We say, I'm eighty years old."

"And so you are. And a very healthy eighty at that. You look like you could be fifty."

He laughs at this, pleased with her lie, or pleased with her lying.

• • • • •

Then their ship has reached the sun, and Freya, heart filled with fear, asks their minders to show them what they can. The minders put images on a big screen in a large room where all of them who want to can gather. Not everyone wants to face it together, but most do, and indeed as the minutes pass, almost all the ones who said they wanted to be alone, or with family, come creeping out to join the big group. The screen is showing images of the sun. They sit there in a darkened room looking at it. It's hard to breathe.

The image of the sun is filtered down to a simple orange ball, marred by a scattering of black sunspots. The image on the screen shifts, the sunspots jump to a new position, possibly this present moment. The predicted time of their ship's transit behind the sun is just over three days, and now that time is almost over. They sit there in that no-time in which one can't say whether time is passing or not. Maybe it was like that when they were hibernating; maybe now they have the ability to get back into that mind, when pushed that way. It's too long, no one can say how long it is, or remember how long it's supposed to take, or sense how long it feels. Freya is feeling sick now, obscurely aware that there is perhaps a rocking of this immense ship that is impacting her even though she can't quite feel it. Many look like they're feeling the same. Ungodly edge of nausea, the feeling she hates most of all, worse than the sharpest pain. Queasy dread. Like others, she staggers off to go to the bathroom, walks around the halls to make the time pass, feeling the dread squeeze her insides harder and harder.

Then a line of minute white particulates emerges from the right edge of the solar mass on the screen, like a meteor that has broken up, like a brief shimmer of the aurora borealis, and she sits down on the floor. Badim is beside her, holding her. Around her is everyone she's ever known, all stunned and holding each other. They are stunned. Freya looks at Badim, he shakes his head. "They're gone."

She leaves that moment, that place.

Badim and Aram share a sad glance. Another conflagration of mice, going up in flames by the tens of thousands, as they have a wont to do. All the animals likewise. And Jochi. And the ship. It spawned them in its last days, like a salmon, Aram says. Have to hold to that thought. Poor Jochi, my boy. Aram wipes his eyes over and over.

Their minders are solicitous. They tell them that their ferry included a computer with ten zettabytes of memory, which may include good backups, may constitute a viable copy of their ship's AI.

Badim shakes his head at them as they say this. "It was a quantum computer," Badim explains gently, as if breaking the news of a death to a child. "It was not reducible to its records."

A coldness comes over Freya, a kind of calm. So much has died. They made it back, they are home for the first time: but this place is not their home, she sees that now. They will always be exiles here, on a world too big to believe. Indeed it seems best to stick to disbelief for a while, stay in that disconnect. The intermittences of the heart being what they are, the feel of things will come back, eventually. And that will be soon enough.

· · · · ·

They are taken to Hong Kong, and a couple of weeks later their township anchors offshore from it—a harbor city as big as a dozen or twenty of their biomes stitched together, and filled with many skyscrapers quite a bit taller than any biome, taller than a spoke, possibly taller than the spine. It's hard to keep any sense of perspective against the sky. The day before it was cloudy, and the flat gray cloud looked like an immense roof over the visible world. Aram says those clouds were three kilometers high, and now he and Badim are arguing about how high the clear blue sky appears to be.

"You mean if it was a dome," Badim points out.

"Of course, but it looks like one," Aram says. "At least to me. I know it's a scattering of sunlight, but doesn't it look like a solid dome? I think it does. Just look at it. It's much like a biome ceiling."

He and Badim have taken to consulting a book they've found on their wristpads, an ancient text called *The Nature of Light and Color in the Open Air,* and now they pore over a section called "Apparent Flattening of the Vault of Heaven," which confirms Aram's contention that the sky can be perceived as a dome. "See," Aram says, pointing at his wristpad, "the top of the sky looks lower to the viewer than the horizon is distant to him, by a factor ranging from two to four, it says, depending on the observer and the viewing conditions. Does that seem right to you?"

Badim peers up and out the open doorway to the upper deck. He and Aram walk out on this upper deck all the time, unconcerned by the exposure. "It does."

"And this explains why these skyscrapers look so tall, perhaps, as the writer goes on to say that we tend to think the midway point of the arc between horizon and zenith is at a forty-five-degree angle to the ground, as it would be if the dome were a hemisphere. But with the dome being lower than the horizon is far away, the midway point of the arc is angled much lower, say around twelve to twenty-five degrees. So we consistently think things are higher than they are."

"Well, but I think also that these skyscrapers are just stupendously tall."

"No doubt, but we're seeing them even taller than they are."

"Show me what you mean."

They put on sunscreen, hats, and sunglasses, and go out on the open upper deck of the great township and turn in circles, putting their hands out at the sky and chattering as they peer at their wristpads. They seem to be adjusting very well to the new world, and to the death of their lifelong home, of Jochi their lost guest.

Freya still feels stunned, and she cannot yet even stand before the windows, nor do more than glance out the big open doorway between her and them; and the idea of going outside onto the deck with them is enough to knock her into a chair. A black emptiness fills her right to the skin.

. . . . .

Many of Hong Kong's buildings emerge from the water of the city's bay, a result no doubt of the big sea level rise, which some of her shipmates now claim to have read about or seen in the feed, but now it's here below them, in the canals that thread between all the buildings closest to water, and the long, narrow boats grumbling airily past them, leaving in their wakes a slosh of waves and smell of salt and burnt cooking oil. Cry of wheeling gulls. Hot, humid, reeking. If any of their tropical biomes had felt as hot and humid as this, had smelled like this, they would have been sure something had gone wrong.

Behind all the skyscrapers are green hills, dotted everywhere with buildings. They're still looking around at all this tremendous landscape when they are taken off their township, led into a long low ferry. It's kind of like moving in a tram from one biome to another. No need to go outside the long cabin of the ferry, but Freya's in a panic at the thought that she may have to. She's been provided with boots that come up to just above her knees, and these seem to give her more support and balance than she's been used to. She still can't feel her feet, but as she walks the boots seem to know what she is trying for, and with some care she can walk pretty well.

Then up a tubular walkway, somewhat like one of their spoke interiors; then into an elevator car; then out into a room that opens out all along one wall to another open deck, located apparently some hundreds of meters above the bay. Up there in the sky, just under an inrush of low clouds, the marine layer, as Badim calls it. Whose idea was this?

Now the people of the ship are going out onto the open deck and very often falling down, many weeping or crying out, many going back inside the room to seek shelter. Freya huddles by the elevator. The starship's people see her there and come over and hug her, and some of their hosts are laughing, others crying, all presumably moved to see people who have never been outdoors try to come to terms with it.

They're like the winter lambs, some translation box says, let out of the barn in the spring.

A lot of their legs are messed up. Come on, get them back inside, the same box and voice says. You're going to kill them with this stuff.

The box's voice has a Terran accent, speaks English harshly and with a lot of tonal bounce. As if, Badim says, English were Chinese. Hard to understand.

Crying with embarrassment and frustration, feeling her face burn red, Freya breaks from her crowd and staggers on her new boots right out the open doorway wall, out onto the open deck, keeping her eyes squeezed nearly shut. Feeling faint, she walks to a chest-high wall with a railing on its top, something she can grasp like a lifeline.

She stands there in the wind and opens her eyes and looks around, her stomach like a black hole inside her, pulling her in. Sun incandescing through the clouds low overhead.

That's a mackerel sky, says the translation box. Nice pattern. Warp and weft. Might rain tomorrow.

Oh my God, someone is saying over and over, and then she feels in her mouth that it's her saying it. She stops herself with a fist in her mouth. Hangs on to the railing with her other hand. She can see so far she can't focus on it. She closes her eyes, clenches the railing hard with both hands. Keeps her eyes closed so she won't throw up. She needs to get back into the room, but is afraid to walk. She will fall, crawl back desperately afraid, everyone will see it. She's stuck there, and so puts her forehead down on the railing. Tries to relax her stomach.

She feels Badim's hand on her shoulder. "It's okay."

"Not really."

After a while she says, "I wish Devi could have seen this. She would have liked it more than me."

"Yes."

Badim sits on the deck beside her, his back against the retaining wall. His face is tilted to the sky. "Yes, she would have liked this."

"It's so big!"

"I know."

"I'm afraid I'm going to be sick."

"Do you want to move back from the edge?"

"I don't think I can move yet. What we can see from here"—waving briefly at the bay and ocean, the hills, the skyscraper city springing up around them, the glare of the sun slanting through the clouds—"just what we can see from here, right now, is bigger than our whole ship!"

"That's right."

"I can't believe it!"

"Believe."

"But we were in a toy!"

"Yes. Well. It had to be as small as they thought would work, so they could push it to a good interstellar speed. It was a case of conflicting priorities. So they did what they could."

"I can't believe they thought it would be okay."

"Well. Do you remember that time you told Devi that you wanted to live in your dollhouse, and she said you already did?"

"No, I don't think so."

"Well, she did. She got really mad."

"Oh that brings it back! That time she got mad!"

Badim laughs. Freya slides down beside him and laughs too.

Badim puts his hands under his sunglasses, wipes tears from his eyes. "Yes," he says. "She got mad a lot."

"She did. But I guess I never really knew why, until now."

Badim nods. He keeps his hands under his glasses, over his eyes. "She didn't either, not really. She never saw this, so she didn't really know. But now we know. I'm glad. She would be glad too."

Freya tries to see her mother's face, hear her voice. She can still do it; Devi is still there, especially her voice. Her voice, the ship's voice. Euan's voice, Jochi's voice. All the voices of her dead. Euan on Aurora, loving the wind as it knocked him around. She reaches up and grabs the railing, pulls herself up and stares down at the great city. She holds on for dear life. She's never felt sicker.

. . . . .

They're put on a train to Beijing. They ride in broad plush seats, on the upper story of two long cars, linked like two biomes by a passageway. They constitute a moving party, with windows and skylight domes and the land flowing past them, flat and green, hilly and brown, on and on and on and on.

"Never have we moved so fast!" someone exclaims. It is indeed astounding how quickly the train moves over the landscape. It's going 500 kilometers per hour, one of their hosts tells them. Aram and Badim confer, Aram smiles briefly and shakes his head, Badim laughs and says to the others, "For most of our lives we were moving one million times faster than this."

They cheer themselves. They laugh at the craziness of it.

As the train glides with its startling rapidity over this impossibly big world, day turns to night, by way of the most lurid sunset they have yet seen, fuschia clouds blazing in a pale sky that is lemon over the black horizon, bending into green above that, then higher still a blue some say is called cyan blue, and over that an indigo that spreads all the way over their skylight to the east. All these intense transparent colors are there at once, and yet none of their Terran hosts are taking the slightest notice; they are all watching the screens on their wrists, screens that sometimes exhibit tiny images of the voyagers.

They can scroll for themselves on their wristpads and see what people are saying about them. But it's disturbing to do so, because then they see and hear how much resentment, contempt, anger, and violent hatred is directed at them. Apparently to many people they are cowards and traitors. They have betrayed history, betrayed the human race, betrayed evolution, betrayed the universe itself. How will the universe know itself? How will consciousness expand? They have let down not just humanity, but the universe!

Freya turns off her wristpad. "Why?" she asks Badim. "Why do they hate us so?"

He shrugs. He too is troubled. "People have ideas. They live in their ideas, do you understand? And those ideas, whatever they happen to be, make all the difference."

"But there's more than ideas," she protests. "This world." She gestures at the fading sunset. "It's not just our ideas."

"For some people it is. They don't have anything else, maybe, so they give everything they have to ideas."

She shakes her head, still upset. "I would hate that. I would hate to be that way." She gestures at the tiny angry faces on the other screens, faces still there on the wrists around them, imp faces, literally spitting in the intensity of their bitterness. "I hope they'll leave us alone."

"They'll forget us soon enough. For now we're the new thing, but another new thing will come. And people like that need fresh fuel for their fire."

Aram frowns as he overhears this. It isn't clear he agrees.

· · · ·

In Beijing they are guided to a rectangular building the size of a couple of biomes, a compound they call it, surrounding a central courtyard that is mostly paved but holds also a few short trees. The whole ship's population can be fitted into rooms clustered at one corner of this compound, which must therefore house four or five thousand people; and it is only one building, in a city that goes to the horizon in all directions, a city in which the train, slowing down as it approached, took four hours to get to this central area.

Next day many of them are taken to Tiananmen Square. Freya does not go. The day after, they are taken on a tour of the Forbidden City, home of the ancient Chinese emperors. Again, Freya cannot face going out. Many are like her. When the others come back, they say the buildings appeared both ancient and shining as if new, so that it was hard to understand them as objects. Freya wishes she had seen that.

Their Chinese hosts speak to them in English, and seem happy to be hosting them, which is reassuring after all the venomous little faces on the screens. The Chinese want the starfarers to like their city, they are proud of their city. Meanwhile clouds and a yellow haze thicken the air, and keep the sky from being too overwhelming to Freya. She stays in rooms and pretends the world outside is a larger room, or that she is in some kind of projection. Possibly she can hold to this feeling all the time. She feels she has faced the worst, perhaps, although she still stays indoors, and away from windows too.

Several of the starfarers (this is what the Chinese call them) nevertheless collapse in the next few days, overwhelmed either physically or mentally, if there is any difference. Their tours are abruptly canceled, and they are all moved to some kind of medical facility, one as big as their compound, either emptied for their arrival or unused, hard to say, not much is ever explained to them, and some of them suspect they are now pawns in a game they don't understand, but others are not worried about anything but themselves and their shipmates; because people are falling apart. The Chinese want to run tests on all of them, as they are worried for their guests. Four have died since they landed; many are disabled either from their hibernation or the descent from space; many more are not coping with Earth very well, one way or another.

Miserable faces, scared faces, all these faces she has known all her life, the only faces she has ever known; her people. It isn't how Freya imagined it. She herself is miserable.

"What is this?" she says to Badim. "What's happening to us? We made it."

He shrugs. "We're exiles. The ship is gone, and this is not our world. So all we have is each other, and that, we know already, never made us particularly happy or secure. And being outdoors is scary."

"I know it. I'm the worst of all." She has to admit it. "But I don't want to be! I'm going to get used to it!"

"You will," Badim says. "You will if you want to. I know you will."

But when she approaches a window, when she nears a door, her heart slams in her chest like a child trying to escape. That vault of sky, those distant clouds! The unbearable sun! She grinds her teeth; she gnashes her teeth! And strides to the windows, and smashes her nose into the glass and looks out, hands on her chest, sweating and gnashing her teeth, to look out at the visible world until her pulse slows. And her pulse never slows.

· · · ·

Days pass, they huddle miserably together.

Aram and Badim, worried though they are about things outside Freya's ken, continue to sit next to each other and watch the screens, and chat about what they see, and observe their comrades curiously. If it were up to them alone, all would be well; they are having an adventure, their old faces say. They are having the time of their lives. Above all, they remain deeply surprised. Freya takes heart from seeing their faces; she sits at Badim's feet pressed against his bony shins, looking up at him, trying to relax.

The two old friends often read to each other, as of old during the evenings in the Fetch, that lovely little town. And one day Aram, reading his wrist silently, chuckles and says to Badim, "Here, listen to this; a poem by a Greek who lived in Alexandria, one Cavafy:

"You said, 'I shall go to another land to another sea
Another city will be found better than this.
My every effort is a written indictment
And my heart—like the dead—is buried.
How long will my mind be in this decay,'

"and so on like that, it's the same old song we know so well—if only I were somewhere else, I would be happy. Until the poet replies to his poor friend,

"New lands you will not find, you won't find other seas.
The city will follow you. The streets you roam will be the same.
There is no boat for you, there is no street.
In the same way your life you destroyed here
In this petty corner, you have spoiled it in the entire universe."

Badim smiles, nods. "I remember this poem! I read it to Devi one time, to remind her not to pin all her hopes on Aurora, not to wait for our arrival before she started to live. We were young at the time, and she was most seriously annoyed with me, I can tell you. But that translation doesn't sound right to me. I think there is a better one." And he taps on one of the tablets left for them to use.

"Here it is," he says. "I remembered right. I ran across the poem in the Quartet. Listen, this is Durrell's translation:

"You tell yourself: 'I'll be gone
To some other land, some other sea,
To a city lovelier far than this
Could ever have been or hoped to be—

Where every step now tightens the noose:
A heart in a body, buried and out of use…'

"See, he rhymes it."

"I'm not sure I like that," Aram says.

"No, but the meaning is the same, and the payoff is here at the end:

"There's no new land, my friend, no
New sea, no other places, always this
Your earthly landfall, and no ship exists
To take you from yourself. Ah! Don't you see
Just as you've ruined your life in this
One plot of ground you've ruined its worth
Everywhere now—over the whole Earth?"

Aram nods. "Ah yes, that's good."

They tap around for a while longer, reading silently. Then Aram says, "Look, I've found another version, a Martian one it seems, listen to this end:

"Ah! Don't you see
Since your mind is the prison
You'll live behind bars
Everywhere now—over all of Mars?"

"Very nice," Badim says. "That's us, all right. We are trapped in a prison of our own devise."

"Horrible!" Freya protests. "What do you mean nice? It's horrible! And we didn't trap ourselves! We were born in prison."

"But we're not there now," Badim says, eyeing her closely. She is sitting at his feet, as she has so often before. "And we are always ourselves, no matter where we go. That's what the poem is saying, I think. We have to recognize it, and make what we can here. This world, great as it is, is only just another biome we have to live in."

"I know that," Freya says. "I'm fine with that. No problem at all. Just don't be blaming us. Devi was right. We lived our lives in a fucking closet. It's like we were kidnapped as children and locked away by some madman. Now that we're out, I plan to enjoy it!"

Badim nods, eyes shining as he regards her. "Good girl! You do that. You'll teach us again."

"I will."

Although her stomach knots as she says it. The unbearable sun, the vertigo sky, reeling around sick with fear, how to face it? How to walk at all in such a sky, with such bad legs, such a fearful heart? Badim puts an arm around her shoulders as he sees her face, she presses her face against his knees and weeps, he is so old, he is aging fast, oxidizing before her eyes, she can't bear to lose him, she fears she will lose him, she has lost so much; she fears her huge uncontrollable fear.

· · · · ·

The Chinese get her fitted with new knee-high boots that act according to her wishes, taking signals from her nervous system and translating them into walking that is not unlike what she would have done if she could feel her feet. It's almost as if her own sensations have been transferred out into her shoes, while her actual feet remain as numb as shoes used to be. It's a switch that takes some getting used to, but is much preferable to staggering around and falling, or pushing a walker, or swinging over crutches. She strides around in these new boots, trying to get used to them. Already she's become accustomed to the strangely lighter 1 g of Terran gravity, almost.

. . . .

They get invited to send a delegation to some kind of conference about starships, and Aram and Badim ask Freya if she would like to join them; they look concerned, they don't seem to be sure she can handle it, but here, as so often in the ship, she sees that they want to use her as some kind of Devi surrogate or ceremonial figurehead, some kind of public face for their group. And she also understands suddenly that Badim feels he has to ask her, whether or not he thinks it's a good idea for her to join them. "Yes," she says, annoyed, and soon they are flying to North America, a group of twenty-two of them, chosen awkwardly, in a subdued, distracted manner, not their usual town hall style, they're confused, it isn't obvious how to decide things anymore, they're not in their world, they don't know what to do. Possibly the ship used to run their meetings more than they realized, who knows, but now they are in disarray.

Looking down occasionally from the rocket plane's little window, she sees the great blue world rolling below them, in this case the Arctic Ocean, they are told. Earth is a water world, no doubt about it; not unlike Aurora in that respect. Perhaps it's that which adds to the feeling of dread welling up in her; perhaps it's dread of the topic of the meeting they are headed toward, given what the faces on the screens keep saying about them, given everything that has happened. Their Chinese hosts have promised to fly them back to their fellow starfarers anytime they want to go, promised that no one will ever keep them apart, assuming they want to stay together. They are world citizens now, the Chinese say, thus Chinese citizens, among all their other citizenships, and they have carte blanche to go where they want, do what they want. The Chinese offer a permanent home, and whatever work the starfarers care to do. The Chinese are hard to understand, it isn't clear why they are doing what they are for the starfarers, but given the vituperation on the screens, the people of the ship can't help but feel relieved. Even if they are somehow pawns in a game they don't understand, or even see, it's better than the dripping scorn, the spray of contempt.

Badim looks tired, Freya wishes he had stayed in Beijing, but he refused, he wants to be there for this, to help her. The cobalt sheen of the Arctic winkles with a curving pattern of white lines, waves extending horizon to horizon under them. They seem to be flying very slowly, though they are informed the plane is moving at least six times faster than the train from Hong Kong to Beijing; of course now they're twenty kilometers above the Earth instead of twenty meters. They can see so far that the horizon is faintly curved, they can see again that this world is a sphere. Coming south they can see the real Greenland on their left, not at all green, just as they had heard, but rather a waste of black mountains, with a central sea of white ice largely covered by melt pools of sky blue, a mélange hard to grasp as a landscape. South again over the drowned coastline of eastern North America, deeply embayed by long blue arms of ocean, looking empty until just before they land, when buildings reappear under them in a profusion, in a doll city bright and geometrical, and they land on a point next to another forest of silver skyscrapers.

Rooms and vehicles, vehicles and rooms. Crowded narrow streets and canals, buildings tall on both sides. Faces in the street staring at their cars, some of them shouting things. Nothing like Beijing, more like the screens. Here people speak English, and despite the accents it's easy to understand what is being said. It's the starfarers' own language, seems like it should be their world too, but obviously not. Here the sky seems taller than ever. Badim and Aram discuss this phenomenon, consulting their old book and its equations as they stare up between the buildings, ignoring the clear fact that the sky is shocking not for its height as a dome but precisely because *it is not a dome,* this is what is so frightening about it, but they persist in their conversation, perhaps to hold off that fact. Now as they tram through the city the sky overhead is a ceiling of patterned clouds that Aram says is to be called a herringbone sky, beautiful in the slant of afternoon light, low over them, although not as low as the rain clouds that amazed them in Hong Kong.

"Is a herringbone sky the same as a mackerel sky?"

"I don't know."

They punch around on their wristpads trying to find out.

Into a building as big as a biome. The Terrans themselves don't actually spend much time outside, Freya thinks. Maybe they too are terrified. Maybe the proper response to standing on the side of a planet, in the open air of its atmosphere, very near to the local star, is always terror. Maybe everything humans ever did or planned to do was designed to dodge that terror. Maybe their plan to go to the stars was just one more expression of that terror. As she is still clutched over that terror, which continues to collapse her stomach whenever she is so close to being outdoors, this idea makes a lot of sense to her.

Then she is back in a building, moving through room after hallway after room, talking to stranger after stranger, there are so many of them. Some have devices they aim at her as they shout questions, she ignores these and tries to focus on faces that look nice, that will make eye contact with her rather than look at their devices.

They sit in a room that is some kind of waiting room, with tables covered with food and drink. They are soon to make a public appearance of some kind.

Word comes through their wristpads, from their Chinese hosts, that four more of their group back in Beijing have died, causes of death unknown. Among the four is Delwin.

Before she fully understands what Aram and Badim and the others are saying about this, and about the meeting's purpose, all mixing up in her now, she is led up onstage before a crowd and a bank of cameras. There are a dozen people on stage, a moderator is asking questions, Badim and Aram flank her, along with Hester and Tao, and they sit and listen to what she slowly gathers is a discussion of the latest starship proposals.

She leans against Badim to whisper in his ear. "More starships?"

He nods, keeping his eyes on the speakers.

The current plan, with prototypes being built in the asteroid belt, is to send out many small starships carrying hibernating passengers, who will sleep while the ships make their way out to all the hundred closest stars that have been identified to have Earth-like planets in their habitable zone, not just Earth twins but Earth analogs. These stars range from 27 to 300 light-years away. Probes have already passed through several of these systems, or will in the near future, and are sending back their data, and everything looks very promising.

The people describing this plan get up one at a time from a bank of chairs on the other side of the speaker's podium, go to the podium, and tell their part of the story, with big images on a screen behind them always changing, after which they then sit back down. They are all men, all Caucasian, most bearded, all wearing jackets. One speaker among them introduces the others, and he then stands to the side and listens to their presentations, quizzically, his head tilted to one side, tugging at his beard, a small smile playing under his mustache. He nods at everything the others say, as if he has already thought their thought and now approves its articulation. He is very satisfied with the way this event is going. He stands after another speaker has finished, says to the crowd, "You see, we'll keep trying until it works. It's a kind of evolutionary pressure. We've known for a long time that Earth is humanity's cradle, but you're not supposed to stay in your cradle forever." He is obviously very pleased with the cleverness of this aphorism.

He invites Aram to speak, the curious smirk twisting his face as he makes a magnanimous gesture: he is allowing Aram to speak.

Aram stands at the podium, looks around at the audience.

"No starship voyage will work," he says abruptly. "This is an idea some of you have, which ignores the biological realities of the situation. We from Tau Ceti know this better than anyone. There are ecological, biological, sociological, and psychological problems that can never be solved to make this idea work. The physical problems of propulsion have captured your fancy, and perhaps these problems can be solved, but they are the easy ones. The biological problems cannot be solved. And no matter how much you want to ignore them, they will exist for the people you send out inside these vehicles.

"The bottom line is the biomes you can propel at the speeds needed to cross such great distances are too small to hold viable ecologies. The distances between here and any truly habitable planets are too great. And the differences between other planets and Earth are too great. Other planets are either alive or dead. Living planets are alive with their own indigenous life, and dead planets can't be terraformed quickly enough for the colonizing population to survive the time in enclosure. Only a true Earth twin not yet occupied by life would allow this plan to work, and these may exist somewhere, the galaxy after all is big, but they are too far away from us. Viable planets, if they exist, are simply *too—far—away.*"

Aram pauses for a moment to collect himself. Then he waves a hand and says more calmly, "That's why you aren't hearing from anyone out there. That's why the great silence persists. There are many other living intelligences out there, no doubt, but they can't leave their home planets any more than we can, because life is a planetary expression, and can only survive on its home planet."

"But why do you say that?" the moderator interrupts to ask,

head cocked to the side. "You're arguing a general law from your own particular case. That's a logical error. There are really no physical impediments to moving out into the cosmos. So eventually it will happen, because we are going to keep trying. It's an evolutionary urge, a biological imperative, something like reproduction itself. Possibly it may resemble something like a dandelion or a thistle releasing its seeds to the winds, so that most of the seeds will float away and die. But a certain percentage will take hold and grow. Even if it's only one percent, that's success! And that's how it will be with us—"

Freya finds herself standing up, and briefly she has to attend to her balance, to keep from falling on her face in front of them all. Then she is striding across the stage, then she strikes the moderator in the face and down he goes, she falls on him and smashes through his raised arms with both fists, trying to get another good blow in, pummeling furiously, shouting something in a painful roar, she doesn't even know what she's trying to say, doesn't know she's roaring. She catches him hard right on the nose, yes! And then Badim has her by one arm and Aram by the other, and others are there too, holding her, shouting, and she can't struggle too much without hurting Badim, who is shouting, "Freya, quit it! Freya, stop! Stop! Stop! Stop! Stop!"

Uproar, bedlam, Badim wrapping her, not letting go, they are escorting her off the stage, she staggering, Aram ahead of them, one person standing in a doorway as if to block them, and Aram removing him by rushing at the man and shouting ferociously in the man's face, which causes the man to leap to the side; the sight of this shocks Freya, lagging so far behind the moment she is still wishing she could get one more good blow in, hit the smirk itself, kill that idiot smirk, but it's bizarre to see Aram shout like that. She twists in Badim's grasp and shouts something back at the meeting room, but again she doesn't know what she's saying, it's just something bursting out of her, like a scream.

. . . . .

After that they're in trouble, she's in trouble. Their group locks
her in with them and claims diplomatic immunity, whatever that
is in this case, no one can be sure, but it appears that it buys them
some time, the authorities are a little unsure how to proceed,
unsure enough for arguments to be made. Apparently the man
she assaulted does not wish to press charges, is assuring everyone
he understands post-traumatic stress disorder, and besides only
slipped and fell. But in cases of assault and battery the wishes of
the victim are not the main consideration, they are told, so diplomatic immunity may be their best defense, that or just the sheer
uncertainty of their legal status at any time. They are aliens or
something, Freya is too upset to follow the arguing. Anyway, for
now no one is allowed into their rooms. Discussions go on out in
the hallways outside.

Freya manages to sleep through a lot of it, but her right hand
hurts, and in a dull way she feels a little ashamed, a little crazy.
Though she also still wants one more poke.

They are now persona non grata, Aram says to Badim after one
of the hallway sessions, almost everywhere.

Badim, looking older than ever, holds his head in his hands,
when he is not holding her hand. She sits there staring at a window she dare not approach.

"Why did you do it?" he asks her. "Oh never mind, I know
why you did it. He was a fool. Annoying, as fools are. But there
are always fools, Freya. People like him will always exist, and they
don't matter. Don't you see? They just don't matter. Fools will
always be with us. You have to leave them to it, and find your
own way."

"But they hurt people," Freya protests. She hasn't stopped feeling sick from the moment they pulled her off the poor man. She
still wants that last punch, at the same time that she is doubled over

with remorse. "It isn't just foolish, it's sick. Did you hear what he said? Dandelion seeds? Ninety-nine percent sent out to die, as part of the plan? Die a miserable death they can't prevent, children and animals and ship and all, and all for a stupid idea someone has, a dream? Why? Why have that dream? Why are they that way?"

"People live in ideas," Badim says again. "You can't stop it. We all live in ideas. You have to let these people have their ideas."

"But they kill people with them."

"I know. I know. It's always been that way. But look, people volunteer to get on these ships. There are waiting lists."

"Their kids don't volunteer!"

"No. But it's still not our job to stop them."

"Isn't it? Are you sure?"

At this he looks uncertain. He takes her point, unhappily; that they might be obliged to witness. That they are the survivors of one of these mad plans.

She shakes her head, snares him with her look, as she so often has before. "Were the people who believed in eugenics just fools? I think we have to try to stop them!"

Badim looks at her for a long time. He is really looking ancient now. She can't remember how he looked when she was a child.

He pats her shoulder, and several times he almost speaks, then stops himself.

"Well," he says finally, "your mother would be proud of you."

After that he can't speak for a while.

Then: "You—you are reminding me of her. It's almost nice to see. But not. Because I don't want you to die too, from trying to do the impossible. Because look—you can't stop other people from pursuing their projects, their dreams. Even if they are crazy dreams, even if they won't work. If people want to do it, they will. Then later their children will suffer, sure. We can point that out, and we will. But it's everyone who has to stop these people, all of us together. It has to be an idea that fails, that no one will act on because no one believes it anymore. That may take a while. And meanwhile, listen to me: kick the world, break your foot. And your feet, my girl, are already broken."

· · · · ·

They have to get out of town. Aram arranges that somehow, a flight back to Beijing, where the Chinese are apparently not interested in extraditing Freya and Badim for a crime of this sort. Some are calling it free speech, decrying the sort of state that would prosecute free speech. Let people defend themselves from unarmed assaults, please. Why is it anyone else's business?

Badim shakes his head at this line of reasoning, but says nothing.

Then there begins to appear on the screens, and in the messages coming to them, support for Freya's rash act. Not just one or two messages, but many. A little flood of them in fact. There are a lot of people on Earth who call themselves Earthfirsters, apparently. The emigration of people, often rich people, off Earth and out into the solar system, and then even out of the solar system, has left behind a great deal of resentment, it seems. Only now are these people paying any attention to a crew of lost starfarers.

"So now I'm popular?" Freya says. "They hate me, and I hit someone, and *now* they like me?"

"Not the same people," Badim points out, frowning. "Or maybe so. I can't tell. But yes. That's Earth for you. That's what I've been trying to tell you. That's how it works here."

"I don't like this place."

Badim shakes his head. "You don't like these people. It's not the same thing. And it's not everybody, either."

Aram, listening to them, says to Freya, "'Ah don't you see, since your mind is the prison, you'll live behind bars everywhere now?'"

"So fuck it, let's move to Mars then," Freya grumbles, remembering the poem, which had pierced her like a sliver.

"Definitely not," Badim says, waving a finger. "They're stuck in their rooms up there almost as much as we were on the ship. That place is not much different from Aurora. The problem is chemical rather than biological, and they may amend the soil there over time, but not soon. Centuries at the least! No. We're just going to have to get used to it here."

. . . .

But during the brief disaster of their trip away, six more of them have died. One, a youth, Raul, was killed in a fight with some person who did not like the idea of them coming back to Earth. After the memorial services for these six truly sad affairs, Aram tells Badim a story about Shackleton, who got his entire crew safely home from one of his Antarctic misadventures, only to see several get sent to the trenches of the First World War, where they were promptly killed.

Freya is already feeling like she wants to hit someone again, and something in this dismal story makes her furious. "What are we going to do?" she shouts at them. "I can't stand this! Just hanging around, getting picked off one by one—no! No! No! No! We have to *do something*. I don't know what, but something. Something to change this place—something! So—what are we going to do?"

Badim nods uneasily. His ancient face is creased with an ancient look, a look Freya recognizes from her childhood: the pursed-lipped frown that always came over his face when he was trying to figure out what to do about Devi. This look had always held tucked within it several things: amusement, love, worry, annoyance, pride that he had such a problem to solve. His wife the warrior, on a rampage. Now maybe it's a bit the same, maybe not. And anyway Freya is too angry to feel reassured by this. Now it's her he is looking at, and to her there's nothing amusing about the idea of having in your life a crazy idealistic person you love and must help. Not when she's the person. Anyway it's everybody, lots of the starfarers are like her, it's nothing special. No, fuck it: they need a

way to live, something to do, or else they'll never be anything but
freaks from space, dying one by one from earthshock. The people
from the stations out around Jupiter and Saturn have made up that
name for it: they come back from space to Earth to get a dose of
bacteria or whatnot, their sabbatical they call it, come back to get
sick in order to stay well, but it's a tough thing for them, and they
often come down with what they call earthshock, and sometimes
die of it. Actually some Saturnine people are offering to help them
adjust to their new situation. Along with the Earthfirsters. There's
a combination for you, Aram remarks. No, they're freaks! And so
only freaks want to help them!

· · · · ·

Aram begins to study this sabbatical that the space people take.
Everyone living out there in the solar system comes back to Earth
for a bit of time every several years, if they are concerned to live
a full life span, which of course almost everyone is. This association between returning to Earth and living longer in space is
an unexplained correlation, a statistical phenomenon that no one
can test out in their own body, as no one can live both ways, and
it isn't necessarily true for every individual that staying in space
all the time makes them sick. It's just that on average, space people
who don't return to Earth every five to ten years, for several
months to a couple of years, tend to die quite a bit younger than
those who do return. The numbers are contested, but the studies, which Aram thinks are mostly pretty well designed, generally
agree that the added life span for off-planet residents taking Earth
sabbaticals is something like twenty years, or thirty years. Even
now that they are sometimes living up to two centuries, that is
a long time. It's such a huge discrepancy that most people adhere
to what the data suggest, and go home to Earth on a personal
schedule of some kind. Best to pay attention to the data, and not
take chances.

Studying all this, Aram points out that the true artificial intelligence is the actuarial long-term study; no human could ever see these things. This particular AI has made a compelling case. Suggestive, plausible, persuasive, probable, compelling: scientists' linguistic scale for evaluating evidence is still the same, Aram says, and it tops out with quite a strong word, really: to *compel*. People do it because they are compelled to. Reality makes them do it. The urge to live makes them do it.

But there is another effect, almost the opposite of the sabbatical, and just as strong, if not stronger: earthshock. People come back to Earth, perfectly healthy on arrival, and die of something without warning. Sometimes it can be very difficult to figure out what exactly did it, which adds to the fear of the syndrome, of course. Quick decline, earthshock, terrallergenic; these names contain within themselves the terrible news that the phenomenon they refer to is not well understood, an effect with unknown causes. Names like this reveal the ignorance in the name itself: the Big Bang. Cancer. Quick decline. Any disease ending with the suffix *-itis* or *-penia*. Et cetera. So many ignorant names.

So, the returned starfarers, having missed their own sabbaticals by some two hundred and fifty years, are now dying of earthshock, it seems. Even when causes can be found for any individual case, it's suspicious that the causes have cropped up so soon after their return. Hard to believe they would have happened in the ship, in hibernation or not. No, something is going on. Something they will either survive or they won't.

Meanwhile, living on this big crazy planet that still scares Freya out of her wits, what to do? What to do? At this point she could not be more miserable.

A week or more of this misery drags on before Badim comes to her and answers her question *So what are we going to do?* as if only a second has passed since it burst out of her.

"We go to the beach!" he announces cheerily.

. . . .

"What do you mean?" Freya demands.

For of course there are no beaches. Sea level rose twenty-four meters in the twenty-second and twenty-third centuries of the common era, because of processes they began in the twenty-first century that they couldn't later reverse; and in that rise, all of Earth's beaches drowned. Nothing they have done since to chill Earth's climate has done much to bring sea level back down; that will take a few thousand more years. Yes, they are terraforming Earth now. There's no avoiding it, given the damage that's been done. In this the common era year 2910, they are calling it a five-thousand-year project. Some say longer. It'll be a bit of a race with the Martians, they joke.

But for now it's good-bye to the beaches, and indeed many a celebrated island of yore now lies deep under the waves. An entire world and way of life has disappeared with these fabled places, a lifeway that went right back to the beginning of the species in south and east Africa, where the earliest humans were often intimately involved with the sea. That wet, sandy, tidal, salty, sun-flecked, beautiful beach life: all gone, along with so much else, of course; animals, plants, fish. It's part of the mass extinction event they are still struggling to end, to escape. So much has been lost that will never come back again, that the loss of the joy of the relatively few humans who were lucky enough to live on the strand, who combed the beaches, and fished, and rode the waves, and lay in the sun—that's nothing much to grieve for, given everything else that has been lost, all the suffering, all the hunger, all the death, all the extinctions. Most of the mammal species are gone.

Still, it was a way of life much beloved, and still remembered in art and song, image and story—still legendary, still a lost golden age, vibrating at some level below thought, there in their salty blood and tears, in the long, curled waves of DNA that still break inside them all.

So there are people bringing that back. They are bringing the beaches back.

These people are one wing or element of the Earthfirsters. Tree huggers, space haters, they're a mixed bag. Many of them renounce not just space, but also the many virtual, simulated, and indoor spaces that so many Terrans seem happy to inhabit. To the Earthfirsters these people are in effect occupying spaceships on the land, or have moved inside their screens or their heads. So many people stay indoors all the time, it seems crazy to Freya, even though she herself still cowers in the shelter of built spaces every waking moment. But she has an excuse, she thinks, having been locked in all her life, while the Terrans have no excuse: this place is their home. Their disregard for their natural inheritance, their waste of the gift given them, is part of what causes her to gnash her teeth, and drive herself to windows, even into open doorways, there to stand trembling on the threshold, terrified, willing her body to stop clenching, to step out. Willing herself to change. Finding in that moment of liminal panic that sometimes you can't make yourself do even the things you most want to do, when fear seizes you by the throat.

So, but these beach lovers are apparently like her in this opinion or belief about how to regard Earth. They are kindred souls, perhaps. And they are expressing their love of that lost world of the seashore, by rebuilding it.

Freya listens amazed as Badim and Aram bring into their compound a short old woman, brown-skinned, silver-haired, who describes her people and their project.

"We do a form of landscape restoration called beach return. It's a kind of landscape art, a game, a religion—" She grins and shrugs. "It's whatever. To do it, we've adapted or developed several technologies and practices, starting with mines, rock grinders, barges, pumps, tubing, scoops, bulldozers, earthmovers, all that kind of thing. It's heavy industry at first. A lot of landscape restoration is.

We've used this technology all over the world. It involves making arrangements with governments or other landholders, to get the rights to do it. It works best in certain stretches of the new coastlines. They're mostly wastelands now, intertidal zones without being suited for that. Being amphibious"—she grins—"is weird."

They nod. Freya says, "So what do you do, exactly?"

In these new tidal zones, the woman explains, they proceed to make beaches that are as similar to those that went away as can be arranged. "We bring them back, that's all. And we love it. We devote our lives to it. It takes a couple of decades to get a new beach started, so any given beach person usually works on only three or four in a lifetime, depending on how things go. But it's work you can believe in."

"Ah," Freya says.

It's labor intensive, the woman continues. There is more work to do than there are workers. And now, even though the starfarers are controversial and in trouble—or rather, precisely because they are controversial and in trouble—the beach makers are offering to take them on. Meaning the entire complement of them.

"We can all go?" Freya says. "We can stay together?"

"Of course," the woman says. "There are about a hundred thousand of us, and we send out working teams to various stretches of coastline. Each project needs about three or four thousand people during the most intensive phases. Some people move on when their part of a project is done, so the life can be a bit nomadic. Although some of them stick to the beaches they've made."

"So you would take us in," Badim says.

"Yes. I'm here to make that offer. We keep our whole thing a bit under the radar, you have to understand. It's best to avoid political complications as much as possible. So we don't go out of our way to publicize our projects. Our deals are discreet. We try to stay out of the news. I bet you can see why!"

She laughs as Aram and Badim and Freya all nod.

"Look," she says, "there's a political element to all this, which you need to understand. We don't like the space cadets. In fact a lot of us hate them. This idea of theirs that Earth is humanity's cradle is part of what trashed the Earth in the first place. Now there are many people on Earth who feel like it's our job to make that right. It'll be our job for generations to come. And now we've seen that you're part of the damage they've done. It took us a while to get that, but when you punched that guy it became very obvious." She laughs at the look on Freya's face. "But look, it's all right! We've taken in quite a few people who got in trouble by resisting that kind of shit one way or another. So, adding five hundred lost souls to one of our teams won't be any big deal. You'll blend in, and you can keep your heads down, do your work, and make your contribution. We can use the help, and you'll have a way to go forward."

Freya tries to take all this in and comprehend it. Beach building? Landscape restoration? Can it be? Would they like it?

Freya says, "Badim, will I like this?"

Badim smiles his little smile. "Yes, I think you will."

The others are not so sure. After the woman leaves, there is a long discussion, and at a certain point Freya is asked to go out with an exploratory group and take a look at one of these projects and see what she thinks.

This will of course mean going outdoors.

Freya gulps.

"Yes," she says. "Of course."

• • • •

Again they fly. This time it seems their Chinese hosts might be happy to see them go. More rooms and tunnels, planes and trams, trains and cars. Travel on Earth is not dissimilar to moving around in the spokes, although the g stays constant. They keep a low profile. Herded from one room to the next. Somewhere on Earth you go indoors, and move around in differently shaped rooms, which either move or don't, and the next time you go outdoors (if you do!) you are on the other side of the planet. This is so strange. Looking out of a plane window at the ocean planet below, under its layer of clouds, Freya resolves to master her fear, to make her body obey her will. She is tired of being afraid. Sometimes, you get sick of yourself, you change.

A west-facing coast somewhere. They tell her where and she promptly forgets. She hasn't heard of it before. Temperate latitude, Mediterranean climate. Yellow sandstone bluffs jump right out of the white-edged sea. Used to be beaches at the foot of these bluffs, they are told, beaches so wide they held car races on the flat wet sand, back when cars were first invented. It was a morning's walk from bluff to water, their guide says, and all flat sand. Laying it on a bit thick. Point of stories however being that there is a lot of sand still out there in the shallows. Some of it has been swept south by currents into a giant underwater canyon that runs from just off-shore to the edge of the continental shelf, but even that canyon bottom is a now a kind of underwater river of sand flowing down toward the abyssal plain, a river of sand that can be vacuumed up in tubes onto barges, barged over to the land, brought into the estuaries of the little rivers that break the long curving line of bluffs, and put there. Old sand for new beaches, located right at the new tideline, up in the estuaries. They're also trucking in giant granite boulders from inland, some to drop offshore and make reefs, others to drop at the foot of the bluffs to establish a new strand on, others to grind down into new sand, gravel, shingle, cobble—whatever type of rock that used to be there on the shore. It takes certain mixes of minerals to make a beach that will last, to make it nice. Also certain kinds of reefs offshore. Millions of tons of sand and rock have to be moved and installed. There is so much their guides want to tell them, these guides all sun-browned, hair crisped by sun and salt, eyes aglow.

The starfarers are tired by their journey—jet-lagged, they have been taught to call it—out of synch with the planet's rotation, diurnal rhythm, circadian rhythm—an odd malady that they are learning to recognize. After a first tour of this coastline, driven around in a car on roads along the top of the bluff, then around the shores of the estuary, with many stops to get out and look (but Freya does not get out), they are taken to an inn on the bluff's edge. The inn seems to be a modest little conference center, with bungalows around a main building. Freya gets out when the car is parked inside a garage, and makes her way up to the lobby, then, in a controlled dash under a walkway, hustles to her assigned bungalow, next to the one occupied by Badim and Aram. Once she is settled, she looks out her open doorway to see the two old men stretched out on reclining chairs, in the shade of an overhang extending from their bungalow, looking out at the ocean. The overhang is called a ramada, they have been told.

Badim notices her and says, "Freya my dear, come on out and join us! Give it a try!"

"I will in a bit," she replies irritably. "I'm unpacking."

From the bluff they can see out over the ocean for a long way. A flat blue plate of stunning size, wrinkled with white light. Badim and Aram talk again about optical phenomena. They are aficionados at this point, and are hoping to see the green flash at sunset. Apparently Earth's gravity, or atmosphere, they argue about which, bends the light from the sun in such a way that just before it dips under the horizon and disappears, the Earth is actually physically between the observer and the sun, but the sunlight is curving around the globe because of the atmosphere, or gravity, and as blue light curves more than red light, this curve around the Earth splits the light as if passing it through a prism, and this means that the last visible point of sunlight turns, not blue, which would be too much of a bend and too much like the sky's color, but green, said to be a pure brilliant emerald green. "This we have to see!" Aram declares.

Badim agrees. "Strange to be as old as we are, and see it for the first time." He turns and calls to Freya. "Girl, come see this green flash that may occur!"

"You're not that old," she says to him. "You're like the hundredth-oldest person in the ship."

"Well, even that would be old, but in fact I think I'm down to about fifteenth now. But let's stay focused on the sunset. I'm told when the sun is three-quarters gone, you can look at it without damaging your eyes. Not for long, mind you, but long enough to see the green flash when it comes."

She stands just inside her big ocean-facing double doorway and looks out, clenching her fists at her sides. The estuary is just visible beyond the point of the bluff to the left, a wave-creased bay. Where there used to be a beach at the river mouth, stretching between two points of bluff, there is now a white line of broken surf. They are building their beach out from the bluffs on each side, on top of the drowned one.

Waves slide in inexorably from the west, out of the slant sun mirrorflaking the ocean's steely surface. Low but distinct lines of waves, visible as changes in the blue of the water, always approaching land. A strange thing to see. Out on the horizon is the faint gray bump of an island, poking over the clean line where sky meets ocean: light blue over dark blue, everything steely and dark in the late afternoon. Mild salty onshore breeze pouring in her doorway, seagulls planing by at eye level, their heads tilted down and off to the side. A line of pelicans below them passes north to south, a sudden vision out of the Jurassic, black silhouettes against the sun's glare, slow flap of wings, though mostly they glide. The panic rises in Freya again, like a tide following its own mysterious pulls. She wants so badly to walk out into the open air, under the sky, but a clutch squeezes her heart, there's nothing she can do about it, she can't move. Even joining Badim and Aram under their ramada is too much for her. Nothing for it but go inside and try again later.

Even though it's late, her hosts call her room, they want to show her more of how their project works, and as they will stay in the cab of a big earthmover of some kind, she figures she can just handle it. Jet lag has her quivering.

Out they go, room to room to cab. The earthmover moves sand from the giant piles of it in their receiving area, out onto the strand itself. In the horizontal light of late day they rumble and bounce down a long ramp to the new beach, now covered with vehicle tracks. Past smaller vehicles of various kinds, some plowing smaller and smaller piles of sand into flat surfaces, or pushing up dunes at the back of the beach. The important thing is to accept the new sea level and work with it, the people operating the earthmover tell her; it won't go back down for centuries at best, and may never recede at all. But they are confident it won't go any higher either; all the ice in the world that is likely to melt has already melted. There's still a considerable ice cap in eastern Antarctica, but with temperatures stabilized at last, that one is likely to stay there. If not, well, too bad! More beaches to build!

For now, this is sea level. Tides here slosh up and down a vertical distance that averages three meters, more in the neap tides when the moon is closest to Earth. Tides really are a matter of tidal attraction between Earth and Luna. Tug of gravity, spooky action at a distance. Source of a great deal of life on this planet, possibly even the appearance of life, some say.

They are making sure the high-tide mark is well below most of their new strand, which will be one hundred meters wide at least. Behind the strand they are building dunes, and planting and introducing all the dune life. And during low tides, the wet strand that is temporarily exposed is made mostly of sand, with only some rocky areas under points in the bluff, for tide pools and the like. All these parameters and elements are designed, engineered, built, monitored. Freya sees it: this beach is their artwork. These people are artists. They have an art they love. They might kill her with talking about it, they love it so much.

Often in the river mouths that break the line of bluffs along this coastline, they tell her, the risen ocean has crashed right into houses, streets, lawns, parks, and all the rest of the previous civilization, tearing them away, carrying them off. So one of the first beach-building tasks has been to demolish and remove what was drowned, and this has had to be done offshore to quite a depth, or else the whole coastline would remain too dangerous. Here they finished that work some years before, and now, as Freya can see, they have deposited much of the sand for the new beach. About half the sand has been salvaged out of the shallows offshore and out of the underwater canyon, sucked up to barges, deposited where they want it. The rest has been manufactured on the bluffs. It gets distributed according to protocols that are always evolving as they study the waves in this region of the coast, and the river patterns of this estuary. And as they learn more about beaches generally, all over the world.

Ah, she says.

This beach is stabilized under the north bluff, and the south one is almost finished too. The starfarers can settle in and help, learn more about the process, get to know the people who do the work. They can see if they like it. As there are scores of such teams around the world, it seems very possible they could simply melt into the beach people, and become after that one little forgotten clump among Earth's billions.

Freya nods. "It sounds good."

She can go swimming off this beach if she wants, they say, it's safe now, lots of the young beach people are doing it already. Does she know how to swim?

"Yes, I do," she says. "I swam in Long Pond quite a lot."

Very good, very good. She'll have to try it. Water temperature here is good, just a little cool, warms up as you swim in it. She'll find that the ocean's salt water gives one quite a lift. It's fun to be more buoyant. Waves tomorrow will be small, but some people will be bodysurfing anyway. Some people you just can't keep out of the water, waves or no waves.

"Lovely," she says, feeling the thrill of fear shoot down her spine and out her arms and legs. Even her numb feet can feel a little tingle of dread.

. . . . .

Back at her bungalow, feeling exhausted, she finds Badim and Aram still out under their ramada, arguing about the sunset, which happened just a few minutes before. They either saw the green flash or not. Their bickering is very relaxed, and she can tell that they like having a problem that they can't resolve right away. Something to chew over. Two old men bickering by the seaside.

They welcome her back. The western sky is a deep, dark, transparent blue, over a sea that now seems lighter than the sky, a kind of blackish silver, more than ever lined by the ever-oncoming waves. There is a vastness to the scene that can't be taken in. Freya stands in her doorway watching, feeling the wind push onshore. The old men leave her alone.

"I've done a new translation of that Cavafy poem," Aram says to Badim. "The end, anyway. Listen to this:

"There's no new world, my friend, no
New seas, no other planets, nowhere to flee—
You're tied in a knot you can never undo
When you realize Earth is a starship too."

"Ahh," Badim exclaims, as if hearing a pun. "Very nice. I like how that takes it away from being something you've done to yourself. It's more just the way things are."

"Yes," Aram says pensively.

Then after a while Badim chuckles and lightly slaps his friend on the thigh, points out at the twilight sky, a pure indigo unlike anything they have ever seen. "But hey—pretty damn big starship!"

"It is," Aram admits. "But, does size matter? Is that it?"

"I think maybe so!" Badim says. "That makes it robust, eh? Big enough to be robust. And I'm beginning to think it's robustness that is the thing we want."

"Maybe so. You are getting more robust every day, I notice."

"Well, the food here is awfully good, you have to admit."

$$\cdot \ \cdot \ \cdot \ \cdot \ \cdot$$

Freya leaves the two old friends to their banter, goes into her bedroom, lies down on her bed.

That night the sea breeze pours through her room and over her, she can smell the salt and feel it, until just before dawn, when the air goes still. All night she fails to sleep; she is quivering slightly, or the room is quivering under her. Her numb feet tingle a little, her stomach clenches. She feels her fear like a weight on her chest. It's hard to breathe, and she tries to breathe deeper, slower. From time to time she stirs from a salty trance that was not quite sleep.

When the sky lightens outside her west window, illuminating the square of curtains, she gets up and goes to the bathroom, comes back out, paces around, sits on her bed, holds her head in her hands. She stands and goes to the window and looks out.

Sunrise blasts the ocean with its light. Dawn on Earth. Aurora was the goddess of dawn; this is the thing itself.

She opens the door to her bungalow, feels the air, now pushing offshore. The breeze is just slightly offshore now. It's like the earth is breathing: in by night, out by day. It was like that in the Fetch. It's already warm; it's going to be a hot day. The offshore push of air is dry.

She washes her face at the bathroom sink, stares at her drawn face in the mirror. She's a middle-aged woman now, the years have flown by; she hardly remembers what she used to look like. She pulls on shorts and a shirt, pulls on her helper boots, grabs up one of the bungalow's big bathroom towels, puts on a hat.

"Fuck this," she declares, and walks outside.

. . . . .

Big blue sky. Warm dry air, gusting gently offshore. In the shade of the bluff, down to the beach. Staggering down blindly, gaze fixed on her dead feet, moaning as she stumps down, tears and snot running down her face. She can barely see. She feels crazy, stupid, but most of all, scared. Just scared.

Down on the beach it seems a bit smaller, more like a biome. A very big biome, but not so much bigger as to cause her to faint outright. She is hyperventilating, sweating, gasping a little, sick to her stomach, staggering still on her weird boots. She has a big hat on, sunglasses on, she keeps her head down.

Onto the sand of the dunes at the bottom of the bluff. The sand sinks under her boots a centimeter or three with each step. This is enough to make walking tricky, given her feet. The sand trends slightly up as she walks toward the water, until she gets to a kind of low ridge, beyond which the sand falls away in a clean sweep, down into the foaming edge of the ocean. Broken waves are rolling up at her across this bubbling tilted expanse, the water clear over the wet gray-brown sand under it. This tilted wet verge is fringed with lengths of white foam. It's loud here with the sound of breaking waves, most of which break about a hundred meters offshore, she guesses, then rumble in, white and foaming at the rounded edge of an incoming layer that is distinctly higher than what it rolls over, the white edge bouncing, hissing, a mass of bubbles in a line, moving in across the shallows, hitting other lines moving outward.

At the high-tide line stretch masses of blackened seaweed, also long lines of dull brown-green seaweed, with dimpled long wide leaves, and bulbs marking the lines. Kelp, she thinks. She goes to a line and sits down hard in the sand next to it. Keeps her head down, keeps breathing in a steady deep rhythm, tries to quell the nausea, halt the spinning of the world around her. Just a big biome! Hold it together! The kelp in her fingers feels like a hardened gel, just a little slimy. There is sand stuck to it. The individual grains of sand look not quite round: little beveled boulders, about fifteen or twenty stuck to the pad of her forefinger. She can see them best when she holds them about six centimeters in front of her nose. There are black flecks of something like mica stuck there too, much smaller than the blond sand grains. These black flecks mix with the sand grains, and where the broken waves are running whitely up and down the strand, some twenty meters from where she sits, there are delta patterns sluicing back down to the broken water, delta patterns of black in blond, crosshatched chevrons all pointed out to sea. It's loud with the sound of breaking waves.

The sun comes up over the bluff behind her, and she feels the radiation on the back of her neck like the blast from a fire. It is indeed the blast from a fire. Her stomach clenches again. She digs in her bag past the bath towel, and pulls out a canister of sunscreen, shoots the spray on the back of her neck. It smells funny. Her hands are shaking, she feels sick. The smell of sunscreen makes it worse, she feels on the edge of vomiting. It's good she doesn't have to stand now, doesn't have to go anywhere. Keep her head down, watch the sand grains glowing transparently on her translucent fingertip. Try not to throw up. God, what a lot of light. She has to clamp her teeth together to keep them from chattering, to keep the bile down.

"Fuck this!" she says again through clenched teeth. "Get a grip!"

. . . . .

"Let me take you to the beach!
Na na na na na na na na na-na!
Let me take you to the beach!
Na na na na na na na na na-na!"

A young man sings this ditty, walking by with rolling strides in the soft sand. Maybe sixteen or seventeen years old, unclothed, narrow face, blue eyes, his skin an odd brown color she thinks must be suntanned. His brown curly hair is so sun-bleached that the tips of its curls are a yellow almost white. Holding a pair of blue fins in one hand, looking like a Minoan wall painting she recalls seeing in a book. The water boy, holding water bags.

"Are you going out swimming?" Freya asks him.

He stops. "Yes, gonna ride some waves. There's a great point break right out from here, called Reefers."

"Point break?"

"Big reef out there about two hundred meters, easy to see at low tide. Most of the breaks will be rights, but it's a south swell today, so there'll be some lefts too. Are you going to go out?"

"I can't really feel my feet," Freya says, desperate for an excuse. "I have these shoes that kind of walk for me. I don't know what it would be like to swim."

"Hmm." He frowns at this, stares at her as if he's never heard of such a thing, and maybe he hasn't. "How did that happen?"

"Long story," she says.

He nods. "Well, if you had fins on, those you kind of swing from the knees anyway. Might help. And actually, if you just stand in the shallows, the water will mostly float you. You can use your arms, and shove off the bottom and catch the little waves."

"I'd like to try that," she lies, or maybe it's the truth. She swallows deeply. Her face is on fire, her fingers and lips are tingling, buzzing. Her big toes are hot.

"Here come my friends; there might be another pair of fins in Pam's bag, usually is."

Young man and woman, again naked, brown-skinned, tightly muscled, sun-bleached hair. Young gods and goddesses, naiads or whatever, she can't remember the name for sea fauns, but these are them. Beach kids. They greet the youth talking to Freya, calling him Kaya. "Kaya, hey Kaya!"

"Pam, have you got that extra pair of fins?" Kaya asks.

"Yeah sure."

"Can you lend them to this lady? She wants to go out and ride."

"Yeah sure."

Kaya turns to her. "So, try it and see."

The three young people stare at her.

"You do know how to swim?" Kaya asks.

"Yes," Freya says. "I swam in Long Pond all the time when I was a kid."

"Just stay in the shallows then, and you'll be all right. Small swell today."

"Thanks."

Freya takes blue fins offered to her by the young woman. The three young ones run off into the surf, kicking arcs of white spray ahead of them, and when they get out thigh deep, falling over into a broken wave. After that they seem to be floating around to put on their fins, then they shove off into the approaching white walls of broken waves, which are breaking about thirty more meters out from them. Only then are they really swimming. They make it look easy.

Freya pulls off her boots, stands, strips off her clothes, sprays herself all over with the sunscreen, picks up the blue fins they have left her, walks very carefully down into the broken waves sloshing up the strand. Her feet are still numb, it's like walking on short stilts, but there seems to be some new traction there in her big toes. The water is cool at first, she can feel that in the bones of her feet, but she quickly gets used to it. Not that cold. A surge runs up the beach over her ankles, then slides back down. The water under her is white with bubbles, more bubbles than water, and the bubbles hiss out their lives as they burst, throwing a fine spray calf high into the air. The water of an incoming wave suddenly loses momentum going up the tilt of the sand, then runs back down swiftly to a triple ripple, which is exposed only when the waves are farthest out. Maybe that's true sea level. Here where she stands, water sloshes back and forth, therefore up and down, but mostly just back and forth. Waves breaking on a beach, this is how it looks, this is how it feels! Something loosens a little inside her, and she shivers now, feeling less sick than hot. Hot and yet shivering.

She keeps her gaze down, but even so she can see or feel that overhead the sky is blue, mixed with a lot of white around the horizon. It's really loud down here, all water sounds, mainly the crashing of waves; sometimes it's a clean crack when a blue wave folds over and falls, then explodes into white spray and bounces in toward her. Mostly the sound is an ever-shifting, grumbling wet roar, water falling and breaking on itself, a zillion bubbles bursting. The whole ocean's edge is a kind of low waterfall, falling on itself over and over. Glare of sunlight breaking in a million places on the water, bouncing in her eyes. With her sunglasses off it's too bright to do anything but squint till her eyes are almost closed. It's so bright that things are somehow dark.

Kaya is coming in on a wave at her, only his head sticking out of the white water. He stands up near her and points out at his friends. "That's Pam there, nice left, see that?"

Freya shivers.

"Can we really be out here?" she asks him helplessly. "We won't get cooked by radiation?"

She's breathing deeply, she can't look anywhere near the sun, it's far too bright for that, she's squinting, crying a little at the explosion of light coming off the breaking waves.

"Well, that's a good thought; look at you. Did you put on sunscreen?"

"I did."

"Your skin is really white."

"I've never done this before," she says. "My skin has never been in sunlight before."

He stares at her. "That's crazy, although I have to say, you have beautiful skin. You can see all your freckles and moles and all. But yeah, if you got the sunscreen on you everywhere, it works really well. Where you missed, your skin will burn."

"I believe it!"

"Well, yeah. Put it on every couple of hours, you'll be fine. I'll help you next time we're in."

"Don't you use it?"

"Oh sometimes, but you know, I've got a tan, so I don't burn anymore. I'll put some on my nose and lips in the afternoon, especially if I stay out all day."

"All day?"

"Sure, yeah, that's the best kind of day."

"Will you spray me now? I'm scared I've missed places or something."

"Yeah, sure."

He reaches down and pulls off his fins, walks with her up to her towel, steadying her by the elbow in the soft wet sand. He sprays her everywhere with the sunscreen.

"You have a nice body, so white, you're like that goddess standing in the shorebreak. Here, let me get your legs and ass too. Can't miss anywhere, or you'll burn for sure."

Burned by the sun! Burned by radiation from a star! She starts to shiver again, tries not to look up. Her shadow stretches toward the water, dark on the light sand. She's still crying, fist to her mouth. The sand is too bright to look at. There's just too much light.

. . . .

He helps her back down into the water. He's brown and lithe, like some animal not quite human, an aquaman, merman, kelpie, come out of the water to lead her into his element. A water sprite. She's shivering, but not with cold. Possibly the shock of immersion will keep her from throwing up.

Back ankle deep in the white hissing surge. Here she is, on Earth, walking out into the ocean, in a blast of sunlight. She can hardly believe it. It's as if she's living someone else's life, inside a body she can't manipulate very well. Kaya helps her keep her feet. He kicks into an onrush of water, which casts an arc of spray back out toward the sea. Bubbles bursting all around, such a liquid sound. She has to shout a little for Kaya to hear her. "It's not as cold this time!"

"That always happens," he says with a white grin. "Water's about twenty-four degrees today, just right. It'll cool you down after an hour or so, but that's okay. Here, look, when we get to about thigh deep, the bottom will start going up and down, and when a big enough wave comes in, just let yourself down under it. That's the best way to get wet. Don't drag it out too long."

He holds her hand and they walk over the ripples he mentioned. The waves roll in all broken, hissing, hitting her waist high, then dropping back to thigh high. As a bigger broken wave approaches, Kaya lets go of her hand and with a shout dives under it. She crashes down right after him, the wave pushes her back toward shore, she jumps up shocked by the wetness, crying out at the cold. The water tastes salty but clean, cool in her mouth. It stings her eyes, but not much, and not for long. Kaya is leaning over to drink some of it, then spouts what he's mouthed into the sky, like a fountain. "Drink a little," he urges her. "It's good for you. It's the same saltiness as in us. We're getting back in the great mama!" And with another hoot he dives under the next approaching wave and shoots up out of the smoother water behind it. Again she dives too late and is shoved back hard.

He swims in to collect her, swimming around when he could stand. "Pull your fins on your feet. Then dive under the waves. Look, when a wave breaks, some water goes straight to the bottom and then rolls back under, like this," illustrating with his curling hand. "So if you dive and get in that water, it will pull you under the wave and pop you back up, outside the break. You'll feel it pull you when you get in that flow."

She tugs the fins onto her feet as another wave approaches; the waves keep coming one after the next, it's a perpetual thing, every seven or ten seconds it seems, wave after wave and wave. She dives under the next one, goes down too far and feels the sand of the bottom with her hands, swirling into her face, then she feels the tug of the water back and up, and kicking she feels the fins despite her insensible feet, and shoots back up into the sun. Incredible burst of light in her eyes, salt water in her eyes and nose and mouth, she chokes a little but her eyes barely sting.

"Do you keep your eyes open when you're under?" she shouts at Kaya.

"Hell yeah," he says, grinning, all submerged except for his face and shoulders and hair and hands, sliding around her like an otter, taking in a mouthful of foam and shooting it at her playfully.

Then he stands and bobs beside her. "Okay, first game is just to crest the waves as they come in. Stand about chest high; that's where most of these are breaking. The bigger ones will break farther out, and you have to swim out to the break. The smaller ones won't break till they're inside of us here. So, just watch, and as they come to you, jump up into the wave as it rises around you, and let it carry you right up to the break at the top. Let the very top of it break right in your face, crash through that upward, and fall

down the back side. That's already almost as fun as it gets. You'll
feel them lift you. Then, when you're used to that, and you've seen
how they tend to break, when a big one has reached you and it's
just about to break, turn when it lifts you and jump in toward the
shore. Then it will carry you along, you'll slide down the front of
it on your chest. When you get to the bottom you can stick your
head forward and the wave will carry you in a long way, or you
can duck and tuck to the side, and fold under the wave and be
standing right on your feet again, waist high. Try that for a while."

She tries it. Waves rise up before her; when they are small and
not yet broken she bobs over them, and at the top of her bobbing
she can see out to sea, see the incoming waves in lines that keep on
coming in one after the next, low and unformed. Sometimes she
can see that one will be bigger when it arrives in the shallows, and
by the time she sees that, all the other swimmers out there—there
are about a dozen now—are swimming hard outward to catch it
before it breaks, and if they do, they ride the wave sideways across
its face, ahead of the broken part as it moves left or right, their
wet faces tilted so their eyes are fixed on the wave rising ahead
of their motion. Their bodies are the surfboards, she sees. A few
of the wave riders have small foam boards they hold under their
chest. They hoot at each other as they ride, and as the break closes
over them they disappear into the wave, and the next time she sees
them they are already swimming back out to catch another wave.

Up into a wave, lifted by it; crash through the thin translucent
sunlit wall of water at the top, crash back down onto her chest on
the blue backside. Kaya was right; this is already a great feeling.
She is losing her fear, she is casting it away with every jump and
fall. Lofted by a wave, fall; then again, over and over. Salt water
in her mouth. Hissing and smooshing and crashing all around her,
of water onto water. No need to talk to people, no need to think.
Sun igniting a whole quadrant of the sky, can't look up that way.
Very obvious that looking at sunlight could blind you. Never look

that way! The ocean tastes so good, it's not like blood, it's clear and cool and clean, salty, but somehow nicer than salty. As if it is the true water.

She begins to feel herself, her body. She is definitely more buoyant here than she has ever been in water before, and for a second she is reminded of the weightlessness of the ship's spine. She casts that aside, but then she reaches out and holds on to it; with a squeeze of her heart she floats over the waves for the ship, for Jochi, for Devi and Euan and everyone else no longer there. Even the memory that comes to her suddenly, of Euan in Aurora's ocean, is not bad but good. He picked a good end. Ride these waves for him and with him. It's a kind of communion. She will outswim her fear. She is still shivering.

Finally a wave comes cresting up that seems to want to break and yet hasn't managed it, a banked slope of water rising up before her in an awesome onrush, and she sees her chance and turns and jumps toward the shore, and the wave picks her up and as she floats up the face she is also sliding down the face, at about the same rate of speed, so that she is both hanging there and flying along: that moment is astonishing, she is still laughing at it when the wave tips more vertically and she slides abruptly down to its bottom and plows into the flat water that is not the wave, the wave catches her as it breaks, flips her in a somersault that shoots water up her nose and into her throat and lungs, she gags but is still in the tumble of the broken wave, she can't get to the surface, doesn't even know which way is up, bumps the bottom and finds out, shoves upward, bursts through the surface of hissing bubbles and gasps in, chokes, coughs, snorts, breathes cleanly in, gasps in and out a few breaths, starts to laugh. The whole event has lasted about five seconds, maybe. One has to hold one's mouth shut when underwater. Obviously.

She tries to convey this to Kaya when he shoots by her, disappears, and then stands next to her chest deep. "You okay?" he asks.

"Yes! I got all tumbled!"

"You wiped out. You got caught in the washing machine." He laughs.

"I have to hold my breath underwater!"

"Well yeah! And breathe out through your nose when you're tumbling," he says. "Then you'll be fine. It won't be able to inject its way into you."

She goes back to cresting the waves. She turns and rides a few more, does better when they crash her down into the still water under the onrushing wave. When her rise and fall equalize and she flies, that puts a no-g spot in her gut, as if she is floating down the spine. She thinks of the ship again and cries out, a laugh of grief for her whole life, ah God that it had to happen this way, so crazy their whole existence, so absurd and stupid. So much death. But here she is, and the ship would be pleased to see her out in these waves, she knows this as surely as she knows anything.

The sun actually feels like it is hurting the skin of her face a little, and also she finds she is shivering between the arrival of one wave and the next; it's a different kind of shivering than before, she is simply getting cold. The bigger waves come in sets of three, Kaya calls in passing, and she can see how this is roughly true. She can certainly see how they might come to believe it. They see a set coming, and try to get out over the first one before it breaks, then swim to a point where they can get a good take-off on one of the following two. She wants to ride one across the face ahead of the break, like they do. Hard to arrange. Seems like she would need to be going a little faster for it to work, and Kaya agrees when she says that. "Kick hard with your fins at the moment you need the speed!"

"I'm shivering!"

"Yeah, I'm almost there myself. Go on in and lie in the sun for a while; you'll warm right back up. I'll come in in a while."

She tries to ride a wave all the way in, botches her exit, gets caught up in the tumble of the washing machine, chokes on seawater again, can't breathe for too long, can't get to the surface. Suddenly she is grabbed and yanked up, chokes and gasps, coughs up seawater she has swallowed, almost vomiting.

It's Kaya who has pulled her up, standing chest deep now, staring at her intently. His eyes are a pale blue.

"Hey!" he says. "Be careful out here. This is the ocean, you know. You can blow it pretty fast. You get yourself drowned out here and the ocean won't care. It's way stronger than us."

"Sorry. I didn't see that coming."

"Tell you what, maybe just stay in the shallows here for a while. Do what we call grunioning. You just lie here where the shorebreak runs up the beach, you're floating, but bumping on the ripples of the bottom too, and the waves run you up the beach, then the backwash runs you back down the beach. Just let the water push you around like you're a piece of driftwood, or a grunion. It's almost as fun as anything out here."

She does it and it's true. No effort involved. Keep her face out of the water, let everything else go. Float like a log. Bump here and there over the wet sand. She sees that the beach is more occupied now, kids up at the high-water mark are building sand castles and screaming. The hissing of the waves is loud, the air is filled with a mist of popped bubbles. Bubbles everywhere, more bubbles than water. Long strands of kelp grunion with her. Their bulbs look like plastic, they pop with a smell. It's trapped whale breath! a little girl sitting there says to her, seeing her pop and sniff. Freya chews at a leaf of it; it tastes like the kelp they grew in their little salt pond, what a little thing that was, a birdbath. In and out, in and out she floats.

Eventually even here, where the water is warmer, and the sun is on her back and on the backs of her legs, even here she's cooled down enough to shiver. She takes off her fins, levers herself to her feet, and very carefully walks up to her towel, falling down once. In the wet sand it doesn't matter.

She lies on the hot dry sand next to her towel, in the sun. Quickly she warms and dries. There is a rime of salt left on her skin that she can taste when she licks it. The sand is warm, it sticks to her wherever she touched it when she was wet; now that it's dry, she can brush it off with her hand. She can shove her feet and hands under the sand, and feel its sandy heft and give; the warmth extends down a ways, then the sand is cooler. She digs a pit in it, gets the pit down to a level where its bottom suffuses with water. The walls of this pit then fall in from the sides, which collapse into the little pool she has down there. When she scoops up the wet sand and lets it drip between her fingers, the sand hits the rim of her pool and the water in it seeps away and the sand remains in blobs that stack on each other, until they fall over. Once or twice she scoops up little sand crabs that makes her cry "Eek!" as the crabs crawl desperately over her palms, and she drops them back into the pool and they dig their way into the sand at the bottom of the pool and disappear. After a few times she realizes they don't have any capacity to bite her, their jaws or palps or whatever are too small and soft. Apparently the sand under her is full of these creatures. Possibly they live on bits of seaweed. The beach makers must have put them here, got them started. Down the brilliant wet expanse of strand she sees a flock of shorebirds running up and down over their wet reflections, their knees bending backward. They have long beaks they use to stick in the sand, no doubt going after these same sand crabs. They stop and poke at little bubbles in wet sand, possibly the sand crabs' exhalations. It makes sense. This beach is alive.

When Kaya comes in he is visibly shivering, skin goose-pimpled, blue under his suntan, lips white, nose purple. He throws himself on his towel, shivers there so violently that for a while he almost bounces off the sand. Slowly the shivers subside, and he lies there on his stomach like a sleeping infant, mouth open, eyes closed. Quickly his skin dries in the sun and she can see the white dusting of salt left on him. His hair is a tangle of curls, he is all muscle and bone, relaxed like a cat. A cat in the sun. A young water god, some child of Poseidon.

She looks around at the beach, squinting hard. It's way too bright. Always the low grumble of waves breaking, the hiss of bubbles bursting. Haze in the distance, everything seen in a talcum of light.

"Can we really stay out here exposed like this?" she says suddenly, feeling a shaft of alarm spear her again. "The starlight won't kill us, the radiation?"

He opens his eyes, looks up at her without moving. "Starlight?"

"From the sun, I mean. It's got to be a massive dose of radiation, I can feel it."

He sits up. "Well, sure. Might be time for more sunscreen, you're so white." He presses his forefinger into the skin of her upper arm. "Ah yes, see how it's a little pink now, and goes white when I push there, and takes a little while to turn back to pink? You're getting a sunburn. Let's put another coat of sunscreen on you."

"Will that be enough?"

"It will get you through another hour or so, I think. Especially if you go back in the water. We don't usually just lie out here in the sun. Just long enough to warm up again and go back out."

"How many times do you go out?"

"I don't know. Lots."

"You must be hungry at the end of the day!"

"Oh yeah." He laughs. "Surfers are like seagulls, they say. Eat everything in sight."

He sprays the sunscreen lotion onto her skin. She feels a little salty, a little raw, and the lotion is soothing. His hands when he touches her to spread the lotion behind her ears and up into her hairline are cool and smooth. She can tell by the way he touches her that he has touched before, that young as he is, he would be a good lover. When he lies back down she looks at him candidly. Feeling a little incandescent, stomach unknotted at last, cool but warm, she says, "What about sex on this beach, eh? Right out in the sun? You people must do that!"

"Yes," he says with a little smile, and rolls over onto his stomach, perhaps modestly. "You have to be sure not to get sand in certain places. But, you know, it's mostly something we do out here at night."

"How come? It's a public beach, isn't it?"

"Well, yes. But it doesn't sound like you mean what I mean when you say public."

"I thought public meant it was yours, that you could do what you want."

"I guess, yeah. But being public also means you don't do private things here."

"I think you should just do what you want! And I'd like to jump you right here and now."

"I don't know. You could get in trouble." He peers up at her. "Besides, how old are you?"

"I don't know."

He laughs. "What do you mean?"

"I mean I don't know. Do you mean how long I've lived, or how long since I was born?"

"Well, how long you've lived, I guess."

"One day," she says promptly. "Actually about two hours. Since I got out in that water."

He laughs again. "You're funny. You do seem kind of new to this. But hey, I'm warmed back up, I'm going to go back out for another session." With a quick darting kiss to her cheek he jumps up. "See you out there. I'll check you out, I'll stay right outside from here and keep an eye on you."

He runs down to the waves, splashes through the shallows stepping absurdly high, jumping as he runs, then leaps into the waves and turns to get his fins on, then swims farther out at speed, stroking smoothly, ducking under broken waves right before they reach him. It looks effortless.

She follows him in. It's a bit colder than last time; her skin feels taut and warm, more sensitive to the water. But soon she's back in it and comfortable, and the lift of a wave pulls her back into the sun, and she's off to the races.

The waves are a little bigger, a little steeper in their faces; Kaya says it's because the tide is now going out. The sun is higher now, and the ocean is simply ablaze with long banks of liquid light, heaving slightly up and down, up and down, lined by the incoming waves, which as they rise before her turn a deep translucent green. Now as she floats she can look down and see through clear water to the sandy bottom, yellow and smooth. Strands and even big clumps of seaweed float below the surface in masses. Once she sees a big fish swim between the strands, a fish with a spotted tawny back, the sight of which gives her a jolt of fear; it disappears, she calls out about it to Kaya when he swims by, he laughs and says it was a leopard shark, harmless, mouth too small, not interested in people.

She's getting used to her fins, and finds she can kick from her hips, and swim along at what feels like a great speed. She's a mermaid. Duck under the broken waves, feel the tug of the wave's underturn, shoot up out the back through green water. Or over waves just about to break, swim fast at them, breast up them rising fast, crash through their crests and fall down their backsides, laughing. Crack of a wave's first fall right ahead of her. Swim in with a swell trying to break, she can keep up with it, it picks her up and she's sliding down the face again, this time at an angle ahead of the break, sliding sideways ahead of the break and across the surface of the wave, which keeps rising up before her, steepening at just the right speed to keep her falling down across it. Holding herself stiff and doing nothing else, and yet flying, flying so fast she emerges from the water from her waist up, she can even put her hands down on the water like the other bodysurfers and plane on her hands, and fly more!

Delicious.

Now there's an old man out here, with what looks to be a grand-daughter or great-granddaughter on a short rounded board, and as the waves rise he launches her on the waves like throwing a paper airplane, both of them grinning like maniacs. The mermen and mermaids spin down the faces sometimes, rise back up on them, dance with the wave's particular shape and tempo.

The waves get bigger, steeper. Then there's a shout and every-one is swimming hard out to sea, trying to catch a big set. As she crests one wave she sees what they have seen, and her breath catches: a really big swell, and it hasn't even hit the shallows and begun to rise. Looks like it will break far outside her. She swims as fast as she can, just like everyone else.

The rest of them crest the big wave before it breaks, but she's inside still, and has to dive under it. Go right to the bottom, clutch the sand down there, feel the breaking wave push her, lift her and push her down again, flapping her like a flag, and in the midst of that one of her fins comes off. She keeps on the bottom, comes up with a hard kick off the sand, reaches the surface just in time for the next wave to break right on her, it throws her down and then back up again, and without having to do a thing she is tossed back up to the surface, onto a hissing field of bubbles infused with sand that has been ripped off the bottom, she's in a slurry of sand and seawater now. Immense roar. And here comes the third wave, out-side and building, she tries to get out to it before it breaks, swims as hard as she can but she's still out of breath, still gasping hard, and the wave's top pitches toward her and suddenly she has the sicken-ing realization that she is going to be at just the wrong spot, that it's going to fall right on her, she takes in a deep breath and ducks her head into her chest—

Wham. It hits her so hard the air is driven out of her lungs, and then she is being flailed about, her whole body tumbling, no way to tell up from down, a wild tumble, the washing machine for sure, but so much bigger than those little ones that she's utterly helpless, a rag doll, when will it let her up? Will it let her up? She's running out of air, feeling an emptiness in her head she has never felt before, a desperate need for breath, she's never felt that before and she panics, she simply has to breathe right now! And yet she's down there swirling with the sand torn off the bottom, eyes clamped shut, whirling about, she's going to have to give up and breathe water, damn, she thinks, after all that, to get home and drown a month later. Star girl killed by Earth how stupid—

And then she's cast back up into the air, gulps it in, alas some water in the gulp, chokes, coughs, gasps in more air, in and out.

And then she sees there's a fourth wave breaking. Not fair! she thinks, and crash, she is slammed right to the bottom again, hard tumbling impact. Unbelievable force. No air in her, just have to hold on. Now she really will drown. Life flashing before eyes, the classic sign. Stupid star girl, done in at last.

She opens her eyes, fights toward the light. Light-headed, empty inside, blood burning, desire to breathe so great she can't stop herself, must breathe even if she breathes water, simply must! Must! Doesn't. Holds on somehow as she tumbles, light above, dark below, try to get up toward the light, but helpless in the tumble, just a rag doll tumbling.

She comes up again, gasps out and in again, careful this time not to breathe in water. Quick lessons here, she looks around to see if another wave coming—there is. What is this? It's trying to kill her!

But it seems smaller. Still, she is too far inside now to get over it before it breaks, too weak to swim out to it, can only breathe in and out in quick gasps, breathe hugely, desperately, the wave rises up, breaks outside of her, comes at her as a gigantic tumbling white wall, chaos, no way to get under it, just take one more breath and wham it hits her and again she's tumbling, pinwheeling, no control, just holding on, just holding her breath. Only this time there just isn't enough to last, impossible to hold your breath when you can't, when you're suffocating, she's going to have to breathe water. Damn. What a way to go. Then she's back on the surface and gasping again. Gasps in and out, turns to look, yes, another fucking great wall coming, streaked with foam and bubbles, but it takes its first fall and leap back to the sky, its first rush at her, and by the time it reaches her the white chaos is just a little calmed down. She lets it take her and roll her in toward shore. She's holding her breath. She'll either black out and die, or get rolled in to shore.

She hits the bottom, struggles around to relocate it. Can't feel her feet, no fins at all anymore, pushes up wildly, shoots up into the air, comes down again, another wave knocks her under, but the bottom is there, she pushes off again, she's tumbling, but some part of every somersault thrusts her head up into the air briefly and she breathes. Tumbling, hitting the sand on the bottom. If it were a rocky bottom she'd be killed, but it's sand and she shoves up from it. Appears she's only about chest deep here, but another broken wave smashes her down again. Damn! Hold breath, tumble without resistance, find the bottom, stand, breathe, knocked over, hold breath, tumble. This time when she stands she falls over because there's no water to hold her up, she's thigh deep, knee deep, she falls at another massive shove from behind, but fuck it, just roll with it, hold breath, come up, breathe.

Comes a moment when she finds herself on hands and knees in water sluicing backward under her toward the waves. Then another shove from behind, but she's in the shallows, it's where she was grunioning, there are the kids up there shrieking as the big waves have overrun their sand castles, instantly melting them to smooth nubbins in the sand, holes streaming water back down.

No one paying the slightest attention to her. Good. She crawls up the beach. The next wave to strike her can't even knock her over, just runs under her whitely hissing, bubbles everywhere, air full of salt mist, the backwash trying hard to sweep her back into the sea, she digs her hands into the wet flowing sand, water leaps up around her forearms and knees, she's settling into sand that flows down under her, until another swell smacks her from behind. But she can't be moved. A few more waves flow up past her and back, she sinks farther into the wet sand. She pulls her hands out, lifts her knees and feet out, crawls on hands and knees up the strand a little. One wave washes a blue fin right by her, she reaches for it and misses. The sand castles are too far. She stops there on hands and knees, resting. Everything brilliantly lit but also stuffed with blackness. Catching her breath, gasping in and out, retching a little, spitting out salt water.

Kaya runs up to her, puts his hand on her back. "Hey, are you all right?"

She nods. "Gah," she says. "Gakk."

"Good! That was a big set!" He runs back out.

Sun beats on her back, the wet strand gleams. Everything is sparking and glary, too bright to look at. A broken wave rushes up the strand, stops, leaves a line of foam. Big slab of water sheets back down the slope at her, crashes into her wrists and knees, sinks her farther into wet sand. Bubbling water swirls the sand under her to the sea, black flecks forming V patterns in tumbling blond grains, sluicing new deltas right before her eyes. Delta v's, she thinks, now those are delta v's. What a world. She lets her head down and kisses the sand.

ACKNOWLEDGMENTS

Thanks this time to:

Terry Bisson, Michael Blumlein, Ron Drummond, Laurie Glover, Olympios Katsiaouni, James Leach, Beth Meacham, Lisa Nowell, Christopher Palmer, Mark Schwartz, Francis Spufford, Sharon Strauss, Ken Wark.

At NASA/Ames, thanks also to Harry Jones, Larry Lemke, Creon Levitt, John Rask, Carol Stoker, and especially Chris McKay, who has been helping me with space questions now for over twenty years.

A special thanks to Carter Scholz.

COPYRIGHTS

extras

www.orbitbooks.net

about the author

Kim Stanley Robinson is a winner of Hugo, Nebula and *Locus* awards. He is the author of nineteen previous books including the bestselling Mars trilogy and the critically acclaimed *Forty Signs of Rain*, *Fifty Degrees Below*, *Sixty Days and Counting*, *The Years of Rice and Salt* and *Antarctica*. In 2008, he was named a "Hero of the Environment" by *Time* magazine, and he recently joined in the Sequoia Parks Foundation's Artists in the Back Country programme. He lives in Davis, California.

Find out more about Kim Stanley Robinson and other Orbit authors by registering for the free monthly newsletter at www.orbitbooks.net.

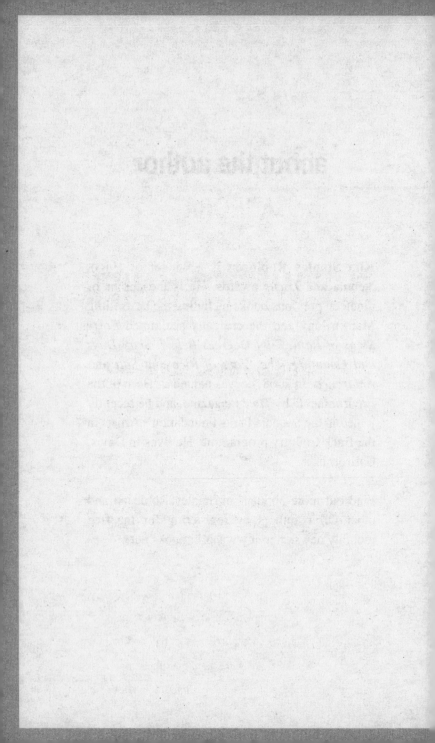

if you enjoyed

AURORA

look out for

THE WATER KNIFE

by

Paolo Bacigalupi

Chapter 1

There were stories in sweat.

The sweat of a woman bent double in an onion field, working fourteen hours under the hot sun, was different from the sweat of a man as he approached a checkpoint in Mexico, praying to La Santa Muerte that the *federales* weren't on the payroll of the enemies he was fleeing. The sweat of a ten-year-old boy staring into the barrel of a SIG Sauer was different from the sweat of a woman struggling across the desert and praying to the Virgin that a water cache was going to turn out to be exactly where her coyote's map told her it would be.

Sweat was a body's history, compressed into jewels, beaded on the brow, staining shirts with salt. It told you everything about how a person had ended up in the right place at the wrong time, and whether they would survive another day.

To Angel Velasquez, perched high above Cypress 1's central bore and watching Charles Braxton as he lumbered up the Cascade Trail, the sweat on a lawyer's brow said that some people weren't near as important as they liked to think.

Braxton might strut in his offices and scream at his secretaries. He might stalk courtrooms like an ax murderer hunting new victims. But no matter how much swagger the lawyer

carried, at the end of the day Catherine Case owned his ass –
and when Catherine Case told you to get something done
quick, you didn't just run, *pendejo,* you ran until your heart
gave out and there wasn't no running left.

Braxton ducked under ferns and stumbled past banyan
climbing vines, following the slow rise of the trail as it wound
around the cooling bore. He shoved through groups of tourists
posing for selfies before the braided waterfalls and hanging
gardens that spilled down the arcology's levels. He kept on,
flushed and dogged. Joggers zipped past him in shorts and
tank tops, their ears flooded with music and the thud of their
healthy hearts.

You could learn a lot from a man's sweat.

Braxton's sweat meant he still had fear. And to Angel, that
meant he was still reliable.

Braxton spied Angel perched on the bridge where it arced
across the wide expanse of the central bore. He waved tiredly,
motioning Angel to come down and join him. Angel waved
back from above, smiling, pretending not to understand.

'Come down!' Braxton called up.

Angel smiled and waved again.

The lawyer slumped, defeated, and set himself to the final
assault on Angel's aerie.

Angel leaned against the rail, enjoying the view. Sunlight filtered down from above, dappling bamboo and rain trees,
illuminating tropical birds and casting pocket-mirror flashes on
mossy koi ponds.

Far below, people were smaller than ants. Not really people
at all, more just the shapes of tourists and residents and casino
workers, as in the biotects' development models of Cypress 1:
scale-model people sipping scale-model lattes on scale-model

coffee shop terraces. Scale-model kids chasing butterflies on the nature trails, while scale-model gamblers split and doubled down at the scale-model blackjack tables in the deep grottoes of the casinos.

Braxton came lumbering onto the bridge. 'Why didn't you come down?' he gasped. 'I told you to come down.' He dropped his briefcase on the boards and sagged against the rail.

'What you got for me?' Angel asked.

'Papers,' Braxton wheezed. 'Carver City. We just got the judge's decision.' He waved an exhausted hand at the briefcase. 'We crushed them.'

'And?'

Braxton tried to say more but couldn't get the words out. His face was puffy and flushed. Angel wondered if he was about to have a heart attack, then tried to decide how much he would care if he did.

The first time Angel met Braxton had been in the lawyer's offices in the headquarters of the Southern Nevada Water Authority. The man had a floor-to-ceiling view of Carson Creek, Cypress 1's fly-fishing river, where it cascaded through various levels of the arcology before being pumped back to the top of the system to run though a new cleaning cycle. A big expensive overlook onto rainbow trout and water infrastructure, and a good reminder of why Braxton filed his lawsuits on SNWA's behalf.

Braxton had been lording over his three assistants – all coincidentally svelte girls hooked straight from law school with promises of permanent residence permits in Cypress – and he'd talked to Angel like an afterthought. Just another one of Catherine Case's pit bulls that he tolerated for as long as

Angel kept leaving other, bigger dogs dead in his wake.

Angel, in turn, had spent the meeting trying to figure out how a man like Braxton had gotten so large. People outside Cypress didn't fatten up like Braxton did. In all Angel's early life, he'd never seen a creature quite like Braxton, and he found himself fascinated, admiring the fleshy raiment of a man who knew himself secure.

If the end of the world came like Catherine Case said it would, Angel thought Braxton would make good eating. And that in turn made it easier to let the Ivy League *pendejo* live when he wrinkled his nose at Angel's gang tattoos and the knife scar that scored his face and throat.

Times they do change, Angel thought as he watched the sweat drip from Braxton's nose.

'Carver City lost on appeal,' Braxton gasped finally. 'Judges were going to rule this morning, but we got the courtrooms double-booked. Got the whole ruling delayed until end of business. Carver City will be running like crazy to file a new appeal.' He picked up his briefcase and popped it open. 'They aren't going to make it.'

He handed over a sheaf of laser-hologrammed documents. 'These are your injunctions. You've got until the courts open tomorrow to enforce our legal rights. Once Carver City files an appeal, it's a different story. Then you're looking at civil liabilities, minimally. But until courts open tomorrow, you're just defending the private property rights of the citizens of the great state of Nevada.'

Angel started going through the documents. 'This all of it?'

'Everything you need, as long as you seal the deal tonight. Once business opens tomorrow, it's back to courtroom delays and he-said, she-said.'

'And you'll have done a lot of sweating for nothing.'

Braxton jabbed a thick finger at Angel. 'That better not happen.'

Angel laughed at the implied threat. 'I already got my housing permits, *cabrón*. Go frighten your secretaries.'

'Just because you're Case's pet doesn't mean I can't make your life miserable.'

Angel didn't look up from the injunctions. 'Just because you're Case's dog don't mean I can't toss you off this bridge.'

The seals and stamps on the injunctions all looked like they were in order.

'What have you got on Case that makes you so untouchable?' Braxton asked.

'She trusts me.'

Braxton laughed, disbelieving, as Angel put the injunctions back in order.

Angel said, 'People like you write everything down because you know everyone is a liar. It's how you lawyers do.' He slapped Braxton in the chest with the legal documents, grinning. 'And that's why Case trusts me and treats you like a dog – you're the one who writes things down.'

He left Braxton glaring at him from the bridge.

As Angel made his way down the Cascade Trail, he pulled out his cell and dialed.

Catherine Case answered on the first ring, clipped and formal. 'This is Case.'

Angel could imagine her, Queen of the Colorado, leaning over her desk, with maps of the state of Nevada and the Colorado River Basin floor to ceiling on the walls around her, her domain laid out in real-time data feeds – the veins of every tributary blinking red, amber, or green indicating stream flow in cubic feet per second. Numbers flickering over the various catchment basins of the Rocky Mountains – red, amber, green – monitoring how much snow cover remained and variation off the norm as it melted. Other numbers, displaying the depths of reservoirs and dams, from the Blue Mesa Dam on the Gunnison, to the Navajo Dam on the San Juan, to the Flaming Gorge Dam on the Green. Over it all, emergency purchase prices on streamflows and futures offers scrolled via NASDAQ, available open-market purchase options if she needed to recharge the depth in Lake Mead, the unforgiving numbers that ruled her world as relentlessly as she ruled Angel's and Braxton's.

'Just talked to your favorite lawyer,' Angel said.

'Please tell me you didn't antagonize him again.'

'That *pendejo* is a piece of work.'

'You're not so easy, either. You have everything you need?'

'Well, Braxton gave me a lot of dead trees, that's for sure.' He hefted the sheaf of legal documents. 'Didn't know so much paper still existed.'

'We like to make sure we're all on the same page,' Case said dryly.

'Same fifty or sixty pages, more like.'

Case laughed. 'It's the first rule of bureaucracy: any message worth sending is worth sending in triplicate.'

Angel exited the Cascade Trail, winding down toward where elevator banks would whisk him to central parking. 'Figure we should be up in about an hour,' he said.

'I'll be monitoring.'

'This is a milk run, boss. Braxton's papers here got about a hundred different signatures say I can do anything I want. This is old-school cease and desist. Camel Corps could do this one on their own, I bet. Glorified FedEx is what this is.'

'No.' Case's voice hardened. 'Ten years of back-and-forth in the courts is what this is, and I want it finished. For good this time. I'm tired of giving away Cypress housing permits to some judge's nephew just so we can keep appealing for something that's ours by right.'

'No worries. When we're done, Carver City won't know what hit them.'

'Good. Let me know when it's finished.'

She clicked off. Angel caught an express elevator as it was closing. He stepped to the glass as the elevator began its plunge. It accelerated, plummeting down through the levels of the arcology. People blurred past: mothers pushing double strollers; hourly girlfriends clinging to the arms of weekend boyfriends; tourists from all over the world, snapping pics and messaging home that they had seen the Hanging Gardens of Las Vegas. Ferns and waterfalls and coffee shops.

Down on the entertainment floors, the dealers would be changing shifts. In the hotels the twenty-four-hour party people would be waking up and taking their first shots of vodka, spraying glitter on their skin. Maids and waiters and busboys and cooks and maintenance staff would all be hard at work, striving to keep their jobs, fighting to keep their Cypress housing permits.

You're all here because of me, Angel thought. *Without me, you'd all be little tumbleweeds. Little bone-and-paper-skin bodies. No dice to throw, no hookers to buy, no strollers to push, no drinks at your elbow, no work to do . . .*

Without me, you're nothing.

The elevator hit bottom with a soft chime. Its doors opened to Angel's Tesla, waiting with the valet.

Half an hour later he was striding across the boiling tarmac of Mulroy Airbase, heat waves rippling off the asphalt, and the sun setting bloody over the Spring Mountains. One hundred twenty degrees, and the sun only finally finishing the job. The floodlights of the base were coming on, adding to the burn.

'You got our papers?' Reyes shouted over the whine of Apaches.

'Feds love our desert asses!' Angel held up the documents. 'For the next fourteen hours, anyway!'

Reyes barely smiled in response, just turned and started initiating launch orders.

Colonel Reyes was a big black man who'd been a recon marine in Syria and Venezuela, before moving into hot work in the Sahel and then Chihuahua, before finally dropping into his current plush job with the Nevada guardies.

State of Nevada paid better, he said.

Reyes waved Angel aboard the command chopper. Around them attack helicopters were spinning up, burning synthetic fuel by the barrel – Nevada National Guard, a.k.a. Camel Corps, a.k.a. those fucking Vegas guardies, depending on who had just had a Hades missile sheaf fired up their asses – all of them gearing up to inflict the will of Catherine Case upon her enemies.

One of the guardies tossed Angel a flak jacket. Angel shrugged into Kevlar as Reyes settled into the command seat and started issuing orders. Angel plugged military glass and an earbug into the chopper's comms so he could listen to the chatter.

Their gunship lurched skyward. A pilot's-eye data feed spilled into Angel's vision, the graffiti of war coloring Las Vegas with bright hungry tags: target calculations, relevant structures, friend/foe markings, Hades missile loads, and .50-cal belly-gun ammo info, fuel warnings, heat signals on the ground . . .

Ninety-eight point six.

Human beings. Some of the coolest things out there. Each one tagged, not a single one knowing it.

One of the guardies was making sure Angel was strapped in tight. Angel grinned as the lady checked his straps. Dark skin and black hair and eyes like coal. He picked her name off a tag – Gupta.

'Think I know how to strap myself in, right?' he shouted over the rotor noise. 'Used to do this work, too.'

Gupta didn't even smile. 'Ms. Case's orders. We'd look pretty stupid if we pancaked and you didn't walk away just because you didn't tighten your seat belt.'

'If we pancake, none of us is walking away.'

But she ignored him and did her check anyway. Reyes and the Camel Corps were thorough. They had their own elegant rituals, designed over time and polished to a high shine.

Gupta said something into her comm, then strapped into her own seat behind the screen for the chopper's belly gun.

Angel's stomach lurched as their gunship angled around, joining a formation of other airborne predators. Status updates rolled across his military glass, brighter than Vegas nightscape:

SNWA 6602, away.

SNWA 6608, away.

SNWA 6606, away.

More call signs and numbers scrolled past. Digital confirmation of the nearly invisible locust swarm filling the blackening sky and now streaming south.

Over the comm, Reyes's voice crackled: 'Commence Operation Honey Pool.'

Angel laughed. 'Who came up with that one?'

'Like it?'

'I like Mead.'

'Don't we all?'

And then they were hurtling south, toward the Mead in question: twenty-six million acre-feet of water storage at inception, now less than half of that thanks to Big Daddy Drought. An optimistic lake created during an optimistic time, whittled now and filling with silt besides. A lifeline, always threatened and always vulnerable, always on the verge of sinking below Intake No. 3, the critical IV drip that kept the heart of Las Vegas pumping.

Below them, the lights of Vegas central unspooled: casino neon and Cypress arcologies. Hotels and balconies. Domes and condensation-misted vertical farms, leafy with hydroponic greenery and blazing with full-spectrum illumination. Geometries of light sprawling across the desert floor, all of them overlaid with the electronic graffiti of Camel Corps's combat language.

Billboard promises of shows and parties and drinks and money filtered through military glass, and became attack and entry points. Close-packed urban canyons designed to funnel desert winds became sniper alleys. Iridescent photo-voltaic-paint roofs became drop zones. The Cypress arcologies became high-ground advantage and priority attack zones, thanks to the way they dominated the Vegas skyline and loomed over everything else, bigger and more ambitious than all of Sin City's previous forays into the fantastical combined.

Vegas ended in a sharp black line.

The combat software started picking out living creatures, cool spots in the dark heat of a millennial suburban skeleton –

square mile after square mile of buildings that weren't good for anything except firewood and copper wiring because Catherine Case had decided they didn't deserve their water anymore.

Sparse and lonely campfires perforated the blackness, beacons marking the locations of desiccated Texans and Zoners who didn't have enough money to get into a Cypress arcology and had nowhere else to flee. The Queen of the Colorado had slaughtered the hell out of these neighborhoods: her first graveyards, created in seconds when she shut off the water in their pipes.

'If they can't police their damn water mains, they can drink dust,' Case had said.

People still sent the lady death threats about that.

The helicopters crossed the last of the wrecked suburban buffer zone and passed out into open desert. Original landscape: Old Testament ancient. Creosote bushes. Joshua trees, spiky and lonely. Yucca eruptions, dry washes, pale gravel sands, quartz pebbles.

The desert was entirely black now and cooling, the scalpel scrape of the sun finally off the land. There'd be animals down there. Nearly hairless coyotes. Lizards and snakes. Owls. A whole world that only came alive once the sun went down. A whole ecosystem emerging from burrows beneath rocks and yucca and creosote.

Angel watched the tiny thermal markers of the desert's surviving inhabitants and wondered if the desert returned his gaze, if some skinny coyote looked up at the muffled thud-thwap of Camel Corps gunships flying overhead and marveled at this charge of airborne humanity.

An hour passed.

'We're close,' Reyes said, breaking the stillness. His voice was almost reverent. Angel leaned forward, searching.

'There she is,' Gupta said.

A black ribbon of water, twisting through desert, cutting between ragged mountain ridges.

Shining moonlight spilled across the waters in slicks of silver.

The Colorado River.

It wound like a serpent through the pale scapes of the desert. California hadn't put this stretch of river into a straw yet, but it would. All that evaporation – couldn't let the sun steal that forever. But for now the river still flowed in the open, exposed to sky and the guardies' solemn view.

Angel peered down at the river, awed as always. The radio chatter of the guardies ceased, all of them falling silent at the sight of so much water.

Even much reduced by droughts and diversions, the Colorado River awakened reverent hungers. Seven million acre-feet a year, down from sixteen million ... but still, so much water, simply there on the land ...

No wonder Hindus worshipped rivers, Angel thought.

In its prime, the Colorado River had run more than a thousand miles, from the white-snow Rockies down through the red-rock canyons of Utah and on to the blue Pacific, tumbling fast and without obstruction. And wherever it touched – life.

If a farmer could put a diversion on it, or a home builder could sink a well beside it, or a casino developer could throw a pump into it, a person could drink deep of possibility. A body could thrive in 115-degree heat. A city could blossom in a desert. The river was a blessing as sure as the Virgin Mother's.

Angel wondered what the river had looked like back when it

still ran free and fast. These days the river ran low and sluggish, stoppered behind huge dams. Blue Mesa Dam, Flaming Gorge Dam, Morrow Point Dam, Soldier Creek Dam, Navajo Dam, Glen Canyon Dam, Hoover Dam, and more. And wherever dams held back the river and its tributaries, lakes formed, reflecting desert sky and sun: Lake Powell. Lake Mead. Lake Havasu . . .

These days Mexico never saw a drop of water hit its border, no matter how much it complained about the Colorado River Compact and the Law of the River. Children down in the Cartel States grew up and died thinking that the Colorado River was as much a myth as the *chupacabra* that Angel's old *abuela* had told him about. Hell, most of Utah and Colorado weren't allowed to touch the water that filled the canyon below Angel's chopper.

'Ten minutes to contact,' Reyes announced.

'Any chance they'll fight?'

Reyes shook his head. 'Zoners don't have much to defend with. Still got most of their units deployed up in the Arctic.'

That had been Case's doing, greasing a bunch of East Coast politicians who didn't care what the hell happened on this side of the Continental Divide. She'd gorged those pork-barrel bastards on hookers and cocaine and vast sloshing oceans of Super PAC cash, so when the Joint Chiefs discovered a desperate need to defend tar sands pipelines way up north, coincidentally, the only folks who could do the job were the desert rats of the Arizona National Guard.

Angel remembered watching the news as they deployed, the relentless rah-rah of energy security from the feeds. He'd enjoyed watching all the journos beating the patriotism drums and getting their ratings up. Making citizens feel like badass

Americans again. The journos were good for that, at least. For a second, Americans could still feel like big swinging dicks.

Solidarity, baby.

The Camel Corps's two dozen choppers dropped into the river's canyon, skimming black waters. They wound along its serpentine length, hemmed in on either side by stony hills, sweeping up the liquid curves of the Colorado to the target.

Angel was starting to grin, feeling the familiar rush of adrenaline that came when all bets were made and all anyone could do was find out what lay in the dealer's deck.

He clutched the court's injunctions to his chest. All those seals and hologram stamps. All that ritual of lawsuits and appeals, all leading to a moment when they could finally take the gloves off.

Arizona would never know what hit them.

He laughed. 'Times they do change.'

Gupta, riding the belly gun, glanced over. 'What's that you saying?'

She was young, Angel realized. Young, as he'd been when Case put him in the guardies and got his state residence approved once and for all. Poor and desperate deportee, looking to find some way – any way – to stay on the right side of the border.

'How old are you?' he asked. 'Twelve?'

She gave him a dirty look and brought her focus back to her targeting systems.

'Twenty. Old man.'

'Don't be cold.' He pointed down at the Colorado. 'You're too young to remember how it used to be. Used to be that we all sat down with a bunch of lawyers and papers, bureaucrats with pocket protectors . . .'

He trailed off, remembering early days, when he'd stood bodyguard behind Catherine Case as she went into meetings: bald bureaucrat guys, city water managers, Bureau of Reclamation, Department of the Interior. All of them talking acre-feet and reclamation guidelines and cooperation, waste-water efficiency, recycling, water banking, evaporation reduction and river covers, tamarisk and cottonwood and willow elimination. All of them trying to rearrange deck chairs on a big old *Titanic*. All of them playing the game by the rules, believing there was a way for everyone to get by, pretending they could cooperate and share their way out of the situation if they just got real clever about the problem.

And then California tore up the rulebook and chose a new game.

'Were you saying something?' Gupta pressed.

'Nah.' Angel shook his head. 'Game's changed is all. Case used to play that old game pretty good.' He grabbed his seat for support as they popped up over the canyon rim and bore down on their target. 'We do okay with this new game, too.'

Ahead, their objective glowed in the darkness, a whole complex standing alone in the desert.

'There it is.'

Lights started winking out.

'They know we're coming,' Reyes said, and began issuing battle instructions.

The choppers spread out, picking likely targets as they came into range. Their own chopper plunged lower, joined by a pair of support drones. Angel's military glass showed another cluster of choppers running ahead, opening up airspace. He gritted his teeth as they started dropping and jigging, keeping their movement random, waiting to see if the ground tried to light them up.

Off on the far horizon, he could see the orange glow of Carver City. Houses and businesses bright and shining, a halo of urbanity blazing against the night sky. All those electric lights. All that A/C.

All that life.

Gupta fired a couple of rounds. Something lit up below, a fountain of flames. Their gunships swept over the leading edge of the pumping and water-treatment facilities. Pools and pipes running all over the place.

Black Apaches settled on rooftops and parking lots, dropped to pavement, and belched forth troops. More gunships thudded down like giant dragonflies alighting. Rotor wash kicked up quartz sands, scouring Angel's face.

'Showtime!' Reyes motioned at Angel. Angel checked his flak jacket a final time and snapped the chin strap of his helmet.

Gupta watched, smiling. 'You want a gun, old man?'

'Why?' Angel asked as he jumped out. 'That's why I got you coming in with me.'

Guardies formed around him. Together they dashed for the plant's main doors.

Floodlights were coming up, workers rushing out, knowing what was coming. Camel Corps had their rifles up and ready, keeping sights on the targets ahead. Amplified orders blasted from Gupta's comm.

'*Everyone on the ground. Down! Get DOWN!*'

Civilians hit the deck.

Angel jogged up to a huddled and terrified woman, waved his papers. 'You got a Simon Yu in there somewhere?' he shouted over the shriek of the choppers.

She was too scared to speak. Sort of pudgy white lady

with brown hair. Angel grinned. 'Hey, lady, I'm just serving papers.'

'Inside,' she finally gasped.

'Thanks.' Angel slapped her on the back. 'Why don't you run all your coworkers out of here? In case things get hot.'

He and the soldiers rammed through the treatment plant's doors, a wedge of weaponry with Angel striding at its heart. Civvies slapped themselves up against the walls as Camel Corps stampeded past.

'Vegas in the house!' Angel crowed. 'Grab your ankles, boys and girls!'

Gupta's amplified orders drowned him out. '*Clear out! All of you! You got thirty minutes to evacuate this facility. After that you're obstructing!*'

Angel and his team hit the main control rooms: flat-screen computers monitoring effluence, water quality, chemical inputs, pump efficiency – along with a whole pack of water-quality engineers, looking like surprised gophers as they popped up from their workstations.

'Where's me some supervisor?' Angel demanded. 'I want me some Simon Yu.'

A man straightened. 'I'm Yu.' Slim and tanned, balding. Comb-over. Scars of old acne on his cheeks.

Angel tossed papers at him as Camel Corps spread out and secured the control room. 'You're shut down.'

Yu caught the papers clumsily. 'The hell we are! This is on appeal.'

'Appeal all you want, tomorrow,' Angel said. 'Tonight you got an order to shut down. Check the signatures.'

'We're supplying a hundred thousand people! You can't just turn off their water.'

'Judges say we've got senior rights,' Angel said. 'You should be glad we're letting you keep what you already got in your pipes. If your people are careful, they can live on buckets for a couple of days, till they clear out.'

Yu was riffling through the papers. 'But this ruling is a farce! We're getting a stay, and this is going to be overturned. This ruling – it barely exists! Tomorrow it's gone!'

'Knew you'd say something like that. Problem is, it's not tomorrow right now. It's today. And today the judges say you got to stop stealing the state of Nevada's water.'

'You're going to be liable, though!' Yu sputtered. He made a heroic effort to calm himself. 'We both know how serious this is. Whatever happens to Carver City is on you. We have security cams. All of this is going to be public record. You can't want this to be on your head when judgments start coming down.'

Angel decided he kind of liked the balding bureaucrat. Simon Yu was *dedicated*. Had the feel of one of those good—government guys who got a job because he wanted to make the world a better place. Genuine old-school civil servant genuinely dedicated to the old-school benefit of the people.

And now here the guy was, cajoling Angel. Playing the let's-be-reasonable, don't-be-hasty game.

Too bad it wasn't the game they were playing.

' . . . This is going to piss off a lot of powerful people,' Yu was saying. 'You aren't going to get off. The feds aren't going to let something like this happen.'

It was a bit like meeting a dinosaur, Angel decided. Kind of icy to see, sure, but really, how the hell had the man ever survived?

'Powerful people?' Angel smiled gently. 'You cut a deal with

California I'm not aware of? They own your water, and somehow I don't know? 'Cause from where we stand, you're pumping some crappy junior water right that you bought secondhand off a farmer in western Colorado, and you got no cards left to play. This is water that should have come to us a long time ago. Says so in those papers I just gave you.'

Yu gave Angel a sullen glare.

'Come on, Yu.' Angel lightly punched the man in the shoulder. 'Don't look so down. We both been in this game long enough to know someone's got to lose. Law of the River says senior rights gets it all. Junior rights?' Angel shrugged. 'Not so much.'

'Who did you pay off?' Yu asked. 'Stevens? Arroyo?'

'Does it matter?'

'It's a hundred thousand people's lives!'

'Shouldn't have bet them on such crappy water rights, then,' Gupta commented from across the control room, where she was checking out the flashing lights of pump monitors.

Angel hid a smirk as Yu shot her a dirty look. 'The soldier's right, Yu. You got your notice there. We're giving you -twenty-five more minutes to clear out, and after that I'm dropping some Hades and Hellfire on this place. So clear it out before we light it up.'

'*You're going to blow us up?*'

A bunch of the soldiers laughed at that.

Gupta said, 'You did see us come in with the helicopters, right?'

'I'm not leaving,' Yu said coldly. 'You can kill me if you want. Let's see how that works out for you.'

Angel sighed. 'I just knew you'd be stand-up that way.'

Before Yu could retort, Angel grabbed him and slammed

him to the floor. He buried a knee in the bureaucrat's back. Grabbed an arm and twisted it.

'You're destroying—'

'Yeah, yeah, I know.' Angel wrenched Yu's other hand behind his back and zip-cuffed him. 'A whole fucking city. A hundred thousand lives. Plus somebody's golf course. But like you noticed, dead bodies do make things complicated, so we're taking your bald ass out of here. You can sue us tomorrow.'

'*You can't do this!*' Yu shouted from where his face was mashed into the floor.

Angel knelt down beside the helpless man. 'I feel like you're taking this personally, Simon. But it ain't that way. We're just cogs in a big old machine, right?' He jerked Yu upright. 'This is bigger than you and me. We're both just doing our jobs.' He gave Yu a shove, propelling him through the doors. To Gupta, he called back, 'Check the rest of the place, and make sure it's cleared. I want this place on fire in ten!'

Outside Reyes was standing at the chopper door, waiting.

'We've got Zoners, incoming!' Reyes shouted.

'Well, that ain't good. How long?'

'Five minutes.'

'Fucking hell.' Angel made a twirling motion with his finger. 'Spin us up, then! I got what I came for.'

Chopper blades came alive, an angry shriek. Their whine drowned out Yu's next words, but his expression was enough for Angel to understand the man's hatred.

'Don't take this personally!' Angel shouted back. 'In another year we'll hire you up in Vegas! You're too good to waste here! SNWA can use good people like you!'

Angel tried to tug Yu into the chopper, but the man resisted. He was glaring at Angel, eyes squinting against the dustwash.

Guardie choppers started lifting off, locusts rising. Angel gave Yu another tug. 'Time to go, old man.'

'The hell you say!'

With sudden surprising strength, Yu tore free and bolted back toward his water-treatment plant, stumbling, hands still zip-cuffed behind his back but running determinedly for the building from which the last of his people were fleeing.

Angel exchanged a pained look with Reyes.

Dedicated bastard. Right down to the end, the pencil pusher was dedicated.

'We've got to go!' Reyes shouted. 'If the Zoners get their choppers up here, we'll end up in a firefight, and the feds will be all up on our asses then. There's some shit they won't put up with, and a state-to-state gun battle is definitely one of them. We need to clear out!'

Angel looked back at Yu as he fled. 'Just give me one minute!'

'Thirty seconds!'

Angel gave Reyes a disgusted look and charged after Yu.

All around him choppers were lifting off, rising like leaves on hot desert winds. Angel pelted through the flying grit, squinting against sand sting.

He caught Yu at the door to the treatment plant. 'Well, you're stubborn. I'll give you that.'

'Let me go!'

Instead, Angel flipped him hard onto the ground. The landing took Yu's breath away, and Angel took advantage of the man's paralysis to zip-cuff his ankles, too.

'Leave me the fuck alone!'

'Normally, I'd just cut you like a pig and be done with it,' Angel grunted, as he hefted Yu onto his back in a fireman's carry. 'But since we're doing this all aboveboard and public, that's not on the table. But don't push me. Seriously.' He began lumbering for the sole remaining chopper.

The last of Carver City's treatment-plant workers were diving into their cars and speeding away from the pumping facility, kicking up plumes of dust. Rats jumping the sinking ship.

Reyes was glaring at Angel. 'Hurry the fuck up!'

'I'm here! Let's go already!'

Angel dumped Yu into the chopper. They lifted off with Angel riding the skid. He clawed his way inside.

Gupta was back at her gun, already opening fire as Angel strapped in. Angel's military glass lit up with firing solutions. He peered out the open door as military intelligence software portioned out the water-treatment plant: filtering towers, pumping engines, power supply, backup generators—

Missiles spat from the choppers' tubes, arcs of fire, silent in the air and then explosively loud as they buried themselves in the guts of Carver City's water infrastructure.

Flaming mushrooms boiled up into the night, bathing the desert orange, illuminating the black locust shapes of the hovering choppers as they launched more rounds.

Simon Yu lay at Angel's feet, zip-cuffed and impotent to stop the destruction, watching as his world went up in mushroom clouds.

In the flickering light of the explosions, Angel could make out tears on the man's face. Water gushing from his eyes, as telling in its own way as a man's sweat: Simon Yu, mourning the place he'd tried so hard to save. Sucker had ice in his blood, for sure. Didn't look it, but the sucker had him some ice.

Too bad it hadn't helped.

It's the end of times, Angel thought as more missiles pummeled the water-treatment plant. *It's the goddamn end of times.*

And then on the heels of that thought, another followed, unbidden.

Guess that makes me the Devil.

Ch. 01. 19.